"This superb novel of light, gla[...] that Jeff Noon is one of our few[...]"
Warren Ellis

"A disturbing and bizarre journey by one of the great masters of weird fiction."
Adrian Tchaikovsky, Arthur C Clarke Award-winning author of Children of Time

"Every Jeff Noon novel is a wonderful, precious thing. These are bad times, and we need him more than ever."
Dave Hutchinson, British Science Fiction Association Award-winning author of the Europe series

"Style has always been Noon's strongest suit, and in creating the varied cityscapes of *A Man of Shadows*, his talent for hallucinatory imagery has found a perfect match. This book is absolutely drenched in arresting visuals."
Barnes & Noble Sci-Fi & Fantasy Blog

"Manchester's delirious prophet returns with scripture written in shadow and light."
Kieron Gillen, co-creator of The Wicked + The Divine

"Noon has written a kaleidoscopic noir novel of dizzying dream logic."
Publishers Weekly

"Noon's prose takes you to weird and scary places other novelists don't go, a reminder why he's so revered."
SFX magazine

"This is a beguiling introduction to a strange new world, and a trip worth taking."
Sci-Fi Now magazine

"While *Vurt* was undeniably the in-your-face work of a brash wunderkind, *A Man of Shadows* is arguably even better: the product of a more mature, surer writer with less desire to awe the reader for the sheer sake of showing off his chops, and more intent on producing emotional resonances, more vivid storylines, and imparting whatever hard-earned wisdom the writer has garnered."
Locus

"Clocks and watches form a recurrent motif in this artful, eerie novel that infuses the mystery genre with symbolism and soul."
Financial Times

"This novel – and the double city contained within it – is an immersive and addictive experience; one that, despite the tension of the narrative, the reader will miss once it's all over."
British Fantasy Society

"Wonderful and uniquely absorbing."
Starburst

"Noon takes the concept of time and plays with it from every possible angle."
Strange Alliances

"*A Man of Shadows* is a quite extraordinary novel. Its world building is absolutely fantastic – intricate, complex, moody and disturbingly real. Dayzone and Nocturna are brilliantly visualized and would have been sufficiently impressive on their own but the skill of Jeff Noon astounds even further with his treatment of time."
For Winter Nights

JEFF NOON

THE BODY LIBRARY

A Nyquist mystery

ANGRY
ROBOT

ANGRY ROBOT
An imprint of Watkins Media Ltd

20 Fletcher Gate,
Nottingham,
NG1 2FZ • UK

angryrobotbooks.com
twitter.com/angryrobotbooks
The cut-up method

An Angry Robot paperback original 2018

Distributed in the United States by Penguin Random House, Inc., New York.

ISBN 978 0 85766 673 4
Ebook ISBN 978 0 85766 674 1

Printed in the United States of America

9 8 7 6 5 4 3 2 1

For Karen, Grant & Alfie

THE UNTOLD MAN

One night in the late summer of 1959 a young courting couple were seeking a place of calm and secrecy. Hand in hand they darted round corners, through narrow unlit passageways, along subways. They fled from the words, the endless words, the stories that filled the air of every street, public square, household, café and bar. They wanted only the warmth of contact, the young woman's mouth against the man's ear, and then vice versa: one tale told in two bodies, two minds. So it begins. They found a doorway at the end of a litter-strewn alley, a metal door long given over to rust, the framework buckled, the door cracked open just a little, enough to get a hand inside. They entered and walked along a corridor to find themselves inside a small disused library. The place was dark and dusty, filled with the smell of mildew and rot. They didn't notice the spots of blood on the floor. The only noise was the couple's own footsteps and a quiet, almost silent rustling sound from all around.

The young man was called Marcus, the woman Andrea. They were eighteen years old, both from the town of Lower Shakespeare, both lost in the realms of first love.

Marcus set aflame an oil lantern and the flickering yellow light dispelled the gloom. Stacks of tall shelves divided the room into series of aisles and these shelves were packed with books: old volumes in the main, both hardback and paper, novels and reference books, the covers dotted with mold, some with the spines cracked, others pristine. All thoughts of physical pleasure had now left the two intruders, for here was a treasure trove, a place of countless stories, untold for many years. Marcus imagined the constant rustling sound was the pages rubbing together in the dark of the covers, desperate to be opened, to be read once more. He told this to Andrea and she smiled at the thought. They pulled novels off the shelves and read the titles to each other. Yet when they opened the books they saw only blank, empty pages. No words. No stories. Here and there they noticed the trace of a single letter, light grey in color, merging into the page even as they watched.

Yet this didn't stop them. They were young, they loved life, they saw everything as a possibility. They read to each other, making up the opening paragraphs according to the titles, extemporizing, weaving words together. Andrea began: "I stood on the threshold of a new world, nervous of where my next step might take me. I faltered, and then found my faith. I stepped out into the unknown." Marcus countered this with, "I have visited many other planets on my travels, but only one can I truly recall, now, many years after my wandering days are over. Its name? Planet Earth."

They laughed and kissed and moved on, becoming separated, each seeking their own delights, each wondering if one book in the library still contained words, and what those words might be. Andrea ventured further into the library than her friend, further into the dark. She had no source of light with her, but she wasn't scared, even though the shelves were now so close together she had to move between them sideways, shuffling her feet. Again, a patch of blood smeared on a book cover went unnoticed.

The blank pages rustled even louder, so many lost voices murmuring in her ears, yearning, yearning. Was it really the lost stories talking, as Marcus had suggested, or merely an illusion? It might be mice, moving behind the walls. Or a hive of wasps in the eaves. Or thousands upon thousands of bookworms slowly destroying the volumes from within. Andrea possessed the kind of imagination that very quickly overflowed its own boundaries. She stopped moving. Something had disturbed her. Squeezing out from the shelving units she found herself in a small enclosed space at the rear of the library. The darkness was complete here. Yet some object glimmered, close by, lower to the floor: one object, and a second. She knelt down and reached out with a careful hand, her fingers pressing against some kind of material, clothing perhaps. Was somebody sleeping here, a tramp seeking warmth and comfort? But no sound was heard, no breathing. Marcus came to her, carrying the lantern. Now the shape was more clearly seen. Andrea crept closer and the two objects came into focus – a pair of eyes, staring at her from a darkened face.

A man's eyes. Unblinking in the light. Drained of color.

"Is he dead?" Marcus said, in a whisper.

"I think he must be," Andrea replied. "He's just staring ahead. Bring the lamp closer."

Marcus did so.

"There's something on his skin."

"What is it?" he asked.

Andrea examined the man's face. "Words," she answered. "Hundreds of them. They're all over his face, his neck. And look... on his hands. Everywhere."

"Tattoos?"

"No. No, I don't think so."

She took the lamp off Marcus and held it just a few inches above the man's face, and she gasped at what she saw there.

"What is it?"

"They're moving," she said. "The words are crawling on his skin."

Marcus didn't believe her at first; he thought she must be mistaken. But he knelt down at Andrea's side and saw the truth, and he felt sick. Neither of them spoke for a while. The only sound in the library came from the pages of the books as they rustled on the shelves.

All the empty pages.

Among them lay a man covered in stories.

PART ONE
ACROSS CALVINO ROAD

SUBJECT MATTER

They came from all directions, from all parts of the city. From the northern quarter, where people told stories only in the dark for fear of awakening the creatures they talked about; from the southern towns, where stories dealt only with the crudest, most base aspects of life; from the east of the city, where novels were written only to make money for the teller and those who profit from the storyteller's art; and from the west, where the whisper poets lived with their softly spoken narrative ballads and their barely heard rhymes. From all directions the travelers arrived. From the city and beyond, from the nearby hills and farmlands, from faraway towns and villages and from other cities worldwide – the people gathered here in Storyville Central to partake of the Twenty-First International Festival of Words.

Every road, lane, avenue and cul-de-sac was crowded with listeners and storytellers alike, with fables, with myths and legends, with murder mysteries and tales of horror both human and supernatural, with two-line parables and epic sagas which took a day or more to relate, with yarns and anecdotes and accounts of genuine true fictions, with lies galore, glorified. On corners, in kiosks, outside bars, in vast concert halls and tiny wooden sheds that held two people only, one teller, one listener: here the people shared their stories. Joy filled the streets. The stories merged and mingled where narrators vied for the same audience, events and characters migrating from one tale to another, as they often will.

The night was liquid, flowing with words, with language itself, dissolved and shared like wine amongst the poor. Tongues danced, lips moved, arms and hands made expressive gestures. Eyes, ears and minds were alive to all suggestions, to thrilling adventures, to romantic trysts, to fights and clinches and kisses and gunshots and hidden clues and sudden twists in the tale that caused the audience to swoon with delight. They listened to stories of demons, ghosts, heroes, villains, winners and losers. The city was born and made from all these stories, both fictional and real. Stories. Nothing more. And the people were lost in them, lost in words. Talking and listening, they pushed against each other, desperate to hear yet one more tale, further adventures, endless narratives.

John Nyquist was one face among many that night, but with this difference: his story was entirely personal, told only for himself and the man he was following through the crowd. A silent story. He kept his distance, slipping from one group of auditors to another, from one tale to another along the boulevards and pathways, always keeping his subject in sight. The man he was shadowing walked on, never looking back, unaware of his part in the private eye's tale. This subject's name was Wellborn. Patrick Wellborn. That's all Nyquist knew. It was enough.

He reached Rabelais Plaza. A sudden influx of listeners blocked the lane ahead as they tried to follow an itinerant storyteller in his wanderings. Nyquist lost sight of his target. He was held in place, pressed in on all sides. Words exploded into life around him as the listeners repeated the latest tale to each other, sentence by sentence. The crowds congregated here. Endless echoes and comments swirled around him, and he was caught momentarily in at least five different narratives. Nyquist panicked. He shrugged off the other tales and kept to his own. He hurried on, forcing a way through the crush of people, finding the entrance to a narrow alleyway. A few more steps released him at last from the crowd's hold. Now he was alone. And the further he walked down the alley, into darkness, the further he moved into silence. It was a strange sensation after the evening's constant barrage of intersecting voices, as though a tide of sound had flowed away, leaving only a deathly quiet in its wake. But there was no sign of Wellborn. Nyquist reached the end of the alleyway and emerged onto the feeder road for a high-rise estate. It was part of the city's nature, that the old town with its fancy hotels and high-end stores, and the central plazas where visitors and residents mingled together so easily, were all located so close to the poorest areas. He saw that he was standing on the edge of Calvino Road. Before him rose the five towers of the Melville Estate. It was an area that marked the edges of the tourist maps issued by the city council. Not that Nyquist paid any attention to such fears: his job had taken him down shadier avenues and he knew that life was good and bad all over, high or low. Still, he remembered the warnings from when he had first arrived in town: *Don't stray off the marked story paths. You'll never know what happens next.* These warnings were always recited with a shiver of fearful excitement.

Nyquist crossed the road, heading towards the high-rises. He scanned the area and saw a lone figure moving away from him. He recognized the white scarf the man was wearing, and the green suitcase he always took with him on his travels. It was Wellborn. Nyquist set off at a

quicker pace, making sure to keep his subject in sight –
one shadow following another. Four of the towers were
lit up, one in darkness. In the central courtyard a crowd
of people were gathered, sharing stories between them.
Nyquist heard at least four different languages, as faces of
varied shapes and hues glimmered in the lamplight. He
kept on, weaving between dark-eyed teenagers and their
families until he saw his quarry entering a doorway to one
of the apartment blocks, the one with no windows alight.
Nyquist started to run. He'd been in the city for less than
three months, and this was his first well-paid job. He'd
been given the case four days ago, working freelance for
an investigative agency. He wasn't used to having a boss,
but what else could he do? Work was work, and money
was money, half upfront, the rest on completion.

Each day Wellborn had visited a different precinct,
moving through the highest echelons of society and
the poorest ghettos. Nyquist's task was simple: observe,
but never engage. Do not reveal your presence, do not
speak or make any kind of contact with the subject. Just
follow, observe, report. Beyond that Nyquist knew very
little. Patrick Wellborn looked to be in his mid-forties,
of medium height, with long hair, far longer than was
currently fashionable. Nyquist sensed that he was looking
for something or someone; there was an increasingly
desperate air to the man's wanderings, to the way in which
he talked to people, almost interrogating them – once or
twice Nyquist had thought Wellborn might actually start a
fight, but on each occasion he pulled away from violence
at the last moment, and on he went, searching, searching,
often well into the night.

Nyquist reached the entrance to tower block number
five and slipped inside. The lobby was empty. The elevator
door stood closed, its indicator light ascending: it had

already reached floor two. There were seventeen floors altogether. Nyquist needed to find out which apartment Wellborn was visiting; that was important. The more detail he included in his reports, the more he got paid. It was that simple. So he set off climbing the stairs, reaching the first floor and continuing on, keeping his pace steady and even. But he was already out of breath, and the stairwell was hot and sweltering. He looked down the length of the second floor corridor and saw it was empty. In fact, the entire building looked to be abandoned. He decided that the elevator was still rising. He put on some speed, taking the steps two at a time up to the third floor, and on. He was wheezing and holding his side by the time he reached the fourth landing, but he could see the elevator door halfway down the corridor: it was open. He approached warily, walking past apartments 41, 42, 43 and 44. There was someone stepping out of the elevator car. Nyquist stopped moving. He was expecting to come face to face with Patrick Wellborn. Instead he saw a young boy, standing alone. Nyquist was taken aback. He didn't know what to say.

The boy had white hair in a pudding-bowl style, and the letters *ABC* on his shirt.

"Hello. Are you lost?"

Nyquist smiled, he couldn't help it. "I think I am," he answered.

"It's easy to get lost in here."

"Tell me, did a man come up with you? In the lift?"

"Yes, sir."

Nyquist looked down the corridor: the far end seemed to disappear into a haze of hot air, like a desert mirage.

"What's your name, son?"

"Calvin."

"You live here?"

"Yes, I do. I'm supposed to be at home right now,

doing my chores." The boy spoke in a precise and careful manner, each word fully pronounced. "But playing out is much more fun."

"Calvin, do you know where the man went, after he left you?"

The boy nodded.

Nyquist bent down to the youngster's level. He was perhaps six or seven years old, with blue-grey eyes, and his fingertips were black and smeared as though he'd been playing with ink. The boy put on a brave but nervous smile as the private eye's face neared his.

"Can you show me which door it was. You only have to point."

The boy nodded. He said in a now confident voice, "I know the number."

"That's very good. Why don't you tell it to me."

Calvin moved nearer and he whispered, "Number 67."

"Apartment 67? But that's not on this floor, is it?'

"It's the truth, sir. That's where you'll find him."

Nyquist was puzzled. He had the sudden impression the boy might be lying. Maybe he was just making up stories, as any rascal might? Yet how innocent he looked and sounded, as he sang a children's rhyme to himself:

There was a crooked man, he told a crooked tale…

The boy walked away down the corridor.

Nyquist stepped inside the elevator and pressed the button for floor six. Just as the door was about to close the boy reappeared. He laughed, a repeated leap of two notes, low then high. It was almost a melody. He handed over a small object, saying, "You'll need this." And off he ran before Nyquist could even formulate a question. The car started to ascend.

The boy had given him a key fob inscribed with the number 67.

When the elevator reached the higher floor, Nyquist stepped out and walked down the corridor until he reached apartment 67. The door was closed. He tried the bell push, receiving no response. He put the key in the slot and turned it. The door opened. He entered the hallway of the apartment and waited there, listening. He could hear a rustling sound in the darkness. Warily, he stood in the doorway of the living room. His hand groped along the wall, finding a light switch.

At first he couldn't process what he was looking at: a large tree trunk was growing out of a hole in the floor, reaching up to disappear through a matching hole in the ceiling. Nyquist stepped closer. He saw that the edges of both holes, above and below, were jagged, the carpet and floorboards having been broken and smashed by the tree as it grew upwards. The tree was gnarled and ancient, the bark rotten in places and squiggling with worms, yet it looked healthy enough and a good number of branches reached out into the room, the leaves abundant despite being entirely black in color. He pulled one loose. It crackled in his hands and left behind a smear of inky sap. The tree's twigs and leaves rustled in the breeze that came in through the room's open window.

Nyquist reasoned it was some kind of weird art decoration. But it felt more like he had stepped into a dream world, a separate story from his normal reality.

He searched the rest of the apartment. There was no one there. In the main bedroom he found five sheets of manuscript paper arranged on a table, set out in a line as though in sequence. Each sheet contained a mixture of text and images. He picked up the nearest one and tried to read the writing it contained, but he couldn't make any sense of it; the words seemed to be in the wrong order. Yet as he scanned the sheet he felt a pleasant sensation, his skin was tingling all over. He wanted to read more. And then he noticed that a smaller piece of paper had been glued to the first, forming a pocket in which some object was lodged. He felt at it with his fingers, and he started to tear the sheet in two, to reveal the object: it was a tooth, a human tooth. But he hardly had time to process this strange discovery, when a noise disturbed him.

Someone had cried out in sudden agony.

Nyquist stood where he was. He shivered, cold. His hands trembled, and when he looked at them a trail of blood ran down his fingers. He couldn't understand it; where had it come from? It wasn't his blood. He wasn't wounded. The red droplets stained the paper.

And then the painful cry sounded again.

"Who's there? Show yourself."

The room was plunged into darkness. Nyquist spun, his entire body wired and ready for action, for defense, or attack. Eyes wide, seeking answers.

But the room was empty. The moonlight through the window painted one wall in a soft, silvery glow, edged with shadow.

And then a voice spoke. "Who are you?"

Nyquist turned at the sound to see that a man was standing in the doorway. He stepped forward revealing his face: it was Patrick Wellborn. The man's eyes were filled with dark intent and he spoke in a fierce whisper: "Why are you hurting me?"

It was a question that Nyquist couldn't answer.

Wellborn's eyes moved to the sheet of paper that Nyquist held in his hand, and the muscles of his face twitched in irritation.

"Don't hurt me."

Nyquist still didn't respond. This was the closest they'd ever been, observer and subject matter, face to face. He braced himself for a fight. Wellborn's face creased with anger. Rage. Pure rage. Nyquist managed to speak calmly: "I don't know what you're talking about." This was the truth, but it was a remark too far. Something snapped in the other man. Wellborn stepped closer, one hand coming out of his jacket, an object held loosely within it. Nyquist couldn't make it out, not at first, not until the object was raised up, offered, a gift, a prop in a story.

Moonlight illuminated the knife.

It flashed forward.

TURN THE PAGE

He was lying on the bed in the moonlit dark, hardly breathing. Not daring to move, just lying there. His eyes were tightly shut, his hands clenched at the sheets. Sweat ran down all over his skin so that his clothes stuck to him. The heat barely stirred in the room. There were colors moving behind his eyelids, and his head ached. But he couldn't open his eyes, not yet. Instead he lay there on the tangled sheets and listened.

He could hear his heart beating madly, nothing more.

Nyquist was still in shock, in panic. He had not yet put together the events. He couldn't think properly.

Now he heard another sound: the ticking of a clock.

Most of all he wanted to hear someone talking, or laughing, or a cry of pain even. Any sign of life would be welcome.

There was nothing.

He let his eyes come open and the room formed around him. The glow of moonlight through the half-open curtains at the window, a portion of wall and a corner of the ceiling. By turning his head he could make out the dial of the clock on a bedside table, but he couldn't see the time clearly. How long had passed since the attack? A few minutes, an hour, maybe more? There was no way of telling.

He lifted his hand up towards his face. The hand was wet, something was stuck to his fingers. It was a clump of hair. Long dirty, greasy hair.

Wellborn's hair, torn out at the roots.

His stomach churned in revulsion and he shook his hand vigorously. But the hair clung to him. He scrabbled at it with his other hand, until at last he was free of it. He managed to sit up and then get to his feet. He stood beside the bed, shivering still, and not knowing what to do next, feeling sick inside. He wanted to scream out loud. *What can I do? Help me.* It would be a useless cry. Nobody could help him.

Nyquist made his way to the bathroom. The strip light buzzed into life. The extractor fan whirred. It sounded like something alive, something caught in a trap. The water dripped from the leaky tap. He turned it full on and washed the blood off his hands.

The blood. The water swirled with it.

The color looked unreal, too bright, too vivid. He felt faint.

The patterns in the water. His own blood and the victim's, mixed together.

He glanced upwards to meet his face in the mirror and then turned away quickly from what he saw there, the splashes of red across his skin. He looked terrible, haunted. His eyes were cold. There was a cut on his cheek. He waited until the water ran clear and then he filled his palms and washed his face. For a long time, he remained as he was, bowed down. If only he could stay this way forever, his face cold from the water, his eyes closed. But in the end he had to stand back upright. He wiped his face and hands. There was another cut, deeper, on his left forearm. He shook his head at this. Nothing could get any worse than it already was. He held a wet flannel against the wound, pressing hard. He tried tying it around his arm to no avail; it kept slipping off. He gripped the sink unit with both hands and held himself against the pain, forcing it to the back of his mind. He placed the flannel down on the sink unit, laying his left arm down upon it. He used his right hand to tie a knot, grabbing one end with his teeth, the other with his fingers. He pulled. He pulled it tight.

His reflection looked back at him one last time.

Nyquist went back into the bedroom. He saw a splash of blood on the wall. According to the bedside clock it was ten minutes past midnight.

This room, this terrible situation. How the hell did it turn out like this?

He rested for a moment as he thought of the task ahead.

He was afraid.

John Nyquist was afraid.

He had killed a man.

He clicked on the overhead light and moved round the bed and stared down at the dead body that lay on the floor, half in shadow. He took it all in. The dreadfully still form, the knife on the carpet, the torn sheet. The unholy mess of it all.

The blood was everywhere.

His one remaining hope – that the whole thing had in some way never happened, that it was all a vision or a nightmare – now vanished. His life seemed to be at an end, as though he had killed himself, and not some other person.

It came to Nyquist then: he would have to phone the police, he would have to confess. It was self-defense, that was evident. Wasn't it? Of course. Of course it was. Yes, he would explain to them just what had taken place here. The truth.

But what was the truth?

He'd been following Wellborn. It looked bad. And he'd already had a few run-ins with the squad, even in his short time in this city. It was part and parcel of the nature of his job. Could he chance it? And even as he stood there looking down at the body, he found himself changing the details. The truth wasn't enough, it wasn't good enough. He was inventing, making up a story. He felt his lips growing wet, a taste of salt in his mouth. His eyes were stinging. He made a promise with himself, that he would sort all this out by his own endeavors. No police. Not yet.

He knelt down beside the bed. The lower half of the corpse was visible, while the chest area and the face were still partially hidden in shadow. Nyquist had a hope, that the man would suddenly move, that a hand would reach out, the eyes open.

He touched the skin. It was already cold.

The spirit had left the flesh.

Nyquist knelt down to examine the body. Patrick Wellborn had very distinctive features, the look of a 1930s concert pianist: long hair swept back from a high brow, arched eyebrows, bony cheeks. It was easy to imagine him dressed in black jacket and tails, playing a Beethoven sonata. But there was no music in the air, not now, no elegies. The man's hair was matted where the wound showed, and blood was pasted on the skirting board nearby.

Nyquist tried to think about the attack. Why had it happened? It had all taken place in the dark of the room, a vicious struggle to survive, a whirl of violence.

The knife slicing at his arm. A sudden cold electric shock. But he wasn't ready yet, he wasn't ready to die. He could remember being trapped in the narrow space between the bed and the wall, holding the other man close, desperate to stop him from taking another swing with the blade.

The two bodies struggling. The knife falling to the carpet. Now he had his chance: Nyquist gripped Wellborn's neck with both his hands and smashed his head over and over against the wall, as they both half-collapsed to the floor, and still he kept on until at last the man lay still within his grasp. And then Nyquist must've fallen back onto the bed and lain there, or fainted away. Some other realm took charge of him. He felt that half a funeral veil was drawn across his eyes, holding the full extent of the pain at bay.

Speaking to the police seemed even less of a possibility.

He went through the man's pockets. There was nothing of interest except for a wallet with a little cash inside it. No driving license, no photographs, no items of a personal nature. And then he found, tucked in an inside jacket pocket, a folded sheet of paper. Nyquist opened this and saw it was similar to the pages he had tried to read earlier, a mass of words all mixed up together. Again he felt his skin tingle slightly as he read a few lines of text. He placed the paper in his own pocket and rubbed at his eyes to clear them of sweat, of grit. There was something lying on the floor just to the side of the corpse: a key. It must've fallen out of Wellborn's jacket. The fob was printed with the number 66. Nyquist made his decision. It was time to turn the page, to see where the story led. He walked through to the hallway and opened the front door and stepped out. The corridor was empty. He locked the door with the key the young boy had given him. Then he walked to the next apartment along. Number 66. He leaned in and pressed the side of his head to the door panel.

He listened.

Silence. The door was firmly locked. He knocked lightly and waited a few more moments. Then he slipped the key into the lock. The door clicked opened and he walked through into the hallway.

For a moment he was worried: exactly whose story was he stepping into?

He looked into the living room, but could see nothing of interest. A jazz ballad played quietly from a radiogram in the corner. Nyquist moved down the hallway, glancing in the bathroom, also empty. He pushed open the bedroom door and was searching for the light switch when a voice called out from within. A woman's voice.

"Patrick. Is that you?"

FAR-OFF LONGING

Nyquist stayed where he was, more than halfway through the door, his hand resting on the wall. He could hear someone moving about inside, the rustle of linen sheets. And then the bedside lamp came on.

In its muted glow, they stared at each other, the man and the woman.

Her face was cast in soft red light, her voice slurred.

"Where's Patrick?" she asked.

Nyquist entered the room. "Patrick?"

"Where is he?"

The woman was lying in the bed. She gathered the sheets around her and cried out, "Get out of here!"

Nyquist closed the door. He turned on the main light. The woman covered her eyes.

"Hey. That hurts. Turn it off."

She was partway drunk, he could tell that. Nyquist went over to her. Despair made him angry. He grabbed her by one wrist, pulling her up.

"Hey!"

"Who is he?"

"What? Leave me—"

"This guy. This Patrick. Who is he?"

"I don't—"

"Tell me!"

"I don't know! He's just–"

"Just what?"

"He's just some guy…"

Her voice trailed off. Nyquist let go of her. She fell back. He could see the look in her eyes. Desperation. He could sense the need, the need to live. The way she slumped down, the way she moaned to herself and rubbed at her eyes. He looked round the room. A half empty bottle of booze stood on the bedside cabinet. The woman's clothes were strewn across the bed. The suitcase resting on a small table next to the wardrobe was the same case he'd seen Wellborn carrying, when he'd entered the tower block.

Nyquist tried to breathe more easily. His voice softened. "What's your name?"

"Zelda."

"You're his girlfriend?"

She laughed. "Me? I'm nobody's girl."

"I see."

"Oh, is that right?"

"You're a hooker."

"Well that's a very nice thing to say, I'm sure."

Nyquist laughed. It was all he could do.

"What're you laughing at?" she asked. "Creep."

"Wellborn tried to kill me."

"Oh." Her eyes opened in shock and she started to ramble, the words tumbling out like she was trying to purge herself of bad feelings:

"You can't trust anyone. Right? That's the trouble with this town, everyone's got at least five or six or more stories they're involved in, all at the same time. It's crazy, I mean how am I supposed to know who I'm dealing with? This name, that name. Character arcs, roles, aliases. Oh, it gets so confusing! Sometimes I wake up and I don't know who

I am, like, what's my part today, what do I say, when and where and how, in which accent? Don't you ever get like that, mister? You must do."

"No."

Nyquist went to the suitcase. It was old and tatty, a faded green. The two locks clicked open. "This is Wellborn's case?"

Zelda nodded. She was getting out of bed. "That's right. He brought it with him."

There wasn't much inside: a few items of clothing, a paperback novel, a gentleman's wash bag. He rummaged through the clothing and emptied out the wash bag. There was nothing suspicious, nothing that would give him knowledge. He looked at the lurid cover of the book, a pulp detective thriller called *Deadly Nightshade*. Nyquist riffled through the pages, searching for anything between the leaves: a motorbus or train ticket, a dry-cleaning stub, a parking ticket, a clue of some kind.

But there was nothing.

"What're you looking for?" asked Zelda.

"Answers."

"Why, what is it? What's happened?"

She was getting dressed, pulling on a tight cotton dress, a pair of heels. The dress was decorated with red and yellow flowers. She pinned a brooch to her collar.

"Where's Patrick?" she asked. "What have you done to him?"

He threw the suitcase across the floor. Zelda looked scared. She froze.

"What's wrong with you?"

"Just shut the hell up!"

He felt faint, he had to press one hand against the wall to steady himself. His sight blurred, the room growing hazy. And then he moved suddenly, his fist slamming into the wardrobe door. The wood splintered, buckled.

Zelda cried out.

It was all happening at once, all going wrong.

He stood there, helpless, waiting for his breath to steady. The knuckles of his right hand stung, the skin was ripped open.

Zelda watched him. She was fully sober by now, the shock cleansing her. And when he'd finally settled, she said, "Another tough guy. Just what I need."

Nyquist slid down the wall, further, until he was sitting on the floor, one hand covering his eyes. He was whispering to himself, reciting the story that had led him here, to this place, his back cold from the damp in the wall. It was pitiful.

Zelda came over to him. She knelt down at his side and put her hand on his shoulder, and she spoke in a tender voice.

"What is it, darling? What's wrong?"

Nyquist answered quietly. Zelda had to lean in real close to catch his words.

"I've killed him."

"Patrick, you mean?"

"Yes. He's dead. I smashed his head against the wall."

She took a breath and held it.

Now he looked at her. He was shivering. "He attacked me. I had to defend myself."

"Of course. It's always that way."

"Always?"

"When a man kills someone. Every story in the newspapers, or the radio, on the street, there's always some reason or other. Nobody ever admits to the simple pleasure."

Her face loomed over his, her makeup smudged, her eyeshadow lime green in color, her lips smeared with red.

He could smell the alcohol on her breath. It sent a jet of desire through his heart, both for women, and for drink. The various combinations.

"There must be something," he said. "Something you can tell me about Wellborn. Who is he? What's he doing here?"

"Come on, let's get you up. You're in shock."

She reached out a hand and Nyquist took it. She helped to pull him up. He was still trembling, his body seeking release or shutdown after the fight, the giving out of death. She sat him on the bed.

"You'll need a few minutes. To calm yourself."

"I've got none to spare."

"Minutes?"

"No time at all."

"Ah well, you know what they say…" She was checking her face in the dressing table mirror. "The road is a long tongue. I shall never reach the end of it."

Typical bloody Storyville sentiment, he thought. And he said, "I'll get there, don't you worry."

Her eyes glanced sideways at him as he continued:

"There's always a way."

He stood up from the bed. At the window he looked out over the city, which seemed a place of far-off longing. Lights were still gleaming on the main streets even at this late hour: the Festival of Words was still going on. He pictured all the various stories of the night being told, his own among them: himself, this room, the prostitute, the dead body lying beside the bed in the room down the corridor.

Where was it leading to?

He turned back to the room. Zelda was standing there, looking at him. She was waiting for something to happen.

"What's your back story?" he asked.

"My what?"

"Isn't that what they say around here?"

"Sure, sure it is."

"Then let's hear it."

She held her hand around her body for comfort. "Wellborn picked me up on a corner. About a month ago."

"Had you met him before?"

"No. That was our first time together."

"Tell me what happened."

"What are you, some kind of peeping tom?"

"A private eye."

"Same species, different family." She gave a little smile as she said this, as though she knew him already, his failures, his needs.

He asked, "So he took you somewhere?"

"We went to a hotel."

"Keep going. What next?"

"What do you think?"

"I don't know. You tell me."

"We did the business, of course. What is it with you?"

Nyquist's face screwed up. "I'm trying to work out why he attacked me, with a knife."

"A knife? You never said…"

"There it is. Maybe I did you a favor."

"You mean… it could've been…"

"Sure, why not. He needed a victim."

Zelda bit her lip. She looked anguished. "OK then, here's the deal. I didn't see him after that for a week or so, and then we met up again. But he'd changed."

"In what way?"

She hesitated. "He was… well, he was strange. Driven, taken over."

"Like an addict?"

"I thought that. But it wasn't like anything I've seen

before. He wasn't skittery, or sweaty. He was just... pure.
Whatever it was that had taken him over, he was enjoying
it. But he was scared at the same time. Something was
bothering him. Oh, I can't explain it."

"Did he bring you here, to Melville?"

"Only tonight." Zelda sat down on the bed. "He gave me
the address, and the date and the time. It was prearranged.
But he was late, see. That's why I had a little drink. He was
an hour late."

"But then he turned up?" Nyquist asked.

"He did. I thought he'd want to get down to business
right away, but I could tell he wasn't in the proper mood.
He was more agitated this time. I think he was scared."

"Of what?"

"I don't know, but he was pacing the room back and
forth like an animal caught in a trap. And then he left."

"Did he tell you where he was going?"

"No, but that he'd back in a short while, and that I was
to wait for him here."

Nyquist thought for a moment. "Did he take anything
with him?"

"Not that I could see, no."

"What then?"

"What then? Well, nothing. I had another wee drink."

"And then I turn up?"

"That's right, and now you're telling me you've killed
him. I mean to say, this is getting out of hand. This is *not*
the kind of affair I like to get involved in, not at all."

"What about the times before?"

"What about them?"

"Anything at all. Tell me who he is. What did you talk
about?"

"Oh, the usual. What we thought of the latest big stories,
and so on. He'd had trouble at work, I knew that."

Nyquist had never seen Wellborn go to any place of work, not on any of the days he'd followed him.

"Where did he work, any idea?"

Zelda shrugged. "He never told me. But he'd left there recently. Maybe he was sacked, I don't know."

Nyquist nodded and he cursed the job he'd been given, and his reasons for taking it on, pure poverty, boredom, the need to get out of the office before he went stir crazy. He should've asked the agency for more information. He should have realized that all was not clear.

Zelda looked concerned. "Look, mister. You're absolutely sure that he's dead?"

"Yes."

"I mean, you checked, and all?"

"He was dead."

"He wasn't breathing? You felt for a pulse?"

"I didn't need to."

"Oh bloody hell. You see, now we have to go in there and make sure. Well, *you* do, anyway. I'm not looking at some poor bugger with his head caved in, no thank you."

Nyquist closed his eyes. For a moment he felt again his hands around the man's neck, the shuddering impact of the skull against the wall transferred through the man's body, to Nyquist's wrists, to his brain. He'd felt the force of life leaving his attacker.

Nyquist looked at Zelda and asked, "Did Wellborn mention any other people to you, friends, colleagues, family? Any names?"

"No, nothing."

She fell silent. He did the same. She was looking at him eagerly.

"What do you want?" he asked.

"I need my money."

"You want paying?"

"Didn't you take Patrick's wallet?"

"No, it's next to the body."

"Well, I need paying."

"Didn't he pay you before, at the start?"

"Of course. But I need more now, don't you see? Danger money."

He stared at her.

"Oh, don't give me that look! I'm involved in a murder. I'm one of those accessories, like in the movies – before and after the fact."

She started to search through the bedclothes.

"I've lost an earring."

"I think you should leave here, Zelda. Run. As fast as you can, and get as far away as possible."

"What about you?"

"Don't worry about that."

"I always worry," she said. "It's part of my job."

He looked at her closely for the first time. He saw the beauty hidden away, and the tenderness, the inner need. He saw the sparkle in her eyes, almost lost, almost darkened, but not quite, not yet. He saw the loving nature, still there, held deep. And most of all he saw the loneliness. It matched his own. They had both given their best years to a dirty, thankless but necessary task. And now very little remained that was good.

His left arm was hurting. He could feel the blood soaking through the flannel under his jacket sleeve.

Drop by drop, goodness drained away. That was the fact.

He had a sudden urge to hold the woman, Zelda: to take her in his arms, to exchange some kind of comfort in the night, in the hot, drowsy, feverish, blood-stained, story-filled night. It would offer proof of life, to counterbalance the death.

But he kept his distance. "Have you got any pills?" he asked.

"What kind are you looking for?"

"Something to take the pain away."

She rummaged through her handbag. "I'll get you some water."

He looked at the floor, at the emptied-out contents of Wellborn's suitcase. The clothes, the razor and shaving soap, handkerchiefs, a bottle of cologne, the paperback novel. A thought came to him: this was a strange place to do business with a prostitute, this abandoned tower block.

Zelda returned from the bathroom with a tumbler of water and a couple of tablets. He took them and drank them down.

"Where does it hurt?" she asked.

"Everywhere."

"Pinpoint it, why don't you?"

"My arm."

"Let me have a look at it for you."

But he moved away from her touch and settled in the chair.

"Play the moody one then, see how far it gets you."

He took the folded piece of paper from his pocket and stared at the lines of text on it, some of them typed, others written out by hand. The sentences were jagged, as though they'd been cut into fragments.

"Did you see Wellborn reading this?" he asked. "It's a letter, maybe. Or a page from a manuscript, a novel."

Zelda didn't respond, not in words. But her features were contorted: was it fear they held, or something else, something more desperate, passionate even?

"Do you know about this, Zelda?"

She shook her head.

He could tell that she wasn't being completely truthful. Again, his eyes scanned the page and this time a word jumped out at him: *Wellborn*. The man's full name was written there: *Patrick Wellborn*. Now why should that be? Perhaps it wasn't a novel, or not purely fictional: the real world infiltrated the story in some way. He read on a little further and found a phrase he could make out clearly amid the jumble: *He told a crooked story*. It brought back a memory: the boy in the elevator who had directed him towards apartment 67.

"None of it makes sense," he said. "How can anyone read this?"

Zelda came close. "Let me see."

But her words were cut short as the doorbell rang.

ONE VOICE AMONG MANY

Nyquist held her back. He put a finger to his lips. Zelda's eyes widened as she looked first at him and then at the open door of the bedroom, as though expecting someone to walk in at any moment. Nyquist hurried into the hallway and then stopped. The bell rang a second time. And then a fist banged on the door.

A man's voice called out: "Wellborn? Did you bring the woman? Are you in there?"

Zelda stood just behind Nyquist. He could hear her breathing cease.

The fist rapped again. "Wellborn! Come on, open up. Dreylock wants a word, there's a good fellow." It sounded like a threat.

Another knock, even louder this time.

Then silence.

Dreylock? Nyquist committed the name to memory. He walked to the door and listened closely: people were talking to each other, the words unheard. And then footsteps moving away. He peered through the peephole and then waited a while longer. He opened the door as quietly as he could.

Behind him he heard Zelda whisper, "What are you doing?"

He peeked out and saw a group of people walking away, two men and a woman. They stopped further down the corridor at the door of apartment 67, where they appeared to be in conversation. One of the men had a key; he used it to open the door and all three went inside. Now the corridor was empty.

Nyquist had to make a decision. The door to the stairwell wasn't too far away. He turned back to Zelda and said, "Come on, I think you should follow me."

"Oh you do, do you?"

"They mentioned a woman. I presume that's you."

"Like I'm the only one in the world, you mean?"

"You want to take a chance?"

"Maybe I should. Maybe I'd be worse off with you."

"They're going to find Wellborn's body."

He slipped out of the apartment and walked the short distance to the stairwell door. He started down, taking the steps two at a time.

"Wait for me."

Zelda caught up with him. They passed the door to the floor below and carried on down. A noise rattled down the stairwell after them, the sound of feet pounding on the steps. He could feel the metal framework vibrating. Voices echoed against the peeling walls.

Zelda cried out, "They're after us. This way."

"No, we carry on down. The ground floor. Outside."

But she insisted. "We'll never make it that far."

Zelda led the way through the door to the next floor down and together they ran along the corridor until they reached the elevator. She pressed at the button over and over, but the car was in use: the indicator light showed it was stuck on a higher floor. Nyquist looked back to see that the corridor was still empty: the pursuers had not yet reached this floor, or else they had moved further down, not realizing. He looked back to see that Zelda had already moved on, away from the stairs, past one closed door after another.

"In here!" she said.

There was a door a few feet away that looked to be partway open. She went to it and urged Nyquist to follow. He did so and she closed the door behind them.

Here they waited in the dark.

And waited, his hand on her shoulder, his other hand at her side. He held her like that and felt that he was being held in turn, by her, her hands mirroring his in their positioning on his body, as though they were about to start waltzing. But they stood where they were, staring at each other. Zelda's eyes were wide and glinting and fearful, and Nyquist imagined his must look the same. Or worse.

In the dark.

In the silence.

In the silent dark of the hallway they waited, close together.

Her breath, his breath, coinciding.

In the dark.

Footsteps from outside, and the sound of talking. Nyquist had the feeling it was them, the group of three. Patrick Wellborn's friends or colleagues; or his enemies. It didn't matter which – Nyquist was prey, their quest, and he didn't know why. They probably blamed him for killing Wellborn, that's all he could imagine.

Zelda pressed tighter to him.

The warmth of her skin: it was a balm against fear.

All was quiet now, so they released each other from their embrace. Nyquist dragged the bolts across on the door, one at the top, one at the bottom. Zelda clicked the switch in the living room, while he checked the bathroom and the bedroom: all empty, all dark, no lights working.

"This must be an empty apartment," he said, keeping his voice quiet.

"A lot of them are empty, I think."

They were standing in the living room. She tried the shaded desk lamp: it worked, giving out a small cone of yellow light.

"That's better."

"Tell me who Dreylock is," he said.

"Who?"

"You've never heard the name?" Zelda shook her head. "The guy at the door shouted it. They wanted Wellborn to come out and meet Dreylock."

"I didn't hear. I was too shivery."

Nyquist took steady breaths, trying to calm himself.

"I don't know anyone here," she added. "I took the elevator to the apartment Wellborn told me about, and that was it. I didn't see anybody." Her eyes blinked a few times. "This is block five of Melville Towers. You know it's meant to be a bad place, haunted or something. People warn you about it."

"But you came here to meet Wellborn? Why?"

"Oh, I get asked to go all over. I'm used to it. And he was offering good money. Real good. And you'd be surprised what some men find exciting."

Nyquist frowned. There was something about this woman that didn't quite add up: he couldn't tell if she was telling a true story, or a made-up tale. Maybe that came with her job. He asked, "You've never brought any other clients here?"

"Clients?"

"Johns. Tricks. Whatever you call them."

Zelda clicked her fingers. "Clients, indeed! Cheek. What do you think I am, a service agency?" She'd found a drinks cabinet and was busy selecting a bottle in the dim light. "I call them my lovers, actually."

Nyquist heard the twist of a screwtop cap and then the glug of a drink being poured. The sound made his lips water, but he needed to resist temptation, at least until he was out of this place. Zelda sat down in an armchair. He just stood there a while longer, listening. There was nothing to hear, only the woman's teeth clacking gently against the glass now and then and the sound of the drink going down her throat.

He sat at the dining table, close to the lamp. "What are you drinking?"

"Gin. Do you want one?"

"No."

He leaned back in the chair and tried to relax a little. His body was numb, his arm was throbbing just beneath the veil of the painkillers: it was a predator lying in wait, just around the corner in the shadows. And the more he relaxed, the more he was aware of a noise in his head, subdued, but there: a constant ringing tone. He imagined a violinist's bow being scraped across the rim of a high-pitched bell.

"I've changed my mind," he said.

She poured him a drink and came over and handed it to him. He took a sip.

"Take your jacket off for me."

"Why?"

"Just do it."

He removed his jacket and let Zelda roll up his shirt sleeve for him until the flannel was revealed, already soaked in blood. Gently she undid this. The wound was exposed.

"Don't move a muscle," she said.

"I won't."

She got up and left the room. It was strange, how alone

he suddenly felt, in her absence. The night had been cut up into pieces, sliced by a blade into strips, and then glued back together in the wrong order. Fragments were missing. This is what he felt. Nyquist was bereft, and completely at the night's mercy. And then Zelda came back into the room, carrying a fresh flannel, a bowl of water and a piece of white cloth. She washed his arm with hot water and then dabbed at it with disinfectant. Then she wrapped it in the cloth, a large white handkerchief, making an excellent bandage of it. "I found this in a drawer in the bedroom, and the disinfectant in the bathroom."

It was soothing. "You've done this before," he said.

"Needs must." She tied a knot in the makeshift bandage. "There you are. That should keep you going."

"Yes. Thank you."

Her next words surprised him. They shouldn't have, not really, for they were often heard in Storyville, a common question to ask of someone, even of strangers.

"Have you written anything of your own?"

He admitted to his sins. "I'm trying to. But the words keep stopping mid flow."

"Oh, that's normal."

"Is it?"

"*Let it be. Keep on. Keep writing.* That's what I was taught at school."

"The letter X is broken on my typewriter."

"Well don't use any words with X in then. That's easy."

"Everyone tells me it's important, an important letter."

"For the kiss at the bottom of a letter? Or like XXX, adult rated?"

"More like X the unknown."

"It's like this," she said. "You're either a tale talker, or a tale stalker."

"Is this your own idea?"

"Pretty much. But I stole some bits and pieces."

He rested his head against the back of the chair and said, "Tell me about it."

"Right then, it goes like this. If you're a stalker, OK, all you're ever doing is running around after someone else's story. And that's fine, it's a way of life, but it's not brilliant. But if you're a tale talker, well then, your story is your own, you're making it up as you go along. You see how it is? You're in charge."

"I don't think it's that simple. Not in my business."

"Because?"

"Because I'm always following people, I'm always looking for clues, flaws, cracks in the armor. What else can I do but chase after someone else's story?"

They were speaking quietly, both of them. She looked at him closely in the lamplight.

"I used to think the same about my job, but now, it's all different."

"Why?"

"I found a voice," she answered. "It was my own voice. I didn't even know I had it. It was hidden away, well hidden. I hid it deep inside myself, ever since childhood. But when I found this voice again, a year or so back, well, it turned into a poem." She smiled. "One line of poetry, and then another. I didn't even know what it meant, not really. But the words flowed easily, once I'd started. One poem. Two. Another. I couldn't stop. On and on it went, like a river flowing."

"What do you write about?"

Her mouth downturned. "Well, nothing anymore."

"You stopped?"

"My work was stolen. I used to carry it around with me in my bag, a blue notebook filled with words, scribblings, but then someone took it from me."

"A man, you mean?"

"Of course a man." She tutted. "He took the bag and everything in it. Well, he certainly got his money's worth, that night."

"And since then?"

"Nothing. Not a word. I mean, I've tried and everything, but nothing happens. I just haven't got the inclination anymore." She paused. "The pen is dry."

"That's sad."

"Yes, isn't it."

"So what did you write about, when you were writing?"

"Well, let's see." She put a finger to her brow. "First of all, my life, I guess. I'd write about that. What I saw on the street every night, in the dark, and in men's eyes when they're lying in my arms." She thought a little more. "And then sometimes I'd write about dreams, broken or otherwise. And things that people said to me, or that I overheard, the words. But more than that: the things that are left unsaid, when two people get really close, you know? And other times I'd write about the city, the political situation, this side fighting that side, words against words for control over words, endless, endless fighting." Excitement danced in her eyes. "Other things. Oh, just lots of things, whatever came to mind. Items in the news, for instance, and cats and dogs, funny things I've seen in the daylight, people getting drunk or crying in public over their lost love, erm, what else? Cats, did I mention cats, right, right, and the secret words that people use when they think no one is listening, but of course I would never mention any names, or I'd change the names. And then at other times I'd find myself writing about my past, childhood memories, my long lost parents, whom I bless and curse in equal amounts. Oh, and the games that men and women play, and the limits of the city, where the stories drift away, where the terribly sad stories go when there's no one left to tell them, no listeners, no reciters, only the words themselves drifting away through the trees and the fields. Does that make sense to you?"

"Yes, yes. Of course." Nyquist was astonished.

Zelda caught a breath. "Well, I could go on."

"You could read me one of your poems. If you can remember one, that is."

She looked at his face and smiled and said, "Oh. Right then. Yes. I can do that. Maybe. Are you sure? Yes, OK then."

She steadied herself and took a moment to relax. Then she leaned away a little as she started to recite. Her voice was soft and breathy and tender. And in the half light, in the small humid room, in the echoing space, Nyquist listened to her words.

On the edge of town
where the stories flow away,
they stand alone,
a man and a woman
covered in silence.
They walk alone
with only one word
left unspoken between them
one word unwritten.
Until, on the border
where one breath meets another
a story begins in a kiss –
here, on the edge of town
where the words flow away.

Zelda leaned forward again. She looked nervous. "I've never read my work to anyone before."

"It's good."

"You think so?"

The poem spoke to him but he couldn't explain why; he couldn't articulate it.

"I'm no expert. But I liked the bit about the borderline."

Zelda brightened. "Yes, I like that bit as well. But what does it all mean?"

"Well, you wrote it."

"Exactly. But that's the problem. It's like asking a bee about the building of a hive."

Nyquist finished his drink.

"And anyway," she continued, "I thought you might be able to work it out. After all, isn't that your job?"

"Poetry?"

"Like you said just now, looking for clues and secrets and the like." She came in close. Her voice was filled with the tang of the gin.

Nyquist shook his head. "I think this story's beyond my reach. As yet."

"As yet? I like that. It means there might be a time…"

"For?"

"You know, when you might know… you might know what it means."

He nodded. She smiled. They stopped speaking.

There was nothing else to say.

Their faces were close.

This close…

Only silence held them apart now, and even that was breath-filled, enough for each to feel the warmth of the other, the *life* of the other, on their faces, their skin, a message passed across the tiny gap between. And for a moment he felt his lips moving towards hers: it was a movement stolen from a dream, or from the poem she had just recited.

Passion in slow motion.

Now they touched.

The kiss was held sweetly between them, equally shared, and for that one long moment it felt to Nyquist as though the shadows had drawn back, further into the corners, to let a little more light into the room.

And then they parted once again, he from her, both of them looking embarrassed. Zelda stood up awkwardly. "We still haven't been introduced properly," she said, putting on her poshest voice. "Whatever shall I call you?"

"Nyquist."

"No first name?"

He couldn't help but cover up his feelings. "Read it in the papers," he said, "when they arrest me."

She grinned. "Nyquist. I like it. That's a name with a past."

"You think so?"

"It sounds a little like *night quest*. A journey through the darkness."

"You don't know how close you are to the truth."

"The truth? Oh, I left that behind years ago."

It was a strange thing to say. He wondered what had happened to her, to bring her to this place in life, but he didn't ask.

"Where are you from?" she asked.

"Dayzone."

"Oh my. The place with the strange mist and all that, the dusklands? You poor man."

He smiled. "It wasn't so bad."

"Now you're lying to me."

His lips still tasted of her. "Why do you call them *lovers*?" he asked.

"That's the character most men want to play."

"Of course. And in this city..."

"In this city you're nothing unless you're in a story."

Nyquist finished his drink. "Trouble is, I've only been here a short while."

"I know. I can tell."

"Zelda. How do you know I'm not a cold-hearted killer?"

She thought for a moment before answering; "Because I've met those types of men. Or at least men heading in that direction. And you're not like that, Nyquist. It's in the depths of the eyes…" She touched his face with her hand. "And yours have hope in them, even now, a little bit at least."

Her sight engaged with his in the soft lamplight. She was older than he'd first assumed. He could see the lines at the corners of her eyes, the crinkles above and below, which the makeup didn't quite hide. The long tresses of her blonde hair were dark at the roots. The skin tightened over her cheekbones whenever she smiled. Each mark on her face was a symbol on a treasure map.

Zelda knew that she was being examined. She looked at him with the same intensity.

Quietly she asked, "What brought you here?"

He told her. He told her as much as he knew, the whole sorry tale. How he'd been given the case by Antonia Linden, a woman who ran a top-flight investigative agency; how he'd followed Patrick Wellborn for four days and nights, and how he'd ended up here, in Melville Five, with his subject matter dead, dead by his own hand.

"It seemed like easy money, when I took it on." His eyes stared ahead, seeing nothing.

"You're scared. I can tell."

"I've killed a man." He looked away. "I need time to think, that's all."

He took the piece of manuscript paper from his pocket and placed it under the lamp. He had a feeling the paper was important. Wellborn had been carrying it, perhaps bringing it to the bedroom of apartment 67, where the other papers rested on the table. And he'd been so pained when he'd seen that Nyquist had torn one of the sheets in two.

There was a page number at the bottom: 49. So he had assumed there were many other such pages, all belonging to the same manuscript.

Nyquist started to read. He saw again Wellborn's name and the line about someone telling a crooked story, but beyond that it was a muddle, so many phrases stuck together with neither rhyme nor reason. Sentences started and then broke off, and other sentences of unrelated subject and style took over halfway through. He was reading his way through the maze in a puzzle garden. But the crooked story phrase gave him an inkling: the writing itself was crooked in some way, broken apart and scattered.

"I can't make head nor tail of it," he said. "Everything's jumbled up."

"Let me read it." She took the paper from his hands and gazed at it without speaking. He thought she might be under a spell.

"Zelda?"

Still she stared at the words, her eyes darting from one to another, filled with longing. She started to murmur to herself, and to make little cries of delight.

Nyquist took the paper off her.

"No."

Her fingers clung to it. The paper actually started to tear. "Zelda!"

She breathed again and relaxed. And her hand opened up. He folded the paper and replaced it in his pocket.

"What happened to you?"

Now she looked confused. "I don't know... I don't

know..." And she looked around in a daze, as though waking from a dream.

"Where do you live?" Nyquist asked. "Which part of town?"

It took her a moment to answer. "Christie."

"That's not too far away. Come on." He stood up and was already moving toward the door. "We need to get out of here."

But she sighed and said in a whisper, "I feel so lost."

Nyquist wavered, standing on the threshold of the room. He looked at her face, half in gloom, half aglow in the lamplight. Her voice was so resigned, so adrift on other realms, he didn't know what to think. Doubt triggered his heart. It was bittersweet. Zelda was on his side, he felt that. He had to believe that. She was all that he had, right at this moment, his only connection to simple human kindness. Her story enfolded him, his story in hers – he was already tangled up in it, he could feel the words pulling at him.

"There's something going on here," he said, almost to himself. "Beyond what I know. I just need to work it out."

"How are you going to do that?"

"I'll find out why Wellborn attacked me. I'll prove myself innocent. Self-defense."

Zelda sighed, and then held her breath. "Shhh! Do you hear that?" she said.

The shadows whispered around them.

Words were forming.

Neither of them moved.

And then he came to her, close once more. "What is it?"

"Voices."

"More than one?"

"Yes. Many of them."

"Where?"

She squeezed his arm and she led the way, following the

sound. They went into the hallway. Nyquist stopped at the open bedroom door and peered within at the darkness. It seemed to move – the darkness moved. There was no other way of describing it. The darkness trembled and whispered and the voices called to him.

He entered the room. The shadows hunched in the corners and clung to the ceiling. The voices called from the center of the space, from the air, disembodied. He walked forward a few more steps, expecting at any moment a hand to reach out and touch him, or to strike him, even. But the room was empty. And still the voices called, they swirled around, calling from one side and then another. He tried to listen, to discern one voice from the many, to follow the words, the exact meaning of what was being said. But the voices merged together, male, female, young and old, adult and child, and nothing could be made out, not clearly.

Zelda stood in the doorway, not daring to enter. Her voice was as soft as it could be: "What are they saying?"

He didn't answer. The voices held him in their spell.

"It's the ghosts," she said. "The ghosts of all the people who have lived here over the years, lived and died."

Her very words disturbed the air around him, and the voices fluttered madly before settling back again. It was enough to set him free from their allure, their magic charm, whatever it was. He moved back to the door and said, "We should leave." She nodded in agreement and turned away. But Nyquist stood at the bedroom door one last time and looked back into the solid dark. Again he had the sense of the darkness waiting for him, wanting to pull him closer, to claim him. He would be one more voice lost in the tangled air, a story told forever until the great silence fell upon the Earth. The thought of this troubled him deeply and he was about to move away when one voice in particular called out, and he stopped and stared ahead.

Zelda watched him. "Let's go," she said, her voice as quiet as all the others.

But he remained as he was, frozen, listening. His eyes held such a look of pain that she had to stand near him and listen also. And then she heard it.

…Nyquist… Nyquist… Nyquist…

It was a woman speaking, soft and tender; calling, calling to him. Now another joined with her, this time a man, and this time whispering a different name:

Zelda… Zelda, we're here… We're waiting for you…

Now she too was entranced. They stood close together, not daring to move.

…We're here… Zelda, Nyquist… We're waiting for you… Join us…

Zelda held his arm tightly and felt his body tense up with fear. The words batted against their faces and hair and clothing, living creatures, like moths in the night air.

…We're here… we're waiting…

OTHER PEOPLE'S STORIES

Nyquist was the worst affected. He could still hear the voice in his head, his own name being called. Zelda took charge. She pulled him along. The corridor was empty but she kept looking around nervously, this way and that, expecting at any minute to see the three pursuers, whoever they might be. Wordless sounds came from Nyquist's mouth and when she glanced back at him she could see that his eyes were glazed. His feet were dragging on the carpet. It was so bad, Zelda didn't know what to do to help. And then a door opened a little way down the corridor and she stopped where she was, with Nyquist alongside. A man came out of the doorway. He looked to be in his thirties, with a closely shaved head and a wine-colored blemish on one side of his face. He stood there in silence, his dressing gown hanging open over striped pajamas.

"I'm sorry," Zelda said to him. "Did we wake you?"

The man made no reply, he didn't even look at her. He bent down to place a tin bowl on the floor just outside his door, as he made a clucking noise with his tongue. He called out, "Here, Peterson. Come on, boy." Straight away a tabby cat darted from behind a potted plant further down the corridor and started to wolf down whatever meat or fish the bowl contained. The man smiled and patted the cat's head. Zelda decided that both man and cat were harmless. She pulled Nyquist along until she reached the door of the elevator. They were in luck, the car was at the floor already. She pressed the button to open the doors and she and Nyquist went inside. Nyquist leaned against the wall rubbing at his face and eyes. His mouth felt dry, his throat irritated by a ticklish sensation. He wanted to gag. The voices were now inside him, he could hear them whispering in his skull.

"Which floor?" Zelda asked.

"Ground." The one word took him an effort. "The outside."

Zelda examined the panel. "I'm not sure which it is."

He leaned away from the wall and almost toppled over but she caught him and held him upright. "You feel like a drunken man who still thinks he can perform."

Nyquist glared at the wall panel, willing the buttons to come into focus.

"What floor are we on now?"

"The fourth."

"Press the button."

"There is none."

"No button?"

"Not for the ground floor, no."

Nyquist narrowed his eyes. He saw that Zelda was right: there was no button for the ground floor, only a gap below the first floor.

"There's no button," he drawled.

"What do you want, mister? A prize?"

He pressed the button marked with the number one, and the doors slid to and the car started to descend.

"We'll walk down from the first floor," he said.

"Sure, we can do that."

"What happened to the ground floor button?"

Zelda shrugged. "How would I know? Maybe some kids stole it?"

"Or maybe…"

"What?"

"There is no ground floor."

Zelda shook her head at this. "Nyquist, you're really suffering."

"The building doesn't want us to leave. It was calling to us."

"Oh God, don't say that! What is wrong with you?" She laughed nervously. "I don't want to think about such things."

The car reached the next floor down and stopped, and the panel light remained fixed on the number three. It blinked on and off. Zelda stared at the doors, expecting them to slide open and someone to enter, scared it might be one or all of the gang who had chased them down the stairs. But the doors remained closed. The car was stationary.

She looked at her companion. Nyquist's eyes were closed and his body lolled against the wall. He was trembling. Quietly she said, "It's just the people downstairs, or upstairs, or in the adjacent apartments."

His eyes opened. He didn't understand.

"The voices we heard, in that bedroom. It's just people talking in the other apartments and the voices travel through the walls, or the pipes."

"You think so."

"That's what I think."

"You said the place was abandoned."

"I told you, a few people live here. I mean, we met that man in the corridor, didn't we, with the cat?"

Nyquist glared at her. "You're trying to make me feel better, is that it?"

She shrugged and looked away and said, "Is that the thanks I get?"

"Whoever it was, living or dead, they said my name. Our names! They know we're here."

"I think…"

He waited for her explanation. She didn't have one.

"I think we misheard. We were confused, the gin made us tipsy."

"Both of us?"

"Oh, don't get all uppity. I'm just positing a suggestion."

"Positing?"

"Is that too fancy a word for you?"

Zelda looked defiant and she pressed at the first floor button a few times, hoping to get the elevator moving, or for the door to open. Neither happened.

"I'm getting hot." She wafted frantically at her face with a hand. "Did I tell you I was claustrophobic? No? Well I am. And there's another nice word for you. Four syllables."

"What's wrong?" he asked. "Why aren't we moving?"

"I don't know." She pressed a few more buttons at random. "We're stuck."

Nyquist wiped at his brow with the back of a hand.

Zelda tried a smile. "Well this is a state of affairs, I must say."

He didn't respond. They both fell into silence, each pressed up against opposite sides of the elevator. Zelda fidgeted with her bag. "How long will we be here?" she asked.

"I don't know."

She looked around at the confines of the elevator car, shook her head sadly, and then said, "Can you imagine, as a teenage girl I dreamed of writing, of telling stories that everyone would fall in love with. I'd write my own adventure story and make myself the heroine." She sighed heavily. "And now look at me."

"You're not so bad."

"Is that the best you can do? *Not so bad?*" Zelda grimaced. "I'm plying cheap fantasies to two-bit losers once or twice a night just to make them feel better about themselves, like they're big strong men, or romantic heroes, or whatever else tickles them. Whatever makes them feel alive, for an hour or two."

"You wrote your poems."

"Oh sure. Poetry. Now there's a way to get rich."

The car started again with a jolt, and the elevator descended.

"Thank God." She smiled broadly. "My grandma told me: once a story's started, there's no escaping it. Not until it's done. Not until the very last word is told."

The car stopped a second time.

Zelda groaned. "We should've taken the stairs."

"What floor are we on?"

"I think we're between floors."

Nyquist made a noise, a murmur.

"Are you all right?"

He didn't answer. He was staring at the wall before him, his eyes narrowed. Zelda reached for him, worried, but he pushed her away and continued to stare ahead, and a word, a cry, caught in his throat.

"What is it?"

He spoke in a rush. "I don't know where I am. I don't know which story I'm in."

"Yours and mine, of course."

Her answer did little good and he started to shudder. Zelda had seen this happen a few times before, this sudden fear that took people over, when they felt the city's stories overwhelming them, strangling them.

"Nyquist. It's all right, I'm here. I'm here for you."

He shook in her hands and a line of spittle overflowed his lips. He cried out, "I've got no story. No story!" The car jerked and started once more to descend. The sudden movement set him off worse than ever and he cowered as though the four walls and the floor and ceiling were all closing in.

"This is the story," Zelda insisted. "Our story. Yours and mine, intermingling." She bent down with him and held on tight and said the words over and over: "Our story, in this moment. Zelda and Nyquist. Two adventurers. Our story!" And at last he started to calm down and his body rested in her arms. Slowly, he came back upright.

The car stopped and the doors opened.

"We're here," she said. "The first floor."

The man looked back at them from the corridor.

There was a moment when neither party recognized the other. And then Nyquist was jolted back to life, to full attention, as his body took over in an instinctive movement. His fist banged on the button panels, hitting them at random, willing the doors to close in time.

The man outside stuck his foot between the closing shutters. He was a big guy, at least half a foot taller than Nyquist and built wide and heavy. He moved slowly, but his weight was enough to cause damage, as he barreled into the elevator car. Nyquist was taken off guard. His opponent pummeled him with a red raw fist, a blow that drove Nyquist further into the elevator. The back of his skull connected with the rear wall. There was a moment of darkness and then he was sliding down the wall to the floor. He heard Zelda crying out: she seemed to be a very long way away, in another time, another place. And then the man was at him again, his fist raised to inflict further damage. Nyquist was in the worst position: he could hardly move, the space was too small and his opponent took up too much of it. The air was flashing with colors and sparks. He was blacking out, he was going under. Zelda was there with him now, down at his side, she was screaming up at the man, yelling at him to stop, but he didn't stop, he simply grabbed her and threw her against the other wall and then he bent down and held Nyquist by the throat and lifted him up, almost lifting him off the floor, it was so easy a task. Nyquist felt blood dripping down into his eyes, half-blinding him. The man stared at him, teeth glinting, breath foul and his eyes narrowed almost to slits. He dragged Nyquist from the elevator and into the corridor. Zelda stumbled after them both. There were voices coming from further down the corridor and she looked that way to see the other two pursuers, the man and the woman approaching.

Zelda stood her ground and cried at them to stay away and to leave Nyquist alone. No one listened to her, nobody cared.

Nyquist was down on the floor. Sideways on he saw Zelda being dragged away by the other man, the woman helping him. Down the long, ever-distancing tunnel of his dwindling vision they disappeared, Zelda screaming out at him in silence, complete silence, her mouth wide open but empty of all noise, her eyes filled with anger and despair. Nyquist cursed the words of the world that had brought him here, a helpless case. The big man hit him again on the side of the head and now he could feel the carpet fibers in his mouth, the taste choking him. One last time he called out for Zelda. His hands scrabbled for purchase, but nothing would hold, nothing, nothing at all, the world was slipping away and he was sliding down the incline of his own consciousness as it tipped and tilted crazily. His nails dug into the flesh of his attacker, hung on, but they were ripped away easily. He was being pulled away from everything that was good in life, all light, all warmth, all peace, all love.

All dreams.

Every last dream.

CROOKED MAN BLUES

She was a stranger, haloed by lamplight.

"He's waking up."

An unseen man responded to the woman: "So he is, Amber."

Nyquist forced his eyes open fully.

The woman's hair was jet black and shiny with ringlets on each side, and her skin was doll-white except for the eyes and lips which were painted as dark as her hair. From the look of her, Nyquist felt he might be in a cabaret bar, some place in the post-war years, a dive. The music he could hear – a barrelhouse blues from an out of tune piano – only added to this atmosphere.

He sat up, groaning in pain.

He couldn't move freely, his hands were tied at the wrists with twine.

The unseen man continued: "But he looks terrible, don't you think? A pile of flesh and blood and nothing much else."

This character now loomed into sight, a thin guy dressed in a double-breasted pinstripe suit, a dark blue shirt and a purple tie with a large knot. He smoked a cigarette with delicate ease and gazed at the fingernails of his other hand, searching for dirt, no doubt.

Nyquist tried to speak, to ask about Zelda, but managed only another groan.

The thin man sauntered over. "Don't exert yourself, Mr Nyquist. Not yet."

It was a threat.

"My name is Vito. And this is Amber." The woman smiled with her black lips. "And this is Lionel. Well, you've met him already, I think." Vito smiled with the least possible movement of his facial muscles.

Lionel grunted. He was the big number who had attacked Nyquist in the elevator. His current victim was an upright piano which he pounded with his giant fists, punishing it for some previous misdemeanor, the splayed fingers often hitting two or even three notes at the same time: so it wasn't the instrument that was out of tune, it was the man's hands.

"Igor Stravinsky would have loved it, don't you think?" said Vito. "Oh surely it would've caused a riot in Paris."

Now the blues gave way to a ragtime tune that rattled like a skeleton in chains. Amber started to dance to the rhythm, her lithe body made even more feminine by the man's suit she was wearing. The pearls around her neck swayed in time to the manic beat. Vito watched dancer and piano player with utter disdain in his eyes. His glossy gelatined hair shone under the light. "Such brazen show-offs." Vito's voice was cultured, dripping with decades of privilege; somehow or other, he had fallen on hard times.

He was dangerous.

Nyquist wiped at his face, as best he could with his hands tied together. He could feel the dried blood on the side of his head. The music sounded like a crazed funeral march in his skull, calling him to an early grave. He wasn't ready for such a journey, not quite yet, but the slightest movement made him feel dizzy.

At last he managed to speak. "Where's Zelda?"

Vito tilted his head to one side like an amused bird of prey. "Your lady friend, the drunken whore?"

"Where is she?"

"Of course, you're concerned." Vito smiled and turned to his companions. "Amber, why don't you bring in our other guest."

She nodded and left the room.

"Now, don't worry," Vito continued. "Zelda's been well taken care of."

Nyquist felt his anger biting. He got to his feet and stepped forward, his bound hands clenched into fists and raised up together like a club, ready to strike.

"Steady on, old boy. You'll do yourself an injury."

The room seemed to melt a little. "What have you done to me?"

"A little precaution."

He'd been drugged, that was it. A narcotic of some kind. His veins were heavy with it, his bones also, and his skin was another man's skin that he was living inside for the time being. He sat down again and rested his head on his hands. And when he closed his eyes all he could see was the dead man rising up before him. Patrick Wellborn. He could barely think a single clear thought without it threatening to overpower him.

Amber came back into the room, leading Zelda by the arm. Nyquist looked on as his newfound friend let herself be guided. She shuffled along with her body drooped forward and her head bowed down almost to her chest. Her once-long blonde hair had been chopped at quite roughly with a pair of scissors, so that chunks of it were missing.

"Zelda?"

She made no response to his call, not at first.

"Zelda? What have they done to you?"

Lionel started to play a dramatic melody, something that might accompany a silent movie. He was a real joker.

Now Zelda looked up and Nyquist drew in his breath at what he saw. Her face was bruised in different places, one of the wounds so bad that blood was still wet and pulpy on her skin. Her eyes, when they finally alighted on Nyquist, seemed utterly bereft of life. He got to his feet once more and looked deeply at her, willing at least a spark to be present. But there was only dimness, only a soft unfocused gaze that soon enough drifted away from him, without any proper recognition.

"Why have you done this?"

Vito answered simply: "I might ask the same, actually. I'm presuming it was you who attacked Patrick Wellborn? You beat him to death, from the looks of his injuries."

Nyquist took a step forward, trying to spit out an expletive. But his response was cut off halfway through the word. He felt dizzy. The music stopped suddenly. Lionel had raised his bulk from the piano, and he and Amber and Vito were all standing there looking at Nyquist. What were they looking at? He couldn't work it out. Through a yellow haze he saw Zelda collapse to the floor.

In sympathy, he sat down himself, back onto the seat.

"Will he be all right?" Amber asked. "He looks dreadful."

"I'm sure," Vito said to her.

"He'd better be," said Lionel. "We don't want any trouble, not when Mr Dreylock wakes up."

"There won't be any trouble," announced Vito. "Believe me." He was the leader of this little triangle, but even he was looking worried now.

And still Nyquist couldn't work out why. And then he threw up. His whole body was bent over, heaving and vomiting, right on the carpet.

Amber laughed at him. Vito sneered with disgust. Lionel hopped from one foot to the other, while running the palm of one hand over his silvery crew-cut.

"Clean that up," Vito said.

Lionel puffed out his barrel chest. "Me? Why me?"

"Because you put him in this state."

"I only hit him. You slipped him the Mickey Finn."

Amber chimed in, protecting Lionel: "Vito, don't be a bully. Leave him alone."

"Clean it!"

The edge in Vito's voice acted on Lionel like a trainer's whip. The big man made his way to the door of the room, moaning as he went.

Nyquist felt terrible; he wiped at the vomit on his lips with his bound hands and wished for better times, if he could only find a way out of this state. He scanned the room, seeking a means of escape. It was a large apartment, far more lavish than any he had been in as yet, furnished well in the art deco style. His sight moved to the large window, through which he could see the night sky. He was high up in the tower block, somewhere near the top floor, a luxury suite. Only the old piano seemed out of place; it looked like an instrument salvaged from a public house, or a brothel. Vito stood near the door. Nyquist was caught here, and the drug was holding him back from action.

He looked down at Zelda, where she lay curled up on the floor, softly moaning to herself, and his head cleared a little, seeing this. Her remembered her face as it was before, and her hair, and the beautiful lines around her eyes. That smile. Her spirit. The short time they'd spent together, close, touching, an hour or so, if that. Two lonely people reaching out to each other, in the cold, in the night, that was all it was. Yet it seemed to mean so much more to him, the moments freighted with poetry. Those lines she had recited, he tried to recall them. *A man and a woman in silence. Walking alone, one word spoken between them, one word written.* No. No, he was getting it wrong. Oh damn. He would have to ask her, that was it, when all this was over and they were safe, he would get her to recite the poem again, just for him. And the thought of this future event gave him hope, a way forward.

Lionel came back into the room carrying a mop and bucket. He started to clean the floor around Nyquist's feet, slopping suds into the carpet. This close up, the scabs and blisters were visible on the big man's knuckles, wrapped tight around the handle of the mop. Amber looked on with a look of concern in her eyes. Vito was already bored, he had retreated to the table where he sat quietly, reading a newspaper while idly spooning chunks of corned beef direct from the tin to his mouth. Nyquist's only chance now was to wait, willing his blood to clear itself of the drug, and his mind to settle.

A sudden noise startled him, the sound of a bell coming from another room.

Everyone stopped what they were doing.

Lionel held the mop in mid-stroke, water dripping from it. Vito frowned and folded his newspaper in two. Amber stood to attention, her entire being focused on the sound. No one spoke. The ringing sound continued, this time followed by a man's voice screaming.

"Amber! Amber, I need you! I need help."

Immediately the woman responded. She left the room and hurried down the corridor.

Lionel and Vito looked at each other. Lionel was worried. Vito lit a cigarette; some of his old composure had returned. He stood up and sauntered over to Nyquist, where he blew smoke into a series of blue circles that rose towards the ceiling, drifting apart like a set of faulty halos.

Nobody spoke.

Zelda looked to have passed out. No one attended to her.

Nyquist prepared himself for another attempt at standing up, but his body was still too weak. He had to remain where he was.

And then Amber reappeared at the door. She walked over to her bag on the table and took a few items from it. Nyquist saw a pair of scissors in her hand.

"What does our good master want?" Vito asked.

"First he needs fixing up," Amber replied. "And then he wants you to bring the fellow in to see him." She nodded towards Nyquist.

"Will do," Vito replied. "Just make sure Dreylock looks nice for our visitor."

Amber frowned at this and left the room.

Vito turned back to his captive. "Well, well, you are privileged. The great man himself demands your presence."

Just then Lionel started up on his piano once more, vamping a few dissonant chords and singing over them in a gruff voice:

There was a crooked man and he told a crooked tale,
He scratched a crooked story with a crooked nail.

Despite the wrong notes, the song played around in Nyquist's head, tormenting him. Vito grimaced, anger sparking in his eyes. "Not now, Lionel."

"Not now?" The big man's hands hovered over the keyboard. The last notes were still ringing out. "Are you sure?"

Vito stubbed out his cigarette in an ashtray. "There's a good chap."

Lionel, somewhat reluctantly, leaned back on the piano

stool. Vito relaxed. He took out a small, neat-looking pistol from the inner pocket of his jacket and checked it was loaded. Satisfied, he replaced it in his pocket and sat back down to read his newspaper. Nyquist looked from one man to the other – the first elegant and cruel, the other muscle-bound and almost childlike – seeing the tension between them, indeed between all three members of the group, the woman included. This was not a strongly bound unit, not at all, and in the cracks between them all he might find a means of escape, of hurting them even. Resetting the balance.

He said, "Tell me why I'm here."

Vito turned the page of his newspaper. Lionel was still sitting at the piano, his hands folded on his lap. Neither of them looked at him, neither spoke.

Another turn of the paper.

A hand was tempted towards a few keys of the piano, and then removed.

"What do you want from me?"

Vito tutted. He pointed to a section of the paper and said. "Have you seen this? They want to have even more control over the city's stories."

"Who does?" Lionel asked.

"The Narrative Council."

"I hate those bastards. They should leave well alone. Let the people live the stories they want to live."

"Yes, quite. A bold thought. Still…" Vito closed the newspaper. "At least they can't touch us, not in here."

Amber came back into the room. She looked fraught, a little nervous. "He's ready to see you now," she said.

Vito nodded. "Lionel, if you would, a little help."

Lionel got up from the piano and came over to Nyquist and lifted him. He struggled a little, but couldn't find the strength to fight back. Together, Vito and Lionel dragged his inert form over to the doorway and down the hallway towards a closed bedroom door. His hands were still tied, the twine drawing blood from the pinched, raw flesh.

Vito knocked and waited for a cry from within. Then he opened the door and Lionel pushed Nyquist through.

The room was so dark that he couldn't see anything, not to begin with. He was aware of Lionel leaving the room and closing the door behind him. Vito remained at his side, holding Nyquist steady with a hand on his arm. Then Vito moved away a single step and Nyquist remained upright, swaying slightly on his feet. Slowly his awareness was coming back to him and he peered into the blackness of the room, knowing a figure was sitting there, a man, perhaps resting on the bed. But he couldn't yet see the figure clearly. A breath was drawn, a rattle followed by a wheezing, slightly musical sound like a broken piano accordion.

Vito spoke to the shadows in a quiet, referential voice. "Mr Dreylock, sir, this is the man we saw coming out of Wellborn's apartment."

At first the figure made no move. He took a few more breaths, each one as pained as the last, before slowly reaching his hand out to the side, towards a cabinet.

A lamp clicked on and the face of the bed's occupant was revealed.

Nyquist gasped at the sight before him. He felt sick.

STITCHES

The man's hand moved away from the lamp and beckoned
to the visitor, urging him closer. With careful steps Nyquist
did as he was told. He was still a little unsteady on his feet.

"Closer. Closer."

Each utterance was drawn out with an effort.

"Closer!"

Nyquist stepped up to the side of the bed. They were
both in the circle of lamplight, each looking at the other.
Dreylock held the stare easily, but Nyquist felt queasy and
it took all his effort to maintain eye contact.

"Not a pretty sight, eh?"

"I've seen worse."

It was a lie, the best he could do.

Dreylock laughed out loud, which set off a bout of
coughing. He said to Vito, "Do you hear that? I've seen
worse!" More strained laughter.

"He's a comedian, sir."

"He is. He is, that. *I've seen worse.* Oh my!"

Another helpless, rattled-out laugh left Dreylock looking
agonized. He breathed heavily and reached for a tumbler
of water on the bedside cabinet, which also contained a
collection of medicine bottles, salves, ointments and the
like. He took a sip of water and swallowed a white pill.

"Excuse me," he said. "You're not seeing me at my best."

Dreylock was propped up against the headboard, his upper body visible above the covers. He wore a striped pajama top which was stained down the front with drool and foodstuffs. At first he seemed an old man, albeit one of considerable build. But now that Nyquist saw him close up he could see that Dreylock was younger, middle-aged, but his physical features aged him dreadfully. His was a face from a nightmare – the brow, cheeks, chin and shaven skull were all marked by a series of scars set at jagged angles to each other, where the skin didn't quite meet, with each portion of skin held together by stitches. It was a patchwork of a face with a horrible home-made quality to it, something made by a blind, inebriated god on a bad day. The stitches were amateurish, ragged and placed at irregular intervals. A great weight of sadness was hanging upon the man, hooding his eyes, bending his shoulders, and he sighed: a sound carried directly from the heart.

"Mr Nyquist... well, here we are." He took another sip of water. "It's your first time here in Melville Five, I'm guessing? Yes, I thought as much." Dreylock nodded and smiled. "And how are we treating you?" Now that he'd started to speak properly, his voice was charming, almost melodious.

Nyquist didn't answer.

Dreylock turned to Vito. "He looks a little confused. Have you hurt him?"

Vito looked embarrassed. He shook his head. "A little chloral hydrate, that's all."

So that was it, Nyquist thought. Knock-out drops. He must have swallowed them at some point, the drink forced down his throat. His bile rose.

Dreylock tutted at Vito. "You're so primitive, you really are. And what have you done to the poor man's hands?"

"Sir, we need to be careful…"

"Untie him, for God's sake. We're civilized people."

Vito took out a small penknife and cut through the twine. Nyquist rubbed his wrists, one against the other, to alleviate the pain.

"Lean into the light, please. I want to see what you look like."

Nyquist did so. He felt he was being examined by Dreylock as an entomologist might a new specimen, something in a jar, or even worse, twitching on a pin. It was the lack of true expression that unnerved the most: behind the man's scars and wounds, only pain was visible. All other emotions had been exiled from the features, and even when Dreylock spoke with a soft voice, that agony remained in his eyes, in the broken plates of skin that shifted slightly as his muscles moved beneath.

"Mr Nyquist, I only want to know about your part in the story."

"Which story?"

"Really? You're asking me that? Vito here tells me that you killed Patrick Wellborn. Isn't that true?"

"I retaliated."

"Pray tell, what did you do to upset him so?"

"I tore a piece of paper in two."

"Oh, that will do it! That would do it. Nasty. And so cruel."

"I don't know what you're talking about."

Dreylock smiled at some inner joke and said, "Those papers meant the world to him."

Nyquist felt his newly freed hands clench in anger.

"Why should I even talk to you?"

Dreylock sneered. "Oh, we're getting irate now. Vito, I do believe your preparation is wearing off. Yes, indeed. He's showing his teeth."

"Let Zelda go. She's got nothing to do with this."

"We will decide upon this matter in due course…"

Dreylock stopped in mid flow. He moaned and spluttered. His body was racked with pain as his face broke apart at one of the junctures. He was touching at his cheeks and brow, fingers smeared with blood. He called out: "Amber! Amber, I need you! Quickly!" All the pain of his life was collected in his voice. "Amber!"

The young woman hurried in. "What is it?" She looked around and said to Vito, "Can't you handle anything?"

Dreylock pleaded with her: "Amber, help me, please."

She walked over to the bedside and picked up a few items from the cabinet.

Vito said, "Shall I take him outside, boss?"

"No. No, let him stay. Let him see this."

Dreylock's upper body was perfectly still as his eyes glowed with hatred. He wanted to torture Nyquist with the blood on his face, the blood that flowed from the reopened scar. It was a mask of pride.

Amber calmed her boss down, gently patting his shoulder and cleaning his face with a damp cloth.

Dreylock said, "Hold him still. Make him watch."

But Nyquist didn't need to be forced. He looked on as Amber took up a surgical needle and thread. With deft movements she began to sew the two separated parts of her patient's face back together, repairing the damage. As far as Nyquist could tell, there was no anesthetic being used, only Dreylock's own willpower, which must have been immense. He just sat there and glared at Nyquist as the needle moved in and out of his flesh, in and out, and a line of small black stitches appeared. Amber concentrated, Dreylock grimaced. The work continued, from one torn patch of skin to another, a smaller wound this time, the needle moving up and down. Nyquist was hypnotized

by the work, by the extreme nature of the man's life, by
Amber's complete control of the situation, by the obvious
love she was showing her patient. And at last the job was
finished. Amber wiped away the last of the blood and
tidied up.

"Thank you, my dear," Dreylock said to her.

Amber nodded and left the room.

"Vito, go with her."

"Are you sure?"

"Go on! I need to be alone with our visitor."

Vito followed Amber, closing the door behind him.
For a moment silence took over. And then Dreylock said,
"Please, sit down. We need to talk."

Nyquist stayed on his feet.

Dreylock nodded. "As you please. You know, I really
must apologize for showing you that operation. But I
wanted you to know of the nightly ordeal I have to go
through."

"I can't imagine. I really can't."

"Oh, it's particularly bad tonight. Other times I'm quite
lively. Up and about, strolling down the corridors. Now
then..." He smiled. "You have a good few questions, I
imagine. The first, as you brought up, concerns the safety
of your companion, Zelda."

Nyquist nodded. "There's no need to hurt her. No need
for her to be here."

"I have to disagree, I'm afraid. Zelda is important to me,
in my present task." He licked at a spot of blood on his
upper lip. "Now then, second question..."

"There's no other question."

"You do disappoint me. I rather thought you'd be
curious about my face. Most people are."

Nyquist didn't respond. But Dreylock carried on,
obviously enjoying his captive audience. "The thing is, it's

not just my face." He undid the top buttons of his pajama jacket to reveal his upper chest and neck. Nyquist saw the scars that spread across the skin: he was a jigsaw of a man, a person of fragments. "But of course," he continued, "the face is the worst. I really need to contain any strong emotions, for they cause me such trouble. Such is my... burden." He put a special emphasis on this last word, as though the very speaking of it caused him agony.

Nyquist knew that his only way out of this predicament, the only way to help Zelda, was to go along with the game. "Who did this to you?" he asked. It was a key question, for it brought a fierce tremor to Dreylock's face, such that the freshly tailored scars might break open once more. Nyquist tried a guess. "Was it Wellborn? Is he to blame?"

"In a sense. In the sense that he introduced me to this place, this building. And to the boy who lives here."

"The boy?"

"Calvin. That evil little runt."

"He did this to you?" Nyquist couldn't believe what he was hearing.

"Oh, you've met him, have you?"

"Yes, I have."

"The little sod tempts you, he leads you on, he makes such promises, such treasures to be had." Dreylock coughed again and shook his head. "Stories, beyond stories, beyond stories." His voice was brittle, weighted by anger. "And when it's all over and the deed is done, you hardly ever see the boy again, not unless he's got some job for you. He darts about here and there like that scallywag Puck from *A Midsummer Night's Dream*, making mischief. That's his job, see, entrancing, goading, luring. And now..." He raised a hand to his scarred features. "You see what happens, when it all goes wrong? The consequences."

Nyquist still didn't understand.

Dreylock continued, "Patrick Wellborn held my one good chance at being cured. He was given a task: to bring Zelda to the tower. This is what Oberon wanted."

"Oberon?"

"Calvin's father, or grandfather, or great grandfather. I really don't know. He's the owner of this whole place. And evil through and through."

"And he wanted Zelda brought here? Why?"

"For his pleasure. For his collection. God knows." Dreylock dismissed the thought with a wave. "What matters is this: that Oberon will be pleased with the task completed, with Zelda's delivery, and that in his mercy he might make me whole once more."

Dreylock's eyes lit up at the thought. Nyquist saw the truth, the threat. He didn't know how precisely, but Zelda was in danger: right from the beginning they were after her, and Nyquist had simply gotten in the way.

Dreylock studied him. "I believe that you and I were destined to meet. It was written."

It was written…

It was a phrase Nyquist had heard a good few times in the past months; the idea that some life stories were already written out, waiting to happen in reality. This was seen as both a good thing and a bad thing, depending on the circumstances, and the teller. The whole idea angered him.

"I have a great desire to hit you right now."

The man in the bed stared back at him, quite calmly. "The more you hurt me, Mr Nyquist, the angrier I become. And the angrier I become, the more blood flows from my body." After a slight pause he added, "Do you really want to witness that?"

Nyquist uncurled his fists and stepped away from the bed. He turned and looked around the room, at the sparse furnishings, the closed curtain at the window, the medicines on the cabinet. He wondered about breaking free of this place, doing damage along the way to Vito and Lionel. But he was trapped here, that was the truth, still suffering the effects of the knock-out drops, his mind skipping from one thought to another.

Dreylock said, "You're not looking too good yourself. Sit down, please."

Nyquist's hands were shaking. He took the offer of the seat at the bedside, looking for all the world like a concerned relative on a hospital vigil. He picked up a paperback book that lay amid the medicines and bottles on the cabinet. It was the same crime thriller he'd found in Wellborn's suitcase: *Deadly Nightshade* by the author Bradley Sinclair. The cover of the novel showed a young woman wearing a tight purple dress. She was holding a gun in her black-gloved hand. A typical *femme fatale*. Some poor victim cowered before her, his face stricken with fear. Nyquist looked up from the book and contemplated the bedridden man. Dreylock shared a reading interest with Patrick Wellborn. It made him think about the real connection between the two people.

Dreylock asked, "Tell me, have you heard the voices yet? The voices whispering to you, calling your name?"

Nyquist nodded. "What do they mean?"

"Yes, I thought so. And Zelda the same, no doubt. You see, that's one of the signs. You've been chosen, both of you."

"For what?"

"You will find out, soon enough. When the story is ready. There's really no escaping it."

Nyquist's head lowered into his hands and his eyes closed, and in the darkness created he found a tiny measure of peace. "I just need..."

"Yes, what is it?"

He looked up. "I just need to get out of this building."

"We would all like to do that, believe me."

"With Zelda. That's all I want."

Dreylock sighed. He ran a hand over his shaven head and worried at the black sutures that lay there, crisscrossed, old and new. The map of a terrible land. "Sadly, there is no way out. *The Body Library* holds us all."

"I don't even know what that is."

"You've never heard of it?"

"No. What is it, a morgue, a cemetery?"

"Both, in a way. And a giver of life, a wellspring." Dreylock smiled at the metaphors. "*The Body Library* is a novel, a book, and a rather special one at that." He reached over to his side and picked up a sheet of paper from the bedcovers. "We found this in your pocket."

"I took it from Wellborn's jacket."

"This is one page from the sacred manuscript. Have you read it?"

"I tried. But it makes no sense, the words are all messed up."

"Quite, quite. Cut-ups and splinters." He paused and sucked in a breath. Pain flickered on his face. "Everything..." He struggled to speak. "Everything that happens in this tower – our meeting here in this room – and all things other than this: every single thing happens because of *The Body Library*..."

Dreylock's expression suddenly changed; anger flooded his face, causing the scars to enflame. He clapped his hands together and pressed the bell at his bedside, and then shouted out loud for good measure. "Bring her in! The woman. Zelda. Bring her!" After only a moment the door opened and Vito entered, dragging Zelda with him. She struggled a little in his grasp, but from the look of her she was still drowsy.

Nyquist stood up from the chair as Vito pushed Zelda forward. She almost fell. Nyquist grabbed her, keeping her upright.

"What a fine pair they make," Dreylock announced. "The king and queen of a tale long lost in time."

Nyquist cried out, "Dreylock, let her go!"

"That can't happen. It's time for payment." Dreylock's eyes blazed as he said this, his entire body taken over by the need to be cured. He started to shout to the room: "Calvin! Calvin, I know you can hear me. Calvin!" His voice ranged higher with each calling. "Calvin! Calvin, where are you! I've brought Oberon a present. Zelda is here!"

It sounded to Nyquist as though the man was calling up a demon, or trying to, reaching out from one world to another.

"CALVIN!"

The name was now a single cry of fear and despair, repeated over and over. Dreylock's hands rose up with each utterance, the way a preacher's might. Zelda was struggling in Vito's grasp, obviously frightened by what she was seeing and hearing, the madness in this room. Nyquist made a move towards Dreylock, but then he stopped, staring ahead.

Dreylock had stopped speaking. He looked feverish, and a tremor came to his eyes, and his cheeks and brow, a signal from far away, a warning sign.

Nyquist asked him, "What is it? What's wrong?"

Dreylock opened his mouth. It stayed open, the words not yet released. His hands were still raised in the air. And then a terrible racking pain shot all the way through him, and his body jerked on the bed, dislodging the covers. His arms thrashed about wildly and the back of his head banged again and again at the pillow and the headboard behind him. His eyes popped wide open, seeing monsters. Blood poured down from the cracks in his face and his pajama top was already red and saturated from the wounds that had reopened in his chest.

At last Dreylock screamed.

Nyquist had never heard anything like it, not in all his days.

Vito let go of Zelda. He moved towards the bed, but it was obvious that he hardly knew what to do. Dreylock was in too much pain, a pain that filled the room with its presence.

Voices could be heard from beyond the bedroom door and soon it burst open and Lionel and Amber appeared. They rushed into the room. Lionel looked as if a ghost had taken up residence in his face: the tough guy was scared stiff. But Amber immediately took charge. Nyquist moved back to let her closer to the bed. She reached for Dreylock, trying to calm him, but it was hopeless. The patient screamed further and knocked his nurse's arms away in a violent spasm. The blood was by now spewing from the visible cuts and from those below, out of sight: the bedsheets were crimson with the flow. Many of the sutures on his face had snapped and the scars were wide apart, revealing the muscles of the face beneath.

Vito came to Amber's side and together they wrestled with Dreylock. Lionel was still frozen to the spot. Vito called to him urgently.

"Lionel! Help us. Come on!"

At last the third member of the party broke into action and joined them at the bed, not that he could do much; his big hands flapped around uselessly.

"Hold him down!"

Vito's orders had an effect at last. Lionel threw himself on the bed, forcing Dreylock to be still. It was the best they could do. Their boss howled from the black pit of his heart. Amber was scrabbling through the medicines on the cabinet, evidently unable to find what she was looking for. Then she bent down and picked up a syringe from the floor. She started to fill it from a bottle of clear fluid. This was Nyquist's cue, now they were all occupied. He took Zelda by the hand and together they made their way to the door of the room. They were halfway down the corridor when Vito's voice called out.

"Lionel, stop him!"

Nyquist pulled open the front door of the apartment and pushed Zelda through, out into the corridor, yelling at her to run. She did, stumbling at first, then picking up speed.

He turned, only to see Lionel barreling down towards him.

Nyquist's mind was empty but for one thought: *Not this time.* Danger acted as a prod to his body and he met the big man's forward motion with a fist. All his attention went into it: those curled fingers, the tensed muscles of his arm, whatever skill he'd picked up along the way, in the streets, the endless nights of peril, the years and years of being lost, alone, in search of peace. Everything. And even in the midst of the long twisted pathway that he found himself on, his body half wrecked by the drug, and by confusion, he made contact.

Pure. Golden. On target.

Flesh on flesh.

There was a crack of bone.

Lionel stumbled back, his eyes dazed. Drops of blood fell from his nose onto the carpet. He leaned against the wall for support, his useless hands still reaching out. Nyquist dodged them, and turned back to the door. Lionel grabbed at his jacket. With a lurch Nyquist pulled away and made it through the doorway. He set off on a staggering run in

Zelda's direction. But he couldn't see her, the corridor was empty. Had she darted into another apartment for safety? Or maybe she'd taken the elevator without him? But where was the elevator? Nothing seemed clear. He ran on and reached the end of the corridor and saw that it branched off, in two directions. These upper floors had a different layout from those below.

Nyquist took a look behind: the way was clear, no one had come out of Dreylock's apartment yet. This was his chance. He chose a direction at will and ran as fast as he could. The breath rattled in his lungs and he rocked on his feet, almost falling. But he steadied himself and felt the need to escape as a powerful force, a surge of energy that carried him forward. He could only hope that he'd chosen the right way to go.

There was a closed door at the end of the corridor. He pulled at the catch, willing his hands to obey him, willing his eyes to stay in focus. He was falling again, going under. But the door opened. He was through. At the end of another, much shorter corridor he saw the door to a service elevator. To each side stood a pair of potted plants, the stems tall and overflowing with leaves. Zelda was standing there, waving at him.

"Quickly. Quickly!"

Her voice was far away, further away than her body was, but Nyquist knew that his only hope now lay with her. He ran on. Her face was cut, dripping red. In a strange state of bliss, he reached up and cleaned a little of the blood away from her cheeks. "Nyquist. Look..." He turned. Vito was standing at the doorway, some few yards away. He glared at Nyquist and then started to walk down towards them.

The elevator car was heard, approaching from below.

It was too late. Vito was already upon them, his pistol in his hand. His suit jacket was stained crimson from

Dreylock's wounds. Nyquist tried to swing for him, but he was suddenly too weak. Vito easily stepped out of the way.

Zelda clung to Nyquist.

The gun moved from one person to the other, making its decision.

Amber called from the corridor, unseen, but her voice loud. "Vito. He's in shock. I need help!"

The elevator doors were opening.

Amber called again. She appeared at the corridor doorway. "Now!"

The gun hand hesitated. Vito looked back towards Amber and that was all that Nyquist needed. With all his remaining strength he took another swing. It was parried easily and Vito pushed back, causing them both to tumble. Here they struggled. Nyquist could see three or four of his opponents at once, each slightly blurred, not quite superimposed. He shoved one of them away and hit out wildly at another, neither action having any effect at all. Sweat rolled down into his eyes. He was passing out.

And then the blows came down.

Vito delivered them methodically, punch after punch. No, not punches. It was worse than that: he was being hit with the gun stock, metal on flesh. Nyquist's eyesight blossomed red and he slipped to the floor, bringing Vito with him. Another blow met his temple and this one worse than the last, the worst of them all. He blacked out for a second, roused only by another hit to his face. This time the side of his head collided with the corner of a wall and he lay there unmoving, only his right hand outstretched showing any kind of life as the fingers twitched on the hard floor: a code that nobody could hear or understand.

Death stood over him, dressed in a smart suit and a purple tie.

From a far-off place he heard his name being called, a woman's voice.

Nyquist.

Nyquist...

And then death stopped moving. Death stood there staring at him. Death tumbled to the floor, slowly, slowly, landing next to Nyquist just outside the elevator.

The mist cleared a little.

Zelda was standing over the two men. Her body was shaking. On the floor lay the smashed remains of a large plant pot, its shards scattered everywhere. "I did it," she said. "I did it." Nyquist stared ahead. Fine grains of soil and root fiber hung in the air, bits of leaf, petals, pollen, strands of cobweb, a dead fly, all suspended. Slowly drifting. It was the dream or a nightmare a plant might have when the sun went down and predators moved in. He saw it all, every tiny green thing, every particle, every speck of dust, his mind fully engaged with the sight. The sound of the breaking pot still reverberated around the space.

There was a hole in the wall some few inches from Nyquist's head. He hadn't even heard the gun go off.

Vito groaned from where he lay on the floor, his head bloodied.

WORMS AND ALL

They were holed up in a room on a lower floor. The service elevator had taken them down only so far and then stopped. For a while they had wandered the endless, empty corridors searching for a stairwell, another elevator or a fire escape even. But there were none of these things: the corridors led only around corners into other corridors. There were no numbers on any of the doors they passed. Nyquist had stumbled on at Zelda's side, kept upright and guided by her. A trail of blood stained the carpeted floor behind them, a marked trail through the labyrinth that only served to show just how lost they were. Something had happened to them both, the after-effects of drugs they'd been given perhaps, or of whatever process had taken place in Dreylock's rooms. Seemingly the building had closed itself around them, holding them in its spell. Yes, it was easy to believe in such things: the story had taken them over.

Zelda offered him a slice from a tin of peaches. "I found this in a cupboard. There's a dozen tins, all the same brand."

Nyquist felt the cold fruit slither down his throat.

"Nothing else on offer?"

"Tins of corned beef. Stacks of them." She smiled. "We could survive here for a few days, eating corned beef and peaches. It's like an adventure novel. Two castaways on a desert island, forced by circumstances into each other's arms."

He looked at her. She was his mirror and he saw her eyes dart from one wound to another on his face. He must look a wreck. He certainly felt it.

"I did what I could with your face."

He nodded his thanks. Her face also showed evidence of damage, but she'd attended to that as best she could.

"How do you like my hair?" she asked. "It's the new style. All the rage." She gave him a half smile. "Ragged Chic."

"It suits you."

"You fell asleep," she told him.

"Did I?"

"Only for a few minutes. You were mumbling."

"Oh right, yes. I was dreaming."

"What about?"

"I saw your face."

She grinned. "Dearie me. What was it, a nightmare?"

"Your face, covered in words. But they were moving around, spelling out different phrases, sentences, whole stories."

"I hope you didn't read any of them. What on earth was I saying?"

"I don't know," he answered in all seriousness. "I can't remember."

They sat in silence, side by side on the bed. She reached for him and pulled him close and from there it was an easy movement to be lying in his arms. They stayed like that for a while, perfectly still, not speaking. Nyquist took comfort from her, and he hoped he was giving something in return.

"It's John, by the way. My name."

"Thank you," she murmured. "I shall call you that from now on. Or maybe Johnny. Yes, I think that suits you more." She settled deeper into rest.

His mind wandered, the worries returned. He slipped away from her arms and went to stand by the window. He was still high up enough to see the city spread out before him. Only a few of the lamps of Storyville remained alight, marking the place where the nocturnal storytellers gathered in bedsits and lofts, swapping their tales of night-bound creatures and demons. He could almost imagine the sound they made, the words breathing through the air, the listeners keen and wide awake to hear the adventure. He felt a longing to return to the streets.

Zelda's voice broke his mood. "What are you looking at?"

"The city, the lights."

"It's always so beautiful. I never tire of it."

"So you were born here, in Storyville?"

She sat up on the bed. "Yes. Born, raised, written about, written off, written out, rewritten by my own hand. You know, the usual biography." She stretched her arms wide and then said, "I haven't seen my mother in such a long time now, years and years. Would you like to see a picture of her?"

"Of course."

Zelda pulled at a chain around her neck, revealing a silver locket. She slipped it over her head and handed it to him. He clicked open the lid. Inside was a piece of white card cut into an oval to perfectly fit the insides of the locket. There was no image, only a line of text handwritten on the card. It said:

A picture of my mother.

He smiled at this. "This is all you have of her?"

"It's my most treasured possession. She looks very good in it, don't you think."

"She's beautiful. And you look just like her."

"Yes." She clicked shut the locket and replaced it round her neck. "People say that."

Nyquist took a seat at the dressing table. He avoided his face in the mirror.

Zelda asked, "What about you?"

"Me?"

"Your parents."

"What's to tell?"

"There's always a story."

"My own mother died when I was very young."

"Oh, I see. I'm sorry."

"And my father walked off and left me a few years later." He held up a hand to still Zelda's voice. "I was brought up in one foster home after another, and then I ran away and looked after myself as best I could, on the street, in hovels, abandoned houses, air raid shelters, wherever a bit of warmth and shelter could be found."

He paused.

Zelda held the silence.

He looked at her and said, "We have walked similar pathways, I imagine."

"Yes. Two versions of the same story." She touched his hand. "How did you survive?"

"I learned. One thing at a time."

"You were alone?"

"Most of the time. I remember..."

Zelda leaned in a little closer. "Yes?"

"He left me a note, my father. I found it when I arrived back at the house, after he'd disappeared. It was propped up on the mantelpiece, above the fireplace. A white envelope, yes, I see it now, addressed to me. I opened it…"

He hesitated, but Zelda let him be. She knew the tale would tell itself, when he was ready.

"I opened it." He stopped again and this time his voice caught on the words and he turned his eyes away from her.

"Johnny… you don't have to…"

But he looked back to her, his eyes fierce now, fierce with the anger of years.

"I read the first line and that was enough. The words… the words blurred on the page, my hands were shaking. Oh God."

Zelda spoke quietly: "What did you do?"

"I tore it up." He laughed bitterly. "Yes, I remember now! I think I must have seen a spy do it with a secret coded message, in a film, or maybe I read it in a book. I tore up the letter into tiny pieces and I put them in my mouth and swallowed them. Neither I nor anyone else would ever read those words. No one."

Neither of them spoke for a while. The night gathered around them, in the corners of the room, in the holes in the floor and walls where the insects crawled, behind the mirror's surface. Zelda played with her locket, turning it over and over in her hand. Far away, a languid strain of music was heard.

And then Nyquist said, "Tell me everything. All that you know about Wellborn, the truth. Can you do that?"

"Yes, I can try." A moment. "Patrick came up to me on the corner of Lawrence and Nin, where the working girls hang out. All that's true."

"But you've been holding something back, haven't you?"

She nodded. "We went back to his place and did the business. Afterwards, he fetched a metal plate from the kitchen and placed it on the table in front of me. He reached into his jacket and pulled out a sheet of paper. He asked me to read the words on the paper. And I tried to, I really did, but they just didn't make any sense, no sense at all."

"Like the one I found in his wallet?"

"Yes. A different page, but just like that. Exactly. All gobbledegook. But he insisted that I read it a second time, all of it, top to bottom, every word. He wanted me to read it out loud. I really felt like I was taking part in some occult ritual, or something like that. I was getting a bit scared, to be honest. But I read through the story again, if it can be called that, and this time... this time, as I read it..."

"Go on. What happened, Zelda?"

Her eyes glinted and her face took on a glow that had nothing to do with the moonlight, or the bedside lamp.

"As I read the words out loud, I got this feeling inside. Right here..." She touched at her heart. "A warmth. A tingle. It was very... it was pleasurable. It was exquisite!" Her eyes closed momentarily. "Johnny, let me tell you... I'd never felt anything like this, not in all my life."

"What happened next?"

"Wellborn placed the paper in the bowl and he set fire to it." She hesitated.

"Keep going."

"He told me that burning a page was a sacred act, that the spirits of the story would be released by it, into the air, into the mind of the reader." She laughed. "Oh, don't give me that look! I know how it sounds. But then..." She breathed in deeply and a look of sheer pleasure came to her face. "He made me inhale the smoke."

"That's weird."

"It was. It was truly weird, actually. But the man was paying, and he was paying well, and I thought, what the hell, what can happen that's so bad?"

"So you did as he asked?"

"I did." Zelda bowed her head slightly as she said this, as though reliving the moment. Now she looked up, directly at Nyquist, and he saw the love of life flooding her eyes. Love, or something darker. It worried him.

She continued, "I could feel the smoke in my eyes, entering my lungs. It stung at first, but then I felt the *words* drifting around inside me. The words on the page, inside my body. It was just incredible. It changed me. I became somebody new. A different person, a better person."

"And Wellborn was doing the same thing?"

"Oh, he was well travelled. I reckon he'd been doing this for a good while. It's why I came here to meet him tonight, because of what he promised me. More of the same, he said, but stronger, more powerful. The story folding around me, taking me in, protecting me."

Nyquist looked away slightly. He needed time to think, to put the pieces together if he could. He recalled the pages he'd seen laid out in apartment 67, including the one with the tooth glued to it. That must've been Wellborn's place of safekeeping. And when Nyquist had torn up one of the pages, Wellborn had then attacked.

Nyquist had destroyed the treasure.

He heard Zelda moaning and turned to see that she was rocking back and forth on the bed, her arms wrapped around her middle.

"What is it? What's wrong?"

"Can't you hear them?"

"Who?"

"The voices. They're calling to me again. Whispering my name. Listen."

He did so. Hearing only silence this time, below the usual noises of the night.

"I can't hear them."

Her own voice took on a harder edge. "I need more."

"Zelda?"

"Where's the page, the one you took off Patrick's body? Where is it?"

"I don't have it."

The need powered her voice, her movements. "We could burn it together, both of us."

"Dreylock took it from me–"

"It's *The Body Library*. It's calling my name."

"Zelda!"

His raised voice stopped her. Now she looked angry. She stood up. "I'm not leaving this place. I can't. Not yet. Not until…"

Nyquist followed her across the room, trying to grab hold of her, but she skipped away. The telling of the story of Wellborn and the burning page and the smoke of words and the voices she had heard, all these things had triggered something in her, a new desire. She was possessed.

"Zelda, you can't stay here."

"You don't understand! How can you, you've never felt it."

He held her against the wall.

"Get off me."

"Zelda…"

"Leave me alone!"

She pushed him away with all her strength. He let himself be pushed. It was true: he couldn't possibly understand the need she felt. Her eyes glared with a sudden lust for whatever it was that drove her. A new personality was taking over, a new *character*, and it wasn't anything good. Yet he was drawn to her. Gently he reached out and she took his hand in hers. The contact was brief, but telling. She relaxed a little and said a terrible thing in a calm voice:

"Story is a demon that visits in the night."

Nyquist was shocked.

"It crouches on your chest, breathing words."

"Zelda, don't say that."

Her eyes belied the calmness of her voice, and he knew that the demon she spoke of had taken up residence.

"I need to find *The Body Library*." Her fingers wrapped tight around his arms, the nails digging in. "Wellborn promised he'd take me there."

"It's a book, that's all. Not a place. Dreylock mentioned it. A manuscript."

"He told me that all my wishes would come true."

Nyquist frowned. "Whatever Wellborn promised you, it was a lie, a story."

"A true story."

"Zelda, you were brought here on purpose. It's nothing to do with…"

"Listen!"

Her passion took him over. He had to stop, he had to listen.

The voices… his own name… now he heard it…

Nyquist… Nyquist…

She saw the look in his eyes.

"You see. The book is calling us, calling to us both."

He quietened her with a gesture.

There was another sound, below the whispering.

Laughter.

One low note, one high. Repeated. Low, high, low, high.

Zelda heard it as well, and she said in a hushed tone, "Who is it?"

He moved away from her and went out into the hallway. It was difficult to tell where the sound was coming from. He checked the living room, the bathroom, the kitchen: all were empty. He opened the front door and went out into the corridor, looking to left and right. There was no one in sight. But he could hear it still, the laughter. Close now, louder. It was mocking him. He walked along the corridor, passing one door after another, each one closed. And then he stopped outside apartment 87. It was the only door in the corridor to have a number on it. The sound came from within. It was the boy laughing. Calvin. The door was ajar. Nyquist pushed it open and stepped inside. He was vaguely aware of Zelda at his back. The hallway was empty. He looked into the living room and saw the tree trunk emerging from the hole in the floor and disappearing into a hole in the ceiling. But this was a different apartment to before, a different part of the tree, with the branches more tangled, the black leaves fuller and more lush. They shone like dark-eyed mirrors, many hundreds of them. Did the tree grow through the entirety of the building? It was all he could imagine.

Nyquist stepped warily into the room. There was a faint wash of moonlight from the window, nothing more. Yet the room was so perfectly lit, so enclosed, so encased, so balanced, so bathed, that he made no attempt to switch on the light. No thoughts plagued him, only that the room welcomed him, it waited for him, it had waited here all night, waited for him to get here, to find the room, the one room, to wander the corridor and stairwells of the tower of broken stories until he walked in through this doorway, as now, these last steps. He was here. This was his place. There was no other way to think of it. He belonged here. The boy's laughter mingled with the sound of leaves rustling and twigs creaking, and the song of a bird, a sparrow sitting on a branch, twittering away. Regardless of its circumstances, the creature was happy in its tiny place in the world.

Zelda stood in the doorway, watching Nyquist. She called

to him softly, asking him to be careful. She had sobered up now. He hardly heard her. Only the leaves, only the birdsong, only the laughter, until they too fell silent, each in turn. And then he saw a shape in the darkest corner of the room, a shadow moving, nothing more.

It was the boy.

Only his eyes were visible in the shadows, two white orbs staring at him. And then he emerged from the dark, stepping into moonlight. The whispers were heard once more, so many of them filling the space with their invisible bodies, the names of both Nyquist and Zelda being called out, called forth. Calvin reached with his hands and Nyquist came to him. Zelda followed after, drawn by the same spell. They both took those last few steps into the boy's world. Now he had them.

The leaves of the tree rustled around Nyquist's head. He was aware of fruit hanging down, of worms in the fruit; he was aware of the boy's face and eyes, his red mouth moving with the words that came from him, the words that lived inside him, that crept out now from between those lips.

"It's taken you a time, crooked man."

"Yes, I know. I lost my way."

The answer came easily to Nyquist. He was in a trance. Lost, lost totally.

Zelda was at Nyquist's side, as bound as he was.

The boy said, "Not everyone makes it this far. I gave you some games to play."

"You did."

"And now, are you ready to step forward?"

"I am."

Zelda echoed Nyquist. "I am."

"We are."

They spoke as one, one body, one mouth. One decision.

Calvin smiled briefly. He intoned his binding spell: "We are gathered here this night to bind these two into our circle of words and magic. Within our story, let them live anew." He reached up to a low hanging branch and plucked a globular fruit from it. The peel was red, the flesh white within when he bit into it. The worms writhed. He fed them, Nyquist and Zelda, he fed them the fruit that he had chosen for them, half-eaten: fruit, flesh, saliva, worms and all. The taste of it, both sweet and bitter, had an adverse effect on Nyquist. He came to, observing himself from afar, seeing himself eating the fruit offered to him by a boy, with Zelda at his side, yes, he saw it all, the tree, the moon-washed room, his own body swaying under the spell as it took him over, whatever it was, wherever it might lead, and he screamed, from the depths of his being he screamed aloud, the sound of it lost somewhere between thought and lips.

There was nothing he could do, no other steps he could take.

Now his body took him back and he was lost once more.

The boy was chanting. "Let us bow down, each of us, to King Oberon. Let us partake of the story. The library of the body beckons."

Nyquist felt one last flicker of recognition: that he was in danger.

And then that too was gone.

His eyes closed.

INK

… his eyes closed and he sank further down into the dark into the flow the fluid all was fluid a black liquid in which his body floated drifted suspended submerged breathing yes still breathing in the liquid in the blackness of the pool he sank down and lay there suspended and dreaming and being read yes being read head to foot every part of him his mind his thoughts his blood and bone his eyes his limbs his heart yes all of him read again and again as a book of flesh where the ink was seeking the stories all the stories of his life every last one being read by the pool of ink in which he lay suspended drifting floating submerged breathing yes breathing still and being read and his eyes opened in the black and all he could see was the black there was nothing else only the blackness of the ink seeping into his skin in which he floated in which his body was read and read over and over again and his stories taken from him and others given to him in return yes words taken and words given as one story mingled with another in the pool of midnight's ink closing over him…

Z

When next he opened his eyes Nyquist saw the open sky far above, the night sky with the moon and the stars visible and the faint wash of the Milky Way. It took him a while to realize that he was outside, that he was lying on the ground outside the tower of Melville Five.

He tried to sit up, and groaned in pain as he did so.

A simple thought came to him: *I'm free. Somehow or other, I got out of that building. I escaped.* He was bruised, cut around the face and hands, aching in his limbs. But most of all: alive. And he prayed to the storytelling gods of the city for letting him get this far.

He looked around, as though seeing the world for the first time. He was sitting on a stone pathway that skirted the outside wall of the building. Strangely, he couldn't remember how he'd ended up here. He racked his brains for an answer, a single memory, a glimpse of meaning, an image. But there was nothing at all, no answers. He remembered the room with the tree and the fruit and Calvin making his spell. That was all.

He stood up warily, a little shaky on his feet.

The courtyard between the five towers of Melville was empty and quiet, and most of the windows he could see were dark. It must have been the early hours of the morning. A humming noise disturbed him. He looked for its source and was drawn to a fissure in the building's wall: an insect was just leaving its nest, crawling along the brickwork. A beetle, it looked like, large and dark of body. But then the creature's wing case clicked open and it launched itself into the night, and its body glowed in the air, transformed into a bright yellow bulb in the shape of the letter *A*. Another glow bug followed, and then one more, these two describing the letters *K* and *M* with their luminous bodies. Nyquist tried to follow them in their flight, but they darted hither and thither around his head.

And then he saw a figure, over by an adjacent tower, a dark figure. This person made a gesture, a signal of some kind, a wave perhaps.

It was a woman, he saw that now. The woman he'd met earlier. His companion on this night's story. Somehow or other, they had both escaped.

And yet. And yet…

He couldn't remember her name.

The lack pained him.

Nyquist started to walk towards her. It was a simple plan: wherever she led, he would follow. He passed a pair of drunken middle-aged men, poor souls who could not give up on the day's stories. Like himself. He felt that he was moving through a dream: he was tired and his mind flickered with a sense of unreality, so much so that he saw more and more of the glow bugs encircling him, each of their bodies lit up with a different letter of the alphabet. He was haloed by language. The bugs flitted about. They stirred his eyes with their colors, and he reached up and actually took one in his hand, quite easily, the letter Z, plucking it from the air, gently, gently. He could feel the insect pulsating in his closed palm, its warmth heating his skin and its yellow light showing between his clenched fingers like a lamp. A single word entered his mind.

The word was *Zelda*.

Yes, that was right. Now he remembered. Her name.

But when he looked up again, when he scanned the streets all around, the woman was gone, lost from sight. Nyquist was alone.

He opened his fingers and the captured beetle took flight. But his palm was not empty: a small amount of pulpy substance remained, of no proper color or shape. He tried to cast it away but the substance clung to his fingers. A residue. The night's tale had left its mark upon him.

He moved on at last, away from the five towers. His heart was heavy.

Zelda, Zelda...

It was like this: a man and a woman had walked the same story path for a while, a few hours. And then parted. That should be enough.

Surely it was.

PART TWO
AT THE END OF PLATH LANE

A SECOND TELLING

Nyquist lived and worked in A. C. Clarke Town, a small precinct some way from the center of the city. It was a low-rent area and he could afford a three-room flat. The front room served as his office, and he lived and slept and ate in the back room. The third room, the bathroom, was tiny, but adequate. It was enough. He had few expectations in life, and merely desired a place to live, to spend time alone, to make himself anew. He existed on small town cases and small town money, and got by, making a few friends along the way and a few enemies. He could handle both, keeping friends and foes at a suitable distance. This was a city where words were currency, and stories the life blood that kept the people and the place moving forward, and he was happy to be one more minor character in the narrative. Yes, the people's flow of words kept him going, it worked as whisky used to work: stirring the soul, hiding the pain. But sometimes, despite all his precautions, the faces of people he had lost along the way – either dead or missing or blurred forever in the mind's eye – would pile in and assail him, most often at night as he lay on the edge of sleep. At such moments he would often get out of bed and walk through to his office. Here he would sit at his desk to type out a few more pages of his own novel, *A Man of Shadows*, based on his experiences in the city of his birth.

Life continued in this manner. Once a week his narrative officer would visit and ask about the stories Nyquist was currently involved in. The officer was called Bella Monroe, a woman of middling years and soft to middling temperament. He could never work out how such a person should end up working for a council department with such a terrible reputation. She always wore the same outfit on every visit: a threadbare brown trouser suit and a white, ruffled blouse buttoned high at the neck, almost tight enough to cut off the circulation. Her hair was long and thick and greying here and there and brushed back from her brow in waves. She kept it in place with a pair of eyeglasses which, when lowered over her eyes, gave her the look of a creature in constant surprise at the world's nature. Nyquist knew her husband had passed away a few years back, that she had no children. From a hint or two he also knew that she was in love with someone, a man whose name he didn't know. Nyquist liked her. He appreciated her understanding of his life, his struggles to fall into step with the city's mode of being; and she seemed to sense within him the darkness, the troubles he'd run away from, the need to conform, to find a good, peaceful story and settle into it. No doubt she'd witnessed such a need many times in newcomers.

He watched Officer Monroe now, as she worked. She carried with her at all times a selection of notebooks, a slide rule, and several pens of different colors. Storylines were notated, locations marked on a street atlas, the names of all known participants recorded. Of course sometimes Nyquist followed the wishes of his clients more than the council's, hiding personal details, changing names and so on, but more or often than not he obeyed the law. Many cautionary tales were whispered about the council's methods of extraction, if a story turned out to contain criminal elements.

Bella Monroe tapped at her notepad. "Anything else, John?"

"That's it."

"If you don't mind me saying, it all seems rather paltry."

"What can I do?"

"Unfaithful husbands, embezzled funds. A lost cat? Really?"

"Stolen, Bella. A *stolen* cat."

"Quite. But still..."

"It pays the rent. Just about."

Monroe looked at the private eye over the tip of her eyeglasses. "You know, you've been here now for what is it..."

"Three months. A little more."

"Usually, after such a period we expect our citizens to be taking part in slightly more complex or intriguing narratives."

"Nothing ever happens to me."

"Well make it happen, Mr Nyquist! Make it happen."

A tremble of exasperation shot through Monroe, but then she settled herself once more and studied her open notebook for a few moments. Nyquist had to feel for her: every week this same conversation took place, and every week Monroe made her notes and went away, back to her office deep in one of the council's buildings.

At last she closed her notebook. "Well, the city's grand narrative will not be troubled by your exploits. Not quite yet. Tell me, how is the novel coming along?"

"Slowly."

"One word a day?" It was said with a smile.

"Two. If inspiration strikes."

Monroe studied the private eye again. "I've been doing

this job for more than twenty years now."

"You've mentioned that, yes."

"And over that time, certain instincts have been honed. And I believe... I truly believe that you're holding out on me."

Nyquist looked back at the officer, hoping not to give anything away.

Monroe kept her voice even as she spoke: "I think you've been involved in another story. A tantalizing story. A dangerous story, even. What do you say?"

He shrugged.

"You know you can be fined for hiding stories. And perhaps, worse..."

"Easy on the threats, Bella. I've got nothing to tell you."

Nyquist's voice had risen, just a little, enough to make Monroe bristle. They stared at each other in silence. The blades of the desk fan made the only noise in the room.

He said, "The last office fan I had, it had a bullet hole in one blade."

"What are you saying?"

"This one hasn't." He paused. "It's how I know my life is better now."

Monroe blew out a breath. "Very well. Nothing to report." She started to collect her things together. "If you insist."

Nyquist stood up to show the officer out. But at the door he stopped her and asked, "Is it possible for a person to be taken over by a story?"

"How do you mean?"

"Say they're having trouble telling where the story begins, or ends. Maybe the story is just as real as life. Just as real, just as vivid."

Monroe shook her head sadly. "There are such conditions, yes."

"Tell me about them."

"Well, some of them are self-induced. Others are brought about by the use of certain preparations."

"Preparations? You mean drugs?"

"Listen to me, John…"

Nyquist moved away from the door. Monroe watched him carefully. The private eye looked agitated; he was rubbing at his face with one hand, while the other, clenched into a fist, rapped at the desktop repeatedly.

"We advise people against the use of such things. Really, we do. They are designed to inhibit the mind's sense of reality, and replace it with another."

"So they can make you believe in things that never happened?"

"Yes, perhaps. But they're unsafe. They can lead to–" She broke off. "Why are you asking this?"

"No reason. None at all."

"Well then." Bella Monroe hovered in the doorway, wondering what to say for the best. In the end all she could manage was, "Tread carefully. Some stories are best left untold."

Nyquist didn't reply. The narrative officer left him there, daylight streaming through the blinds, the desk fan cutting his thoughts into ribbons of black and white.

Zelda…

Often she came to his mind. Her face as it was, as she talked about her real reasons for being in Melville Five: how she needed to escape the story demon sitting on her chest, breathing words into her sleeping face. It was a frightening image.

And he remembered Zelda's story of the burning manuscript pages, the smoke rising, how it made her feel that she was a different person. Perhaps the ink on the paper itself had some property to it, some psychotropic quality?

Maybe it had seeped into Nyquist's fingertips as he read the page from *The Body Library* he'd found in Wellborn's pocket? It was possible. It was easy to imagine the people of Storyville resorting to such practices: anything to make the story come alive, to intensify the drama of their lives. Tricks of the mind. And he thought of his own experiences in the tower – the sense of being trapped in a labyrinth, the helplessness. He remembered it as he might a dream.

Often he felt a sadness within, and it ate at him, daily, nightly. He should never have let Zelda go at the end, he should have chased her through the streets and taken her in his arms and kissed her madly, like some dumb hero in a throwaway romance pamphlet.

But her own story had taken her elsewhere, dragged her away.

Three days had passed since the visit to Melville Towers, since the death of Patrick Wellborn. Memories of that night wavered like smoke before his eyes. How on earth had he and Zelda escaped the building? He could remember plainly the boy Calvin speaking to him, but the words themselves were no more discernible than an ancient text scrawled on a moss-covered stone. They must've been carried out, that was it: perhaps Vito and Lionel had helped. Who could tell what any of them were up to, in that place.

And right there and then Nyquist was standing once more in the bedroom of apartment 67 with Patrick Wellborn lying on the floor, his head a pulpy mess and the blood and hair already sticking to Nyquist's hands.

It sent a shudder through him.

Of course he'd thought about going to the police. Yesterday morning he'd got as far as the main entranceway of the precinct station, only to decide against it at the last minute. And he'd lived in trepidation ever since, expecting them to arrive at his office at any minute, asking questions, blaming him for Wellborn's murder. But nothing had happened, he'd been left alone. And no mention had been made in the *Storyville Reporter* about the body being found. Nyquist could only think that Dreylock or some other party had removed the corpse and hidden it somewhere, covered up all evidence of the death.

And last night, safe in his bed, he had dreamed that Patrick Wellborn was still alive, back at home with some imagined happy family, or else laughing and drinking with his friends in a bar.

The morning's light burned such thoughts clean away.

Nyquist felt sick and weary. He had to be in charge of his own tale, that was the number one rule of the city, everyone had drilled it into him.

Tell your own tale. Make it real, goddamnit!

He left his office. He paced the afternoon streets like a ghost in search of a human body to inhabit. He was tempted by narrators and raconteurs of all persuasions on every corner; prostitutes called to him from alleyways, offering the best story he'd ever been told; young beggars or kids playing truant prattled around him, trying to sell him penny dreadful tales of evil deeds and hideous mutilated corpses. He ignored them all and walked on until he reached Rabelais Plaza, where his own story had taken such a dreadful turn. The festival was coming to an end at last and so the streets were a little emptier, but there were still many shoppers and tourists about. Nyquist felt he was cut off from all their narratives. He walked alone, along a single strand that led through the streets and into the dark alleyway he had taken that night, following Wellborn. Why? Why was he doing this? He was a man who revisits his own wound with his fingers every day, a self-doubting Thomas. He knew well enough that a story path can never be walked twice, not without changes creeping in. Yet here he was, travelling in his own footsteps.

The alleyway, he now saw, was called Betjeman's Way; he couldn't imagine a place further removed from that particular poet's daydreams of a lost England, the sun beating down on young women playing tennis and stopping for afternoon tea. Rather, the alleyway was filled with litter, graffiti, animal excrement, piles of empty boxes, a rat or two, dustbins overflowing next to locked doors. The place stank of rot and filth. He hadn't noticed any of this four nights ago, fully engaged as he'd been with the task ahead, the shadowing.

He stepped out from the end of the alley into daylight once more and looked across Calvino Road to the five towers of Melville. The estate gave off a very different atmosphere in the daytime; looking more benign, and more decrepit. But then as he drew nearer he noticed signs of life: a woman hanging out washing on a balcony of the first tower, two girls playing hopscotch in the car park, a group of men working on a van, the engine lying in pieces around them. They nodded at Nyquist as he passed, and one of the young girls ran rings round him. He stopped outside the entrance to tower number five, but he couldn't bring himself to enter the lobby. The place seemed to have a negative magic about it, a spell to keep out strangers and the unwanted. As he hesitated, two women walked by along the pathway, each one carrying a bundle of laundry. One of them said, "I wouldn't go in there, love, if I were you."

"Why not?"

"Nothing good will come of it," her friend said. "Nothing at all."

"No one lives there."

"No one good, that is."

The women walked on. Nyquist entered the building.

He pressed for the elevator and straight away a bell dinged and the door opened. The car was empty. He darted inside. He saw the buttons for the different floors, all seventeen of them, and he saw that the ground floor was clearly marked. There was nothing suspicious here, nothing to remind him of the night of death and confusion, when he and Zelda couldn't find their way outside, no matter how they tried. Perhaps then he'd been too weak, too beaten, too drugged up, to really see his way forward. He pressed the button for the sixth floor. The car started to ascend. Immediately he felt his stomach cramp with fear, and sweat break out on his brow. The thought of what he was doing set his whole body trembling, head to foot. He had killed a man here, in this building. One thousand tiny incidents made up the story of his life, up to the moment when he had smashed his assailant's head against the wall. Nyquist closed his eyes and prayed for the dread to subside. At the sixth floor he exited the car and walked down the corridor towards apartment 67. Everything looked the same as it had on his previous visit, but perfectly normal now, without any sign of threat. The building was empty, that was obvious: he could smell damp, rot, loneliness and abandonment. He paused outside the apartment and rang the bell. Nobody answered. No one came to greet him, no one spoke or welcomed him inside, or explained the events of the previous night in a perfectly logical manner.

The door remained closed.

Nyquist couldn't face the elevator a second time so he took the stairs, all six floors, down to the lobby. He walked outside and he stood in the clean bright air, trying to calm himself. It took a while, but eventually he traced his steps back through the streets to where he'd parked his car. He drove out to Chaucer, a precinct to the southwest of the city. This was one of the oldest districts, its foundations first set down in the medieval period. Now it was a tumble of crooked houses and churches squeezed into a maze of narrow side streets, many of the older buildings converted into cheap apartments or offices. Among a ragbag of small factories and bargain stores he found the office of A. P. Linden Associates. He'd been here just once before, when he'd first taken on the job of following Patrick Wellborn. Antonia Linden was a tough-natured businesswoman in her thirties. The office gave little away about her personality: a dull job-lot of furniture and fittings, nondescript prints on the wall, a bored assistant called Harvey. But this tumbledown building stacked between two larger premises was the first sentence of a story that eventually led to Melville Towers and the blood on his hands.

Nyquist rang the bell and waited. He looked through the dusty window and saw an empty reception desk, with no sign of activity. This wasn't right; it was only four o'clock, they should still be at work. He was about to walk away when an elderly woman appeared at the door of the tailor's shop next door.

"There's no one there," she said to Nyquist.

"Is that right?"

"The place has been locked up and empty for days. No staff, no customers. A typical fly-by-night, if you ask me."

"How do you mean?"

The woman came forward, obviously keen to impart her knowledge. "Around here companies tend to come and go."

"I see." Nyquist stared at the locked door. "Well, thank you."

"Did she owe you money?"

"No." It was a lie; there was still an amount owing, but Nyquist had cast such demands aside; he wanted only the truth of the story he had fallen into.

Quickly he invented a story. "I'm an old friend of Antonia's. Just looking her up, while I was in town."

"She might come back to work one day, who knows."

Nyquist mused on this. "I heard she ran an investigative agency."

"That's one way of looking at it."

"What's the other way?"

"Linden worked on people's stories. On the narratives of life."

Nyquist must've looked confused, because the next-door neighbor started to explain: "Sometimes she completed people's stories for them, for good or for ill. But most of the time she erased them."

"Erasure?"

"Surely. Don't you have a few incidents you'd rather had never happened? Things you don't want to tell the council about?"

"Of course, of course."

It gave Nyquist much to think about as he drove back to his office, through the now crowded streets. He remembered what Officer Monroe had said to him: some stories are best left untold. Well, it was too late for such caution. The task of following Wellborn was taking on other aspects, it was turning even darker, more mysterious. Just who had employed Linden to unwrite their story? And why had Nyquist been given the shadowing job?

As he walked upstairs to his first floor apartment he saw a man and a woman standing outside the door. Immediately he pegged them as detectives; he'd seen enough of them over the years to recognize that precise mixture of determination and world-weariness.

It was too late to retreat; the female officer had already spotted him.

"John Henry Nyquist?"

"That's what my mother named me. What of it?"

The woman didn't respond at all to his attitude. Her eyes were green and bright and set as the only precious things in an otherwise cold face. They gave Nyquist hope that a human being was alive in there, somewhere.

She showed her warrant card and gave herself a name: "Detective Inspector Molloy. And this..." she nodded to her partner, "this is DS Fabien."

Nyquist looked at them both.

"We need to talk to you," Molloy said.

"Talk away." He made to push past her and unlock his door, but she stopped him with a touch on his sleeve.

"It's about a dead body."

Nyquist could feel again the splatter of Patrick Wellborn's blood and the torn-out hair and no matter how he tried, they would not be removed.

His hands would never be cleansed.

THE BODY IN QUESTION

Not a word was said between them. The only sound came from their footsteps echoing down the bare, grey corridor. Molloy walked at Nyquist's side, Fabien slightly behind them both. They signed in and went through into a viewing room. Nyquist was directed towards a large window, where he stood waiting until a curtain was pulled aside from within, and then he stared through the glass at the inner room. The walls, floor and ceiling were white all over, a room without human atmosphere. He looked at the dead body that lay on the trestle bed just a few feet away, its form covered by a sheet as white and as clean as the walls. All reminders of life had been removed. A morgue attendant folded back the sheet, revealing the upper shoulders and head of the corpse.

It wasn't Patrick Wellborn. It was the face of a woman. Her features were distorted, pulled to the side and upwards as though by a great force, and a darker ring of flesh was visible around the neck, red at the edges and a darker color within. It looked like she'd been strangled. There were some other markings on the face and body, disfigurements of some kind. He couldn't make them out properly. Had she been beaten up, prior to the death?

"We know it's difficult," Molloy said. "Just do what you can."

The assistant tilted the head slightly towards the window. In any other circumstance the act would possess a comic effect; but here the movement was enough to trigger a reaction that struck Nyquist to his core. He raised a hand to his eyes and covered them. He started to shake, his body following its own instructions.

Detective Molloy asked him, "So you know her?"

Nyquist did his best to look beyond the blemishes and distortions, to the woman that he remembered. He nodded, just the once, and his voice broke on a word.

"We need you to speak aloud."

He took in a breath and tried again: "Yes. She's called Zelda. I don't know her last name."

DS Fabien wrote something on the clipboard he was holding.

Molloy said, "Thank you. We need to ask a few questions."

But Nyquist couldn't move. He stayed at the glass, staring ahead. For these few moments he clung to the hope that it was all a horror tale, as so much else was in this city. It was so easy to become confused by the false and the real, the story and the life, that endless feedback loop. Fiction and non-fiction. Zelda existed on the borderline of the two states, and now she'd fallen, fallen into death. Her story was over. The end. Turn the page and close the book. As though in recognition of this the morgue attendant pulled the sheet back over Zelda's face, and the dark blue curtain closed again across the window. Even then Nyquist stayed where he was, until Fabien grabbed him roughly by the arms and pushed him out of the room.

Twenty minutes later he was sitting at a table in an interview room. He had a feeling he was being watched, although the walls were solid, no windows, no trick mirrors. No evidence of a hidden camera. Still, he couldn't help imagining somebody's hidden eye, scrutinizing him, waiting for a sign of guilt, or fear. He'd been left here alone, no doubt as some form of interrogation technique. It gave him ample time to wonder on Zelda's death, and his own part in it, indirect or otherwise. He kept his face as stone-like as possible, hoping to give nothing away as his heart burned with anger and his mind leapt from one scenario to another, seeking an explanation, a culprit, a mistake that he'd made, a reason why, anything that might act as an escape route, a way to break free. There was none. He was trapped at the center of the story web, all the strands converging on him without any explanation.

And he wept, he wept inside. He kept his sadness locked away.

Until Zelda's face appeared once more before him, not as he'd viewed her at the end, white where it wasn't blemished and hollow of life, but as he'd witnessed it before, in the tower block. And strangest of all, he couldn't work out why he was so affected by her, and by her loss. It was a simple act of kindness he came back to: Zelda tending to his wounds, bandaging his arm for him, when really she should have gone her own way, left him alone to face whatever else the night might have thrown him. He recalled the pain and troubles they'd shared in those few hours as they'd moved from room to room to room, searching for a way out, her hand in his on the stairs as they ran down, her voice as she'd screamed at Lionel, her bravery then, yes, call it that, and her smile even in the heart of danger. Her face was a message that he didn't have time to decipher, and then he knew the truth, the unwritten truth: he had seen a potential in her, in the two of them together; they were made for the same type of narrative, tattered and torn and dirty and cast aside to fend for themselves,

the two of them, yes, their lips meeting once more in
that kiss, that poem, the one sweet poem of a kiss, and
of course he was living inside his own head inside the
small grey interview room in a police station, he was
living a fantasy, yes call it that, because only in the
fantasy could he see the way forward, towards love, or
at least the possibility of such a thing, such a feeling, a
future, yes dare to call it that, a doorway opening on the
lighted passageway ahead, where Zelda waited for him,
her arms wide, her eyes, her lovely eyes on his, her soft
voice calling to him, calling...

The door of the interview room opened and the two
detectives entered. Immediately Nyquist's internal prayer
ended and the vision of Zelda vanished like a moth's wings
in a candle flame. She was dead. The world was a cold,
harsh place once more.

They sat down across the table from him. He held the
gaze of them both, and hoped that his own eyes wouldn't
betray him.

Molloy spoke at last: "So then. Zelda?"

He nodded.

"And you don't know her surname?"

"No. I told you."

Fabien leaned back in his chair, seemingly at ease.
Molloy made a note on a writing pad.

"And where did you meet?"

"Where does any man meet a prostitute?"

"You tell me."

"On a street corner." He was not yet ready to tell the
truth, not until he had sorted this out, not until he'd found
out why she'd been killed.

"Which one?" Molloy asked.

He remembered Zelda's words: "Where Nin Street meets
Lawrence."

Fabien smiled. "The most popular red light district in the city."

Molloy asked, "You were her client?"

Nyquist didn't answer at first. The question was repeated.

"No. Not as such."

"Really?"

"We talked."

"That's all?"

"That's all. We talked for an hour or so."

Fabien sneered at this. But Molloy kept on: "And you paid for this service?"

Nyquist's eyes closed. From a distance he heard himself say, "That's right, I paid for the pleasure of her conversation."

Now Fabien laughed out loud. "Can you believe this guy, Molloy?"

"He's a puzzle, that's for sure."

"He's more than that. He's a liar."

Nyquist shifted forward. "I need to know why I'm here. Am I a suspect in Zelda's murder, or not?"

Neither of the detectives answered him.

"Do I need a lawyer?"

Molloy responded. "We're just asking questions, that's all."

Fabien added, "Do you think you need a lawyer?"

Nyquist was in the dark. Patrick Wellborn's name hadn't yet been mentioned, and asking for a lawyer would surely force things out into the open.

"No," he answered. "I just want to get out of here."

Molloy nodded. "We all do." She looked through a sheaf of notes and asked, "How many times did you meet with Zelda?"

"Once. That's all. Like I said, I paid my money and we talked. Then we parted."

"And where did this conversation take place?"

"A hotel room."

"Which one?"

"A cheap one. I can't remember its name. I was drunk. And depressed. Everything was going wrong for me, in my business, and my personal life. I've only been in Storyville for a few months, and you know how difficult it is to make friends."

Perhaps, if he added enough details to the lie, it would become true.

"I was lonely. I drove out to the district and met with Zelda. She seemed to know what I wanted."

Fabien hunched forward in his seat. "Conversation, you mean?"

"It's more common than you might think. Zelda told me that, lots of men… they just want to be paid some attention. So we talked. I liked her, she was spirited and she listened and said all the right things back to me, whether she meant them or not, and if she didn't mean them, well then she was a bloody good actress."

Nyquist stopped. He'd said enough. It was a story born from blood and darkness, half real, half made-up.

"I don't know why she died," he added. "I really don't."

Molloy answered him in a matter of fact way: "She killed herself."

Nyquist felt the cold run through him. "She… you mean…"

"Yes, it looks that way. She hanged herself. Are you surprised?"

"But she was…"

"Go on."

"She was full of life." It sounded strange even as he said it, almost pathetic.

Molloy shrugged. "Well, there it is."

"As far as we can tell," Fabien added. "It all has to be checked out."

Nyquist didn't know where to look; the two detectives had him in their power. And the world was a smaller place, suddenly, smaller even than this tiny grey room.

"So…" Molloy stacked her notes. "You saw her just the once?"

"That's all, yes."

"And she didn't appear suicidal?"

"No, no. Not at all. Why would she do that? Why? I can't believe she'd do that."

They were both looking at him. He felt his anger building, and his mind reeled. Everything that had happened that night in Melville Five was now a chaotic tumble of events and images, scattered like the words on the page he'd found on Wellborn's body. And the sudden thought of the dead man almost made him confess. He could feel the words on his tongue, the tingle, the relief waiting just one sentence away. But he stopped himself. This wasn't the time. Not yet.

DI Molloy placed a sheet of paper on the table. "This is why we asked you to come in. We found it on her body."

Nyquist narrowed his eyes in concentration. It was another page torn from *The Body Library*. He glanced over the lines of text – the usual mixture of handwriting and type – and almost immediately he noted one particular word standing out from all the others.

It was his own name.

Nyquist.

Nyquist read the entire sentence to himself: *Cut price shadow man John Nyquist none other walking darkness bound.* His name was circled again and again in blue pen, and in the margin in the same color was a simple two-word plea: *Find him!*

"Looks like Zelda was desperate when she marked your name," Molloy said.

Fabien cut in: "We just need to know if it means anything to you?"

Nyquist tried to make sense of it all. "Zelda needs... she needed my help."

"With what?"

"I wish I knew. I wish she'd... O God, I wish she'd come to me."

The two detectives stared at him. "How about Marlowe's Field?" Molloy asked. "Did Zelda mention that to you, ever?"

"Is that where you found her?"

Molloy kept her eyes on him. "She was found swinging from the branch of a tree, right over a sewage overflow pipe."

"Hell of a place to choose," Fabien added. He had a mocking smile on his face. "She must've really hated herself. Mind, that's hookers for you. Live in the shit, die in the–"

Nyquist was out of his seat before either of the two detectives could react. He grabbed Fabien by the neck and dragged him up and away from the table, against the nearest wall.

Molloy got her arms between the two men.

"Sit down. The both of you. Sit down!"

Fabien started to laugh.

Nyquist held the other man's stare for a moment and then followed the order, taking his seat back at the table. Fabien remained standing. He tugged his jacket straight and pulled his tie away from his neck. He still had the smile written across his face as he lit a cigarette. Nothing meant much to him, Nyquist could see that. The smoke floated around the strip light above the table. A fly buzzed at the tube, angered by the limits of its world.

Nobody spoke for a moment until Nyquist mumbled something under his breath.

Molloy leaned across the table. "What's that?"

"I was close to her. To Zelda..."

"But you only knew her a few hours, isn't that right?"

He nodded in reply. "Yes, but she reached out to me. We connected."

"Two sparks in the night?"

He looked at her. Molloy's expression was entirely serious, perhaps in reaction to a similar story of her own.

He whispered, "Yes, something like that."

"Good, good." She placed a large photograph on the table. "What do you make of this?"

It took Nyquist a while to make out the object in the image. It was a gently curved expanse of off-white material, marked all over with words. At first he could only think it was some kind of book or manuscript, perhaps another page from *The Body Library*. But then he realized: it was a close-up photograph of a piece of skin covered in writing.

"This... this is Zelda? Her body?"

Molloy nodded. "This is her lower back. And this..." Another photograph. "Her face. It's unusual, don't you think?"

The disfigurements Nyquist had noticed earlier were now plainly seen: a smattering of letters and words on the cheeks, brows and neck. Not as many as on the body, but enough to make it shocking.

"They're not tattoos," Fabien said.

Molloy placed another two photographs on the tabletop. "We don't know what they are, to be honest," she said. "But it's not the first time we've seen this. There have been a number of similar cases in the last few weeks."

Nyquist didn't know what to make of it. "Is it a sickness? Was she suffering?"

"More likely a side effect," Fabien told him. "From a drug."

"Thankfully, Zelda is the only infected person to kill herself. As yet." Molloy tapped at the table. "Come on, Nyquist, can you tell us anything about this? Anything at all? What was she taking?"

He heard the buzz of the strip light more than he heard the human voices in the room. The fly rubbing his wings together was louder in his mind.

He still hadn't responded to Molloy's plea.

DS Fabien helped him out: "She's covered more or less all over." He was reveling in the description. "Her entire body. Can you imagine that, the words creeping up towards her face? The woman must've been terrified. No wonder she took the easy way out."

Molloy hardened her tone. "All right, Fabien. Let's keep this civil."

"I'm just saying."

"Well don't."

Fabien raised his hands in mock apology to his superior.

Nyquist paid them no mind. He was looking only at Zelda's eyes in the second image. He imagined that if he could reach into the photograph and open the closed eyelids, memories would be held there, pooled like ink in the black pupils. The reason for her death would be made plain.

He scratched at the back of his neck. His whole body was reacting badly, running with sweat. He needed desperately to get out of this room, to breathe in clean air.

"Are you all right, Nyquist?"

He looked at Molloy's concerned face, seeing only a blur, and shook his head. He wanted to break the world apart with his bare hands. But the anger he was feeling quickly burned away, to be replaced by despair. He spoke quietly.

"I could have helped her."

He looked from one detective to the other, and then down at his hands on the table, and the photographs below them.

"I let her walk away, into the night. I let her get away."

The black fly landed on the table and started to wash itself.

Nyquist stared at the scattered images. All these different sections of Zelda's body, each one covered in letters, words, symbols. He knew for certain: there was story here, an explanation waiting to be unlocked if he could only find the key.

But the darkness of the text held too many secrets.

OVERFLOW

He drove out to the eastern part of the city, through Brontë Town, through Blakeville, taking the Asimov Bypass, until the houses and offices gave way to factories and warehouses, and then further on, past isolated shacks and empty-looking garages and roadside cafés. It took him a good hour and a half to get there, fighting against the last of the morning's rush-hour traffic. The dashboard radio crackled with ballads and stories from the years gone by, the heroes and villains cut from broader cloth than was currently popular; their emotions boiled over, men and women shouted at each other in arguments on the very edge of love, and a gunshot sounded through the tiny speaker. Nyquist turned the radio off. He drove on in silence, only his own thoughts to plague him now, the tumult of words and imagery that played like a moving picture show in his head: knives entering flesh, bodies cut open, a bullet's pathway through the heart. The images were spliced into fragments, and projected in a random order. Blood splashed across the road ahead like a torn curtain. Nyquist closed his eyes to escape the sight, and his hands tightened on the wheel. Still the blood flowed behind his eyelids. He was roused from the madness by the sound of another car's horn blaring out and he swerved to avoid the oncoming vehicle. He steered the car back onto the straight road and did his best to empty his mind of violence.

He pulled over into a lay-by and studied the road atlas once more. He was on the right road, and he placed in memory the various turnings he would need to make and the street signs he would have to look out for: Collins, Wharton, Shelly, Sappho and Plath. He set off once more, thinking back to his time in the police station. They'd finally let him go at one in the morning, having nothing at all to lay on him. He'd slept fitfully, troubled by dreams he couldn't remember one second after waking. But now sunlight sparkled on the windscreen, and the terrible noises and images quietened and faded at last in his mind, and he suddenly felt wide awake, committed to action.

The miles sped by, the story awaited him. He would live it by his own words, no one else's.

The car was bumping over rough tarmac. There was a rundown farmhouse on the right, surrounded by rusting tractors and other dilapidated machinery. A dog barked ferociously. Nyquist took another turning and headed along a narrow lane, with trees on one side and waste ground on the other, where a small mountain of household goods had been dumped: refrigerators, armchairs, vacuum cleaners and the like. This was blighted land, neither city nor countryside.

The car slowed a little as it left the road and took to an earth driveway. Nyquist saw a mud-spattered street name sign that read *Plath Lane*, and he knew he was close to his destination: the field should just be at the end of the lane. He parked. The sun warmed the land and the trees all round him, and the birds were singing brightly from the branches. He walked to the end of the lane and opened a farm gate and then walked across the grass that was wet underfoot: the land was waterlogged. This was Marlowe's Field. Sheep stood around in ones and twos, paying him no mind. Ahead he could see where the field suddenly dipped down into a large ditch lined on one side by stunted trees, their clutching roots exposed in the brown dirt like X-rays of a brain. Two kids were playing nearby, a boy and a girl, throwing stones into the fetid water; a noxious stench rose up whenever a stone landed. They were chanting a rhyme, and they eyed Nyquist suspiciously as he neared, but he ignored them and walked on, over to where a strand of crime scene ribbon fluttered, caught on a hedge. The ground on the other side of the ditch was slightly firmer, and emerging from the bank was the end of a large outlet pipe. This must be the place, as Molloy and Fabien had described it. Dirty, clay-colored water dribbled from the pipe into the pool of wet mud that lay in the bottom of the ditch. A number of iridescent beetles were scurrying around. Nyquist looked up at the tree that loomed overhead. Its leaves were far healthier than its neighbors', and more plentiful, as though the tree had learned to feed off the sickened ground, the roots going deep in search of sustenance.

This is where the body had been found, hanging from a branch.

Zelda's body.

A phrase came to his lips, something he'd heard before or read about, but he couldn't remember where or when: *On the edge of town, where the stories flow away…*

He batted away a fly and scratched at the back of his neck. He had to wonder why Zelda had travelled so far from her home, why she'd chosen this godforsaken place. Perhaps she didn't want any of her friends finding her strung up, which made a kind of sense given what he knew of her personality.

He tried to think back on the night they'd spent in Melville Five. Was there any clue at all in her behavior, that might point to suicidal tendencies? He knew that she'd changed towards the end, in their final conversation, when he'd seen her addiction plainly. Maybe all the lost promises had piled up, and tipped over? Or maybe DI Fabien had told it true: she'd been ashamed of the word sickness that was spreading over her skin.

Poor Zelda. And now all he could see were her final moments, the legs jerking, the body arched upwards in a last attempt to claw at life. He shuddered. One thing was certain: the events of that night in Melville were in some way to blame for Zelda's death.

His thoughts were disturbed as the two kids walked over to join him at the outlet pipe. The girl told him, "This is where they found her, that woman."

The boy laughed. "She was naked."

"Did you see her?" Nyquist asked.

"I did. I saw her. I found her."

"It's true, he did." the girl said. "But she wasn't naked. He's making that bit up."

"I'm not!"

"He's lying, mister."

Nyquist watched their contest. They were eight or nine years old, already hooked on telling tales, early addicts of the city's overriding desire to write itself into all the history books that have ever existed, in as many different versions of the truth as possible. Turning words into action, the girl punched the boy in a half playful, half threatening manner, and they scrambled together on the mud bank, their shoes slipping on the wet ground. Nyquist pulled them apart before they fell.

"What do you know about this place?" he asked.

"What do you mean?"

"Who comes out here?"

"Just the two of us, really. It's a bit of a dump, isn't it."

The girl butted in. "They used to kill people here, in the old days. I know that. There was a gallows pole, right where we're standing."

Her friend agreed with this. "It's true. We learned it in school. And now it's where all the bad stories end up."

Nyquist asked him what he meant.

"All the stories, mister... all the lousy, unwanted, lonely, disgusting, forgotten stories, all the tales that no one wants in the city, they flow through the pipes, they get flushed clean away and they get pumped out, right here, in the mud and the dirt and the shit."

The two kids giggled at the word.

Nyquist was confused.

The girl added her own pennyworth. "It's why we like to come out here, and throw stones in the pond, because you never know what's going to turn up. Show him, Luke."

The boy looked left and right, checking for eavesdroppers. But Marlowe's Field was empty for miles around. Satisfied, he reached into his satchel and pulled out an object wrapped in a dirty handkerchief. This was unwound, revealing a jam jar holding a captured insect. Nyquist took the jar from the boy's hand and held it up to the light.

"It's an alphabug," Luke explained. "We found it yesterday."

"But I don't think it's going to last for much longer," the girl added.

"It's dying."

The insect was black with gold markings, a beetle of some kind. It moved sluggishly over the leaves and soil the kids had packed in the bottom of the jar. Nyquist studied it closely: the markings on the folded wing case resembled the letter Y.

"You should see them at night, mister, when their bodies light up. It's special! You can see the letters they make in the dark."

"They write in the darkness."

"I know," Nyquist said. "I've seen them in the city."

"Nah, that's not possible."

"They don't like the brightness and the heat. It confuses them."

"Well, I've seen them. Do you have any more of these?"

The girl nodded. "Sure, we catch them all the time. But they don't live long, that's the trouble. Pretty much one day and a night, and then they're gone."

"They're just trying to find a mate, Debbie."

And they both laughed at that, even if they didn't quite know what it meant.

Luke listed their findings. "We had an A and a B. But we couldn't ever find a C. But we did have a G, and a K."

"We had a Z once," said Debbie, proudly. "Those are rare."

"Not as rare as the X, though. Nothing's as rare as that."

"No one's ever seen an X beetle, not ever!"

"The alphabugs were crawling all over the dead woman's face and body."

"They were not."

"They were. Right there, as she was dangling from the tree, stark naked. One of them went in her mouth!"

"She wasn't naked, why do you keep saying that?"

"OK, but the rest is true. And best of all, the woman's face was covered in words."

His friend groaned. "You're making it up."

"Everything's made up, silly. The whole world."

And so the two stories continued, one in battle against the other. Nyquist handed the jam jar back to the lad, asking, "Did you notice anything else, anything strange about the scene?"

"It was strange enough, just on its own."

It was a good answer. Nyquist looked around in all directions at the flat expanse of the field, this lonely place. A cold chill could be felt, the first hints of the coming autumn.

He said, "Tell me about the rhyme I heard you singing."

"That old thing? Everyone knows that one."

The two kids started to sing together.

There was a crooked man and he told a crooked tale,
He scratched a crooked story with a crooked nail.
He wrote a crooked sentence on a crooked page
And sang a crooked song in a little crooked cage.

Their young, pure, exuberant voices mixed in a fragile harmony that drifted far over the field as Nyquist made his way back across over the sodden grass towards his parked car at the end of Plath Lane. Thoughts stirred inside him. He imagined a file on a dusty shelf in an unlit storage room at the police station: *Death by her own hand.* That was all, Zelda's memorial.

One more prostitute off the streets. Last name: unknown.

He stopped moving, and wondered about the scrawled remark she had made on the page of manuscript: *Nyquist. Find him!* But what then, if she had managed to locate him? What did Zelda want? Advice? His help? Something more? He couldn't know. It was a message from the grave.

An intense awareness came over him; of the land around him, the field he was standing in, each blade of grass, each flower, each sound below and above the kids' far-off chanting. Bird song, insects buzzing. The humming of the world. Knowledge trembled at the edge of his mind. It was something to do with the story he'd found himself in; or more truthfully, the stories, so many of them, a vast web of connections made up of every separate narrative he was currently occupying, crisscrossing, making the air shimmer with colors and sounds.

He was standing on a nodal point, a hub.

Zelda had died here in this field.

He knelt down. His fingers moved through the blades of wet grass. Something had drawn him, a sparkle in the undergrowth. It was a piece of jewelry, a silver locket. He recognized it as the one Zelda had shown him, or identical to it. He clicked open the lid and looked at the words written inside:

A picture of my mother.

The chain of the locket was broken, snapped. Pulled loose.

He held it tightly within his closed palm, allowing a new story to form in his eyes.

A struggle. A woman fighting back, fighting for life. Perhaps being carried here, across the field towards the gallows tree. A victim.

A single thought came to him: perhaps Zelda had not taken her own life.

THE WORDS LEFT BEHIND

Nyquist found a narrow alleyway at the end of the row. It was pitch dark. His hands groped ahead of him along the mossy, damp brick walls on each side until he reached the rear of the buildings.

It was almost one in the morning and as far as he could tell he was the only person still awake in the area. There were no street lights, but he managed to locate the back of the office by counting each doorway as he passed. He examined the ground floor window and, as he suspected, the frame was old and rotten, like most things in the district of Chaucer. He used a small chisel to chip away at the wood around one of the panels until the square of glass fell out intact onto his palm. He put a hand through the gap and turned the catch and the window opened. He climbed through and lowered himself down to the inside floor. Only now did Nyquist turn on his torch.

By its light he saw a tiny kitchen and dining area. He walked along a corridor until he reached the main office, where Antonia Linden would meet her clients. It was here, in fact, where Nyquist had first met her, at the start of the Wellborn job. If he had any chance at all of finding out the secrets of Zelda's death, then this was the place to start: the beginning of the story. The torch beam flitted across the desk and shelving units. A wall calendar showed this month's chosen writer to worship: James Joyce. Nyquist had tried to read a short story by him once, but nothing much happened in it: no fights, no car chases. He moved on, searching the room. He was hoping to find why Linden had left the office, and where she'd gone to. A home address would be perfect. He opened a filing cabinet and took out a few paper folders: each one held the details of clients, people who wanted their stories to change or disappear: such and such a tale to be erased. He searched through the Ws, but there was no folder marked with Patrick Wellborn's name. He tried the drawers in the desk, finding pens, pencils, bills, receipts, invoices. The usual paraphernalia.

Nyquist sat down in the chair facing the desk and he turned off the torch. This simple act was enough to bring his previous visit to this office back to life.

Linden had rung Nyquist and asked him to come in and see her, tempting him with the offer of a substantial fee. It had been a clear, warm day when he'd arrived, the sunlight peeking into the narrow walkways and overhanging eaves of Chaucer. He was welcomed in by Harvey, a man who seemed far too damaged and world-weary to merit the word "assistant": perhaps he'd had his own story erased at some point.

Nyquist had sat here in this same chair, facing Linden across the desk. Her face proudly showed off its age, the wrinkles and lines and the hard-won achievements they hinted at.

"I require you to follow a person of interest for me."

"What've they done wrong?"

"Oh nothing serious, I can assure you. On occasion our more established clients require discretion, above all else. I hope you understand?"

"I can understand most things, for a price."

Linden had smiled at this. "This is the subject." She placed a photograph on the desk before him. "His name is Patrick Wellborn. This is his current address."

Nyquist had studied the man's face and the address, and nodded. Normally, he would demand further information, but he was still struggling to make his living in Storyville and he agreed to the job without much thought; the fee really was too good to turn down.

"Will you be capable, Mr Nyquist?"

Linden had looked at him with eyes that held secrets, and Nyquist didn't like too much of what he glimpsed there.

"What exactly is it that you do here?"

"I help people out of difficult circumstances."

"Are we in the same business then?"

Linden shrugged. "Let's say this, shall we: you do the dirty work, and I clean up."

And so the details were arranged: "The subject matter is to be followed from his place of residence each day and evening, with the various routes noted, the places visited, the people met with, descriptions thereof, names if you have them; your report will be handed to my assistant Harvey each morning. He will come to your office for this purpose. Is that clear?"

"It's clear." Nyquist shrugged. "But what if something goes wrong?"

"What can go wrong?"

"Maybe this Wellborn doesn't take to having two shadows."

"Well then, Mr Nyquist..." Her teeth were on view. "Don't get too close."

These had been her final words. Nyquist never saw or spoke to Antonia Linden again; he'd dealt only with the assistant. And now, as he sat alone in the darkened office, he felt that he'd been led a merry dance, he'd been hoodwinked. And all he had to show for it was a dead man and a dead woman, and a whole series of questions. He spent a while going over them in his mind. Wellborn and Zelda had both reached the blank page, to use a typical Storyville phrase. The way it goes.

Or rather, the way Nyquist had let it go.

He stood up and was about to leave when he spotted a wastepaper basket under the desk: it was filled with scrunched-up sheets of typing paper. He unwrapped each one in turn, finding nothing of interest. But then he reached down to the bottom of the bin and found a book, a paperback novel, a copy of *Deadly Nightshade* by Bradley Sinclair. This was the third copy he'd seen since this case had begun, and that puzzled him.

Nyquist took the book with him as he made his way back towards the kitchen. A narrow stairway led upwards from the corridor; he hadn't noticed it before. He walked up it and found a storeroom filled with a few odds and ends, cardboard boxes, piles of magazines and files and the like. A smaller room off to the side was empty except for a table and a chair. The wallpaper was a garish flowery design in yellow and blue. He clicked on the art deco reading lamp on the table. It shone down on the bare surface beneath. The room struck him as strange in some way, almost haunted, and he shivered. He thought of Antonia Linden's true job: erasure. And he imagined stories disappearing here and there across the city's vast network, the threads breaking apart, one character disconnected from another.

This room was filled with ghosts.

THE NEXT PAGE

Nyquist woke late, exhausted from a dream that prowled through the darkness of the skull, leaving no traces in the light other than the sense that his skin was covered in ink, jet black ink. He got up, washed, cooked breakfast, checked the mail: junk, junk, junk, a bill, another bill – he pushed them all in a drawer unseen. Within an hour he had set off on his day's task, retracing the various routes that Patrick Wellborn had taken around Storyville. He hoped to find a pattern, a type of behavior. But Wellborn had been a true wanderer, moving from one story to another seemingly at random. Conan Doyle Park, Poe Terrace, Austen Promenade: from place to place, genre to genre, sentence to sentence, ever moving. Nyquist followed the same twisting routes, passing through different areas of narrative as storytellers sang and orated from the corners, bandstands and soapboxes, some with eager, attentive crowds around them, others with sparser audiences. But whenever Nyquist asked anyone along the way if they knew of a Patrick Wellborn he received only suspicious looks and shakes of the head. Where was he going, what was he looking for, what was Wellborn's goal? Was Melville Towers his final destination all along? Or had he been drawn there by someone he'd met along the way? Only once did Nyquist get a positive recognition and that was from one of the prostitutes who worked the corner where Nin Lane and Lawrence Road met. He'd seen Wellborn talking to them once or twice, but never to pick any of them up; he always walked on after a brief conversation, and Nyquist had moved on as well, following his subject matter. But now he stopped and talked to the women.

"Patrick Wellborn? No, sorry, pet, never heard of him."

"He's not a regular, not that I know of."

"Patrick who?"

One after another they spoke up, all answering in the negative. And then he met with a woman who stood apart from the others, hunched in the shadows of a shop doorway as she lit a cigarette for herself. Nyquist joined her in a smoke.

"Let me finish this, love. If you don't mind waiting?"

"I'm not looking for company."

"That a fact? What's your story, then?"

"It's not my story."

Now she looked at him with interest. "Well whose is it, then?"

"A man called Patrick. Patrick Wellborn."

"Oh yeah. I talked to him once."

"You did?"

She blew a trail of smoke from her lips. "He was quite chatty, as it happens."

Nyquist looked at her. She was in her mid-twenties and dressed in a fake fur stole and a dress of shimmering blue fabric. Her face still held a certain amount of innocence, kept in account from her youth.

"What did you talk about?"

"This and that."

He pulled out a couple of bank notes from his jacket pocket. But she pushed his hand away and said, "It's not your money I'm after. I just need to know what you're doing with another man's story? That's stealing, in my book. Plagiarism."

Nyquist thought for a moment. "Wellborn started the story, but he couldn't finish it."

"And you're trying to finish it for him?"

"I am."

"And why can't he finish it himself?"

"He's dead."

The prostitute tutted. "Oh, I knew it! I just bloody well knew it! I said to myself, Gabrielle, I said – that's me, by the way, Gabrielle – I said to myself, Gabby, that man is not long for this Earth. And wasn't I correct?"

"How did you know this?"

She drew Nyquist further into the shadows and lowered her voice. "I can read a few pages ahead, into the future. I can see it in a person's eyes, or in the words they say. Sometimes I just have to touch them and I get this flash of light and then I see a vision. Not clearly, but like through a mist or a dirty window."

Nyquist smiled at this.

"Oh, you can laugh."

"I'm not laughing. I'm smiling."

"Smile all you like, I don't care. I saw it when Patrick Wellborn talked to me, when he touched my hand."

"And what did you see, exactly?"

"Oh, it was horrible. His head was all bashed in, all bloody like."

Now Nyquist gave her his full attention. "Who did it to him?"

"I can't see everything and everywhere, I told you that. Just a few pages ahead, that's all, but the pages are torn and the ink is faded. That's all I can say."

Nyquist didn't know what to say, or what to think. This case was opening up new areas for him, new ideas about just how deep the storytelling went in this city. It wasn't just about beginnings, middles and endings – rather, everything was tangled up, one story wrapped around many others in an endless Celtic knot.

"So, what did Wellborn say to you?"

Gabrielle thought for a moment. "He was confused. But he was looking for someone, for a woman."

"Any particular woman?"

"Sure. Zelda. But she wasn't here at the time. So I thought I might as well ply my trade with him. But he wasn't interested. It was Zelda he wanted. But…"

What is it?"

Gabrielle looked suddenly thoughtful. She said, "Do you know that feeling, when the story gets too much for you, and you can't escape it?"

"A little."

"Well it was like that with Mr Wellborn. That poor man was trapped in a story and he couldn't escape it. That was the feeling he gave me, anyway. And that's when I touched his arm and I got the vision in my head, of where he was heading." She shuddered. Then she leaned close in to Nyquist and continued in a whisper, "Now don't you go telling the other girls about this, will you, about what I can see and all that? They all think I'm a bit weird, as it is. That's why I stand over here, on my own."

"It's our secret."

"Well, I'd better get out there, I suppose. Earn some money."

"You've been very helpful."

"Just find out who killed Mr Wellborn, that's all I ask."

Her demand made Nyquist's heart lurch. It cut to the raw center of what he was, of how deep he was caught up in these events, and how guilty he was.

Gabrielle folded her arms around herself: "Seeing something

like that, something so awful, his head all caved in and bloody like, it was truly frightening. I can still see it, as clear as daylight. It won't go away." Her eyes were filled with the vision, the fear. "I can't get to sleep easily. Not if I'm alone."

Again, Nyquist offered her money and this time she gave in and took it off him. "I don't even know your name."

He told her. She looked deep into his eyes and said. "I know what you're going to ask. And the answer is yes, I can see what lies on the next page for you."

"What is it?"

Her eyes narrowed and a single line creased her forehead. "The next page is fine, no trouble. But the one after that…"

"Yes?"

"Take care, Mr Nyquist. Stay away from libraries." And with that she walked away.

He was alone in the shadows, in the sudden cold of a summer's day that only he could feel. He waited until the moment of dread had passed, before moving out of the doorway. The other prostitutes were grouped together a little way along Nin Lane. A car pulled up and one of the women peeled away and leaned in at the driver's window. A deal was struck and she climbed into the vehicle. Nyquist walked up to the remaining women.

"Do any of you know Zelda?"

Most of them did and they bombarded him with voices.

"Zelda? Oh yeah, we all know her," said one.

Nyquist asked, "What can you tell me about her?"

The first woman replied, "Well, she wasn't a regular on the corner."

Others joined in, all speaking at once: "She came and went, working her own pickup spots, pretty much keeping to herself."

"Thought she was too good for us. Stuck up cow–"

"Oh shut up. Zelda wasn't that bad. We've all got to survive, how we can."

"That's all right for you to say, Daisy. You're still young."

Nyquist asked, "What was her second name, does anyone know?"

The one called Daisy told him: "Courtland."

Nyquist logged it away: *Zelda Courtland*.

"What about in the last few days?"

"Oh we haven't seen her," one of the older women said. "Not lately. I reckon she's hanging out with a fancy fellow, someone with money."

"Maybe she's gone and got herself married!"

They all laughed at this.

Nyquist asked if they knew where Zelda lived.

It was Daisy who answered again "Christie Town."

"Do you know which street, the number?"

But the older woman stopped any more conversation. She gave Nyquist the evil eye and asked, "Here, why do you want to know all this?"

"I'm a friend. And..."

"We've all got friends. I need more than that."

"Don't you know what's happened to her?" he said.

They gathered around him, evidently seeing bad news in his expression.

"Tell us."

And for the second time in ten minutes he found himself giving news of a death. The women on the corner fell silent. They looked at each other, frowning, and one of them cursed, another spat at the pavement.

Nyquist told them the truth: "The cops are happy to think she hanged herself."

"But you think different?"

"I do." He paused. "I think she was killed."

This caused a few gasps.

"Oh, you mean murdered?"

"May the Lord above gather her story."

"It's always the same, no one cares about us, alive or dead."

"But who did it? Do you know?"

"That's what I'm trying to find out." Nyquist said. "Anything you can tell me would be really useful."

They turned to each other and huddled together and spoke in whispers. Nyquist waited. The oldest woman turned back to him: "Are you legit? You're not some pervy sort?"

"No. I really liked Zelda."

She gave him one last up and down look and then nodded. "Zelda lived on Eliot Road, number 17. It's not far from here."

"Thank you."

"Only…"

"What is it?"

"Lately, she was acting strange. These last few days, I mean. Daisy, you knew her best. Tell him."

Daisy came forward, a nervous look on her face. "That's right. Really strange."

"In what way?" Nyquist asked.

"I live in the same boarding house, see, and sometimes we'd walk out together. But just a couple of days ago now, she locked herself in her rooms, and she wouldn't answer when I knocked on the door."

"What was wrong with her, do you know?"

Daisy shook her head. "Well I can't say, not for sure. She wouldn't even show me her face, not properly. One time she did speak to me a little, but only through a crack in the door. I think she'd taken badly to the job. Well, it happens, God help us all. I mean, she didn't want to show herself to anyone, not to any man, not even to her best and favorite clients."

Nyquist thought about the state of Zelda's corpse, the words on her skin. She was probably in pain, or scared or ashamed even, especially as the words reached her face and became visible.

"She said one thing that really upset me," Daisy added.

All the women were clustered around Nyquist now. "What was it?" he asked.

"She said that time was running out for her. That she was scared."

Nyquist urged her on. "Daisy? Scared of what? Another person?"

"I think so. Yes, maybe. But worse than that. Much worse." Daisy's eyes filled with tears. "She told me that she was scared of words."

The other women were shocked by this.

"Never!" one of them exclaimed.

"That's terrible," said another.

"She had to be lying."

The eldest rhapsodized: "Words make us, and keep us. Words embrace us." It was, Nyquist realized, a prayer. "Words save us from our true selves, covering us in story. Words deliver us from everyday life."

"It's true," Daisy insisted. "Zelda was scared to death of words. That's what she said, exactly that. Scared to death."

The prayer continued: "Words enfold and improve us. I am what I speak. My tongue is a long road; I shall never reach the end of it. Words fall in the night like a soft rain, like a balm. I am comforted."

The women all joined in, their voices raised up as one. Nyquist could hear them as he walked away.

Like a page left unturned, I am hidden away...

It used to be, he had no use for prayers. Now he wasn't so sure.

NO LONGER LIVING

Nyquist found Zelda's boarding house easily enough. He spoke with the landlady, who told him that Miss Courtland hadn't been home for a couple of days. Obviously she hadn't yet heard the news of the death, and Nyquist kept it to himself.

"Can I see her room?"

"What are you, a cop?"

"No."

The landlady, a no-nonsense woman in her forties, tutted loudly. "Well, you're too late anyway, I've already rented it out to another lodger. Needs must, and all that. So I don't think it would be appropriate."

"How was Zelda, these last few days?"

"A mess. But what can I say, Miss Courtland was always behind on the rent." The landlady muttered under her breath, "Dirty little good for nothing."

She closed the door in his face.

Nyquist moved on, once more following Wellborn's path through the city. The streets turned darker, the people poorer. Even the stories were different: outrageous, bawdy tales passed on gleefully. Here, life and story coexisted as equal partners, feeding off each other constantly.

He made one last turning. He was now standing

outside the residence of the late Patrick Wellborn: a small rundown hotel in the Orwell district. He watched the building for a while, sitting on a bench across the way and eating a sandwich, as he'd done each morning when actually following Wellborn. Alone or in pairs, down-at-heel men of a certain age entered and left the building, never women: Nyquist assumed it was a rooming house for unemployed or divorced gentlemen, perhaps a last resting post before the steep decline set in. After his disappointment with Zelda's rooms, he wanted to make sure he did this right, and as he sat there wiping crumbs from his mouth a new story formed in his head, a possible means of entry. He stood up and walked across the road towards the entrance. His neck was itching again; the irritation, whatever it was, seemed to be spreading. But he felt emboldened; the city's narrative spirit was taking him over and by the time he'd reached the entranceway he'd already invented a voice, a suitable tone and attitude to go with a new character.

The lobby was badly lit, smelling of damp and boiled cabbage. Somewhere, no doubt, a clock was striking thirteen. With his scant white hair and his shipwreck of a face, the old man behind the reception desk had the look of someone whose best stories had run out a long time ago, and he was now living on the dregs. He eyed Nyquist as though he might be a criminal, come to rob the place. A plump and very furry white cat was curled up on the ledger.

Nyquist brushed down his lapels and said, "I'm looking for Mr Wellborn. Is he in?"

"Ain't seen him, not in a while."

Man and cat looked at him, both with one eye open, the other half-closed. Nyquist gave them the same look back and said, "I'm Patrick's brother."

The man smacked his lips. "Funny, he never mentioned any family to me."

"We're estranged."

"Figures." The old man suddenly picked up a flyswatter and whacked it down on the desk, full pelt. The cat jumped a foot in the air. "Got it." He inspected the swatter, a look of satisfaction on his face. "Little buggers. Now then, sir, what did you require?"

"It's like this. My brother stole a gold wristwatch off our dear father, and I would like to retrieve the item."

Now the old man's eyes were fully engaged. "What are you, a con man?"

Nyquist held up his hands in surrender. "Sir, you have found me out, good and proper."

"How does this sorry tale end?"

"I give you a small amount of cash. You let me see the room. I steal something from there of value."

"That's it?"

"That's all."

"There's nothing of value up there."

"You've looked?"

"I clean the rooms, now and then. When Gladys can't make it in."

Nyquist placed three banknotes on the counter. "Here's the payment."

"You still want to see the room?"

"I do."

The man stared at the money somewhat distastefully. "They're fresh out of the bank only yesterday," Nyquist told him. But the manager still hesitated. Nyquist nudged him along. "Here's the thing: you can watch me the whole time I'm in the room."

The man picked up the money. "I must be a fool, but the trouble is, I can't see where the story's going. Can you?"

"I never can. That's the curse of my life."

"Well then, I guess I'm the same. Otherwise, I'd still be living in sin with an exotic dancer."

Together they walked up the stairs to the second floor. The old man stopped outside a door at the end of the landing and fished in his pocket for a set of keys. The door was opened and Nyquist went inside.

It was a small room. Very neat, very tidy, with a few items of furniture, and nothing on the walls to alleviate the peeling wallpaper or the bare plaster seen in patches. There wasn't a book or a magazine in sight, which struck Nyquist as odd; in this city, books were as essential as food. Or air.

The hotel manager was standing in the doorway. Nyquist asked him his name.

"Travis Gilly."

"Travis, how long has Wellborn been staying here?"

"Four weeks, roundabout."

"I guess most of your tenants are short-stay?"

"Most of them, yes. We have a few long-timers."

"And did Wellborn receive any visitors during that time?"

"Not a one, as far as I recall."

Nyquist opened the wardrobe, finding three identical suits, the same color and style as the one he'd seen Wellborn wearing every day during the last week of his life. He was a man of strict habits and tastes.

"How about money? Did he pay his rent on time?"

"He paid a month in advance, plus a deposit. All in cash."

"No questions asked?"

"Not a one." The manager frowned. "I stopped asking questions many years ago." He took a step into the room. "You gonna tell me what you're really looking for yet?"

Nyquist examined the desk, opening each drawer in

turn. There was nothing of interest.

"What about your maid?"

"Gladys."

"Did she notice anything strange about the room, or the tenant?"

"There was one thing, yes."

"Go on."

Travis settled himself against the wall. "She disturbed Wellborn one day, when she thought he'd gone out. She was hoping to clean his room, you see."

"And?"

"It's like this: Wellborn had his shirt off. His entire upper body was covered in tattoos, or so she said."

Nyquist looked over at the manager. "Did the maid say what the tattoos represented?"

"Well, Gladys is a very religious person."

"Meaning?"

"She called him a *walking bible*."

Nyquist thought about this. So Wellborn was suffering as well from the word sickness, just like Zelda.

"Of course," Gilly continued, "I'd already seen the words on his hands."

"On his hands?"

"Sure, all that writing he had on there. Bizarre, if you ask me."

Now this was puzzling: Nyquist couldn't recall seeing any words on Wellborn's hands in Melville Five. Perhaps the sickness moved around the body, from one section to another? Unless in some way Wellborn had more control over it?

He stood in the center of the room and looked around. The window was tightly closed and the air was thick and slightly grey-looking. Yes, this felt like the room of a seriously diseased person.

Travis fidgeted. "Like I told you, there's very little here."

"That's true. It's like a monk's cell."

Nyquist saw that the carpet under the bed was thick with dust; obviously Gladys's broom didn't reach that far. A handprint was visible in the dust, just under the edge of the bed. Someone had leaned down there, quite recently.

Travis hopped from one leg to another, his nerves getting the better of him. "You're not from the Narrative Council, are you?"

Nyquist didn't reply; he let his silence speak for him.

"Bloody hell! You're a story cop! I knew you had a stink about you. Now listen, I run a pure house. I do. Good clean stories only, no funny business. Nothing non-linear, nothing experimental. Just good old-fashioned narrative, do you hear me?"

Nyquist got down on his hands and knees to look under the bed. "Did Wellborn ever tell you anything about his life, before he came here?"

"Nothing."

"You didn't ask?"

"Mister, this ain't the Hilton or the Mayfair. Plenty of fellows come here to get lost in a tale of their own choosing, and that's their God-given right as a citizen of this fair and lovely city of ours, and we here at Gilly's Home From Home are happy to offer them that service at a fair price."

Nyquist reached under the bed with an outstretched arm and pulled loose a cloth bag that was taped to the metal strut of the bed frame. He stood back up and peeped inside the bag.

"What've you got there?" Travis was genuinely intrigued. "Nothing illicit, I hope?"

"This is all I need, thank you."

"Hey, come on. That's my treasure trove."

"Payment was made."

"That's not fair. What if Mr Wellborn returns? What do I say to him?"

Nyquist stared at the manager. "He won't be coming back, not any time soon."

"Now what does that mean? Mister? Just what does it mean? Is Wellborn's story done? Is it finished? I have to know!"

Nyquist was already heading down the stairs to the lobby. He exited the building and kept on walking until he'd put at least three streets between himself and the rooming house. Only then did he stop to sit down on a motorbus shelter's bench and to look inside the bag. It contained a bundle of paper. Eleven sheets in all, each one covered in words and images, and each page with a number at the bottom, none of them in sequence. He knew that he held in his hands a portion of a lost manuscript. There was also an extra sheet of paper, wrapped sideways around the others. It served as a makeshift folder. Someone, Wellborn presumably, had handwritten on this: *The Body Library*. And below that the name of the author: *A novel by Lewis Beaumont*. One more item fell out of the bag: a council worker's identity card. Patrick Wellborn's face was seen in a photograph attached to the card. Nyquist studied the information: date of birth, status, current employment.

At the time of his death Wellborn was working for the Storyville Narrative Council as a narrative officer.

READING MATTER

A much dented, second-hand Smith-Corona typewriter. A pile of foolscap paper, the title page of the manuscript uppermost: *A Man of Shadows by John H. Nyquist.* Anyone reading this work would see that the author has avoided as much as he can the letter X. An ashtray holding seven stubs, and one cigarette resting on the rim, still burning. A cup of black coffee, a packet of Woodbines, a fountain pen. The blades of a fan were slowly turning, sending waves of cool air across the face of the man who sat at the desk reading a few sheets of paper, his hands sliding one sheet behind another as he moved on, his eyes scanning each line and image as though for clues to buried treasure. A frown line etched his forehead as he concentrated.

Nyquist reached the last page. He'd read through them all four times up to now and was still puzzled at their meaning. Judging from this selection alone, *The Body Library* was barely a narrative by any normal account, hardly a story, more a series of fragments taken from other stories and glued together in some haphazard arrangement. Some of the pages were stitched with red or blue thread, others had smaller, torn pieces of paper glued onto them: pages taken from novels, a picture of a canary, a portion of a street map, two lines from a cookery recipe, a portion of musical notation, a section taken from the *Storyville Reporter*. One page even had splatters of blood on it. He started to read once more from the beginning of the first sheet, labelled page thirteen.

Abigail fired at once the poetry gun, scattering metaphors without remorse or moonlight. One hit after another until the wallpaper peels away showing Margaret's face alone in the mirror. We are the gatherers, we are scavengers. At the pool of language we deliver unto the machine what is the machine's, and live with the consequences. How the moon weeps for the dead! A magic spell is cast. Paradise Lily is selling her wounds on the high street, easy prices and fully guaranteed. Beware of shadows creeping over the land, through the lanes, across the hoardings, dancing like dying whore poets in the fading red light. Alas, alas, in the kingdom of birds, I am the man without wings…

It was enough to make Nyquist's head spin. His usual method of working cases – moving from one lead or clue to another, to seek out the hidden truth – could not be applied here. He was adrift in the words, holding on to one story, then another, one character, then another, one style of writing and then another. And this was just eleven pages, he couldn't imagine how it would feel to have to read the whole book, however many pages it might be in total. Where would the pleasure reside? Yet certain themes and objects turned up more than once, and these intrigued him: prostitutes, guns, a magic spell, a dying poet, even a private eye. He felt that a pathway might be available, in the fog, in the night, with himself blindfolded, stumbling forward with his hands outstretched, seeking the next landmark, the next fragment of sense.

He rubbed at his tired eyes. His lips were dry and cracked

and he dreamed of whisky. But he fought back the urge, and read on a little way further. This was his fifth attempt but it did no good; now the words were dancing on the page, losing whatever meaning he had so carefully put together. It was all too fragile, too tentative. He threw the pages down onto the desk in disgust.

There was no truth here, no secret.

He was as lost as ever.

Perhaps after all Zelda had killed herself? It was perfectly possible, and she might have discarded the locket herself on her walk across Marlowe's Field. Yet the way she'd talked about it, and the portrait of her mother inside – surely it had value. It was a precious object, something to take with her on the final journey.

No, it made more sense that someone had murdered her, and staged it as a suicide. He thought of Dreylock as the most obvious candidate, helped by his cronies. But then the name *Oberon* came to mind; this character had been mentioned by a few of the Melville residents, as some kind of overlord or governor of the building. In fact, Dreylock had called him, "Evil, through and through". But the thought of returning for a third time to Melville Tower Five filled Nyquist with dread.

And there was another mystery, surely connected to Zelda's death in some way: the words that that taken over her body. It looked like Patrick Wellborn also had writing on his skin, according to the maid's story. And he remembered Detective Molloy mentioning that other such cases had turned up in the city. Was it a drug epidemic, as more and more people were burning pages from *The Body Library* manuscript?

And why had his own name turned up on the page found on Zelda's body?

It felt like a story was being played out right in front of

him and all Nyquist could read were these hidden glimpses.

He stood up and started to pace the room, repeating phrases from *The Body Library* out loud to himself:

...in the mind's eye a room of secrets...

...broken on the stones, broken on the pavements, broken on the walls...

...her life a poem in the darkness of daylight...

The words seemed to inhabit his brain. The text was written on the inside of his skull, all eleven pages. He imagined himself walking around the circular chamber of bone, using a lantern to illuminate the walls, his voice echoing as he read one line after another, seeking connections. God help him, he even imagined setting fire to a page from the manuscript and breathing in the smoke. Where would that take him?

...trouble followed him everywhere...

...he was the eye, the dark eye of privacy opened up to the moon...

...on the borders where one breath meets another, a kiss...

Nyquist stood still. He stopped talking to himself.

That last line... yes, now he remembered.

Zelda's poem.

He tried to picture himself, back in the living room of an apartment in Melville Five: Zelda reciting her work for him, her words in the air so quiet, and even quieter now in memory, as he tried to recall them.

They walk alone...

Yes, two people, walking alone. That was it. But where?

On the edge of the city where the...

Where what?

Where the stories flow... where the stories flow away...

The words appeared, one by one, conjured up before him as surely as if Zelda were in the room with him, alive and well, reciting her poetry.

One word unspoken, one word unwritten... until...

Until? Until? It came complete, the line he needed the most to remember.

Until, on the border where one breath meets another, a story begins in a kiss...

That was it.

He went back to his desk and skimmed through the collection of pages from *The Body Library* until he'd found the passage:

...there is no other route, said the rainbow man, only this: on the borders where one breath meets another, a kiss moves across without papers or passport, a refugee from the steel towns to the north...

He was certain now: that particular phrase about borders and breath and a kiss, it had been stolen from Zelda's poem – stolen, sliced into pieces and rearranged and placed back into the flow of the novel as whole, lost or almost lost, until Nyquist's eyes and his memory had found it again, allowing it to rise to the surface.

It could only mean one thing: Zelda's poetry had been used as one of the elements in *The Body Library*. He remembered her tale of how her notebook had been stolen along with her bag. Yes, it made sense. She was connected, intimately, to the strange novel.

Was that why she'd been murdered?

He didn't know. He just didn't know! The story always slipped away.

Nyquist sat at his desk and read through the eleven pages one more time, looking for further clues, any other lines he might recognize, from books he had read, or things overheard. But there was nothing, only that one phrase of Zelda's. He clung to it – those ten words. And every so often during the rest of the day, as dusk fell and then darkness, he found himself repeating the phrase aloud.

on the borders
where one breath meets another
a kiss…

His neck started to itch. He was getting tired of it. He stripped off his shirt and stood in front of the mirror, trying to twist round far enough to see his own back. He couldn't quite make it – the painful area was always out of view no matter which way he turned. He looked in his bathroom cabinet for a salve or ointment, but there was nothing suitable. Another sort of medicine was available however, and he found it in the bottom drawer of his filing cabinet: a half bottle of Dewar's. He no longer hesitated and within an hour he'd finished it off. That night he lay awake in bed for a while, thinking about his next steps. The drink had brought him clarity, and some kind of temporary relief from his guilt over Zelda's death. He reached across for the copy of *Deadly Nightshade* he had found in Antonia Linden's office. The book must be important in some way; it had also turned up in two different rooms in Melville Five. Nyquist read the first few paragraphs of chapter one, even as his eyes started to close.

The young woman ran down the street, keeping to the shadows whenever she could. She darted into an alleyway and kept on moving. The footsteps echoed behind her. She reached the end of the alley and found herself on the main street of the town. There were too many lights! One of her heels was broken, and she was out of breath. She stopped under a street lamp and her figure was bathed in the yellow glow. Her face was fear-stricken. Her dress was torn at the shoulder. Her wild dirty blonde hair was in disarray.

Paradise Lily was trapped. She couldn't move another step.

Joe Creed approached her. He smoked the last drags of a cigarette and threw it to the sidewalk. With a grin he said to her, "There's nowhere left to run, Lily."

"Get away from me!" Her voice rose to a scream.

"Either you trust me, or Madame Leclair will find you again. She'll throw you to the wolves."

"I don't care," she cried. "I don't trust you, Joe. I never have!"

Creed shook his head. This was always the trouble. Nobody trusted him. There must be something wrong with his face. He looked like a bad case of the shakes trapped inside a bag of skin dressed in a cheap blue serge suit and a battered trilby. But what could he do? The war had messed up many a guy. All he possessed was what he saw in front of him, the things he could grab hold of.

He reached out for Paradise Lily and took her by the arm. "Let's go. I'll buy you a drink."

"But what good will it do, Joe?"

"Very little. The world is made by a cruel god and people like you and me, we're at the bottom of the pile."

From one shadow to another they walked on until the night claimed them.

The words blurred into a haze. The book dropped from his hands. Nyquist had one last thought before he succumbed to sleep.

Paradise Lily. Paradise Lily. The same woman. Two books...

A dream arrived.

He was back in Melville Towers. He was staring in the mirror of apartment 67, washing the blood off his hands. He looked up and saw his face in the dirty, cracked glass. He was covered in black marks. They were moving just under his skin like an infection of worms or insects. The letters slithered on his skin, forming words, forming stories.

He tried to read them. He tried to read his own face for a message.

His own face was a cry for help.

His face was a cry for help in the middle of a novel.

His own face was a short story with a sad, sad ending.

His own face was an experimental text without sense or meaning.

His face was written by a mad man.

His face was a gunshot described by a drunk.

His face was a penny dreadful.

His face was a horror story.

His face was a ghost story haunted by his own living self.

His face was a SCREAM written in colored letters ten feet high.

His face was a suicide note.

His face was a cheap romance novel thrown in the gutter on a rainy night, the pages sodden, trampled underfoot by high heels and brogues.

His face was a list of things to buy and keep in storage in case the bomb should ever fall.

His face was an instruction leaflet for a self-destruction device.

His face was a science fiction story about a robot who started to feel emotions.

His face was a racy pulp thriller starring femme fatales and doomed private eyes.

His face was a dialogue between a dead man and a living woman.

His face was a love message written in lipstick on a mirror.

His face was a page torn from an encyclopedia filled with useless information about things that no longer existed.

His face was a screwed-up page from a manuscript tossed in a wastepaper basket.

His face was a fading page of words turning to grey letters, disappearing...

His face was a blank page.

His face was a blank page.

His face was a blank page.

His own face in the mirror was a blank page and he clawed at it with his fingernails, desperate to find the words once more, under the skin, under the flesh, one word, another, any words at all to save himself from reaching the last page, and one by one they reappeared, daubed in blood, the black letters, one by one he read them on his skin:

On the border where one breath meets another, a story begins.

His face was a poem written by a prostitute and he loved it, he loved the words on his face, her words, her softly whispered words.

Zelda's words.

Nyquist opened his eyes in the dark of the bedroom.

He was trembling. Sweat covered his body.

Something had woken him. A noise of some kind, a continuous tapping sound. He sat up in the bed. His movement caused the paperback novel to fall to the floor, but he didn't notice it. He listened. Yes, there it was again, still going, tap tapping away, insistent, metallic, a clicking sound, a beat, but slightly irregular. The sound a human being makes when activating a machine.

It was the sound of a typewriter.

He got up and padded across the room to the door of his office and he opened the door a crack and peeped through.

The lights were out. Shining through the window, a neon sign's glow illuminated part of the room, a rectangle of flooring, one side of the filing cabinet, a portion of the desk. The typewriter was silvered by the light, like an object discovered on the moon. Like the ghost of a machine.

The sound of the keys stopped as soon as he opened the door fully and walked into the room. All was silent now. The shadows moved away from him as he approached the desk. He looked down at the typewriter. There was a sheet of paper in the grip and a few lines of text visible, the individual letters stark on the page.

He stood there and read the message.

Johnny, I wouldn't ask if I wasn't desperate, but I need your help. I'm trapped here, under a spell. I have to do what the boy Calvin says, it never stops. The ink never dries. Please, please help me!

Below this, the writer had typed her name.

Zelda

PART THREE

NABOKOV, THIRD DOORWAY ALONG

THE MUSE

They came for him first thing, the doorbell cutting into his sleep. He woke up bleary-eyed, and it only took the act of sitting upright to bring on a headache. The bell rang on and on, a far higher pitch than normal. At last he got up and pulled a dressing gown over his pajamas. He walked through into the office to let the two people in. The man was a stranger, but the woman was Bella Monroe, and she gave him a weary smile. But he saw something else in her eyes: fear. He'd never seen such an emotion on her before, she was usually calm and quite professional. She told him to get dressed.

"What?"

Her mood changed. "Quickly, Nyquist. Come on."

"You woke me up."

The man was looking around the office, an expression of distaste on his face. Nyquist took an instant dislike to him.

"Aren't you going to introduce your friend?"

Monroe frowned. "Just move."

He did so, walking back into the bedroom. He started to get changed and then turned when he sensed someone behind him. It was Monroe's colleague, standing there watching Nyquist intently. "How about a little privacy?"

There was no response. The man's eyes never left him. Nyquist turned round and pulled on the first clothes he could find. He walked back into the office, following the man, and he sat at his desk looking at his two visitors in silence.

"Mr Nyquist…"

Monroe paused, licked her lips and glanced at the folder she was holding. The file was closed, so he couldn't imagine what she was looking at.

"What is it?" he asked.

"I have to ask a question about the narratives in which you're currently involved."

"Go on."

"Mr Nyquist, have you been completely truthful to us about the nature of those stories?"

He tried to stay calm, to not react in any obvious way, but he felt his throat constrict. He held her stare and smiled and nodded and thought about what he should say next. He came up with a blank.

"I'm afraid… I don't know what you mean…"

"I think you do."

Monroe's expression had changed, she looked fierce, irritated. It worried him.

"As far as I know, I've mentioned everything. But of course, it's not always possible to remember every detail."

"Well, remember them now, why don't you?"

Nyquist looked from her to the man, who gave no clue as to what he was thinking, or what he wanted. He was a few years younger than Monroe, yet he was obviously her superior. His hair was neat, combed into a very precise parting. His features were as tidy as his hair, the eyes, nose and lips perfectly placed, highly symmetrical. It was an unnerving effect, almost masklike. Nyquist had to turn away from it, lest a sudden crack appear in the dull perfection.

"Can you give me a clue, Bella?"

"It's Officer Monroe."

"Right. Of course. Officer. What am I looking for?"

She didn't answer him. Instead she looked over to her colleague and waited. Another moment passed, and then this man approached the desk and spoke at last.

"I see you've been typing recently?"

Nyquist panicked. He couldn't help it. His eyes darted over to where the typewriter sat on his desk. He'd forgotten about his night-time vision. Yes, there was a piece of paper in the machine, but it had to be blank, a blank page. Surely he had only dreamed the words were there. But he could see the few lines of text, quite clearly.

The man bent at the waist and tapped at the sheet of typing paper with a single finger. "You've been busy."

"No."

"No. Really?"

Monroe spoke in a calm but determined voice: "Officer Drake needs to know, John. Help him all you can, I beg you."

Her use of his first name was a blessing. "I think... I think I wrote it in the night."

"You think?" Officer Drake loomed over him. He was a tall man and up close his eyes had a washed-out, early morning greyness to them. "Well?"

The headache was even more pronounced by now, close to the forefront of his brain. Nyquist couldn't answer, but Monroe helped him out:

"Mr Nyquist has been writing a novel for two months now."

He pounced on this. "I have. It's true. It's based on a real-life case from my past."

"I see." Drake nodded. He repeated the boy's name to himself, taken from the sheet of paper. "Calvin... Calvin.

Yes, interesting." He and Monroe shared a look.

"I have a character called that," Nyquist explained.

"And this... this letter, this desperate plea for help... this is a part of that novel?"

"It is. I was dreaming and I woke up in the middle of the night with those few lines in my head and I thought they'd fit into the next chapter, so I got up and typed them."

"So, it was a brainwave? A visit in the night from the muse?"

The man's voice was becoming an irritation. Nyquist felt angry. "Sure. One muse or another often comes to visit me, in the night."

Monroe covered her eyes with a hand. Officer Drake stood where he was and he tore the sheet of paper from the typewriter. "Do you think this is a humorous event?"

"I don't know if the event is humorous, do I?" His voice grew tighter. "Because I don't actually know what the event is, in any form. So why don't you sit down and tell me."

The two men stared at each other.

And then Officer Drake moved away from the desk, carrying the sheet of typing paper with him. Taking this as her cue, Monroe came forward and asked in a quiet voice: "John, do you have any knowledge of a man called Patrick Wellborn?"

"I've heard the name somewhere."

"He's a fellow officer, working for the Narrative Council."

"And what's happened to him?"

"He's gone missing."

Monroe looked devastated by the news, now she'd said it out loud. But once again, Nyquist did his best to not respond, neither to her words, nor to her obvious distress.

"He hasn't been in work for weeks, and his apartment is empty. And we think you're involved, John."

"What is this based on?"

"We know you visited his apartment, for instance, and that you took some items away from there."

Officer Drake interrupted, "That's enough, Monroe. Let's take him in. Vaughn!" He called to the doorway and another man appeared there, ready to help with the arrest.

With a shock, Nyquist recognized this new officer.

He'd seen him at Melville Towers.

NO OTHER OUTCOME

His hands were cuffed and his head forced down into his chest. In this manner Nyquist was led out to a black sedan parked directly in front of his residence. The building's supervisor stared at Nyquist, frowning, and complaining bitterly to his wife about the riffraff they had to put up with these days. Other residents and neighbors watched him go, all peering through their windows at the sight, or standing on the pavement, and they whispered to each other of the shame they felt, and the fear that they themselves might be called up next. It was the most terrible of crimes, to be caught up in the wrong story, a bad story, a story that reached out and stopped other stories from reaching their proper endings: a dreadfully selfish undertaking. One woman spat at Nyquist as he passed by, before Officer Vaughn pushed him into the back seat of the sedan.

They moved away from the curb. Bella Monroe drove, with Drake sitting next to her in the passenger seat. Vaughn sat in the back with Nyquist, but the subordinate officer made no eye contact with him, said not a word, gave no recognition at all that they had previously met. Nyquist thought about saying something to him, but realized that their previous meeting might become useful, depending on how the day's events played out. He had to be careful, to say exactly the right thing at the right time, to tell the right tale. He looked out through the window and watched the city pass by. Another warm day; the sun heated the pavements and sparkled on the awnings of the shops, and the women wore their prettiest dresses and smiled at the men they chatted to. The complex array of the city's grand narrative was evident to Nyquist's senses – in the details as they intertwined, in the moments, in a single gesture or a sudden explosion of sound. It gave him a bittersweet feeling, that such beauty could exist in the city and yet to be denied its pleasures. And every so often one or more of the citizens would turn and look at the black sedan with its tinted windows, and they would know that inside sat a sinner, an abuser of the narrative; they would know that a very different kind of story was heading towards its sorry conclusion.

The car drove on, leaving behind the central areas. He knew they were heading for the Grand Hall of Narrative Content. He had never visited it before, he'd never seen it except in photographs in the *Storyville Reporter*, but he knew that people feared the place, that children were told cautionary tales of what happened to people who strayed off the proper story paths. People referred to the council as the "word police" or the "story cops", and they were seen as being far worse than the real police. It set Nyquist's mind reeling. If only he'd confessed straight away about Wellborn's attack, and his death. But it was too late now, he had made his decision and would have to live with it.

He looked across at Officer Vaughn, but the officer was still turned away.

At last they reached Kafka Court, the large square to the south of the city which housed the governmental buildings. Nyquist looked at the edifices on each side of the square and the hundreds of people who hurried to and fro between them, carrying papers, notebooks, or parchments rolled into tubes and tied with red ribbon. The sedan entered a passageway between two of the buildings and headed down a ramp into an underground car park where the vehicle came to a halt. The side door was opened and Officer Drake pulled him out. He was pushed ahead, and momentarily he lost contact with the officers. He set off running. It was crazy, his mind was reeling. He knew he didn't stand a chance of getting away, but the act of defiance itself was important.

All the roads he'd never taken, all those brilliant stories he should've been a part of, they all wavered in front of him like a mirage, a haze of possibilities. He ran towards it, his head down, his feet almost stumbling on the concrete floor of the car park. He heard footsteps behind him, the sound echoing loudly in the underground chamber, but he ran on and on until he could no longer hear any noise at all, no footsteps, no shouts, no alarms or sirens, and he realized that he was alone. But he didn't slow down, believing in this moment that he was once more in charge of his life. On and on and on. And then he slipped. He slipped on a patch of oil and fell heavily to the ground, the air thrust from his lungs, his cuffed hands landing awkwardly. The pain was barely noticed. He rolled over and saw only a bright light over him, a sunburst he couldn't see beyond, and this was his despair, this light, he was trapped within, incapable of moving one more inch. And he waited there, slowly getting his breath back, until the sound of footsteps made him alert. They stopped close by. He got to his feet once more and stared at the three officers. Vaughn stepped forward but Drake said, "No, let him go. Let his story play out." The statement was followed by a laugh. Nyquist set off once more, at a much slower pace now, little more than a walk. He reached the far wall of the car park and headed for a green metal door. It opened at his touch, with no effort needed, no struggle, and he walked through into a covered alleyway. He staggered down it, gradually picking up speed, running just for the sake of it, in love with the idea of running, of escaping. He turned a corner and hit another brick wall. It was a dead end. A fire escape was his only way out of there, wherever it might lead. He clambered up it and kicked open the first door he came to.

It opened onto the main hall of the building.

The noise was deafening: the sound of cogs and ratchets clattering, wires and springs spinning and leaping, engines stuttering and purring, wooden boards clapping against each other, and people shouting orders.

He was standing high up on a narrow walkway that ran along the edges of the vast hall, and from this height he could see the many workers at their tasks, scurrying here and there along pathways and in between machines. A complex array of wires crisscrossed the open space of the hall, stretching from machine to machine, from portal to portal, and each shining wire carried along its length hundreds of index cards that travelled at speed before being deposited onto workbenches and counting desks. Workers examined these and clipped new cards to the wires and sent them on their journey. All the time, brass cylinders rattled along clear plastic tubes that clung to the hall's ceiling: a monstrous intestinal tract.

Nyquist couldn't move. He was hypnotized by the sight that lay before him. For this was the Grand Hall of Narrative Content, where the millions of stories that currently threaded their way through the city were represented and accounted for. He'd heard about it in late-night whispers in bars and storytelling cellars. Fear, shame, despair: tales of horror.

The hall was so expansive and sprawling it seemed to his eyes like a megalomaniac's palace, or a giant's playroom. More workers dashed around the floor, picking up files and papers, consulting documents, reading new cards and injecting cylinders into tubes. The workers talked incessantly to each other, their voices raised to be heard over the rumble and din of the machines in their operation. The hall sounded like a stock exchange at the height of the trading hour, and it wasn't very different in intent; here stories were swapped and shared, bought and sold, examined, read aloud, edited, added to, re-examined, taken down, removed as waste, rewritten, with new stories arriving every minute through doors and portals in the walls that clattered open and shut like so many mouths. Everything that made Storyville great and wondrous and perilous was contained here. It was a giant shout hurled in the face of an uncaring god. Here was *story* itself in full flood. Nyquist searched through his vocabulary down to the bottom layers, but there was no single metaphor that could contain or describe the hall and its operation, and he felt dizzy from the effort. A fog appeared before his eyes and he almost fell forward, over the rail, into the building's monstrous embrace.

He caught himself at the last moment and he moved along the walkway until he reached a flight of steps leading down to the factory floor. Surely here, amid the confusion, he could slip away, become lost, one more person in the vast crowd. If only his hands were free. But he had no time to think of that, all he could do was move forward, find another way out and from there to the street.

The chaos engulfed him. The noise, the constant movement, the smoke, the smell of oil, the roaring and pummeling of engines, the chatter and cries of the workers, the whizzing of the story cards along the web of wires:

all combined to take charge of his body, his five senses. Workers nearby had turned away from their bench to stare at him. He kept on with the last of his strength, running along an aisle between two of the machines, pushing past the startled operatives. A whistle blew, loud and piercing.

A warning: *Intruder in the midst!*

They closed ranks against his progress. Nyquist's hands were bound together so he used them as a ram, a club, to force a way through, making it a little way, taking off down another aisle, searching for a way out. He tumbled forward and reached out blindly to keep himself upright, and his cuffed hands grabbed at a cluster of wires, pulling them down, snapping them in two. He landed on the floor. Index cards started to slide off the broken wires. Papers scattered. He was surrounded by stories, so many of them, falling, cascading, tumbling over and over like a fall of leaves. And he lay where he was, his eyes taking in episodes described on the cards nearest to him.

Patterson, H.J. Moved in with mother. Both hate each other.
Coleman, Leo. Lost his job due to misconduct. (Connect to Ives, John, Card 347-BCP)
Jeffries, Susan. Extramarital affair with Naylor, Andrew. (Keep watch)
Evans, William. Still missing from family home. (Seek other strands)
Odette, Ronald. Dead. His own hand. Tablets. (Infected)

And suddenly he was thinking of Zelda again. How their own separate stories had connected for a short period of time.

Why? Why did she have to die?

The words on the cards blurred, and he felt that he was losing consciousness, as all around the hall continued with its elaborate, neverending task. Nyquist was hardly aware of its operation anymore. The machines and the workers were silent, even as they sounded, even as they shouted, even as they clamored and cried out. He was cut off from them, from any hope of recognition. Just another scattered man in a scattered land.

There was a scattered man, who took a scattered path...

He clambered back to his feet, using his cuffed hands as support. He felt weak, tired beyond any normal measure as though he'd been on a five mile run. He swayed from side to side, but managed through sheer willpower to stay upright. He was trapped at the center of a mirage. A group of workers surrounded him, keeping him penned in. And yet just a few yards away he saw a face that he knew, and his heart broke at the sight.

It was Bella Monroe.

His friend, his officer, his trusted story collector.

She waited there with the two other officers.

Nyquist waited for her. For what was the use of progress? There was nowhere to go. And he knew then that this building was designed only with capture in mind: the labyrinth of stories always led back to its own beginning, its own end. Only the words carried on. This was why the three officers remained where they were, staring at him, waiting patiently. And knowing this, Nyquist walked towards them. Monroe smiled at him and held out her hands, and he walked towards her, his own hands outstretched and still connected by the cuffs, and the two sets of hands joined as one, hers and his.

He was here, in this building.

There was no other place and no other time.

Only one story was possible from now on.

John Henry Nyquist willingly gave himself to it.

BETWEEN W AND Y

Nyquist felt his hands tighten on the arms of the chair as the overseer asked him for a second time, "When did you first meet Patrick Wellborn?" But every possible answer he could give seemed wrong, except for the truth. A sharp pain needled away at the back of his skull.

"Can you answer me?"

He hadn't been given the overseer's name, only her title. She was old and withered in face and body, with lined features and fragile limbs, but despite her outward appearance she exuded power and confidence. Yet Nyquist kept seeing glimpses of something beneath that, shown in an occasional facial tic, or the sudden trembling of her hands. She was nervous. Something was troubling her, and her colleagues, and anyone with any kind of authority on the council.

"You've kept me here all day," he said. "Locked up."

"Yes, I'm sorry about that. I needed to meet with my fellow seers, to discuss your case."

"And now you expect me to just answer your questions."

"Yes, that would be useful."

Nyquist had been searched and photographed, and then placed in a tiny cell with a bench along one wall and a toilet in the corner. The walls were covered in scrawled writing: names, dates, slogans, lines from favorite stories and poems, made-up rhymes both dirty and heartfelt, nonsense limericks and misspelt cries from the heart. These were messages left there by previous occupants, other poor souls called in for questioning. The walls of the cell were a novel in themselves, a book of escape with no ending. No food or drink had been offered to him beyond a jug of water. At one point Nyquist had howled in frustration, howled like a wild beast at the covered light bulb above his head, a cheap substitute for the moon. Nobody heard him. And so the hours went by; he had no way of knowing how many. At one point he'd lain down on the bench and managed to fall asleep, at least for a little while. In a dream the walls of his cell had spoken to him: a wordless, blighted, hopeless dirge, and he awoke feeling even worse than before. Some time later the door had opened at last, and he'd been marched to the overseer's office, on some upper floor of Kafka Court.

"Useful in what way?" he now asked.

"To the city's wellbeing."

"I don't believe that's the case."

The overseer peered at him. She said, "There is something terrible and possibly very evil happening to our city. For all of our knowledge of the city's stories, none of us here really know what it is that threatens us. But we fear for the people. A number of them have already fallen ill, one or two have died. That's the truth, Mr Nyquist."

Still he hesitated.

"Or perhaps you would prefer to go back to your cell?"

"I'll speak." He took a moment to locate the start. "I was given the job of following Wellborn. I had to find out where he went during the day, and at night, to note the kind of people he talked to, to remember streets and districts he traveled through. And so on."

"Who employed you in this task?"

"An agency run by a woman called Antonia Linden."

"And the purpose of this agency?"

"Erasure."

The overseer bristled. The word sent a shiver through her. Her mouth, hardly visited by joy to begin with, folded inwards to a thin straight line, and her hands curled around into claws. She groaned. But with an effort she managed to relax.

"Good. You're being very cooperative."

The overseer rested her elbows on her desk and put her hands together in an attitude of prayer. She had the look of a corpse found in a Saxon grave or a peat bog, her face creased and folded in many places, peppered with liver spots, her eyes rheumy, her teeth discolored when she opened her mouth. Nyquist couldn't imagine which god or goddess she was praying to – probably to a deity of words, or writing, or writers – but nowhere in her face could he make out a sign of beatitude.

"Why did this Linden woman want Patrick Wellborn's story erased?"

"She never said. I believe she was doing it on behalf of a client."

"And who would that be?"

"I have no idea."

"Well... Linden was certainly very successful at her job. You already know, I think, that Officer Wellborn has disappeared."

Nyquist felt uneasy. The hours of isolation were catching up on him; he was hungry and tired and his body ached from the hard bench and the confines of his cell. Yet he needed to test the case they had on him, so he said in a calm voice:

"Perhaps he's dead."

There was little reaction. "Yes. It's a possibility." The overseer picked up a sheaf of papers from her desk. "These were found in your office. Do you know what they are?"

"They're part of a manuscript, from the draft of a novel called *The Body Library*."

"And you've read it?"

Nyquist nodded. "Only those few pages. I've tried to."

"It doesn't mean anything to you?"

"There's no proper sense to it."

The overseer smiled. "Exactly. And that worries us. You see, we have no record of this book, and no real knowledge of the person or persons involved in its creation, nor of the people who've read it."

Nyquist knew what this meant: "It's outside of your control."

"It appears that way."

She nodded to herself for a second, and then said: "Is there anything else you'd like to tell me?"

Nyquist answered, "The pages of the book can be burned and the smoke inhaled."

"I see."

"It has an effect on the reader."

The overseer nodded. "We know of such things, actually. It's a property of the special ink they've used in the manuscript. Addicts refer to as midnight's ink. For a short period – a few minutes or hours or even a day, depending on the individual's sensitivity – a user will believe that they are actually *inside* a story. Not reading it, not listening to it. But actually a *part* of it. A vital part. The leading role. The user is incapable of distinguishing between real life and fiction. The two separate worlds will merge, here..." She placed one finger on the side of her brow. "Here, in the mind."

Nyquist wondered how far he'd been affected himself.

"The only clue we have is the name *Calvin*. A boy. He's been mentioned by a few of the word sickness sufferers. And now..." She held up another sheet of paper. "Here he is again, typed out by yourself in the night, in a dream, apparently..."

She stopped speaking and stared at Nyquist. His hand had reached round to to scratch at the back of his neck. He was hot and feverish, and he could feel slight bumps just under the skin.

"Are you uncomfortable?"

He shook his head. Yet his whole sensory experience was targeted on those few square inches of flesh. With an effort he pulled his hand away.

The overseer stood up from her desk and gestured for him to do the same. He did so, following her over to a glass display case fixed to the wall. They both stared at it. The box contained twenty-five beetles, all of the same species, each specimen mounted with a pin to the green baize beneath. Depicted on the folded wing case of each beetle was a different letter of the alphabet, from A to Z. Only one example was missing, that carrying the X design. There was a space on the backing where the absent beetle might be pinned one day, if the overseer should ever find one, right between W and Y. Nyquist was fascinated by the collection. Many of the beetles had jet black carapaces, but others were colored bright blue, green or orange and glittered with electrical effects; they shone like jewels, like an oil spill in paradise. The empty space reserved for the missing letter especially held Nyquist's interest, as though it contained everything that was missing in his life, all the lost details.

The overseer said: "There are twenty-six administrative areas in Storyville, each one with its own overseer. My name is K. My job is to look after all the stories in the area, to make sure they mesh together properly, that they are evenly distributed between the different classes, races and creeds, so that no one group or individual is favored. Most of all we try to ensure that stories make sense, that they have their proper outcomes, regardless of their individual moral nature. Without our guidance, the city would quickly descend into chaos."

Nyquist turned to her. "Why am I here? What have I done wrong?"

"I think you know that already."

"I'm not sure if I do."

Overseer K sighed. Nyquist looked at her face. He saw her features in a new light: every wrinkle and crevice was the path of a story, and those contained within them smaller stories, and so on, down to the core, the dark red heart. Her face held the city's tales within it and the weight of this burden over the years, the many years of her career, had affected her deeply. Thus, she was bent and battered, and only willpower kept her functioning. Yet she spoke proudly: "Almost every story connects to another story, even if it's only in the tiniest way, a glance, a tangent, or a ricochet. Do you understand what I'm saying?"

He nodded.

The overseer continued: "Your story has tangled with Patrick Wellborn's one too many times. We've followed your progress, from linkage to linkage, event to event – as told to us by this person and that, in the plazas, in bars, cafés, on street corners. Yet nothing of this was ever mentioned to Officer Monroe in your weekly briefing. And so, it made us curious."

"You know everything?" he asked. "Everything that we do?"

"Not everything. Many events are still personal, still private, unseen by any witnesses. Some parts of the city, certain buildings for instance, are entirely unknown to us. There are nodes of silence, blind spots, dead ends. This is how erasure works. A story's connections are severed one by one, until it stands alone. And then it disappears."

Almost without thinking, Nyquist had started to scratch at his neck again.

The overseer smiled. "You should know, Mr Nyquist, that we found some marks on your body. Precisely where you're feeling the pain."

"Marks? What do you mean?"

"To be precise: letters."

He stared at her blankly as she continued with her description.

"Sometimes these letters form into words, moving around on your skin. Or rather, just beneath the epidermal layer. They act very much like a virus."

"A virus?"

"I'm afraid so."

Nyquist pulled his hand out from his collar; there was blood smeared on his fingertips. The sight of it made him feel faint.

"But that's not possible. I don't understand."

The overseer removed a speck of dirt from her jacket. "Sadly, neither do we. A few other sufferers have been examined, but the underlying cause remains a mystery. We do believe, however, that it's tied up in some way with *The Body Library*. In fact, it's possible that book is the cause of the sickness. Maybe as some serious after-effect of the drug usage, or perhaps something more than that. We are still looking into it."

Nyquist was filled with horror. He remembered Zelda's corpse at the morgue, and the photographs he'd seen at the police station.

Words. Words in the flesh, eating at her body…

He felt dizzy. The office whirled around him.

"Get them out of me!"

It was a raw cry from deep down. He said it a second time, this time unheard by anyone but himself, a whisper inside.

Please. Get them out of me.

The overseer remained calm. Her eyes were clear and focused; she didn't even blink. She said, "There's very little hope for you, I'm afraid. The words are alive in your body, and there's no cure. Not yet."

He could hardly breathe. He felt that his skin was on fire. He'd never felt so weak, or so helpless. His whole body screamed against the sense of being invaded, of being taken over, but there was no escape.

The overseer guided him back to the desk. She sat down opposite him and pulled open a drawer, from which she removed a series of story cards.

"The sickness is the least of your worries."

She laid the cards on the desk, one by one.

"These are various story fragments, each from a different witness, each relating to a journey that you undertook in your car some four days ago."

"Four days?" He tried to think where he was on that date, but his mind was blank. "I don't understand."

"It's quite simple. Here, you see…" She nudged one card forward so he could read it. "You are seen picking up the woman in your vehicle. And here, in another precinct, you are seen driving out towards the east of the city. Do you see?" She pushed more of the cards forward. "There are numerous accounts, all tallying. It's quite linear, once you put it all together. Here, and here. Look closely. The woman is described plainly. One account gives us her name."

Nyquist read the words on the card: *Zelda Courtland*.

He started to protest, but the overseer simply carried on with her laying out of the cards, like a fortune teller consulting the Tarot. "This final witness places you and Miss Courtland driving out towards Plath Lane. Marlowe's Field is quite close by, I think."

Nyquist felt cold inside, as though he already knew what was coming next.

One last card was placed on the table. He read it himself, a description given by two children, a young boy and girl, both of them describing a man dragging a woman across the field, towards the tree. She was struggling to escape.

"I think they describe you quite well, don't you think?"

He stared at the final card without speaking.

The overseer pursed her lips. "It's very sad, such a young life taken from us. I imagine poor Zelda had many stories left to tell."

At last he managed to say, "I didn't do any of this. I didn't kill her."

"The narrative is plain." She looked at him. "All the evidence points to one conclusion, one ending."

The words were breaking out on his skin, he could feel them moving around, spreading down from his neck to his back, around to his chest and from there crawling up towards his face. He was covered in sweat and his whole body itched terribly.

"You've made this up," he managed to say. "The whole thing… it's fiction."

"Of course…" She studied him dispassionately. "A story can be seen from many angles. And the slightest change of focus might well produce an entirely new explanation of the events. Does that make sense to you?"

This time Nyquist stared at her without answering. His fingernails were scratching away, first at one shoulder and then the other. The words swarmed over his hands.

"All it takes is for the eye to shift slightly, and there it is. Suddenly, it doesn't look like murder at all, or it wasn't you in the car, or perhaps another person was seen in the vicinity. And so on and so forth, the patterns are woven, and unwoven, as we choose."

Nyquist hardly heard himself speak. "What do I have to do?"

"It's quite simple." Overseer K leaned back in her chair. "I want you to find *The Body Library* for me. And destroy it."

NIGHT DRIVE

It was dark by the time Officer Monroe's car left Kafka Court. She drove the vehicle along Jules Verne Way, back towards the city center. Occasionally she would glance in the rearview mirror at Nyquist, who was slumped in the back seat. The street lamps cast his face in a sulphurous, intermittent glow. His eyes were closed. He looked to be asleep, and she could only imagine the terrible dreams he might be having. But then his eyes opened slightly and he spoke in a tired drawl.

"Where are you taking me?"

"Home, John. Home."

They drove on in silence, but the day's events proved too much for Monroe to bear. She had to speak out.

"I'm sorry," she said. "I'm truly sorry."

"That's all right, Bella. I survived."

"You did, you did."

"And it's over now, isn't it?"

"Of course. You're free again."

Nyquist laughed bitterly. "Free? That's a good word for it."

The lights grew darker as they took the turning towards Clarke Town. The car drove on and on and Nyquist was lulled by the motion. He looked at his hands and saw they were clean, no sign of the words that had crawled there earlier. He had imagined the illness taking him over completely, a vision real enough to cause him to almost black out.

"I don't feel too good."

"I know."

"I'm infected. Bella. There's something inside me. It's eating at me."

"You just have to…"

"Can't you help me?"

"Just do as the overseer asked. That's all."

"That's all?"

"Nothing more. She's a woman of her word."

"She wants me to find *The Body Library*. Do you know of it?"

"Only a little. Enough to know it's a dangerous task to take on."

"But some poor bastard's got to do it, right?"

"What choice do you have, John?"

"The overseer's got something on me, a made-up story."

"She wouldn't do that. It's against all our rulings."

"Well, it's being used against me."

"There must be a reason. There must be!"

He groaned. "Don't give me the party line, Bella, please."

"It's for the city," she said. "For the good of the city, and the people who live here."

He watched the buildings pass by, the few people strolling along in the evening air. They were moving through a quiet part of town and most of the stories of the night had fallen quiet, or asleep, with no one to tell them. And he wondered how the city would operate if the stories were ever to fall into chaos, as Overseer K had envisioned.

He said, "I feel like I've walked into the wrong bar at the

wrong time of night and been hit around the head, and now I'm to blame for it, somehow."

Monroe just kept on driving.

"Stop the car."

She wouldn't. He leaned forward and put his hand on her shoulder. "Stop the goddamn car, Bella. We need to talk. Give me that at least."

Something in his voice made her follow his command. She pulled over to the curb and cut the engine and the silence folded itself around them like an animal's shadow.

A few moments passed before Nyquist said, "I've messed up, haven't I?"

"It looks that way."

She was as quietly spoken as he was, two people living in a place of whispers.

"What's really going on?" Nyquist asked.

"Patrick... Patrick Wellborn went crazy. We're trying to find him, that's all."

A car drove by along the road. The lamp above a nearby bar flickered a welcome in blue and gold. But there was too far to go before Nyquist could get to such a place.

"I'm scared, Bella."

"I know."

And then at last he said the words he should have said a long time ago: "Wellborn's dead."

Monroe froze. He saw her shoulders hunch forward and her head bow. A single sob escaped her throat.

"It's the truth, I'm afraid."

She turned in her seat. Pain moved across her face, from one expression to another. Her emotions would not settle: fear, doubt, despair, and the faint glimmer of hope clinging on.

"You're wrong. He's still missing..."

"I saw his body."

Her eyes glistened as another car passed by: teardrops in the headlights.

Nyquist asked, "Did Patrick mean something to you? He was more than a colleague?"

She nodded in response. A tiny move that he only just noticed. "We were engaged. We were going... we were meant to get married, next year."

"Bella, I'm sorry."

She turned back to face the windscreen, hiding her face. "Where was he found?"

"Melville. Tower five."

All Nyquist could see was the mass of her hair, the grey streaks, the clip that held it all in place. The trembling of her body with each breath. He felt the need to confess, to help her along, but wondered how far he could go. But she turned to face him again and said, "I don't understand. Melville is one of the city's blind spots. We never hear of any stories that happen there." She frowned. "What was Patrick doing in such a place?"

"The same thing I was: looking for something."

Her voice rose, panic taking over. "It's out of bounds for officers. There's no control there! No beginnings, no endings, things just happen at random."

"And the tower is tied up with the novel, *The Body Library*. The two go hand in hand. But how? What's the connection?"

"Nobody on the council knows."

"Haven't you been inside the building?"

"Not lately. A few expeditions were made, but officers were attacked. One almost died. And now it's seen as a no-go area." A faraway look came into her eyes. "Secrets take you over, don't they?"

"What do you mean, Bella?"

She didn't answer him. Grief overwhelmed her in a

sudden wave of anger. She hit at the steering wheel with the flat of her hands and she cried out in such despair that Nyquist could only let her be, to let her feelings write themselves aloud.

And he waited.

A young couple walked by along the pavement, hand in hand, two stories that he hoped would never be disentwined.

Monroe was breathing in heavily, her emotions still raw, but contained for now.

He waited another moment and then said, "Bella, I need to know everything about Wellborn, all you can tell me."

She settled back in her seat. Nyquist couldn't see her face, but he could imagine her expression, the brave smile. "You know, despite the name, Patrick wasn't at all *well born*. He came from the lowest of circumstances, and he worked very hard to climb out of them. He was kindly, polite beyond measure, at least in the beginning. And yet very committed, and quite passionate." She paused to gather herself. "Sadly, that commitment didn't last long. Not after he became addicted to that horrible stuff."

"Midnight's ink?"

"Yes. Oh God…" Her body heaved. She sobbed, choking on her next words. "He said something to me once. He said, 'What if there was a way in which a person could become fictional? *Fictional*, Bella! Would you welcome such a thing, such a journey?'" She brought a hand up to wipe a tear away. "He asked me to go on that journey with him. But of course…"

"You didn't believe him?"

"How could I? It was madness talking. Or the drugs."

"And now?"

"Now I'm not so sure. Maybe he did find something. Maybe."

Nyquist made his decision. He said, "I helped him along the way."

Monroe turned to look fully at him. He leaned forward in his seat so their faces were just inches apart.

"What do you mean?" she asked. "You helped him?"

"I helped him to die. I defended myself."

She stared at him, without any comprehension on her features. "You mean... you mean he attacked you?"

"He had a knife. He was going to kill me."

"But why would he do that? He was a good man."

"Good or bad, he came for me."

"And you fought back?"

Their eyes locked. "Bella, listen to me, he was drugged up, that's all I can imagine. He took too much of the story. I had no choice."

In a hush she repeated his phrase. "No choice..."

"None. None at all. It was kill or be killed." He paused and then said, "Not even the overseer knows this. Not as far as I know, anyway. Only you, Bella. Only you."

She didn't respond.

Nyquist said, "Now it's up to you, Bella, what happens next. You can call the police, or tell your boss. Or you can let me go, let me carry on, and I swear to you on everything that's good and proper that I'll find out what Patrick was doing there, at Melville Five, what made him so desperate that he was hooked on the ink, and so messed up that he tried to kill me. I'll look for the cause, the root."

She kept on staring at him. Her eyes held such darkness, he could hardly look at her.

"Bella, something pushed him over the edge. Something drove him mad. And someone put that knife in his hand."

At last she spoke. "You think you can find out?"

"I hope so. But I'll need your help."

"Of course."

"Step out of the car."

"What?"

"Bella. Step out."

His voice was suddenly cruel. She climbed out and he did the same and they faced each other in the street, her body in darkness, his lit by a nearby lamp.

"I need to know everything."

"I don't know what you mean. Nyquist! I've told you..."

Now he was close to her, his eyes unblinking. "Tell me the truth."

"The truth?" She spoke in a frightened hush. "The truth scares me so. It scares me half to death."

"That's all right. Tell me now."

Monroe did so, starting slowly, haltingly, but gaining in certainty as the story went on, as though she was relieved to be telling it.

"There is a faction working in secret at the Narrative Council, six of us altogether. We were, all of us, pledged to secrecy, which is why I couldn't tell you any of this before." A slight pause. "Patrick Wellborn was our leader. Even before he discovered the power of *The Body Library*, he was plotting and planning the overthrow of the council. He wanted to release the city's stories from such dreadful human control, to return them to their natural state. We all wanted this, myself included. Others were involved in this rebellion, but we at the council felt we were at the very center of the struggle, working to destroy the institution from within."

The headlamps of a passing delivery truck moved across her features. She stayed silent until the vehicle had vanished once more into the night.

"In reality," she continued, "it was little more than a pipe dream. But Patrick changed. The novel changed him, that damned book of cut-ups."

Nyquist could hear her true pain emerging now.

"Once he succumbed to the burning of the pages and the terrible delirium they brought on, there was no stopping him. He started pushing *The Body Library* as the true way forward, and that we should all work together to realize the book's ultimate purpose."

"Did he say what that purpose was?"

"No, he didn't. At least, not in my hearing."

"And if someone should get in the way of that purpose, what then?"

There was no answer. But Nyquist couldn't help thinking: what if Zelda had in some way fought against the book, and all that it stood for? Perhaps a member of the group had taken action against her?

Monroe continued, "The thing is, John, by this time it was no longer a political struggle for Patrick, but a personal journey. He was taken over, possessed." She faltered. "I feared that I'd lost him. Lost his love, his companionship. He was associating with prostitutes, criminals, the low life of the city, seeking a deeper, more powerful experience from more dangerous stories. And always he would return to me, and fling these stories in my face. He sickened me. I demanded that he leave, but he never would, not until the final word had been spat in my face. I could not recognize him anymore. He would not even answer to his given name, demanding that I call him Joseph, or Joe Creed, whenever the mood took him over. He'd become obsessed with one particular character in *The Body Library*. Someone like you, John."

"Like me?"

"A private eye. But a fictional version. He was staying off work more and more. It got so bad that I considered informing on him. Only by so doing could I possibly save him. But of course I had to think of the others, the other members of the group. I would be betraying them as well. So I let things be. And now… and now he's gone forever."

Monroe had calmed a little. She wiped at her face with a hand.

Nyquist asked, "Tell me about the Melville Tower."

She nodded. "Melville Five is the center of it, the source of the trouble, whatever it might be. I am no longer a part of the group, but I know they still meet up all around the city, gathering members, whispering in basement rooms. Plotting and planning, as such people are wont to do. Some of them are suffering, the words growing under their skin. I have seen it happening before. I saw it with Patrick. They are no longer in charge of their own lives. But it was different with Patrick, worse in a way, because he seemed to have control of the sickness, control of the words that burrowed in his flesh. It was frightening."

Her expression hardened.

"Some great calamity awaits us, I'm certain of it. The group talked incessantly of a day fast approaching when the revolution will take place. They spoke of coming together with one purpose, of being the special ones, the chosen ones. The messengers. Through them the new story will live."

Monroe turned away again, hiding her face in the darkness.

She said in a strained voice, "You're not far from home. Can I leave you here?"

"Of course."

He thanked her, and watched as she got back into her car. But she had one more thing to say before she drove away: "Be careful, John."

He remembered a similar warning from Gabrielle, the prostitute he'd spoken to on Nin and Lawrence. *Take care. Take care.* The trouble was, just now it seemed like the wrong advice. Zelda's death was tied in with *The Body Library*, and with the word sickness that he now shared with her, and possibly with the revolutionary group. And if he was ever to find her murderer he would have to walk into places where care didn't even exist. It couldn't be taken, or stolen, or borrowed.

He would be alone.

LILY AND JOE

Nyquist set off walking towards his block but stopped outside the doorway of The Final Word, a drinking den on De Quincey Lane. It was an easy decision to make. He entered the bar and took his usual seat. The barman, a silent skeleton named Tagget (first name forever unknown) placed a Virgin Mary on the counter. No words necessary. Nyquist held back from temptation: he wasn't here for a drink, he was here for a story or two, or three, or four, however many it took to get his head cleansed of the dirt of Kafka Court. Matthew Le Skin was currently on stage, regaling the punters with his gory tales of derring-do in the Empire. Jacquie McQueen followed him, rousing the audience even further with her lesbian pirate revenge erotica. And by the time the night's headliner, Ursula Bloom, had come on, Nyquist and the rest of the listeners, drunk or otherwise, were well on their way to story heaven: beginning, middle and end, all the events following one another in natural consequence, the characters acting like real people do, when real people are exaggerated, and loving, greedy, lustful, crazy, inspired or despairing. And he was reminded of why he'd chosen this city for his second home: after the misadventures of his younger days, he needed a story to settle down with, to fall into, to be comforted by. It was a stupid dream, perhaps, and one that was already falling apart, but this club and this crowd and this night of revelry and narration gave him hope: he was alive, he was listening, he had a role to play.

Ursula finished her act with a story from her childhood, and after the applause had died down she added as an afterthought:

"There is one simple truth that my mother taught to me. She told me that every woman, man and child on this good earth has two stories, one in their real life, and one fictional. The one in life comes to a natural end, but the fictional story carries on for as long as people will tell it, or read about it."

Nyquist thought about this as he walked home.

Death meant very little in the light of the city's grand narrative. But for this to be true, Zelda's story had to be narrated, beginning to end, right down to the reason why she had been killed. The story had to be told, it was that simple.

He got home around eleven thirty to find his office and living quarters a tip: the council officers had searched through it, leaving the contents of every drawer on the floor, the filing cabinet emptied out, his desk in disarray, his suits and ties scattered on the bed, every pocket turned out for clues.

He sat at the desk and lit a cigarette and drew some consolation from it.

It wasn't enough.

After the night's innocent libations, he longed for a slug or two of whisky.

There wasn't any. The bottle was empty.

He yearned for a woman's comfort.

There was none.

He longed for escape, or even more so, a revelation. An

answer to his problems.

None. None. And none.

He slotted a piece of foolscap into his battered old typewriter and stared at it, willing another communication to appear, for Zelda's ghost to send him a message from the other side. Or more likely for his own subconscious mind to force his hands to start hitting the keys. It didn't happen. The paper was blank. But he had to do something, at least to write a word or two, as evidence that he was alive. And so he made his fingers move slowly from key to key, typing out the exact same line three times over:

The quick brown fo jumps over the lazy dog.
The quick brown fo jumps over the lazy dog.
The quick brown fo jumps over the lazy dog.

And the only letter that mattered was the missing X. He stared at the gap on the paper, falling under its spell, its emptiness, its eternal mystery.

The unknown, the unknowable.

He thought of one thing only. He didn't care about uncovering the source of midnight's ink, he didn't care about the cut-up novel, he didn't care about the death of Patrick Wellborn, he didn't even care about the words that were infecting his body. No, he only cared about Zelda. Zelda and the kiss, the only good moment in his whole goddamn story.

He typed again.

The quick brown fo jumps over the lazy dog.

And again, over and over.

Fo fo fo fo fo fo fo fo fo…

There was no such creature, quick, brown or otherwise.

It was late and he was tired, and the events of the days clouded his memory. As he took off his shirt he thought once more of the writing on his back. His skin was calm, untroubled, but when he angled his shaving mirror just so, opposite the bathroom cabinet's mirror, he saw the letters at their play across the nape of his neck and his right shoulder: yes, they were spreading. He went to bed, thinking that he would have to find Lewis Beaumont, the author of the cut-up text – it was his only way forward, and his only way of escaping from Overseer K's control. But as weary as he was, he struggled to sleep: the nightmare was in the world outside, not inside his head. He turned on the bedside lamp and leaned over to find the paperback book lying on the floor: *Deadly Nightshade*. He reread the first few paragraphs, and then stopped and sat up in the bed. The female character was called Paradise Lily, and he'd seen that name before, in one of the manuscript pages he'd found hidden in Wellborn's room. The name of the novel's private eye also sounded familiar.

Joe Creed.

It took Nyquist a moment to recall Bella Monroe's story: this was the name of the man that Patrick Wellborn had become obsessed with, another character from *The Body Library*. Yet here was the same name in a very different kind of book, a detective story.

It set up questions in his mind. And possibilities.

He would sleep fitfully now.

A METHOD OF WRITING

Cleland North began at the far end of the Woolf Housing Estate, where the road straddled the old canal and where every day the neologists shouted their wares: "New words for sale! New words. All the latest creations, get yours here!" It was Nyquist's first visit to the area. Bella Monroe had given him the address that morning, after he'd telephoned her for information. He parked his car and entered the maze of streets on foot. From every open window and doorway he could hear the tapping of keys and the rapid almost angry return of typewriter carriages, the curse of the authors, the scrunching up of papers as another page was ruined, the clink of wine and whisky glasses, the raging arguments, the lonely monologues, the slammed doors as the latest partner or collaborator stormed out. Gothic romances, adventures in space, cowboy tales of the Old West, pornography of every stripe and persuasion, dramas of everyday life rendered truthfully in unforgiving detail: the city's incessant hunger was fed in the main from this downtrodden part of town.

Nyquist stopped at a corner to get his bearings, consulting the page he'd torn out of his street atlas. He was about to turn right onto Sackville-West when his eye caught sight of a familiar car parked across the road. He crossed over to it. Officer Monroe was sitting inside, looking at him through the open side window.

"Bella? What are you doing here?"

She climbed out and stood before him. Her skin was puffy looking, her clothes were ruffled and her hair was sticking up in fronds. Black circles surrounded her eyes.

"This isn't a good idea," he said to her.

"I disagree."

"Overseer K ordered you to help me?"

"No. I'm on unofficial compassionate leave."

Nyquist shook his head in dismay. "Bella, this is dangerous work."

"I've faced danger. The story riots of '56. You weren't even here then."

"I know that. But still–"

"You wouldn't have lasted ten minutes."

She started to walk down Sackville-West. Nyquist cursed to himself and went after her. He caught her by the arm. She shrugged him off.

"Leave me alone."

"Bella. This is stupid. This isn't the way to do it."

She looked at him with an intensity he'd never seen before, and he understood just why the Narrative Council employed her. Patrick Wellborn's death had triggered Monroe's rage, and a fierce determination now burned in her, even a need for revenge. And he didn't like the thought of that.

"I haven't slept," she said. "I can't let it go."

"I'm still not sure, Bella."

The noise of a typewriter's keys sounded from the nearest window. "Do you hear that?" she said. "All stories are equally important, mine included."

There was no argument against it.

They set off walking. The address they were looking for

was near the end of the row, one small terrace crammed in among many, roof tiles missing, brickwork crumbling, a missing window pane covered with cardboard. Nyquist rapped on the door continually until it opened up a crack and a pair of eyes peeped out at them.

Monroe said, "We're looking for Bradley Sinclair."

It was a woman, her face still obscured: "He's busy. Writing."

"I'm sure he can spare us a few sentences."

"No, no, I don't think so–"

Monroe thrust her council ID card through the gap in the doorway. Immediately the door was opened fully and the woman in the hallway moved aside, a fearful look on her face. She nodded to the rickety staircase. Nyquist had to admit to himself that working with a council officer had its advantages.

"Upstairs, second on the left."

Monroe led the way. They reached the landing and stood together outside the bedroom door, listening to the sound that came from within. Nyquist said, "I'll do the talking," as he knocked on the door. There was no answer. "Bradley Sinclair?" Still no response. Nyquist tried the door. It wasn't locked, so he pushed it open and walked through into a brightly lit room. A large desk dominated the space. Sitting at it was the bent-over figure of Bradley Sinclair. His head was lowered so far forward that his nose almost touched the keyboard of his typewriter and his arms worked incessantly, bent grotesquely at the elbows and shoulders and wrists like the limbs of a praying mantis. He was a human machine designed for one purpose only: to write. The keys clattered, up and down, up and down; the carriage clanged and rattled, back and forth. The return bell rang out – *Ding!* The letters smashed against the paper in a steady rhythm.

"Mr Sinclair?"

Nyquist might as well have not spoken at all, or even be standing there, some few feet away from the writer at his work. Only the story mattered, nothing else.

Monroe moved forward and touched Sinclair on the shoulder. Immediately he jumped from his seat and turned to face them, almost losing his balance in the process. His eyes were blinking rapidly. He backed into the corner of the room, mumbling to himself, most of the words lost in his panic, his quickly drawn breaths.

Nyquist came forward as well, and together he and Monroe managed to calm Bradley Sinclair down a little. Monroe said, "We don't mean you any harm."

"But you stopped me, you stopped me from writing." Sinclair made it sound like a major crime. "Why? Why would you do that?" He spoke in a high raspy voice, perhaps unused to expressing himself out loud, and he couldn't stop blinking. He rubbed at his eyes with his fingers and his breath came in short, shallow gasps.

"We need to talk to you about Patrick Wellborn."

"He's not here, is he? You haven't brought him with you?"

It was a pure outburst of fear.

Nyquist had an idea about how to pacify the man. "No. He's dead."

It worked. Immediately Sinclair relaxed and he started to breathe normally again. He collapsed into his chair at the desk and settled his nerves further with a cigarette. He was a feeble man in his middle thirties, underfed, lacking all sense of muscle beneath the clothes and skin. A faint breeze or a bad review might blow him away. His mousy hair was long and greasy and combed forward to almost reach his eyes, which continued to stare at the paper in the typewriter's platen. His hands were already twitching with the ghosts of stories yet to be written.

Nyquist sat on the edge of the desk. He said, "Wellborn was obsessed with your Joe Creed detective novels, isn't that true?"

"Yes, very much so."

Monroe examined the writer's setup. He typed not onto individual sheets of paper, but onto a continuous roll that was pulled into the machine from beneath and rolled out again as the carriage moved on: it was a system designed to allow the author to never stop working, not until he wanted to. The space behind the desk was billowing with waves of white paper. Monroe said, "This is the technique that Jack Kerouac used when he was writing *On the Road*."

"Yes, yes, yes! That's the method I use!" Sinclair's eyes sparkled. "The method of spontaneous combustion."

"I think he means spontaneous *composition*."

"Same thing, same thing!"

Nyquist said, "People are falling ill, Sinclair. Even dying. And I think you're bound up in it."

The author muttered to himself without answering.

"When did you find out about Wellborn?"

"He came to see me. I don't know how he found my address, I try to keep it secret."

"He worked for the council," Monroe explained. "He could easily find the address of any writer."

"Wellborn wouldn't leave me alone. Always asking for more stories, more knowledge, all the secret histories, the notebooks, character biographies, hidden back stories, the plans for the next books. All of it. He never stopped."

Nyquist pushed on: "What did Wellborn really want from you? What was he seeking?"

"One thing only: to *be* Joe Creed. To become the private eye, to join in the adventures himself. He was crazy. And then... and then it got even worse."

"What happened?"

"He stayed away for a while, and I was glad of that. But after about two weeks he came back, and this time he'd changed. I mean he was acting just like Creed does, he moved like him, he talked like him, the same phrases, same intonation, even the same accent. I mean, his voice had changed! He even started to look a little like Creed does, in my mind, as I see him. He started to walk the same crooked path."

"How did it happen, this change? Do you have any idea?"

"The story took him over. He had stolen Joe Creed's soul from me. And suddenly, without warning, I could no longer write."

Monroe spoke to Nyquist. "This must be when Patrick started taking the drug. He was becoming obsessed."

"He killed her," Sinclair mumbled. "He killed her."

"What do you mean?" Nyquist asked, suddenly thinking of Zelda. "Who did Wellborn kill?"

The writer gazed at his bent fingers, each calloused tip smeared with typewriter ink. "Wellborn killed my muse, he shot her dead!"

Monroe asked, "Are you reporting a murder?"

Sinclair shouted at her: "In here. He killed her, in here." His fingers pressed against both sides of his skull as though he might force a way inside. "He killed her without mercy."

Nyquist asked, "So you employed Antonia Linden to erase Wellborn from your life?"

"What else could I do? I needed to sever every single link between myself and him. Only then would I be free."

Nyquist tried a few more questions, but Sinclair wouldn't say any more on the subject. He kept glancing at the typewriter, at the roll of paper, the half-finished sentence.

"Sinclair, speak to me."

"I have to write."

His hands reached once more for the keys and started to tap out their feverish rhythm, the words springing into life under his guidance. Nyquist looked at the page, at the text that filled it, letter by letter.

Akdfg kslojf mskh sd ljithjom sd s klsgatw d sljo slkfif s jhs ss skold sda...

He checked the sheets that flowed across the floor; they were all covered in the same chaotic outpourings. Bella bent down to the writer and whispered, "You have to stop now, Bradley. You're not making any sense."

Sinclair's fingers hovered above the keys, convulsing like faulty devices. He murmured and fretted, and sweat beaded his brow. His whole body shuddered into sudden action and with an almighty scream he picked up the typewriter and hurled it across the room. It smashed into the wall, taking out a great chunk of plaster, and then fell down to the floor.

Nyquist waited until the last echo had faded away. Then he asked in a calm voice, "Do you know of a book called *The Body Library*? A sort of cut-up text?"

"Yes." A breath of a word. "Yes, I know it. *Deadly Nightshade* was used in the making of it. They sliced open my books and the words flowed out red with blood on the white page and they took the wounded flesh and re-used it, stitching the pieces together with other parts taken from other books by other writers, all in a jumble. I liken it to Frankenstein's monster. Born out of an evil desire, created only to destroy." The speech exhausted him, and he continued in a quieter tone: "Agatha Christie's second Miss Marple mystery was called *The Body in the Library*. So you see, even the title is taken from another person's words. The scissors at work."

Nyquist thought for a moment, then he said, "You used the word *they*, when talking about the author."

"That's right."

"I thought it was written by Lewis Beaumont."

Sinclair bit at his lower lip. "It's two people. Two writers under one name. Theodore Lewis and Ava Beaumont. They approached me earlier this year to ask about using parts of my work in their own book."

"So they did ask permission?"

"Yes. I thought they were going to quote a few passages. That's what I understood, that they were writing a treatise on my work, or on crime fiction in general. But they took the whole book and tore it to shreds."

Monroe asked, "Do you know where we can find them?"

"They have an office right here in Cleland. I went there once, seeking reparation." He gave out the address and Monroe wrote it down in her notebook.

"What were they like, Lewis and Beaumont?"

"They were always arguing, I know that."

"About the book?"

Sinclair frowned. "That's all they ever talked about. What the book should be, how it should look. They were at odds over it."

Monroe said in a gentle tone, "We're really sorry to find you like this, Bradley. I know from my work on the council that your stories have given much to the city."

The author opened his arms wide, as though to grab and embrace the ghost of his muse.

"Lost. Lost forever."

Nyquist nodded to Monroe and they made their way to the door. The sound of tearing paper stopped them. Nyquist turned. Sinclair was ripping the long roll of paper in two. He gathered up another portion of the scroll and tore at it. And again, in another place. And again. Over and over, this work continued.

He was laughing.

PLACE OF BIRTH

It took them half an hour to find the address, a rickety, tumbledown building in a street where every house looked half abandoned. Across the way was a bombsite, a harsh reminder of the war years. Smoke drifted above a bonfire and two dogs sniffed around a pile of rubbish. Here, Cleland North shaded into the even poorer district of Conrad South. Monroe parked at the roadside and turned off the engine. Nyquist looked out through the window. With its green and red timbers and peeling plaster it looked like a ruined fairy tale house dropped down into reality.

"Let's put it together," he said. "It starts with two writers, Beaumont and Lewis."

Monroe took up the thread. "Together they create *The Body Library*, using parts taken from other books and magazines and so on, pasting them together to make a new text."

"Then your friend Wellborn discovers that the pages have a psychotropic quality. He becomes hooked on the word smoke."

"Through this addiction, one particular character in the book…"

"Private eye, Joe Creed."

"…starts to take over Patrick's mind."

"But Creed was stolen from the work of Bradley Sinclair. So Wellborn seeks out the original author, demanding to know everything there is to know about the character."

Monroe nodded. "He was seeking total identification."

"Right. And then Sinclair employs an erasure company to slice Wellborn from his life story. Which is where I come in. Public sucker number one."

They got out of the car. Nyquist looked up at the house. "I doubt if anyone's home. It's too much of a ruin."

Monroe agreed, but added, "Maybe they're hiding from us."

Nyquist rang the doorbell and waited. He tried again with the same lack of response.

"What now?"

"Now, Bella, we break in."

It took him no more than five minutes to locate the weakest window at the side of the house, and to smash the pane. Bella said nothing. He climbed through the window and opened the back door for her. Together, they searched the premises top to bottom, finding no evidence of life.

"Beaumont and Lewis have moved out," Monroe said. "Or maybe Sinclair made the whole thing up, just to get rid of us."

"Possibly."

Nyquist found a ladder leaning against the wall on the top landing, directly below an attic door. He propped the ladder on the lip, climbed up and pushed open the door. He popped his head through the gap.

"What can you see?"

"This is it, Bella."

"Tell me."

"Their workspace."

They climbed up. The entire space beneath the eaves was filled with the detritus of artistic endeavor. Thousands of torn-out pages lay scattered everywhere in ragged piles, some of them reaching high up the walls like snow drifts. A workbench was filled with tools and accessories: pens, scissors, modeling knives, steel rulers, pots of glue and ink, needles and thread, ribbons, even a vise for some reason. The empty covers of novels, both hardback and soft, lay around in a tumble of cardboard: their printed innards had been torn out. Paper slid against paper as Nyquist moved deeper into the attic. Monroe picked up a pair of scissors from the bench and pointed out the dried red substance on the blades. "Please tell me this isn't blood."

Nyquist couldn't answer. He had recognized the cover image of *Deadly Nightshade* – not one copy, but many, their pages sliced and torn open for material. He picked up one sheet of paper with a handwritten poem on it. The style seemed vaguely familiar to him, and he liked to think of it as being one of Zelda's, although, with no name or signature on display, he couldn't be certain. Other items he saw included a cookery manual, a spy novel, a street atlas of Storyville dated 1917, a children's book called *The Brightest Star in the Sky*, a romance pamphlet entitled *The Wayward Bride*, a number of science fiction story magazines, a spotter's guide to the birds of Great Britain. One half page contained lines of Latin text with diagrams of pentagrams and other magical symbols, probably taken from a book of spells, or a demonology. But he was no expert, and the atmosphere of the room overwhelmed him. This was a private library after a bomb had fallen, a disaster area where stories lay in shreds and tatters.

From all these things and probably from many other sources as well, the authors Lewis and Beaumont had constructed *The Body Library*.

Monroe had fallen silent. She lowered herself to the floor and moved her hands through the scattered pages like a helpless nurse on a battlefield. Nyquist knew how she felt. There was too much pain in this room, too many wounded tales. The officer was weeping now, weeping. And he knew it wasn't only for the mutilated books, but for Patrick Wellborn as well, her fiancé, whose life had also been torn apart by the strange novel created in this attic room.

Nyquist went over and knelt beside her. The ever-moving pages made a whispering sound, like a choir of ghosts. So many words, so many lost half-spoken phrases – he was aware of them, his every sense tuned to the slightest shifting of the layers of paper. And Monroe's sobs were another part of the soundscape of the room. Her own trembles set the papers trembling. He asked if she wanted to leave and she replied, "No. Not yet. We need to find out what happened here, John. This is the starting point of all the troubles these last few months." She picked up a few of the papers. "I think Patrick was buying or stealing some of these discarded pages. This was his main supply."

Nyquist agreed. "But why would an author, or a pair of authors, create a book that's unreadable?"

"It's the search for new ways of telling stories."

"I get that, Bella. But it doesn't explain why *The Body Library* seems to affect people so deeply."

The papers shifted around them and the room sighed. Monroe's hands searched through the off-cuts and found a stack of large index cards. "These were taken from the Grand Hall. A whole section of stories went missing, a few months back."

"You think Wellborn took them?"

"It pains me to say it, but yes, I do. I think Patrick was helping them, helping Lewis and Beaumont. They'd already revealed to him the power of the book, and now they needed his help to finish it: the missing element. Real stories, real people. Real lives."

Nyquist looked at the cards: he saw the names of citizens, he saw the tales they were involved in, the tiny incidents, the fragile connections as one story crossed with another.

"Ah well," Monroe said. "Overseer K will be happy, when I report this to her. I imagine the whole collection will be destroyed."

Nyquist hardly heard her speaking. He was lost in his own realm. This room of broken stories had affected him in ways he couldn't admit to, not even to Monroe. Because of his time in the Melville Tower he felt that he too was a part of the whole – he was listed in the body library, in the library of bodies, in the parts and pages of the book, the one book, the all-encompassing book, the book that contained the city within itself, that *was* the city, the book of the city, the book where the city lived and breathed and read itself aloud and wrote about itself in all its ragged, torn-apart glory.

Life, severed at the roots, scattered, caught on the wind.

And then written down once more as words.

The book was a code, a cipher.

But to what end? Containing which secrets?

He was drawn from his thoughts by the touch of Monroe's hand on his own, and by her murmur of his name in quiet alarm. He looked down and saw her fingers running softly across his palm. The letters were visible there, just under the top layers of skin, he could see them moving about, living creatures, already forming into new words. The sickness was spreading, taking over his body.

The story lived inside him.

ONE EVENING AT WORDRISE

It was well past the end of the rush hour but the streets and pavements were still crowded. This made it easier for Nyquist to follow his target, jumping down from the motorbus as the target did, moving from one cluster of people to another, stopping to look in a shop window if he felt he was in danger of being spotted, or ducking into an alcove or doorway. Dusk had fallen. The town was painted in its softest colors. The two men walked diagonally across a market square and on, one behind the other, into a warren of back streets, until at last the crowds thinned out a little. They were in Lower Shakespeare, a district where people from many different ethnic groups and classes mingled, and several different languages merged together, their stories growing quite naturally from half-understood meanings.

The private eye had followed Officer Vaughn all the way from Kafka Court, watching and waiting until the target had left work for the day. Now he had to be more careful; with fewer people around he had to keep his distance. Vaughn crossed one more road and then disappeared down an alleyway. Nyquist followed half a minute later. The alley was called Nabokov Lane. It was a cul-de-sac, narrow and badly lit. Litter and rags lay in piles against the walls and around the metal waste bins, and the stench of urine mixed with that of rotten food and wet fur. The only light came from a lamp with a cracked shade above the rear door of a restaurant. A dog barked from a nearby back yard. Nyquist was glad that Bella Monroe had finally gone home: he'd lied about his plans for the evening, telling her he was tired, and needed sleep. It was the last thing on his mind.

The target stopped.

Nyquist did the same. He pressed his body into a niche in the wall, held his breath, just as Vaughn looked back down the alleyway, trying to see if the noise he'd heard had come from a person, or a dog or a rat.

The two men stood rooted to the places they had chosen.

One searched; the other prayed for the darkness to hold him.

It did.

Vaughn rapped at a door, the third one down the passage, and it opened up for him. He slipped inside. Nyquist was wondering how to take the next step when he heard voices behind him. A man and woman were walking down the alley, barely noticing him. They both had the hungered look of addicts in need of a fix. Nyquist followed and waited as they also knocked on the third door along. He entered with them, acting as though he belonged here. But each person was being checked by a woman sitting behind a counter. Nyquist approached her. With a yawn she asked: "Your first time?"

He nodded, not daring to speak in case he gave himself away.

"Do you have the mark?"

He wondered what she meant, but then held out his hand where the letters were visible beneath the skin: currently they spelled out a word: *history*. The woman took his entrance fee, a few pounds, and passed him on down a corridor lined with booths half-hidden behind velvet curtains. It had the look of an old-fashioned brothel, but all the beds in the booths were empty. Other pleasures had taken over the place. A hulking security guard looked Nyquist over, searched his pockets and inside his jacket, and let him pass to the inner sanctum. He really didn't know where he was going, or what he was going to find, as he followed people up a staircase and through a doorway that opened onto a small hall, softly illuminated by a few overhead theatre lights. It was a black painted room without furniture or fittings of any kind: an empty space. Music was playing over a loudspeaker, the slow movement of a string quartet. The room was already filled with a crowd of people, perhaps thirty or so attendees, all of them standing around the outer walls, leaving the central area clear. They all had a certain look about them, all carrying the knowing air of being outsiders, cast-offs, exiles from the mainstream, seekers of forbidden knowledge. They were dressed mostly in plain clothing, with little to show for themselves other than their facial expressions, which swung between studied boredom and rampant desire. Many were nervous, on edge, as though waiting for a knife fight or an orgy to begin. One or two looked like they might run at any second; others were long-term users waiting for their latest kicks. A number of the attendees displayed the symptoms of the word virus on their hands and faces.

And then Nyquist spotted his target across the room, Officer Vaughn's facial blemish making him stand out even in such a bizarre setting. Vaughn's gaze seemed to settle on his own, but Nyquist quickly hid himself behind a pair of women who were nervous at being here; they kept joking and pinching each other. The council officer moved on.

Soon the few lights took on a brighter hue and an expectant hush fell over the room. Two ushers moved through the crowd, giving out sheets of paper. Nyquist looked at the one handed to him: it was a single page from *The Body Library*. The usher said to him, "All pages must be handed in at the end of the evening." He nodded and looked around, taking in the various people standing nearby – an older man, a middle-aged woman, a boy in his late teens. No one paid him any mind.

The last hubbub died away, leaving silence.

Everyone in the room was holding their breath, Nyquist included.

The tension rose.

And then people started to read from the papers in their hands: at first a lonely hesitant voice, and then others joining in around the room, one by one, each in turn, passing lines of text between them like sacred offerings:

I am golden, I am folded.
I am alone here, among the many.
The clouds part above the island.
The moon rests each morning with the fire in her eyes.
No one knows my secret, no one cares to wonder why.
Our wings are spread, awaiting flight.

At this point the audience joined in, repeating the line with one voice.

Our wings are spread, awaiting flight!

Nyquist had not yet spoken, not yet said a line. He felt that he wanted to, the occasion demanded it, the room, the space, the people, the page in his hands, all combined to make him take part, if he could, if he dared to. He looked at the paper and chose a line at random and said in a clear voice so that all could hear:

Too late for sleeping, Lady Paradise walks the neon pathway.

As one, the audience chanted the name three times.

Lady Paradise! Lady Paradise! Lady Paradise!

And Nyquist felt a surge of power in his body. He was alive! In this moment, in this place – this, finally, was how he was meant to be. The words possessed him completely and he listened with more intent now, as the various reciters carried on:

The night people crawl on the edge of daylight.
I am looking for a doorway marked No Exit.
Don't run away, not yet my love!
When the library burns down we shall all be wordless.
Until then, let the dawn break your eyes apart, let the
darkness shine.

The audience echoed this last phrase:

Let the darkness shine! Let the darkness shine!

Nyquist joined in. His tongue was no longer his to command. And so it continued, the reading of these thirty or so pages from *The Body Library*. It was liberating, and Nyquist spoke again as the urge took him, choosing lines from the page that he held: *The nearer the sky, the further the moon*. None of it made sense to him, not by any linear or logical standard, yet he felt that each word, each sentence fitted in with the ones preceding it and following it: despite everything, a story was being told. But this was a story that more closely resembled the inner workings of the mind, or a labyrinth of dreams, than any standard narrative. And the audience hung on every word, further activated by certain key phrases here and there, adding their own voices to the mix as needed: it was a collective experience, a giving in to illegal desires. In the vast, all-encompassing city of stories, these few people were breaking narrative into pieces, and enjoying every fractured moment.

Nyquist felt lightheaded. By now, the words were having a strange effect on him. He became disorientated, and as the crowd shifted around into new positions he was taken with them. He looked around in a daze as the recital continued.

Lost in the sky, the words, the broken creatures.
The city opens and closes its mouth.

Nyquist spoke aloud once more, hardly hearing the words he was saying:

Where does the road lead, winding around the body's
collision...

His hands were shaking as he stared at the page. His own name appeared in one line and then faded: his eyes darted back and forth as he tried to find it again. But now the words were shifting around on the paper. They trembled and blurred.

The people were no longer reading and the room grew quiet. There was a strange rustling or whispering sound – the sound of paper fluttering. But was he imagining it? Was it merely an effect of the room, the lights, the recital? He tried to keep the page in focus, but the words seemed to be floating just above the surface of the paper. They were shivering, shifting from side to side. Nyquist was transfixed at what he was witnessing. Everyone was standing as he was, gazing in wonder, in silence, at the pages of *The Body Library*. Only the faint whispering sound could be heard.

And then the first word took flight.

...moon...

It rose from the paper in Nyquist's hand and drifted around in the air right in front of his eyes. The four letters separated and whirled away in separate directions. Other words followed suit, from his page and from all the other pages in the room.

The whispering grew louder, a constant hissing sound.

A woman gasped, a man cried out in joy.

Every word on every page of the book had now risen upwards. They flew around the room, a swarm of letters, a flock of sentences. People were looking around in awe at the sight. One teenage girl tried to reach up, to grab at a word as it flew by, but she couldn't manage it: the word was too quick for her.

Now the air was dark with letters. They moved faster and faster, swirling around in a frenzy. Through the cloud Nyquist saw the blemished face of Officer Vaughn once more. The two men stared at each other and recognition passed between them.

The words settled again onto the pages of the book.

The spell was over, and straight away Vaughn started to move. Nyquist nudged aside the people nearest to him, seeking the council officer, hoping to catch him before he left the chamber. But he was too late: his target was nowhere to be seen. A doorway at the back of the room swung to. Nyquist took this as his lead and hurried through, into a dark corridor. A shadow moved, off to the right. He had to assume it was Vaughn, he had no other option. Nyquist stumbled on in the near darkness until he reached another doorway. A spiral staircase led even further upwards. He was faint by the time he reached the top, as though he'd climbed a tall, tall building. But it was only one floor. He was still recovering from the strange vision he had shared with the audience. His body swayed and he held onto the steel banister for support, willing his body and mind to settle. Rather unsteadily he moved through an open doorway, onto the roof of the building. Here he stopped and looked around.

It was a warm and drowsy evening in Lower Shakespeare. The moon was written low in the sky, a giant letter O. A few bugs and moths circled a lamp. Officer Vaughn was standing in the yellow cone of the lamplight. He stood there perfectly still, looking directly at Nyquist. He appeared to be waiting for him to come forward. The private eye did so, taking careful steps. But then he stopped: something was worrying him and he couldn't work out what it was. Across a narrow gap he could see the roof of the next building along: a young man and a woman were lying face up there, perhaps staring at the stars.

Nyquist felt he was stepping into a trap. "Easy does it," he said.

Vaughn answered, "Of course, of course. There's no other way." The blemish turned a livid pink on his face, and his shaven skull glistened under the glow of the lamp. Across the curve of skin, a single word crawled along and then vanished round the back of his head.

"Do you recognize me, Vaughn?"

The other man nodded. "Of course. I saw you yesterday. I helped take you into Kafka Court."

"Before that? A week ago."

Vaughn shook his head. "No. That was the first time."

"What about Melville Towers?"

"Melville?" A tic worried the man's cheekbone. "I've been there once, a while ago."

Nyquist laughed at this. "I saw you last week. Block Five. You came out of your apartment to feed your cat. I was in the corridor."

"I don't have a cat. Can't stand the creatures."

The whole dialogue struck both of them as absurd, but they were trapped inside it now, with no escape.

"Listen, whatever your name is…"

"It's Nyquist."

"I don't know what you're talking about–"

The last word was choked off as his throat closed up. Nyquist had reached out with both hands, grabbing him by the lapels. Vaughn's eyes went wide and he started to grunt, the only noise he could make.

"I saw you. I was there with a woman, Zelda. We were walking toward the elevator. You fed your bloody cat!"

It was useless. The man was still high from the floating words, high on language. He was plugged into the alphabet like a kid sticking a finger in the electrical socket. Nyquist let him go. Vaughn bent over double as he started to cough.

"Why did you run, when you saw me just now?"

Vaughn came back up. His face was red all over. "Why do you think? Christ, man. You've been following me! Following me since I left work tonight. What, do you really think I didn't see you? I thought…"

"Yes?"

"After I helped to bring you to Kafka Court yesterday, I thought that you were out for revenge. That's all. That's the truth."

Everything about the other man's behavior made Nyquist believe him. He stepped back a little.

Vaughn carried on, "Look, I didn't know that you were part of our group, really I didn't. How was I to know?"

Nyquist made a play: "Can you trust me now?"

Vaughn nodded eagerly in relief. "Yes, yes of course. We're all in this together. May the words live on."

A movement made Nyquist look upwards. The moths were fluttering around the lamp. But then he saw that they weren't moths at all, but tiny black letters – *s, q, d, a, l,* and a few others – stray letters that had somehow escaped the room below. Or was he hallucinating still? He could no longer trust his own senses. All that remained was the one question that could never really be answered in life: what was truth, what fiction? He turned back to Vaughn and said, "So you have been to Melville Towers?"

"Once, like I said. Some months ago. How do you think I got this?" He pulled at the front of his shirt, revealing the words that crawled over his chest and shoulders. "But listen."

"I'm waiting."

Vaughn looked fearful. Droplets of sweat mapped the pathway of the blemish, down his left cheek to his mouth, where they wetted his lips.

"I would never go back there," he said. "Not if you paid me."

"Because of the words?"

"At first, yes. But I've got used to that now, especially after meeting with the other people in the group, and seeing the true power of language."

Nyquist thought about this. "So everyone in the room downstairs, they've all been to Melville, and they've all been infected there?"

"That's it. Every last one. We call ourselves the Church of the Sacred Word. And there are more of us, around the city."

"What's the purpose of the sickness?"

"I don't know."

"Can it be cured?"

"I don't know! I really don't."

"What happened to you at the Melville Tower?"

"I can't remember, not clearly."

Nyquist pressed at him. "You woke up outside the building?"

Vaughn grasped at this as a shared truth. "Yes, yes! Exactly. It's the same for all of us. But I don't know how I got there. All I remember is the kid, the boy…"

"Calvin?"

"That's him. He was waving his hands around and mumbling some spell or other. After that… after that… it's a blank." He paused, his chest heaving with the efforts of memory. Then he explained: "That's why I won't go back there. Once was bad enough."

Nyquist told him, "I returned there."

"You did?"

"In the daylight. It was empty. Just an empty building."

Vaughn nodded at this. "No, you have to go at night, I know that much. The book only comes alive after dark."

Nyquist let him calm down a little. He couldn't work out if the man was telling some kind of truth, or inhabiting a complex fantasy. But one thing was certain, Nyquist had stepped inside the same world, real or otherwise, and he needed to tread carefully.

He spoke calmly: "Overseer K wouldn't take too kindly to you being here, I reckon."

Vaughn stared at him. "You're not going to tell her, are you?"

"That depends. Are you lying to me?"

"No, no! I swear it on every word that's ever been written in this or any other language, now and in the past,

and on all the words yet to be written for now and forever!
I swear it!"

"What about Wellborn?"

"Patrick Wellborn? He introduced me to the book, the
torn-out pages, the smoke, the magic of the ink. He started
this whole thing for me. If anyone is, he's to blame."

"I see."

"He knows more about the Melville Tower than any of
us. Talk to him, not me."

Nyquist was starting to get a picture of Wellborn's
activity, of his desire to spread the word about *The Body
Library* and about Melville Five. He was a kind of prophet,
or an oracle, leading the way forward, pointing to the
future.

He changed tack. "What about a woman called Zelda
Courtland? Did she ever come to a meeting?"

"I don't know. I don't know all the names." Vaughn was
a little more confident now. "This is just a private matter,
me coming here, partaking as I do. What can I say, I like to
feel the flow, the buzz, the story coursing through me, just
a sentence or two! That's all."

"What exactly happened down there, Vaughn? In the
room?"

"You saw it."

"Explain it to me. What about the words? The way
they–"

"The words took flight!"

"How? Why? For what purpose?"

"The council have for too long governed how our stories
must be told."

"How come the words can float off the page? What is it,
some kind of magic trick?"

"No. It's true. It happens."

"Hypnosis, maybe. Is that it? A shared hallucination?"

"I really don't know. I'm just..."

"What?"

"I'm just following the story, seeing where it will take me."

Nyquist relaxed a little. He could see that Vaughn was essentially an innocent, someone caught up in a tale he could barely understand.

He looked across the gap to the neighboring rooftop and saw that the young couple had risen to their feet and were now looking across at him. They were teenagers, nothing more. "You kids get out of here," Nyquist shouted. The boy put a little fight into his voice, but the girl said to him, "Come on, Marcus, we'll find somewhere else." They left by the roof's fire door. Now the two men were alone. Even the letter moths had vacated the lamp's halo. Vaughn was pressed up against the low railing that marked the edge of the building. Nyquist leaned over and looked down: a small courtyard was seen two floors below. Three or four washing lines were stretched across the gap, from one window to another, two of them hung with clothing. Through one of the windows a woman's voice was heard as she started to sing a blues number.

Sometimes I wake up, and my heart is closed up tight.
Sometimes I stumble, yet my eyes are open wide.

The lyrics and the melody were meant for Nyquist alone, or so it seemed, and as he listened he thought again of Zelda.

He asked, "Is it worth killing for, this revolution of yours?"

"Probably, for some of us. Not me, of course. Not me."

"Who then?"

The answer came in a whisper, half of joy, half of fear:

"Oberon."

Nyquist came close. "Tell me about him. Tell me about Oberon."

Vaughn was taken over by a sudden ecstasy. His eyes rolled back until only the whites were showing and the living words crawled madly across his bare skull.

"We await him! We await his return in glory."

"Tell me what you mean!"

But it was too late, the council officer had lost himself totally to language, and his mouth spewed forth a multitude of phrases and sentences, in which obscenities and manic prayers mixed together into a tumult of cries, howls, hisses, chirrups, and susurrations.

Nyquist kept hold of him: "Speak to me."

Vaughn managed one last of moment of sense. "Apartment 14," he said, looking directly into Nyquist's eyes. "14!"

"You mean in Melville Five? What will I find there?"

"Apartment 14. That's where it starts. Wellborn told me this. Always, every time. That's where it all starts."

He broke free of Nyquist's grasp and backed away. He was leaning out over the barrier, over the drop, and at any moment he might overbalance and fall. But instead, he crumpled forward like a doll, bent and broken. He was whimpering.

"Come on, Vaughn," Nyquist said. "It's over now. It's over."

But a few more paragraphs beckoned.

Nyquist heard footsteps at his back and he turned in time to see a man approaching.

He stopped a few feet away from Nyquist, his face and body completely hidden by the shadows that seemed to cling to him like a cloak, or a second skin.

"Who are you?"

The man replied with laughter, a cruel sound, muffled as though by a cloth. And then he stepped forward into the glow of light from the lamp.

Nyquist couldn't move.

A swarm of letters circled around the man's head. His long hair hung down like a halfbroken veil that he peered through. He grinned, his lips slightly parted, his eyes as black as the sky above, and any sign of compassion just as distant.

It was Patrick Wellborn.

The dead man.

His entire facial area was covered in letters, marks and numerals. They writhed madly about, constantly seeking new meanings, new words to spell out. Wellborn tore off his ragged shirt to show that his entire body had been infected, top to bottom, one living story of flesh and blood. He bellowed in rage or glory, it was difficult to tell which, an action that sent the letters swirling across his face, arms and chest.

Nyquist was still bound to the spot. This one moment of time held him completely.

Vaughn was genuflecting to Wellborn, apologizing over and over for his errors. But his superior ignored him. He didn't speak, he didn't need to; the letters on his face and body spelled out his hatred, his agony, his utter despair.

At last Nyquist could move. He took half a step backwards, only to feel the back of his legs meet the barrier guarding the edge of the roof.

And now Wellborn spoke at last, a simple statement.

"You killed me."

Nyquist tried to get away, only to feel Wellborn's hand on his chest, pushing, pushing quite gently. It was enough. He managed a breath, and half a word of untold desperation and then he was tumbling over the rail.

That moment of utter loss, of nothingness.

The shock of it.

The sudden gulf, opening.

And then at last his reactions kicked in and he twisted around as best he could and reached out blindly and he felt his hand hit the railing. He grabbed hold of it. His body swung further down and hit the wall beneath, knocking the breath from his lungs, but he was still hanging on, hanging tight, until he felt the blow to his fingers, his knuckles, the sharp pain of it, the fist that smashed down on his hand.

And he let go. He fell.

He struggled against the air itself, but there was nothing to hold on to, not now, only the washing lines as he broke through them, tangled in the sheets, and then the clothes of another person's life momentarily, his hand gripping hold of a line for a second, but that too broke apart and he was falling, falling on, falling through the words, through word after word after word torn from his wide open mouth, falling, through all the stories he had suffered and struggled with to get this far, to this city, this building, this rooftop, this courtyard, story after story after story until this one moment arrived, the present, the concrete floor reaching out for him with sickening speed even as his brain slowed and slowed, giving him time to work out in mathematical detail the exact moment of impact.

Here: where one word meets another.

THE BOOKS

The wings of an angel fluttered all around.

It was a large white bed sheet that drifted down to cover him. It was followed by a couple of men's shirts, a bath towel, and half a dozen pale blue handkerchiefs. Nyquist lay unmoving, one hand still clutching hold of the washing line which had partially broken his fall. But for that, he might well be dead. This one thought, finding its way into his dream, comforted him.

And then the pain arrived.

It woke him fully.

One eye opening.

His face flat against the concrete, the other eye still hidden.

His mouth crooked, a tooth broken.

A pool of blood that seeped away from his vision, becoming blurred.

He groaned and rolled over onto his back and looked upwards. The face of his attacker, Patrick Wellborn, was seen above, framed by the night sky, the far-off stars. Wellborn was leaning over the railing, looking down. They made contact across the distance. Nyquist panicked. He raised himself as far as he could on one arm, testing each part of his body in turn, moving each limb, his chest, his shoulders and neck. He put his weight on his other arm and fell back and realized that his left arm was badly injured, maybe broken. He sank back down. All he desired was to lie there until sleep took him away forever.

But he had to move. He had to keep alert.

He shook himself awake.

Wellborn would want to finish the job; he was probably already heading for the stairs.

Nyquist looked around at his surroundings.

Four walls, no door. The fallen clothing, the washing line.

A window was open close by.

Nyquist put his good hand on the ledge and pulled himself up, and then used his legs to push his body over the lip, through the window gap, and down the other side, wincing in pain as he hit the floor.

He was in a small bedroom. Cheaply furnished, but clean and tidy. He dragged himself to the door, used the jamb to pull himself upright and more or less stumbled from there into the living room. He landed on the floor, on a soft carpet. The radio was on and he heard the velvety tones of Dame Helena Lauderdale, one of the city's most famous narrators.

And from the skies came a great wingéd creature whose eyes shone with the moon's light. It flew over the city, choosing its next victim…

Nyquist cried out in his pain and sat up, leaning against the wall.

A man, woman and a small child were staring at him.

He stared back.

Nothing was said. The moment stretched out.

And then the mother spoke, saying, "Help him, Ken. He needs help."

But the father wasn't sure. "What if he's a criminal?"

"So what if he's a criminal? In that state, what can he do?"

The father pondered this for a second. "True enough." He got up from his armchair and walked over to Nyquist and lifted him up into a seat.

"Where are you hurt?" he asked.

Nyquist couldn't answer. But their kindness cradled him.

"He's in shock, I think," the mother said. "I'll fetch him some water."

"Yes, that's good, Martha. I'll ring for an ambulance."

Nyquist shook his head. Quickly, he struggled to his feet, casting off the man's helping hands. The child, a young daughter of ten years, looked on in awe, her mouth held open in a perfect circle. The mother came in with the drink of water in one hand and a first aid box in the other.

Nyquist swayed. The room swerved away. He was having trouble focusing. But one thought made it through: *this family's in danger if they help me*. That was enough to get him moving, heading for the one door he could see. The mother tried one last time to stop him on the way, but he was determined now. He thanked them all in the best words he could manage with his lips thickening up, and his hearing busted. He could taste blood in his mouth.

He walked out into a corridor and found the front door and then the street, a narrow alleyway squeezed in between the tall housing blocks. This was Lower Shakespeare – there wasn't one straight road in the place. Every pathway had many twists and turns. But he was walking, that was the thing. He was moving away from the trouble. *Yes, keep moving!* That's all he could think.

His body ached, but it was a duller pain now.

His mind was taking over, doing its best to save him.

His left arm hung limply at his side and he limped a

little: his right leg was damaged in some way, but he
didn't let that stop him. He took another turning, and
one or two more, but only enclosed spaces greeted him.
Shadows crouched in every alcove and doorway. Now
and then he saw the sky through a gap in the overhangs,
but mainly the roads were covered over. Houses had been
built on top of houses, on top of other houses, and so on
in layers, each domicile getting smaller. Rooms were split
in two, then three, then four; rooms attached to other
rooms; walls juxtaposed at strange angles, windows
leaning away from the vertical, the road ahead sloping to
one side and then the other, the chimneys bent over, the
doors crooked. Nyquist staggered along, his own body
twisted just as badly as the streets he walked down, as
much as the buildings he squeezed between. The rhyme
came back to him.

There was a crooked man and he told a crooked tale,
He scratched a crooked story with a crooked nail...

He couldn't remember the rest of the verse, but the two
lines got stuck in his mind and he repeated them to himself
as he walked along.

He glanced behind, reacting to a noise. A figure moved in
the distance, a tall shadow cast against a wall by a lamp. It
must be Wellborn: he imagined the man's anger, knowing
that the fall hadn't killed his victim. Nyquist turned away
from the sight, taking a passage between two houses. He
shuffled along. A light gleamed ahead. A doorway. A few
more steps took him there. The door was open a little way,
the lock broken some months or years before. A short
corridor led to a larger room. At first he thought it might
be a church, that he would find sanctuary there.

He wasn't far wrong: it was a library.

And he thought to himself: what better place to lose a story?

It looked to be a private chamber, a large study perhaps, the walls and fittings covered in dust and cobwebs and smelling of mildew. Nyquist stumbled down an aisle, using the two shelving units on each side to support himself. A cloud of dust rose up around him, disturbed after decades or even longer. The library was long abandoned, given over to decay and rot, to tales of forgotten realms, forgotten peoples. He groaned anew and grabbed hold of a shelf to stop himself from falling as a stab of pain cut into his side: he must have cracked a rib in the fall. Books fell to the floor as his hands scrabbled for purchase, but at last he managed to pull himself upright and he rested for a while, getting his breath back.

He listened.

Was there a noise, coming from the doorway, the corridor beyond? Or in here, even, something or someone hidden in the stacks?

No. All was quiet.

He moved on a little further, reaching the end of the aisle, when he heard the sound again, a rustling noise. The sound of pages being rubbed together, a dry sound, the breath of a ghost. He called out, "Who's there?" But even the act of speaking caused the pain to shoot through him, and there was no answer anyway, a wasted effort. Until he stood as still as he could manage, and he heard it clearly: the whispering. The voices of the dead, the passed over, the lost ones, the disappeared – any and all of these. They were waiting for him between the pages, waiting for him to join their tribe.

Patrick Wellborn was alive. The phrase haunted him. Alive! The blow to the head that Nyquist had inflicted wasn't in fact fatal: he was just out cold, that was the only explanation. Every other possibility involved madness, phantoms, the living dead, horror stories, risen creatures intent on vengeance.

Nyquist dug his fingernails deep into his own flesh to keep himself alert. He would survive this. He had journeyed too far to give up now. He turned to face the door and waited, waited for Wellborn to come for him. He would wait here and fight him, no matter what; at the very least he would go down fighting.

Empty words. Too many empty words, that was the trouble. His childhood, his broken marriage, his parents, mother dead at an early age, his father wandering off into the mist of the dusklands never to be seen again; his time on the streets, bringing himself up alone, darting from shadow to shelter and back again, from one home to another, seeking warmth, clothing, food, a modicum of love where he could find it. His job. Such as it was. Helping others for money, when his own goddamn life lay in pieces around him.

His thoughts came to an end.

Something was floating in the air, in between the shelves.

Glowing objects. Insects. A swarm of them. They made Nyquist's eyes burn and blur, he had to squint to see them properly. Alphabugs. Ten or fifteen, it was impossible to tell how many; each one displaying a letter of the alphabet in red or gold or electric blue, but every bug carrying the same letter this time.

The letter X.

They buzzed and fluttered and hummed and zipped around Nyquist. He stepped back involuntarily until he reached the rear wall of the library. He could go no further, he was too weak, and the glow bugs wove a spell upon him. His hands came up to brush them away but they merely circled back and bothered him again. Their bodies were full of fire, yet their wings were no thicker than a sheet of paper from some ancient volume, torn from its binding and cut and fashioned into a means of flight.

Through the blur of blood and tears he glimpsed a figure at the end of the aisle, watching his distress. It was a silhouette, a shadow that barely moved, and he couldn't tell if it was man or woman, or even a child. The figure raised its arms as though conducting the bugs in their flight.

Nyquist sank down to the floor.

His body gave in at last. The end was near, the final page.

The blank page.

A phrase came to mind: "As one story ends…"

Nyquist completed the sentence in his head: *another story begins*. It was a saying much favored in Storyville, especially by the old.

All around on the shelves of the library the books were falling open, one book after another, allowing the words to escape the pages. Now the air was filled with the letters, with a cloud of scattered words, and the alphabugs swarmed among them, lighting the way. The library was alive with language, with scripture, text, and Nyquist was at the very center of it. He felt the letters landing on his skin, more and more of them, his whole body crawling with words, commas, full stops, phrases, sentences, paragraphs, chapters, a narrative, a novel. He was the story. It was that simple: he *was* the story. And this was where it ended, here in the ruins of a library.

Darkness clouded over his eyes, his breathing slowed.

The pain left him and in these fading seconds he thought only of Zelda.

And then she too was gone.

THE UNTOLD TOLD

Begin. Begin again.

The author begins again.

He begins again to build.

He begins again to build from a mark on the paper or a fleck of ink, a dot, a line, a bar, a curve, a gap, marks and squiggles.

He begins again to build on the paper the life of a letter, a single letter.

He begins again to build from one letter to another, these marks, these letters, lines and bars and curves and commas and stops and dots and dashes.

The author begins again to build a letter, one more, one more, one more until at last a word is spelled out in the dark. In the darkness, yes a word.

Begin again to build a word and one more, another word in the darkness, word after word, begin again to build from word after word after word until at last a sentence forms, one more, one more, the first flicker of a story.

Begin. Begin again.

Nyquist felt it all from the inside. The words of his body keeping him alive, feeding and forming and reforming in his flesh.

He saw the world. Two people approaching, watching

him, discussing his face, his body, his life, his death. The
words he was carrying. He heard them and saw them,
he heard the names they called each other, Andrea
and Marcus. He even remembered seeing them on the
opposite roof, before he had fallen. Yet he could make
no connection to them. He called to them, he called their
names, he screamed their names, but his lips would not
move, nor would his eyes. The message would not leave
his body. No signals could get through to the world outside
his skin. He could only lie there on the floor of the library,
helpless, helpless, caught in the silence, the stillness. So
this is what it's like, he said to himself, this is what it's
like when you step outside of all stories. Nothing happens.
Nothing at all.

He saw it all, he heard it all. He felt his body being
examined and prodded, he saw ambulance men, a doctor,
and police officers clustered around. Talking, endlessly
talking. He was their subject matter, nothing more than
that, one more element in the long night's narrative. The
lamps were bright now, shining down on him, many of
them, yet still his eyes would not react. The light was
blinding. If only he could close his eyes!

And then his body was lifted up and carried away. He saw
only the ceiling of the ambulance directly above and the
medical orderly leaning over him now and then, adjusting
equipment, or checking his condition. But there was no
pain, no physical pain; his body was numb, perfectly adrift
within its own universe, self-contained.

He looked out through the two holes in his skull and he
saw the world.

The world he could not touch or speak to, or drag closer.

He felt the vibrations from beneath the vehicle as
it moved along the road. A journey. And for a dreadful
moment he felt sure that they would take him to the

morgue and cut into him with their scalpels and saws. And the thought of this was too much to bear and thankfully the darkness took him over completely.

He was dreaming.

He saw Oberon. He saw Oberon's face. An old, old man, an ancient being.

The face was upside down for some reason.

Nyquist tried to speak to the wise one, the leader, to ask for forgiveness, to ask that his life be given back to him just this one last time, that he might have another chance, another few days would do it, or a single hour in the sunlight.

Oberon was silent. Silent in the darkness.

And then a voice called to Nyquist from far away. A woman's voice. This was his compass, his lodestar – he would reach upwards toward the voice, he would find the voice, he would speak aloud, yes, he would speak, speak...

The face of Bella Monroe hovered over him.

He cried. Nyquist couldn't help it. He cried out loud.

She did not hear him.

His tears were caught inside his eyes, they could not find their way out through the ducts at each corner. Rather they gathered in a small lake and lingered there, forever on the edge of brimming over.

Monroe did not see him crying.

But she spoke to him, nevertheless. And he could hear her voice. It was a balm from heaven.

"John. Can you hear me? I hope you can. We're doing everything we can to help you."

He nodded his head in reply, he replied to her.

Yes, yes, I hear you, Bella. I can hear you!

But nothing got through. No movements, no words. The walls of the skull were too thick and there were no doors, no windows. Still, she attended to him, wiping his brow and his mouth, and tidying his bedclothes for him, and talking incessantly. He could see a patch of curtain, a number of hospital monitors at the edge of his vision: small colored lights blinking, a constant and steady bleeping sound. His heartbeat. There it was. The simple proof that he needed so much: he was alive.

And Bella talked on and on and he was glad to listen. This was all he wanted. He learned that he was lying in a bed in a ward deep inside Kafka Court, his case taken over by the Narrative Council. He learned also that Overseer K had pulled rank on Inspector Molloy. He knew that his entire body was covered in words, in living words that moved through his flesh, keeping him alive. He knew all this from Bella's explanation of what had happened, of how he'd been found in the old library in Lower Shakespeare. Of how he was now in a coma.

He cried out that he was conscious, that he could hear her. He cried out.

Bella didn't respond in any way.

Her face appeared once more, her eyes looking deep into his; her eyes so dark and beautiful and glistening and ever-moving; and his own, black and still, incapable of passing on any emotion at all.

Yet they stared at each other, this man, this woman. Two beings. One fully alive, the other caught in a strange realm where life and death hovered close together, where life was stitched in place only by the words that travelled through the body.

He could feel them moving. He could sense them, he had such knowledge of them as creatures, as living entities building a new kind of language.

He could read the stories they were telling inside his body.

He was the story.

Word by word, thread by thread, the tiny writers at work, hundreds of them, thousands, millions, multiplying all the time.

He was the story and the book. And one name alone, one character, drew his attention.

Zelda.

He experienced her story as it mingled with his. And he saw far beyond the bed he was lying in, all across the city, and he saw again the fifth tower of Melville Estate. Once again in his mind he walked those corridors. He saw the people who lived in the tower and he knew how they lived there, and why they lived there. He knew the truth at last and it was shocking to him, and also perfectly logical at the same time. Also he knew the truth of *The Body Library*, he knew the secret contained within its chaotic, nightmarish pages. Most of all he knew that another life was being lived, another version of himself was alive in the tower, a life away from the bed and this stillness. Yet he could tell nobody about this; the truth remained trapped inside his head.

He might stay like this forever, or until the doctors turned off the machines.

Or until the words gave up on him.

One thing mattered to him, one question.

Who murdered Zelda?

As the spell of darkness kept hold of him, he would use this question, this quest, this night quest, as a fixed point, a single lamp above a crooked pathway. And he thought of the knowledge he'd gained, just before Wellborn had pushed him off the roof.

Apartment 14. That's where it all starts.

Yet he felt helpless, unable to act. Trapped.

But he couldn't give up, not now.

Stick to the task. Keep going. Don't surrender.

Begin.

Begin again.

Begin again to build.

He kept saying the phrase to himself, over and over. Begin again to build, word by word by word. Find the answer.

Bella's voice had fallen silent at last. He could see a portion of her head and shoulders in the dimmed light, where they rested on the bed sheet. She'd fallen asleep. *Good, good. Let her rest.* There was much to do.

Nyquist lay awake and stared at the ceiling and read the endless, tangled stories of his own flesh, and he saw what he had to do. It was simple. He could still find Zelda's murderer. He could still do it, even as he was lying here wrapped in the sheets, his physical body helpless. He could still work the case. He was certain by now that the key to her death lay hidden somewhere inside the Melville Tower. All he had to do was send a message to his other self. No, not a message. An object, he had to build an object. He would place this object in Melville, yes, that was it. And so he began. In the dark he put together his thoughts, fragment by fragment, and in this way he fashioned his object. It was a photograph. It took him more than an hour to do this, concentrating all the time, and his body was weakened by the effort. The words inside were darting here and there, repairing his flesh wherever a break or fissure occurred. They kept him alive.

Now it was done. He had created a photograph in his mind. He held it there, suspended at the center of his coma. He spun it around slowly with his thoughts. The image was blurred, but it would have to do. And he sent it across the city as best he could, across the city of his mind into Melville Five and he placed it inside a grey folder in a filing cabinet in apartment 49. The action exhausted him completely; he could feel himself surrendering to sleep. Perhaps this time he would never awaken from this realm he was caught inside. Perhaps he would die before morning's light came to the streets. But he had done what he could.

He had left a clue.

PART FOUR

APARTMENT 49, MELVILLE FIVE

PAGE ZERO

Nyquist woke up in the middle of the night. It was a simple fact. One moment he was dreaming and the next he was awake. The room was familiar to him, his own bedroom, his apartment, all things in their place as they should be, the clock on the bedside cabinet, clothes strewn around the floor, a packet of Player's Navy Cut nearby, a paperback novel lying on the sheets. And yet everything felt different somehow, as though he were a stranger here in his own home, a traveler, someone passing through. It was unnerving, but the feeling lasted only a moment or two, and then he was up and coughing from the angry ghosts of last night's cigarettes. He headed for the tiny bathroom and stood under the shower for ten minutes, first as hot as he could stand, and then as cold, using the extremes to jolt himself back to some kind of life. He shaved and combed Royal Crown pomade through his hair and splashed on some Bay Rum aftershave. He was ready, ready for anything.

The dream. Now he remembered it. He'd been submerged in a deep pool of black ink, struggling, drowning and then he'd risen up from the water, gasping for air...

It had scared him.

He looked through the kitchen cupboards, finding

only packets of coffee and tins of corned beef and tins of peaches, so many of them stacked high on the shelves. He made do with this, main meal and dessert. After eating he went through into his office and he sat at the desk and stared at the walls and waited for something to happen, for the telephone to ring or for someone to knock at his door: a client, a stranger or a friend, someone in trouble, in need.

But nobody came, nobody needed his help.

He put his feet up on the desk and smoked his first cigarette of the day and drank his second cup of coffee. He stood up and walked around the office three times, and then twice more. He stared at the wall calendar. Today's date – August 29, 1959 – was marked with a red star, but all the other squares were vacant for this month and the next. He checked the filing cabinet: the top three drawers were empty, the bottom one contained a single folder, that was all. Could things really be this bad? He cursed the good people of Storyville. Did none of them stray from the marriage bed or pilfer funds from the cash till or find themselves the victim of petty blackmail? There had to be something!

The hours ticked by on the clockface. Yet it was night, always night, no matter what time he awoke, it was always dark outside the window, the city lit up in blue and gold for his viewing pleasure. In this building time had one season only.

He opened his front door a few times and stared up and down the lighted corridor, but there was never any sign of life. Once he took a few steps along, away from his apartment door, but then he started to tremble, his body shook in panic and he had to reach out for the wall for support. The light bulb flickered above in time with his stuttering heartbeat.

He ate more corned beef, and even more peaches. He sat down behind his desk and read a few pages of *Deadly Nightshade*, the paperback novel he'd found lying on his bed. If only he could have a life like the book's hero, Joe Creed, a private eye who walked into trouble night after night without a care in the world except for where his next drink was coming from. He reached the end of the chapter, where the hero took a blow to the head from a hammer and was left unconscious in the gutter.

Nyquist couldn't remember how he'd got to this place, he couldn't remember any life at all outside of these few rooms, these corridors, outside of this building, this high-rise tower.

Who am I? What am I doing here?

He slid a sheet of paper into the typewriter on his desk and tapped at the keys until he had a line written out, the first thing that came into his head.

There was a crooked man.

Like an automaton he repeated the action.

There was a crooked man.
There was a crooked man.
There was a crooked man.

He sat there with his head in his hands. The silence was too deep, too intense. He rubbed at his face and a great bolt of pain shot from one temple to the other, across his brow. He cried out and his voice echoed around the room.

There was no answer.

In frustration he walked over to the filing cabinet and reached into the bottom drawer to take out the solitary folder. Apparently, this was all he had, the only case he'd ever filed away. It was marked with today's date, yet he couldn't remember putting it there.

The folder contained one item only, a photograph.

It showed a woman's face, her features slightly blurred, out of focus. For a long time he stared at it as a faint memory stirred. He turned the photograph over and saw a name and a location written on the back.

Zelda Courtland
Apartment 14

The woman's name tormented him.

A bell was ringing, far away, far away: if only he could hear it properly. But no, the knowledge flickered away, time and again.

So why had he opened a file on the case?

Now he stared at the woman's face, willing the image to become clearer. He knew her, he was sure of it. At some point in the past, in some forgotten moment, he had met and talked to her. And more than that, yes, much more. Some moments of intimacy had taken place between them. They had loved each other, no matter how briefly. Nyquist was certain of this fact, and yet it felt as though the memory belonged to somebody else, another man in another place, another life.

His headache threatened to return.

Nyquist turned the photograph over once more.

Apartment number 14?

A sudden thought came to him: *This is where it all starts.*

He threw on his jacket and left the office.

PATHWAYS

Nyquist pressed the call button for the elevator and waited and waited, as the indicator light stayed on floor nine. He took the stairs. Not a soul was seen, neither in the stairwell, nor on the first floor corridor. He might well be the only resident. It was deathly quiet until he reached the door of apartment 14, where he heard voices from within, male and female, two or three people talking. Nyquist pressed the bell and immediately the voices quietened. He had no expectations of who might answer, if anyone, or what he might find. Now he heard another voice, an older woman's, from the other side of the doorway.

"Who is it?"

"John Nyquist. From upstairs, apartment 49."

"Oh right, just a minute. I can't get the door open." An edge of panic crept into the voice. "It's stuck. Oh. Just let me…"

The door jerked open. He stepped into the hallway where the little old lady was waiting for him in the dimmed light. Her body was almost bent in two, and her grey hair was netted with cobwebs.

"What do you want?" she asked.

"I was hoping–"

"Wait, Wait!" She peered out through the open door

and checked both sides of the corridor. "Very well, I think we're alone." She came back inside, closed the door and walked into the living room without another word.

Nyquist followed her. "I'm looking for Zelda Courtland? Is she here?" He showed her the photograph.

"Oh, of course. Yes. Zelda."

"She's here?"

"Not just now."

"But you know her?"

The old lady nodded. "That I do, yes. I know all the people who live here."

"I'd like to ask you some questions."

"As you wish."

He took a chair at the table, where a single mock antique standard lamp gave a little warmth to the room, but very little light. The whole room was filled with an old lady's comforts: antimacassars on the chair backs, puffed-up cushions, a patchwork quilt on the sofa. The lady sat down and pulled the quilt over her legs and lap. There was neither sight nor sound of the other, younger men and women he'd heard through the closed door. He looked around for a radio set or a gramophone, but there was none.

The old lady introduced herself: "Some people call me Alice."

"Is that your real name?"

"Yes, of course. Otherwise, why would they call me that? Would you like some tea?"

She poured him a cup and placed it on a lace doily on the table.

"Milk?"

Nyquist nodded. He didn't know where to start, not properly, but at last he said, "I'm a private investigator."

"Yes, I know that. We've met already, remember?"

"We have?"

"Oh dear. You are having trouble, aren't you?"

Nyquist had to admit this was true. "To be honest, I'm not sure why I'm here."

"You want to know about Zelda, isn't that right?"

"Yes, that's what I want."

"But you don't know why you want to know this?"

He hesitated and then answered, "No. I don't."

Alice stared at him, her eyes alert and birdlike in the lamplight.

Nyquist started to explain: "I found a photograph of Miss Courtland, with your number written on the back. Apartment 14. So I thought I'd start here."

Alice nodded, a brusque pecking motion.

"Zelda came to see me twice, I think. Yes. Twice. She had trouble getting through the first time."

"Getting through?" Nyquist was becoming confused, so he tried to keep the questioning on track. "What can you tell me about her?"

"We became quite friendly in our own little way. But she hasn't been back here since then, I'm afraid."

Nyquist thought about this for a moment. He sipped at his tea.

"Are you all right?" Alice asked. "You look perplexed. Biscuit?"

He looked at her and began to speak, but then stopped himself. He dipped a digestive into his tea. Alice waited a moment longer and she asked a question that startled him:

"Did you know Zelda, is that it? In your other life?"

"In my what?"

Now the old lady's eyes sparkled. "Your life before this. In the world, as they call it."

He stared back at her. "You'll have to help me," he said. "Because I don't understand what you're saying."

Alice held up a finger to quieten him. She turned her attention to the far reaches of the room, to the shadows outside the small glow of yellow light around the lamp. She appeared to be listening.

Nyquist listened also, but could hear nothing.

"Alice–"

"Shush!"

Now they were both giving their full attention to the room and its tiny noises. He felt unnerved: the room appeared to be listening back to him. There was no other way to express the feeling. He was being *listened* to.

Alice whispered, "There. Can you hear? There they are!"

It was true, he could hear something. Voices. Two of them, male and female. They were floating in the air of the room, quietly at first, and then growing louder, clearer and more pronounced with each passing second. Nyquist looked this way and that, seeking the people who were speaking, seeking lips that moved, faces, bodies from which the voices came. But the living room was empty. And then one by one they arrived, forming themselves out of the shadows: two characters in the room's drama. The ghostly figures took on form and flesh, solidifying, becoming real, or as real as they could manage at this time. Now they stood before him and spoke aloud, a man and a woman talking to each other. These were the same voices that Nyquist had heard through the door.

Where are we?

I don't know, Charles.

You must know. You brought us here.

You're blaming me.

Edwina, I'm scared.

I know, darling, so am I.

The two characters spoke only for themselves, paying no attention at all to Nyquist or Alice. He felt he was watching a play in a tiny theatre, with an audience of just two people. The mood changed. The female character, Edwina, was now standing close to Charles by the window and discussing the rose garden they could see beyond the veranda.

I wish we were back home, in the garden. Do you remember?

There was no rose garden, no veranda.

There was only the night sky and the city, Storyville, seen through the window of the living room. The upper floors of two of the other Melville towers were visible.

Alice spoke softly: "Don't disturb them. Don't ever touch them."

Nyquist whispered in reply: "Why not?"

"They don't like it. Not yet. Not in this state. They will go away far too early, leaving the story unfinished."

"Where do they go?" he asked. "Where do they go to, these people, when they leave?"

Alice's eyes glittered sadly. "Why, back into the ink, of course. Midnight's ink." She leaned over towards him so that she could talk in an even quieter voice. "Apartment 14 is very special. It's where the characters first appear, when they arrive at Melville Five. They perform for me, a few lines at the most, to begin with, a gesture or two. Like yourself, Mr Nyquist."

He murmured to himself: "This is where it all starts."

"Exactly, yes. Oh, how funny you looked when you first emerged, your eyes blinking and your hands busily brushing away the ink from your clothes and face. People always do that: they assume that midnight's ink is still on them, still clinging. It isn't, of course." She laughed at the memory and a mischievous look played over her features.

Nyquist told her, "I can't remember any of that."

"Ah well, it affects some that way. Never mind." The light dimmed in her eyes. "They move on. They always move on and it's all very sad. I hate to see them go, I really do, but one must be strong."

"Tell me about midnight's ink," he asked.

"It's where we are born, each of us that resides here." She gave a cry of delight. "Oh, but look! How lovely."

Now the young couple were kissing each other, quite discreetly.

"Oh my, isn't that wonderful? I always like it when newcomers kiss." She clasped her hands together. "It's so rare, these days."

And through the window a faint suggestion of moonlight played. Moonlight and the waft of roses, a scent that lingered.

Alice sighed. "Oh, I do believe they're ready."

Nyquist put down his tea cup. He felt strange. Reality swayed from side to side like a tipsy dancer.

And then the elegant young couple turned away from the window and walked across the room, heading for the hallway door. As they did so, one of them, the woman, passed right through Nyquist's body as a ghost might pass through a wall, or an X-ray through a man's skin. He shivered from head to foot and reached out blindly with his arm. But now it all was over: the spirits or whatever they were had left, and the room was returned to its former state: a perfectly normal living room owned by a little old lady called Alice.

She said, "It's always sad to see them go. Still, at least they'll be at home now. I do hope they find a nice apartment."

Nyquist turned to her, wondering which possible question he could ask.

She reached out and touched his arm. "Don't worry. It's not unusual to feel confused, not in this place. It took me ages to get used to living in the tower." She smiled at him.

"One day soon you will forget everything of your former self, and then at last you'll be free, and at peace. Just give it time, young man."

Nyquist still looked confused.

"Look, it's like this," Alice continued. "We've all been given a second chance, a second chance at life. That's how I see it. I no longer think about my other self. This is me. *This*!" She pressed the flat of her hand against her chest. "Here I live, and here I breathe, in the tower. Alice Johnson."

Nyquist finished off his tea. "Who were you before?"

"I no longer know my other self. Truly, I can no longer recall. Do you see? Oh, she's probably out there somewhere..." Alice gestured to the city glimpsed through the window. "But truly, for me it's all gone. Of my life before I came here, all is dust."

Nyquist saw a tinge of sorrow in the old lady's eyes. "I really need to find Zelda," he said. "I think she holds the key."

"To what, young man?"

He frowned. "I don't know, but I think she might be in trouble. After all..."

"Yes?"

"I am a private eye. Isn't that why people come to me, when they're in trouble?"

"But have you considered that she might be... that Zelda might be dead?"

"Why do you say that?"

"Because that's your job." Alice was excited by the prospect. "Maybe you're supposed to find out who murdered her. Just think, that could be your next case!"

"Perhaps. I don't know. Not yet."

"Well, you could always try number 21. I know many people end up there, when they're lost. Or in search of something, or someone."

Nyquist made a note of the new apartment number. He thanked Alice for her help and for the tea and biscuits, and he walked out of her apartment. Taking the stairs up to the next floor he tried to make sense of what she'd said to him, and for a moment the truth of his situation trembled before him like a vision. He saw a man lying in a hospital bed, a woman at the bedside attending to him. But the man's face was in shadow, his name unknown.

It was real enough to make him come to a halt at the top of the stairs.

And then the vision faded as he heard clattering footsteps from the floor above. He looked up to see a child, a young boy, arriving at the next turn in the stairs. His face seemed familiar to Nyquist. For a moment man and boy stared at each other without speaking. And then the boy gave a strange little laugh, low-pitched then high, and he turned on his heels and scarpered back up the stairs.

"Wait!"

But the boy had gone.

Nyquist walked along the corridor until he found apartment 21. The door was wide open. He stepped inside and searched through each room. The place was empty and he felt disappointed after what Alice had promised.

He stood alone in the center of the living room, staring at each wall in turn. Every available surface was covered in writing, in words, numbers, diagrams, equations and maps. There wasn't a spot left free. Even the glass panels of the window had been covered in plain paper and used as a notebook to record information. A pair of stepladders rested against the wall in the corner of the room, which caused Nyquist to look upwards. The work continued on the ceiling, coming in from all sides to meet at the center around the light fitting.

"I'll be with you in a second."

Nyquist turned at the sound of the voice.

A man had entered from the hallway. He was carrying several large rolls of paper in his arms. "I just needed to get some more supplies. Just give me a minute." He dropped the rolls onto the floor and then pulled a great number of pens from his pockets. "Now then, how can I help you?"

"I'm looking for somebody."

"Good. Excellent. Maybe I can be of service."

Nyquist asked, "Is this a story?" He was referring to the walls and ceiling of the room with their vast array of words and figures.

The other man looked surprised at this. "A story? Why, good lord, no. Alas, I simply haven't got that kind of talent. I'm a recorder, only. A jumped-up office boy! Sam Bradshaw at your service." There was a twang of the North in his accent. "I record the tower and its various movements and conversations."

"You're an eavesdropper? A voyeur."

"Those are not the kind of words I like to use."

"But still…"

"Yes, if you like."

Nyquist swept his hand in a wide arc. "So these are things you've overheard, in the corridors, the elevators and so on?"

"The thing is, I'm not overly concerned with what people say, only where they are. That's my interest. Rooms, the foyer, the stairwells, broom closets, et cetera. Sometimes I even press a tumbler against a door panel or an adjoining wall and have a bloody good listen, just to find out who's hiding themselves away in there. It's terrible of me, but there it is. A lonely man needs a hobby."

Sam Bradshaw had some weight to him: it showed in his belly and in the folds of skin around his face, his cheeks and jowls. His greying hair was long at the sides and back, untidy, and sparse on top. Phlegm rattled in his throat. He bore the look of a middle-aged railway guard or a hotel doorman near to retirement, complete with dusty clothes and a slight air of decay in his bodily aroma. But his lips were always nearing a smile, and his eyes, sunken in their pockets of flesh, were lively and bright.

Bradshaw stretched both arms out wide to encompass the whole room. "Collected here are the various movements of people, here and there, hither, thither, up and down the stairs, out of one apartment and into another, and so on and so forth, ad infinitum, forever and a day. Do you see?"

Nyquist couldn't help but see: he had no choice in the matter. The numbers and words in their columns and rows dazzled and danced all around him, in various colors and sizes, in both pencil and pen.

Bradshaw smiled proudly. "Every word, every number, every line, every marking, all done by my own fair hand."

Nyquist knew enough by now not to question further, nor to ask for motive: this tower had its own rules of living.

"Now then, sir, who or what or where is it that you're looking for?"

"A woman called Zelda Courtland." He handed over the photograph. "I thought she might live in apartment 14."

Bradshaw tutted. "No, that's wrong. I mean, she's been there, this character, most certainly. Everyone's been there at some point."

"So you know where everyone is, which person in which apartment?"

"I keep an eye out, that I do. Residents, visitors, intruders, thieves and vagabonds. And most of all, the poor lost souls who wander in here without realizing. Many never find their way out again. It's very distressing." Not a trace of distress crossed his features. "Now just let me think. Zelda,

Zelda, Zelda…" Bradshaw mused on the name and cast his eyes from one wall to another.

A soft whirring noise was heard and a glowing object moved through the air. Nyquist couldn't make out what it was. But Sam Bradshaw bent at the knees and bounced gently up and down like a wicketkeeper poised behind the stumps. His arms waved slowly in front of him, describing complex, interlocking shapes. And then one arm snapped out at speed and he hit the wall with some force, with the flat of the hand. He shouted in sudden joy. "Yah!" Nyquist watched as the hand was pulled away, revealing the squashed remains of an insect. The wings and legs were broken, sticking out of the crushed thorax and abdomen. The orange letter H glowed among the gooey mess, the only evidence of life. And then that too faded, the light going out.

"Alphabugs," Bradshaw explained. "The bane of my life. They make their nests out of paper, you see. Not blank paper, alas. No, the paper has to have words on it, and then the larvae hatch out and they eat the words. It's horrible! Without a doubt, one of King Oberon's worst creations." He scraped the insect's remains off his hands and the wall, leaving an ugly brown and orange stain on the array of numbers.

Nyquist saw other such stains dotted around the walls and ceiling.

"Now then, let's see." Bradshaw started to walk around the room, checking the rows of words and the columns of numbers, looking at his wristwatch now and then and mumbling the date and time to himself as he did so, his keen, agile mind at work, his eyes narrowed in concentration.

"What are you doing?"

"Hush! Quiet please." He stopped at one section of the

far wall, the fingers of his hand tracking down a column, and then pausing in midair. "Oh, that is weird."

"What is it?"

"I'm not getting any reading for a Zelda Courtland, not just now."

"What does that mean?"

"It means, I'm afraid, that I don't know where she is."

Nyquist swore under his breath.

"But I can tell you where she was three nights ago. If that's any use?"

"Yes, it might be."

"Apartment 37. Can you remember that?"

"Number 37. I've got it."

"Very good. Of course, it's not an exact science." A deep sigh escaped his lips. "Some people have a habit, unfortunately, of wandering off their pathways just for the sake of it. But it is unusual, I must say... to have no presence at all."

"Does that mean Zelda's dead?"

"Yes, sometimes it means that. But not always."

Nyquist stepped closer. He said, "I woke up today in apartment 49, and I can't remember where I was before then. Can you help me?"

Bradshaw stared at him. There was a spot of squashed alphabug flesh on his cheek. He looked embarrassed.

The private eye continued: "All I have is this photograph of a woman, and her name: Zelda. It's my only clue."

"I see."

"I don't know who I am," Nyquist continued. "Not truly."

"Well, that's... well, I don't know what to say..."

"Of all the people in this building, you must know." Nyquist felt suddenly desperate. "You've studied every room, the comings and goings, the layout. You must know!"

A look of frustration entered Bradshaw's eyes and he said in a low voice, "I'm as lost as you are, my friend."

"Help me." It was a simple plea from the heart.

"Of course, of course. In any way I can."

The two men were standing but a few inches apart, lost in two very different narratives, and separated by common goals. Bradshaw nodded in recognition. He turned once more to the wall and explained, "Your mind has been changed by the building. You are no longer in charge of what you can see and hear and touch, and so on. The Melville Tower has this effect on certain people, not all, but only those susceptible to its power."

Nyquist shook his head in despair. "What the hell am I supposed to do?"

"Ah, but the building likes you, I can feel it. It wants you to venture forth, to explore its different apartments and corridors. It has many things in store for you. Yes, Mr Nyquist, the tower likes your story."

"You believe that?"

"I have studied the building's ways, and I've learned one thing above all others." His hands moved rapidly along the walls. "Everything happens according to a pattern."

Nyquist looked around in wonder. "Is this a key, or a code? This whole room?"

"Yes, yes! The labyrinth, every pathway, every floor, every room." Bradshaw smiled. "Every page, every chapter."

"How do you mean?"

"The tower is a book and the book is a tower, they live inside each other, the tower in the book and the book in the tower, and so it goes on, ever turning, ever changing, as the seasons turn and change, as the hours pass, as the pages of the book are rearranged and new names are added to the text, such as your own, each new character given over to the story. As the tower changes with the book, so the book changes with the tower." He looked at Nyquist with a troubled expression. "No one can know everything, I'm afraid. But we learn, little by little, night by night."

Nyquist's eyes followed Bradshaw's hands as they moved across the wall. "So I'm looking for apartment 37 next, is that correct?"

"Yes, but you'll have to hurry. It's nearly time."

"For what?"

"Babel. Quickly! Before the stampede begins."

Nyquist was charged by Bradshaw's urgency. He made his way back to the corridor and was barely outside when the door of apartment 21 banged shut, leaving him stranded. A great roar of noise greeted him, a chaotic jumble of voices, high and low, and he was immediately pushed back against the corridor wall by a mass of people. The space around the door was crowded with them, men, women and children, end to end, and every single one of them talking at once; not listening, not conversing, not communicating, but only shouting and arguing, all at cross-purposes.

Nyquist couldn't move.

COMA

John Nyquist woke up. For a moment he struggled with the sheets on the bed before realizing that the bonds were inside his own body; he was still trapped there, helpless, a coma victim, still lying in the room in Kafka Court. Bella Monroe had disappeared from the edge of his vision but he could hear her talking to somebody; it sounded like Overseer K. They spoke in whispers. He settled back inside his own mind and contemplated the ceiling. In the distance, the far hazy distance, he could see the second floor corridor of Melville Five. He could see his other self in the corridor surrounded by people, many of them, a whole crowd of residents all jostling for position. Nyquist had heard the conversation with Sam Bradshaw, and he knew that apartment 37 was the next destination. The sensation was uncanny, as though he were reading about his own life in a novel, seeing himself as a character in a book. The other self was fictional. A fictional being. But he couldn't speak to this other self, he couldn't cry out or scream, he couldn't pass on a message, or offer help, not directly. Or at least, he hadn't yet found a way to do so.

Nyquist was alone in the silence of his thoughts. He felt the words at play in his body, continually updating and rewriting their stories through his flesh.

He had to concentrate.

Send a message. Give instruction. Reach out towards the tower and make sure this time, make it clear what has to be done. The task.

Inside his eyes that could never close, his eyes closed.

He began to write, conjuring out of the dark the first stroke of the first letter. The others followed one by one, each bringing more pain than the last.

Z   e l   d   a

YGGDRASSIL PRESS

Nyquist struggled along the corridor, trying to force a way through the crowd. From all sides they closed in, pressing at him with their warm flesh, their sweat-stained clothes. The many lips moved incessantly, opening and closing, letting the words out in swirls of nonsense. Everyone had a different opinion about a different subject and a different way of speaking, a different accent. This truly was the Tower of Babel after the fall, language battling against language, each seeking supremacy. Nyquist found himself talking as well, he couldn't help it, even as he pushed on through the crowd as best he could. His mouth moved, the words poured out even though he was completely unaware of what he was saying: his brain had no control over his utterance. He was a mouth, a human mouth, a mouth alone with no other organs; his body had one purpose only, to speak: to speak aloud, to cry, to whisper, to sing, to yell in pain, to spit in anger, to mumble and sigh with pleasure, to orate and recite and pronounce deftly, each consonant perfectly placed when needed or swallowed when not, each vowel clipped or elongated. He spoke the Queen's English, he spoke in slang and jargon, he spoke in a working class accent and he spoke in dialects from the North and South. He spoke the finest rhetoric and he spewed out pure filth, all at the same time. His mouth led him on, past one person after another, exchanging threats and promises, demands and murmurs of undying love. He moved from one story to another, through the maze, his clothes rumpled and torn in places, and the further he went, the more violent, the more determined he was that his story, his subject matter alone, should be the victor! And everyone around him in that tangled mass of humanity had exactly the same desire: to win, to secure through the power of argument their own place in the corridor, the high-rise, the world.

At last he reached the stairwell. It was just as crowded as the corridor he'd left, but it was easier here, as three channels opened up, one ascending, the other descending, and the middle of the stairs reserved for those yet to make up their minds. Nyquist joined the right-hand side, slowly making his way to the next floor. He pushed through the doorway onto the corridor. Thankfully here it was slightly less crowded. He soon found out why: a siren rang out along the corridor and the people responded with joy to the sound: they all fell silent, the clamor of voices dying in an instant. Babel time was over. The residents were moving more freely now, as some of them made their way inside apartments and others headed for the nearest stairs or the elevator doors.

Soon Nyquist was alone once more. He rang the bell of apartment 37. It was opened immediately by a teenage boy who smiled at Nyquist in a beatific manner. This boy said not a word, but simply turned and walked back into the apartment. Nyquist followed him inside. He stood in the living room doorway, watching the scene that unfolded before him.

There were a dozen or so children present, ranged from four or five years old to perhaps twelve or thirteen. They stood quietly in attitudes of prayer around the central object: a tree. Or rather, part of a tree. The trunk grew from a large, jagged hole in the carpeted floor and rose to disappear into a corresponding aperture in the center of the ceiling. Patterns of dust drifted down from above, sparkling in the glow of the lanterns that a few of the children held aloft, the only given light. Nyquist was the only adult present and he thought of himself as an intruder on a private realm, a world cut off from his own. He took a step into the room, being careful not to disturb the prayer meeting. He could hear the tweeting and chirruping of birds and he saw sparrows, a canary and a bluefinch flitting about the branches of the tree. He saw a blackbird grab the letter Y of an alphabug from the bark and swallow it down.

The children present were drawn from different classes and groups: middle-class kids, street urchins, well-behaved boys and girls, a schoolboy holding a catapult, ragamuffins, bullies and swots. Nyquist saw one of the older girls actually talking to the tree. She knelt down before it in an attitude of supplication, her hands raised high above her head and her face taken over by rapture. Now the other children joined with her to sing a rhyme of strange enchantment:

The crying tree, the crying tree
All around the crying tree,
I'll catch you and you'll catch me
All around the crying tree.

The verse ended and the children bowed their heads, the birds fell silent and the insects stopped their buzzing. Only the shiny black leaves of the tree made any sound at all, rubbing against each other in whispers. Only two people remained standing. One was Nyquist: the other was the older teenage boy who had greeted him at the door. Now the boy explained: "If you're wondering, the tree reaches all the way from its roots in the basement up to the roof garden, where it emerges into the night air."

Nyquist asked, "What are they praying for?"

"Salvation. A way out."

"Tell me, is it always night here?"

"Always."

"And in the daytime?"

Instead of answering, the boy gestured for Nyquist to follow him. They walked into the hallway and then through into a gloom-filled box room. The boy stood in the semi-dark and said, "In the daytime we sleep. For the tower is dark in the sunlight, empty, devoid of all movement or sound."

"How old are you?"

"Fifteen this autumn. Yet I will never reach my birthday." For the first time the boy's smile wavered. "Not ever. My story won't let me. It doesn't reach that far." His voice cracked with a sudden hurt. "They tore it out! They tore out the page and they cut it into pieces, tiny pieces. The shreds were cast aside, scattered."

Nyquist looked at the teenager. His face was pale, almost bloodless, and glowed lunar-like in the shadowed room. Long straggles of mousy hair hung down in a fringe. His eyes blinked repeatedly like signals of distress, or warning lights. The smile had by now vanished completely. A lone alphabug crawled along the nearest wall, its glowing letter T acting as a tiny lamp. The teenager held out his hand and the bug flew willingly onto his palm.

Nyquist asked for the boy's name.

"Benedict."

Tears rolled down his barely formed face and his young body shook with anguish.

"What's wrong, lad?"

"The bugs fly out, they travel far and wide and come back home when they please, day and night. But for us, no. Not for us. Here we stay."

"You really can't leave?"

"None of us can. Yourself included. Don't you know that?" The boy flicked his hand and the bug took off once more. "We are born again every night, over and over, and our lives continue in these rooms and corridors, changing by a few degrees only."

Nyquist thought about the information that Sam Bradshaw had told him. "Is it only kids who come here, to this apartment?"

"Mainly, yes."

"Adults?"

"One or two. But only now and then."

"I'm looking for a woman called Zelda Courtland. I think she might've visited a few nights ago."

Benedict nodded. "Yes, she came here to worship at the word tree."

Nyquist looked quizzical.

"Yggdrasil," Benedict explained. "The old Norse name for the great tree that reaches up from the earth to the heavens. I learned about it at school, didn't you?"

"I was playing hooky that day."

"Odin suspended himself upside down from the tree's branches, as a sacrifice." The teenager's eyes retrieved a little light. "And over the nine long days and nights of his suffering, the king studied the tangled roots of the tree and made from their shapes the runes, the letters of the alphabet. In this way, language was born. The letters were passed on, hand to hand and mouth to mouth down the centuries. Many stories were told using them, and in this way the word tree lived on." His face trembled with fear. "Until the good King Oberon, bless his soul, took over the task."

Nyquist felt dazed. He tried to stay in focus. "Can you help me find Miss Courtland? Do you know where she might be right now? Which apartment?"

"Maybe I do. If you'll help me in turn."

"What do you need?"

"What are you going to do, when you find her?"

The answer came to Nyquist without any prior thought. "Get out of this place."

"And you'll take this Zelda with you?"

"Yes."

"So you have a way out?"

"I'll find a way."

"Then just come back for me." Benedict reached out to him. "Come back here, to this room, when you're ready to leave, and seek me out. Take me with you."

Nyquist couldn't find a good response to this. "I'm not sure..."

A single line etched the teen's forehead and his voice broke on a word he could never quite say out loud.

"OK, listen. I'll do what I can."

Benedict nodded at this. He looked to one side, his eyes lost in thought. And then he came to a decision. He said, "When Zelda left here, I took the elevator with her. She pressed the button for the sixth floor. I live on the same floor, so I walked along the corridor with her, a little way."

"You saw which apartment she went into?"

"I did. 67."

Nyquist mused on this. "I'm climbing higher each time."

"Just don't go up to the roof, whatever you do."

"Why not?"

Benedict shuddered. "People are apt to throw themselves over the edge."

"I'll do what I can to avoid that."

The teenager nodded in the gloom and for a moment

he seemed satisfied. Nyquist turned towards the doorway.

"You will promise, won't you?"

Nyquist carried on walking, into the hallway.

"Take me with you!"

He'd taken just one more step when the howling began. The teenage boy cried out with such despair that Nyquist had to steel himself against responding, against turning back and offering some small comfort, or a real promise of escape, even if such a thing might well be impossible. But the children around the word tree also heard this cry of agony and assumed Nyquist was to blame for it, for causing their friend trouble. One by one they came out of the living room and stood before him in the hallway, blocking his route to the front door. Their faces stared at him, expressionless. The lanterns glowed with a subdued, flickering light.

"I don't mean any harm," Nyquist told them.

"What have you done to Benedict?" the eldest girl asked.

"Nothing."

Another one repeated the question. "What did you do?"

"He wants to get out of here, out of the building."

"Did you make a promise?"

"No. I can't do that."

They stared at him, all of them, the lantern light dancing in their eyes. And Nyquist felt helpless before them, because none of his usual tactics applied to this situation. Not words, not actions, not gestures. Not even his old standby, silence. All he could manage was a few syllables of gibberish. And then he was hit in the face by a projectile of some kind. Startled, he looked for the culprit and spotted the schoolboy grinning, his catapult proudly held aloft. Nyquist couldn't believe it, he'd been hit by a pebble or a conker or a penny or something! His cheek stung. And there was nothing at all he could do except stand there

as motionless as the children were. Even the clock on
the wall seemed to quiver between one moment and the
next. Until one of the younger girls broke the silence: "We
all want the same." And that started them all off, all the
children speaking at once, a whisper to begin with: "Take
us with you. Take us with you, when you leave. Take us
with you. Take us. Take us with you, when you leave."
Louder now, louder. "Take us with you. Take us with you!"
They moved around Nyquist, obstructing his way forward.
Benedict joined in from the box-room doorway, lending
his slightly deeper voice to the mix.

Take us with you, take us with you, take us with you...

But now another sound could be heard, over the top
of the kids' voices. It was the sound of a bell chiming.
Benedict was the first to react. He held up a hand for quiet
and one after another the children fell silent under his
wish. He spoke in hushed, reverential tones:

"A page. A page is given to us!"

The children turned their gaze away from Nyquist,
towards the source of the chime, and they filed back into
the living room possessed by a sudden intent, a need that
had taken them over completely. Nyquist followed them.
A bell was hanging down from one of the branches of the
word tree, and was being pecked at by the blackbird. Each
jab of the beak set the chime ringing. The congregation
stood in wonder. They were waiting for something to
happen, that was evident. Nyquist stepped closer, careful
not to disturb the room's atmosphere. In truth, he was
as hypnotized as the youngsters. He saw worms crawling
in the trunk of the tree. He saw wasps mulching at the
softened bark. Spiders working their webs. Birds flittering
twig to branch, caterpillars weaving their cocoons in black
leaves. Reddish water dripped from the hole in the ceiling,
dampening the bark of the tree further. The insects scurried

about. Nyquist saw it all, each minuscule event magnified in his sight. The entire tree was a world unto itself. And where the insects worked the most, the bark was peeling away from the trunk in a thin, almost translucent layer.

Paper.

That most mysterious of all substances.

The home to stories.

That off-white field of dreams.

Parchment drawn from nature for one purpose only: communication.

The sheet was fragile, it trembled in the slightest of breezes. Benedict reached up and gently pulled it loose from the tree. He held it by two opposite corners, his fingers hardly brushing the surface. A few tiny black symbols were visible on the paper: letters of the alphabet. His eyes scanned the writing.

One of the younger kids dared to ask: "What does it say, Benedict?"

The teenage didn't answer. Instead he turned to look at Nyquist. "I believe this..." He held up the sheet for all to see. "I believe this is for you."

Nyquist took hold of the paper. He read through the three short lines of text quickly. All around the children were hushed, their faces expectant, their mouths agape. One boy started to weep, he just couldn't help himself. The branches of the tree were reaching out, the twigs scrabbling for purchase on the wall and ceiling, leaves rustling madly like the pages of books being turned at speed. The birds and bugs flew around the trunk, suddenly agitated. The whole room was alive, listening, waiting.

Nyquist read through the paper's contents a second time.

Zelda Courtland was murdered.

Find out who did it.
Find out!

And it was only on this second read-through that he realized: the message was written in his own handwriting.

THE OTHER

The tower block had fallen back into silent mode. Not a sight or sound greeted John Nyquist as he continued on his way, this time taking the elevator up to the sixth floor. The message taken from the tree drove him forward. *Zelda, Zelda, Zelda.* The name meant so much to him, yet he still didn't know why. But if he believed the message, then she'd been murdered, just as Alice in apartment 14 had predicted. For some reason, the search for Zelda's killer had taken possession of him. Perhaps by finding the identity of Zelda's killer, his own mystery would be solved, that he would find out both why he was here and why his past life was shrouded in such darkness.

When he got there, the door to apartment 67 was closed. He rang the bell and knocked on the paneling. He placed the side of his head against the green painted wood and listened. He banged on the door with his fist. No one responded. He tested the door and wondered about trying to batter it down. But it was firmly fixed in place, with no give to it.

And then someone screamed from within.

It was a man's voice, as far as he could tell. It sounded like a person in extreme pain, dying even. The noise rang out and then stopped abruptly.

Nyquist felt as though the scream had gone right through him like a drill. He felt the pain the man must be feeling and he gasped and folded himself over as though wounded in the stomach. He almost expected to see blood on his hands when he pulled them away; but no, they were clean.

The scream came again, the exact same pitch and duration as before.

Nyquist cried out, almost in sympathy. Somebody was being attacked, or even killed. Was Zelda in there? He didn't know, he just didn't know. He wasted precious seconds banging his shoulder against the door. It did no good at all. Then he ran along the corridor to the next door along, apartment 66. It was open a little way, the wood splintered around the lock. Someone had taken an axe to it. He slipped inside and called out, "Is there anybody here?" He hurried into the living room. The furniture lay scattered about, many pieces broken or upended, and the carpet was littered with papers and the smashed shards of ornaments and mirrors. The place had been ransacked. Nyquist jerked opened the full-length window that led out onto the balcony. He ducked under one washing line, and then another. The night sky lay over the city, bathing in moonlight and mist each story, sleeping or awake, on each and every street and corner. The sight made him feel dizzy. Quickly he turned to look at the balcony belonging to apartment 67. There was a gap between the two balconies, too long for him to jump easily across, especially considering that he would have to leap up on this balcony's metal railing first, and then take to the air, all in one swift movement. He looked down: the ground seemed to be many miles away, an impossible distance. A tiny fire burned in the central space and a couple of ant-like figures moved around. It was a long way to fall.

The man screamed again. It was clearly heard, coming through the open window of the next balcony.

Nyquist rushed back into the apartment and desperately searched among the remains of the occupant's life until he found a coat hook on the wall. He pulled this loose and carried it back to the balcony. Here he untied both clothes lines from the far end of the rail and attached the hook to them. He stood at the rail closest to next door's balcony and swung the double-ply line in a circle and then let it fly though the air until it clattered against the rail of the other balcony. It fell away. He cursed and tried again. On the third attempt the hook caught on the rail and he pulled on the line and felt it was safe, knotted firmly to the rail in front of him and fixed by the metal coat hook to the other rail, opposite. He knew that hesitation was fatal, so he immediately stepped up onto the balcony's rail and pressed one hand against the wall of the building. He had dragged the line close to the wall so he could step onto it, and walk across it, holding onto a series of drainpipes he had spotted fixed on the wall between the two apartments.

It should be safe enough, if he kept his cool.

He took the first step, placing the gap between the sole and the heel of his shoe on the line. One hand clung tight to a metal pipe. He lifted his other foot and placed this shoe in front of the other one. He was now aloft, suspended in space, held up by a double-ply of washing line. It sagged a little as he shuffled along.

Hand over hand he grabbed the pipes that branched off the main drainpipe, moving along slowly, keeping his body as close to the wall as he could.

He forced himself to stare at the brickwork, rather than to glance downwards.

The next apartment was quiet now. The screaming had stopped.

But Nyquist had to carry on, he was committed to this action.

He could see every little mark in the wall, every blemish, discolorment, every bit of chipped plaster, every damp patch where rain had dripped down from a leak, every elongated splodge of yellowing bird shit, the gaps between bricks, the powder of the bricks rotting away and falling as his hands and clothing brushed against them, the speckles of paint long dried, the dirt, the loose screw in the bracket that held the drainpipe in place, the embossed serial number on the pipe: D127. He saw them all, every detail. This was his world and he clung to it for dear life. And then his eyes focused once more on that one tiny screw, on the way the bracket shuddered as his hand reached for a new grip on the pipe.

He could see the tiny gap opening as the bracket worked even looser.

Dust fell from the gap, floating away in the air.

He was going to fall. Both hands clutched at the pipe, his fingers gripping even tighter in a sudden panic. The line sagged further under his full weight, as he reached the middle point of his journey. For a moment he rested there, it was all he could do. His hands and feet were frozen in place. Not a single step could be taken.

And then the bugs came. They came from the night sky, drifting in like pieces broken off the moon, shining yellow with their different letters on display. First one, then another, a third, and then suddenly ten or more of them. A swarm. They circled and buzzed around him, battering against his clothes and his skin where it was exposed, at the hands, the face; he could feel one of the insects crawling in his hair.

Nyquist clung on. His whole body shivered with repulsion at the very thought of the bugs touching him.

Three of them crawled about on the brick wall right in front of his eyes. He could read them, each glowing letter:

Y E S

A fourth joined them.

E Y E S

They moved again, and one took off suddenly:

S E E

It was the world's tiniest ever novel. Yes, he saw it. His eyes knew the truth. Here he was, far above the ground suspended between a drainpipe and washing line, and he was reading a story told to him by insects. It was absurd. The laughter broke him out of his fear. He had to either go back or move on, whichever was best. *Move on. Always! Move on! Keep moving.* It was the only mantra he knew. Jolted into action, he moved his feet, taking a series of steps in quick succession. His hands grappled with the pipe even as it loosened further. He hardly noticed when one of the screws worked itself completely free of the crumbling plaster and fell away on its long journey towards the ground. Once this first screw was gone, the others followed easily, one by one. The bracket separated from the wall and the pipe swung free. For a moment Nyquist seemed to hang in stasis. And then he felt he was already falling, as the pipe broke away from the wall, the other brackets breaking in turn.

The alphabugs swarmed away in panic.

He reached out desperately and managed to get one foot onto the balcony rail. It gave him a little purchase, enough to enable one last jump towards safety. His body seemed far too heavy to make it that far, made of lead, but now one hand gripped the rail, and then the other, and he pulled himself up and over and collapsed in a heap on the balcony floor.

It took him a few moments to get his breath back, and a moment further to feel the pain in his shin where it had banged against the rail. Let that be. He was alive. He got to his feet and walked into the living room of apartment 67.

There was no sign of the screaming man.

The room was empty. But another part of the word tree was growing here, from floor to ceiling, and Nyquist knew he must be directly over apartment 37, where he'd met Benedict and the children. The fact gave him a kind of bearing: he was ascending vertically. He was on a straight track.

The room was quiet beyond the rustling of the tree's black leaves. No birds flew here, no insects crawled in the wood. He made his way to the hallway, but then hesitated on the threshold of the bedroom, suddenly cold and shivering. Memories rose from the dark and fluttered away almost immediately. He had seen this room before, he was certain of it.

And one small step through the doorway caused his heart to flutter.

He was walking in a ghost's footsteps.

Moonlight streamed in through the half-open curtains. The sheets on the double bed were tangled and bloodstained. He saw matted hair and blood on the skirting board next to the bed. Someone had been injured here, or perhaps worse. He bent down close to the floor and touched the blood and felt the ghost take him over once more. He saw through a kind of mist or gauze the events that had taken place here at some previous time. He saw blood in his own eyes, on his own hands. He saw the other man's knife. He felt his hands, bunched into fists, punching over and again at the man's face and head. He felt his hands gripping around the man's neck. And he heard again the scream of pain, as one man killed another. He saw all this clearly as the scene came into sharp focus before him, conjured from the room's memory, and he knew the truth.

This man, whoever he was, had died at Nyquist's own hands.

He stumbled back from the sight.

The scream played out yet another time.

This is what he had heard, from the corridor outside, this repeated scream.

Nyquist imagined a tape loop circling from one reel to another, over and over, forever playing that terrible, agonizing sound.

The vision was all so real he felt he could reach out and touch the flesh of his victim, he could smear his fingers in the blood of the wounds. For a moment Nyquist's sense of balance shifted and he felt woozy, weak on his feet.

The screaming stopped at last, and the horrific vision faded away.

He waited in the cold silence, hardly daring to move.

The bed glowed in the moonlight.

His eyes closed. He tried to come to terms with this act of violence, whatever it might be: a vision, a dream, a part of reality he had forgotten about, blocked out. But something disturbed him, a fluttering at the eyelids, a sparkle of colors. But the room was still empty. Pale moonlight lay across the bed like a discarded wedding gown. From far away he could hear a noise, a regular beeping sound, some sort of electronic device at work. The sheets seemed to move slightly of their own accord and the light intensified over the bed, first as a blur of silver, and then as a darker substance in the air, a shape, a ghostly form, a transparent grey mass slowly forming before his eyes.

Nyquist was entirely held in the spell of the moment.

The beeping sound grew louder.

A definite shape was forming, a figure of some kind. It was lying on the bed in front of him, a person arriving out of some other realm – that was the only way he could think of it.

A man. A sleeping man.

Nyquist stepped closer to the bed.

At first the sleeper's face was blurred, indistinct, a set of crude features. But then the face formed itself as though out of clay: the eyes, the mouth, the ridge of the nose, the hair, the single crease on the brow. The colors of the skin.

Nyquist gasped.

He was staring at himself, his own face and form.

"Who are you?"

It was an absurd question, but the only one he could ask.

There was no answer. The other Nyquist lay there, wrapped in clean white bed sheets, a bandage visible on one arm. The bleeping sound came from a series of hospital monitors halfseen around the edges of the vision. Tiny green and red lights blinked on and off. And the line of a graph pulsed in time with the sleeper's heartbeat.

Nyquist bent closer, face to face.

He could hear his other self breathing. He could see the words that crawled over the face and upper chest area. And then the sleeper's eyes opened wide suddenly, and his body arched upwards, straining against his bonds. Nyquist staggered back and watched in terror as his other self fell back onto the sheets and lay there. And then the man on the bed looked across the room, across some unfathomable space, and Nyquist could only repeat his words from before: "Who the hell are you?"

The other answered quietly with the same question: "Who are you?"

And for a moment Nyquist actually thought he was talking to himself. But then the man on the bed spoke again: "Do you need to ask?" The voice was Nyquist's own, an exact copy, but muffled, heard from the bottom of a deep well.

He reached out and his hand moved through the body of the other, as though it were made of mist, or whatever substance dreams were made from. And into this mirror he looked and looked deep and felt he was falling into his own being at last, becoming real, a creature of flesh and blood. Nyquist couldn't understand the feeling. "Tell me," he said. "Tell me what I am."

But the other ignored this plea, saying instead, "Listen. Listen to me. I haven't got long. Find out…"

The man on the bed coughed and was unable to finish the sentence. Nyquist felt it in his own throat, this painful desire to speak, without being able to speak, not properly.

He moved closer once more, kneeling on the bed. "What is it? What do I need to know?"

"Zelda was murdered."

"Yes, I know that. I've learned that."

"Find out…"

"Find out who killed her? Yes, but how? Where do I start?"

The translucent body of the other self was fading away as smoke on a summer's day. He made a final effort: "Two people."

"Go on. I'm listening."

The other's lips were barely moving as his face merged into the grey light of the room. "Dreylock. And…" He coughed again.

Nyquist reached out, trying to hold onto his other self. It was no use, his hands went right through the shimmering body to touch the bed sheets beneath.

Nyquist cried out. "Talk to me!"

The lips of the other moved on, but silent now.

Two characters who could never quite meet. Two narratives with the same hero, but worlds apart.

And then the other managed to speak further. "Wellborn."

"Dreylock and Wellborn?" Nyquist asked, hoping for confirmation. "Who are they?"

"One of them knows the truth. I'm certain of it..."

That was the last word. Both body and voice had faded away. The moonlight lay across the empty bed once more, the blood stains clearly visible on the sheets. Nyquist was alone. He moved away from the bed and sat down in an armchair. He wanted to remain there for a short while, to think about what he had learned in the last few minutes. But a noise disturbed him.

It was the sound of a key in the front door of the apartment.

THE OTHER SIDE

Bella Monroe's voice woke him from sleep. She was sitting at his bedside, talking over and over to herself, the words neverending. He glimpsed her face in the corner of his unwavering eye. Sometimes she would lean closer to look directly into his face, but he could read very little from her expressions. Her lips were moving, her words a mumble under her breath. He couldn't hear her properly. *Bella*, he said, *Bella, speak to me, speak more clearly, speak louder, let me hear you. I need to hear your voice.* But she ignored his pleas. Nyquist was unheard, unknown. And unknown in the dark he listened to the woman's breath and he gazed at her face, and knew she was his only companion at this time.

He was still reeling from his journey to Melville Five, his meeting with his other self in apartment 67. What had been said between them, between himself and his reflection? He couldn't remember, not fully. He could only hope that enough had been given, enough knowledge, one clue or another, a key, a code. Something, a gesture even. A single word might do it, if only his other self could understand the message.

Did he mention Dreylock as a possible suspect for Zelda's killing? Did he warn him that Wellborn was still alive, still at large in the world?

Monroe talked on and on.

Nyquist could feel himself sinking into a final darkness. He tried once more to view his other self moving through the corridors and rooms of the distant tower, but this time the vision eluded him. Death was prowling at the edges of his story.

Monroe's voice...

He concentrated on her voice. This would pull him up and clear for a little while, that simple human connection. But then he would slip away once more as the word virus worked at his body, never tiring, never expiring, always renewing and merging and mutating. It was doing its best to keep him alive, but he feared now that it was all too little and too late...

Monroe's voice! Listen. Listen to her!

Again, he jerked awake. Her face was close to his. He could see that she'd been crying, or at least holding back the tears. He watched her lips as they moved together and apart, making their different shapes. Now he could hear her. She was telling his story, reading out loud whatever was written on his face and chest and arms. The novel of his own self, this ever-changing narrative.

While she spoke to him like this, there was still a chance.

His story might continue, at least for a while.

He had to hope it was enough.

THE OTHER SIDE OF THE MIRROR

The two men faced each other, the stranger at the doorway of the bedroom, and Nyquist on his feet near the chair. The man spoke calmly: "Did I wake you, Mr Nyquist? I'm so sorry." Nyquist didn't reply. The intruder was stocky and well built and he must've been quite powerful in his youth, but just now he was a poor, fragile specimen. He walked into the room a couple of steps, using a stick for added support. His face was truly shocking to look at: it was scarred all over, the gaps between each cut red with blood, most of them old and dried, a few others streaming anew, and crude surgical stitches held the whole fleshy mask together as best they could.

"I've been following your progress through the building. Young Benedict told me where you were heading. He's easily persuaded." He laughed and held up a key fob. "I let myself in."

"Who are you?"

"My name is Thomas Dreylock."

Nyquist tried to not give anything away. He let the other man carry on speaking.

"I can assure you, we have met previously. In fact, we had quite an altercation."

"I've never seen you before."

"Really? People do say I have a memorable face. Many have remarked upon it. Still, there it is. We have met, we have spoken. We almost came to a business agreement. Sadly, you absconded, you and your lady friend."

Nyquist rubbed at his neck and face. "I don't know what you're talking about."

The smile left Dreylock's face. "I think you do, if you would but make an effort." He wiped a thin line of blood from a wound. "Actually, you saw me in difficult, even humiliating circumstances. That was not one of my finest days, no indeed. I was bedridden. And then I had one of my seizures, right in front of your eyes."

"I need a drink."

"Ah yes, such a tempting plot device. The brave but lonely private eye, his one true lover long vanished, believed dead, the bottle of whisky his only partner as he wanders the rain-washed night streets in search of a case or a clue, something to fill the emptiness."

"A glass of water will do it."

"I'll wait here."

Nyquist went through into the bathroom. He bent his head to the tap and slaked his thirst. He looked in the mirror and listened to his reflection speaking: *Zelda was murdered. Dreylock and Wellborn. One of them knows the truth…*

He took out the photograph and looked at the woman's face. Her features were far less blurred now, as though Zelda Courtland was moving towards him one detail at a time.

Soon, soon he would know everything.

He went back into the bedroom. Dreylock was now sitting in the armchair, his hands folded on his lap, his stick propped at his side.

Nyquist got to the point. "What do you want from me?"

Dreylock considered the question. "A story is being

played out in this building, upon this night, a story of some import. And I believe that you and I, Mr Nyquist, we are both vital to its ending."

Nyquist took a chair at the desk. "Let's hear it."

"Of course, you must be very curious." Dreylock smacked his lips. "Perhaps you've heard of a man called Patrick Wellborn?"

"In passing."

"Well that is strange, I must say. After all, you did kill him."

Nyquist closed his eyes. He was threatened by a memory and it circled in like a knife blade, slowly, from afar.

Dreylock's voice rose up in glee. "Right here in this room. There, do you see!"

He pointed to where the blood and hair were plastered on the skirting board. Nyquist felt faint, looking at this evidence of his own crime. He didn't want to believe it, yet at the same time he knew it was true. He had seen the vision.

"But don't worry, you acted in self-defense. I believe you angered him, by destroying one of his favorite pages."

As though in response the terrible scream was heard again.

Nyquist covered his ears.

Dreylock was smiling. He said, "This room keeps hold of its memories, especially ones created from pain. Just think; Wellborn's cry will replay itself through the night hours, until the building is finally demolished."

Nyquist sat down on the bed and felt his head bowing down. The scream blazed behind his eyelids as a fierce burst of red and orange shapes.

And then at last there was silence once more.

Dreylock watched the private eye. He said in a calm voice, "Look at me, please."

Nyquist did so, raising his head.

Dreylock waved a hand in front of his damaged face. "This is my doorway." The man's scars bunched together. "Through my wounds, I will show you the world." He smiled. "Oh, I have a number of such lines. Would you prefer another example?"

"I just want the facts."

"As you wish." Dreylock nodded. "This face of mine, as ugly and painful as it is, has one advantage. It means that I can see the truth about this place, and what's happening to you, to me, to all of us here – my pitiful gang, dear sweet Lionel; Amber with her skillful, healing hands; and nasty spiteful Vito. All of us! I look through the gaps where my new persona has not quite gelled, and I see the reality."

He was speaking from his heart, as broken and sullied as it might be.

"I was not always like this. Once upon a time I was an actor of some renown, noted for my handsomeness, and my passion. I played all the major roles. Hamlet, Oedipus, Kowalski. Only two years ago I played Vladimir in a new play called *Waiting for Godot*. Do you know of it?"

Nyquist didn't answer.

"It's a most fascinating work, and one that rather chimes with our current predicament." Dreylock frowned. "So yes, I was by all accounts a fine performer. Sadly, I was seduced away from such delights when an old friend of mine met up with me in the theater bar one evening, a few weeks ago, this was. It was a chance meeting, but one which changed my life forever, and for the worse. Of course, I wasn't to know that at the time."

Nyquist found himself interested in the story. "What was the friend called?"

"Patrick Wellborn. He introduced me to a novel called *The Body Library*. Not the whole book however but just a few pages, discards, those deemed unfit for the final volume. Still, even these discarded pages had a power far stronger than the words they contained. And via their power I made my way here, to the Melville Tower, seeking further pleasures."

Dreylock paused. He wiped at his face and his hand came away with a mixture of tears and blood. He stared at the sight as he carried on with his tale.

"Once inside this terrible place, I fell under a spell. Does this mean anything to you?"

Again, Nyquist glimpsed a distant image. But it wouldn't settle, and his eyes closed involuntarily as though to hold what little remained firmly inside his head.

"There it is, you see!" Dreylock cried. "The thought exists, the memory. The boy Calvin has performed the same spell on you, indeed on all of us who live here."

"But I can't remember any of this, not clearly."

Dreylock lit a cigarette.

"Well that's the thing, the actual process is hidden to us. How the spell plays out, in which room, the details thereof, all is hidden. The truth is veiled, even from myself. But tell me, you woke up in your room this morning and all seemed real to you?"

"Yes."

"This is what happens, we lose part of ourselves in the process."

Nyquist felt he was nearing the truth of the matter. "What is this spell?"

Dreylock dragged smoke from his cigarette. "I know only what I have surmised. That we are taken to see a man called Oberon, who lives somewhere in this apartment block. Somewhere unknown. We might think of him as the king of this tower."

"Is this a fairy tale?"

"Of a kind. The cruelest kind." Dreylock grimaced. "Oberon splits us in two."

As these words were spoken Nyquist felt a sharp pain in his guts, as though he had been wounded there.

"Yes, it's painful to think upon it. But there it is, the facts, as you requested of me." He stubbed his cigarette out in an ashtray. "From that moment on we exist as two beings. One who lives out there..." he gestured broadly to the window. "In what they dare to call the *real* world. And the other self stays in this building. Trapped here, for Oberon's pleasure. We become characters, nothing more. Characters in *The Body Library*."

Nyquist wished for something more than water. He got up from the bed and searched the room, finding a half bottle of whisky on a bookshelf. He stood by the window, looking out, sipping the fiery liquid directly from the bottle. His thoughts were spoken aloud, as the truth came to him.

"So we are the discarded ones?"

"If you like, yes. Mere fictional beings, while our real selves carry on out there, in the world. Out there in Storyville, doing what they will, living their lives."

Nyquist remained at the window.

"A sorry state." Dreylock's voice was filled with bitterness. "Fiction and Non-Fiction, the two modes entirely separated. In most cases, the others will have no knowledge at all that we even exist."

Nyquist flinched. He looked back to the bed where only a short while before he'd been talking to his other self – his *real* self, if Dreylock was to be believed. Was it possible that this other self was trying to reach out to him, to send him messages, to guide him, to urge him on? Just thinking about the idea made him wonder whether one of those alphabugs had got inside his skull.

Dreylock continued, "But I am different. I am cursed."

He touched at his broken face with his hand. "The spell didn't take with me, not fully. I was left with these wounds all over my body. I am the broken story and through these scars, I glimpse both sides."

Nyquist turned to face the other man. "Which Patrick Wellborn did I kill? The real, or the fictional?"

"Well there is the question, the number one question."

"Which is it?"

"You killed the fiction. You ended his part in the story. I imagine the real Wellborn is mightily pissed off at this. No more games in the bedroom."

"And what does that mean?"

Dreylock smiled. "For most people, one visit is enough to the tower. They stay well away, leaving us in peace. But Wellborn was different. He knew everything about the two sides of his life. I think he was one of the first people to fall under the spell. Because of this he liked coming to Melville Five. He actually liked meeting up with his fictional self. Can you imagine such a thing? The two of them chatted, they shook hands, they shared stories. And even weirder…" Dreylock lowered his voice. "Wellborn brought women here, prostitutes usually, and he'd hide in the shadows and watch his other self making love to them. Oh Lord. He watched his fictional self having sex."

"That's sick."

"Oh, I agree. It's perverse beyond measure." Dreylock started to laugh. "But you know, that's why your precious Zelda ended up here."

"Zelda Courtland?"

"Wellborn brought her here, just for his viewing pleasure. Of course, it never happened. Thanks to you and your brutal actions."

Nyquist finished his drink and walked towards the seated man. "Why do say *precious*? Did I know Zelda?"

"I believe you loved her. Or whatever might pass for love in a few hours of meeting."

"It's too late. She's dead. She was murdered."

"Which one?"

Nyquist stared at him. It was a simple question. In his mind he could see a tree standing in a field, a body hanging from the branches, a woman's body. He saw Zelda's face, the rope tight around her neck, her skin bulging at the throat.

He spoke in a whisper: "She was hanged from a tree in Marlowe's Field."

Word by word, the story was coming back to him.

Dreylock said, "Zelda's fictional self might still be alive somewhere in the building. But I haven't seen her. And that's unusual; I make it my business to meet with everyone who comes here, to interrogate them. You never know who might be able to help me." Again he probed at his scars.

Nyquist remembered how Sam Bradshaw had been unable to locate Zelda on his wall charts. He said to Dreylock, "I need to find her. I need to find Zelda Courtland."

"That's perfectly understandable." Dreylock looked at his wristwatch. "Well, it's past two o'clock. The reading will have started by now."

"The reading?"

With an effort Dreylock stood up from the chair, using his stick as a lever. "There is one person here who knows more than I do. Who might perhaps know Zelda's whereabouts. That is, if you can find a way of talking to her."

He held out his hand, gesturing towards the doorway.

As Nyquist followed him from the apartment, the strange, ghostly scream was heard yet again, once more hoping for a witness, or a physical body to rest in at last.

A LONG WAY DOWN

They exited the elevator at the top floor of the building and walked down a short corridor. A single door stood at the end. There was no bell, no number, no nameplate. Dreylock walked along slowly, on account of his injuries. He produced a key and opened the door.

"This is the penthouse suite. Very few people come here."

Nyquist followed him inside. "Do you have a key to every room?"

"Sadly, no. But I barter and I steal, where I can."

The main living area was huge. The two longest walls were made entirely of framed glass, giving excellent views of Storyville to the north and south. A long narrow roof garden was visible on one side, complete with chairs, potted plants and a dried-up water feature. The furniture in the room was upscale and yet barely used from the look of it. Clumps of dirt and piles of leaves were scattered over the carpet, and on tables and chairs. The whole place stank of damp, of rain, of rot. The reason was obvious: the word tree ended here, or at least it almost did. Its final flourishing reached up from the center of the floor, the sparse topmost branches disappearing through a hole in the penthouse's ceiling. This high up, the leaves looked to be devoid of wildlife, and the room was quiet. Over the years, rain and snow and dust had crept in through the hole in the ceiling, gradually taking over the apartment. Evidently, no one had lived here, not for a long time.

Nyquist was about to ask a question when Dreylock held a finger to his lips, indicating silence. Nyquist listened. He heard the whispering of a voice. No, not a voice, but something very close to it: the rustle of paper. He walked around the trunk of the tree, following the sound, and through the leaves and branches he saw a woman sitting at a small table, her head bowed as she studied a large book that lay on the table before her, illuminated by an ornate metalwork reading lamp. There was a soft yellowish glow surrounding the seated figure. The woman's face was hidden, and the edges of the room she occupied faded away at the limits of the sphere of light. Nyquist noticed blue and yellow flowers.

Dreylock kept his voice low. "Don't disturb her, whatever you do."

"Who it is?"

"This is the reader."

The woman made no acknowledgment of the two men, but continued with her task in utter concentration. The fingers of her right hand reached out to turn a page. Now Nyquist heard again the rustling noise. He had heard nothing like it ever before. This was the sound of paper speaking, whispering, urging, crying, pleading, praying, dreaming. On top of this the woman was murmuring or breathing each word to herself as her eyes scanned the page. Hush meeting hush. Nyquist was held spellbound. His hand reached out, almost touching the outer rim of the yellow glow of light.

"You won't be able to reach her," Dreylock said. "The reader isn't actually here, in the building. But every so often she visits us. Not every night, sadly, and when she does appear, it's only for a few hours at a time."

Nyquist was reminded of the vision he'd seen in apartment 67, but this was of a different nature: stronger, more defined, and far more exquisite.

"What is she doing?" he asked.

"She's reading. She's just reading. Nothing more."

"And the book on the table?"

"*The Body Library*. The book of the tower."

Nyquist was lost in wonder.

Dreylock explained: "In these pages we all exist. Yourself, myself, and all the other residents. As the spell takes us over, our names enter the book as characters. And the reader keeps us alive. She breathes air into our lungs, forces the blood through our veins. Even the blood that flowed from Wellborn's head when you killed him, this also was conjured from the book's pages."

Nyquist's hand tingled as it touched the glow. It was slightly painful and he knew without being told that if he pushed further, the pain would only increase.

His hand withdrew.

"But where is she, really?"

"Somewhere out there." Dreylock gestured to the nearest window frame. "Somewhere in this vast city, the reader sits in her little room with its blue and yellow flowered wallpaper and she reads from the novel, and she gives us life." He turned back to Nyquist. "I know only that her name is Ava Beaumont. She was one of the book's creators." He pointed to the novel on her reading desk. "And because *The Body Library* is made up of so many other books and magazines and newspapers arranged in a random order, it contains not one story, but an infinite number."

Another page was turned.

Whisper…

Dreylock paused to breathe deeply, and to wipe another trail of blood from a scar. And when next he spoke, the words seem to come from the scars themselves.

"On one page of the book lies the cure to my sickness. A way of putting my face and body back together. Of this I'm certain. But all my various schemes to reverse the spell have come to nothing." He sighed heavily. "My, but I grow weary."

For a few moments, the two men watched the reader at her task.

Whisper, whisper…

"What happens when Ava gets to the end of the book?"

Dreylock took a while to answer. "She starts again, from the beginning."

The woman's hand hovered over the paper. She seemed to react in some imperceptible way to the statement. And then she looked up from the book and looked directly at Nyquist. Her eyes held within them the night sky, a star in each pupil.

And Nyquist looked back at her – two people staring at each other through a magical looking glass. Some kind of recognition passed between them.

"She's never looked at me, not directly," Dreylock said in awe. "And I've never heard her speak. Of course, despite this, I am entirely under her spell."

The woman turned his eyes back to the book and carried on with her reading.

Whisper, whisper, whisper…

"Let's get some air."

Dreylock clicked the lock on the nearest window and a door panel slid across. He stepped out into the garden. Nyquist followed as the limping man slowly ascended a flight of steps that led to the roof of the penthouse suite itself. Here, the highest branches of the word tree were visible, poking up through the small circular hole in the center of the roof.

"When I first came up here, I almost expected to find a star fixed to the top of the tree." Dreylock grinned. "Or a plastic angel."

Nyquist stared out over the expanse of sky and city. Never before had Storyville seemed so beautiful to him, nor more fragile. He was a character on a page, nothing more, a page that might turn at any moment, or be torn and crumpled, or disfigured with spilt ink or blood or tears, or that might be set aflame in order that the dream of the words be taken into the body.

The city trembled as he trembled.

It breathed as he breathed.

Dreylock had lit a cigarette. "Sometimes people try to escape from the tower. Downhearted types like myself."

"What happens to them?"

He let out a trail of smoke from his lips. "You really don't want to know. It's a terrible sight."

Nyquist searched through a tangled web of thoughts. "I have one case on hand, to find out who killed Zelda Courtland."

"And that's all you can do, play out that story?"

"It appears so."

"Welcome," Dreylock said. "Welcome my friend to the body library. Not a book, not a building, but the very world in which we live." Sparks from his cigarette flickered away in the wind.

The moon appeared from behind a bank of grey clouds, washing the city with its pale light. Nyquist leaned over the edge slightly and peered down. There was no barrier on this side of the roof, only a sheer drop to the ground below. His stomach lurched.

"I can tell you this, John," Dreylock said. "Once upon a time you were entranced by Zelda. In a different body, with a different mind."

"I know. I'm starting to feel that once again."

Dreylock threw his half-smoked cigarette away. He stood close by, his arm on Nyquist's elbow. "I have words that reach me from afar, through the scars. You should know that Patrick Wellborn attacked you. That is, the real Wellborn attacked the real John Nyquist. He pushed you off a building's edge."

Nyquist looked at him. "Because I killed his fictional self?"

"Yes, exactly." He turned. "You know, Nyquist, your other self was very cruel to me, at our first meeting. I was in desperate straits. I needed your help. I was suffering badly, in terrible pain, and you could see that clearly, I swear. Instead, you took my suffering only as an opportunity to escape."

Nyquist shook his head. "Am I to blame for the other Nyquist's behavior?"

"Spoken like Cain himself." Dreylock gave a strangled laugh. "But here's the thing, my friends and colleagues all left me after that incident, even the lovely Amber. They've all gone their separate ways. And so, because of you... I'm alone."

Nyquist had placed his feet squarely on the floor of the roof. Again, he stared down.

"It's a long way to fall, isn't it?" Dreylock said.

"I'll take you with me."

"I believe you would." Dreylock's grip tightened. Nyquist could feel his strength, his determination. "And we'd be fighting the whole way." He squeezed Nyquist's arm almost to the breaking point, before letting go.

"Did you kill Zelda?"

"Me? How could I do such a thing? My body is a wreck, and I am trapped here, as you are."

"You have agents. People who can work for you."

Dreylock smiled. "My powers are limited. And anyway, why would I kill her? For what purpose?"

"I don't know. I just don't know."

Nyquist moved away from the edge of the building. He felt weak suddenly, and even more adrift from his true self. He stumbled and almost fell.

Dreylock watched him dispassionately. "You poor sod."

"What's… what's happening to me?"

"It's really quite simple. Your real self is dying."

Nyquist forced his eyes to stay open.

"I'm curious. How does it feel?" Dreylock rubbed at his scars as he said this, drawing a copious amount of blood onto his fingers. "Is it very painful?" He picked idly at one of the stitches, pulling it loose. The skin shifted on his face. "I wonder how your lovely Zelda felt, when her physical body was killed."

Nyquist tried to stand up straight. The uncomfortable feeling was passing a little. He wouldn't give the man any more chances.

"I don't know what you're after, Dreylock."

"Oh that's simple. To be put back together. To be cleansed of this." He drew a bloodied hand down his face from brow to neck.

"You think I can help you?"

"I think you're here for a reason, Nyquist, a central reason. More so than anyone else. I would like a share of that power." He laughed again. His face was ravaged, breaking down, but this time he didn't seem to mind, in fact he gloried in it. He split his lips wide on a hideous grin and his skin followed suit. Nyquist could hear the stitches pinging open. The blood flowed freely from the fissures.

"We'll die here," he said through cracked lips. "That's the truth. We were born here, and we'll die here, each of us alone. There it is, the only story worth telling–"

Dreylock stopped speaking. He froze, unable to move.

Nyquist watched him.

Dreylock put up his hands as though to ward off a blow.

And then they both heard a tearing sound. It was loud and piercing, as though flesh had been torn from bone. Nyquist felt the pain deep within own body and he cried out. Dreylock did the same, to a lesser extent.

"What was that?"

"A page being torn out. It's the reader, but why… why would she do that?"

Nyquist was still reeling from the sudden attack. "I felt it, inside. I *felt* it." He rubbed at his sides, seeking the wound, expecting blood. There was none.

"This is how it works," Dreylock said to him. His voice was strained. "We are bound to the book."

Nyquist viewed the city through his blurred vision, the gold and silver lights wavering. The sky was filled with sparks. The moon looked down, sickened and off-white at the sight of such weakness, and Nyquist had to submit. He bowed over. The stab of pain repeatedly struck him, this time deep in the skull. He tried to speak, to put forth words, but nothing good was said, only fragments, gibberish.

There was a sudden shiver of cold air.

Dreylock called out in surprise.

Nyquist turned.

The reader was ascending the steps to the penthouse roof. The yellow glow of light came with her, like a lunar gown enveloping her body from head to foot, keeping her both safe, and separate. Ava stood there swaying, a single page of the book held in one hand.

The leaves at the apex of the tree rustled in the breeze,

whispering, whispering.

Nyquist moved towards her. Not a strand of Ava's hair was ruffled by the elements that played around the tower's upper stories, not a speck of dirt caught in her eye. She was not of this world, but another one, a place that was more real, more fleshy, bloodier, and infinitely sadder. Nyquist knew this from the look in the reader's eyes.

He came as close to her as the sphere of light would allow. For a moment he thought she might actually speak to him, to pass on some knowledge, or a secret. But her lips remained sealed. Instead, she held up the page she had torn from the book.

Nyquist reached forward. He actually felt the edge of the paper with his fingers.

And then the light closed upon itself, and vanished completely from the rooftop, taking the reader with it.

Nyquist and Dreylock were alone once more.

The single page of the book remained in Nyquist's grasp.

There were stitches of red thread in the paper, and a tiny bird's feather stapled in place. And the words themselves, when he tried to read them, only served to make his head spin. But somewhere on that page he felt certain a clue was given, a way forward. And then he saw a phrase, just three words among many: *what you seek*. And a few lines on he saw the name *Zelda*. It was enough to make him concentrate, to learn how to decode the book's ragged, cut-up style. His eyes jumped from one line to another, across the page, and up and down, and diagonally, putting one word with another, drawing a meaning together from all the different places, only to have it slip away at the last grasp. Yet one thing was repeated more than any other, the number nine, whether written as a word or as a numeral. He counted all the mentions; there were eight of them altogether. But then he saw the number at the bottom of the sheet: page nine. Nine mentions of the number nine.

What you seek.

Zelda.

Number nine.

Dreylock tapped him on the arm. "What does it mean? Anything?"

Nyquist didn't answer. He was already reading ahead across so many invisible pages. Slowly, slowly, from the depths of a lost story, the truth was rising to meet him.

SCISSORS CUT PAPER

It was a long elevator journey with many people getting on and off at the lower levels. Some of them talked to each other, others stayed silent. Nyquist saw them as fellow travelers, fellow residents. For the first time he felt that the Melville Tower might be his chosen home one day, when this current adventure was over. Who knows, he might find Zelda and live with her in some kind of peace. Two fictional people enjoying a fictional life together: there had been stranger unions, he was sure.

At one point the car was entirely filled with people, yet he felt no discomfort as his body was squashed and squeezed between wall and flesh. But for the final stage, from the second floor down to the first, he and Dreylock were alone. Nyquist took out his photograph of Zelda. He was close to recognizing her, and the prospect of seeing her image clearly excited him. The light buzzed and flickered overhead, lending her face an intermittent glow. She had the quality of a dream figure, or a ghost. Which seemed appropriate: her real self, her physical body had passed away. But her fictional self lived on, he was certain of it.

The elevator reached the first floor. They walked down the corridor towards apartment number 9. The door was locked and no one answered the bell.

"Are you going to produce a door key?"

"Not this time." Dreylock's face had taken on a cold, fixed expression within its pattern of cuts, bruises and trails of blood.

"You've got no idea who lives here?"

"None at all."

Nyquist banged on the door with his fist but there was still no response.

"What now, private eye?"

"It's like this: the reader gave me that manuscript page on purpose. She wanted me to come down here, to this apartment. But what's the point of directing me here, if I can't get inside?"

"How does this help us?"

"The reader knows everything."

"So?"

"So there's a key, Dreylock. All we have to do is find it."

He looked up and down the corridor and then set off walking towards the fire door at the far end. Next to the door, fixed to the wall inside a glass cabinet, was a fire axe. Nyquist rolled his jacket sleeve down over his hand and smashed at the glass with his lower arm. It took him just two blows to break the glass. He grabbed the axe and hurried back to apartment 9.

"That's your idea of a key?"

"Stand back."

He didn't give him much time. The axe was already swinging high overhead. It hit the center of the door and broke through the wood paneling. Nyquist yanked the head free and raised it again. Dreylock was cowering against the opposite wall of the corridor. The axe struck home a second time, a third, a fourth. The door was now in splinters, especially around the lock.

Nyquist threw the axe to the carpet and used his boot

heel to kick the door open. It swung back against the inner wall of the hallway.

"Stay here," he said to Dreylock.

"As you wish."

Now he was inside. Nyquist searched the hallway, living room and bathroom. Each was empty, each stripped completely of furniture and floor covering, the walls stripped of paper or paint. The only sound was made by his footsteps echoing on the bare floorboards. He couldn't help feeling angry, and disappointed. And then he entered the bedroom. It had the appearance of a tramp's den. There was a pallet bed on the floor covered with a sheet, and a wooden stool in the corner. No carpet, no wallpaper, very little fresh clean air. The smell of an animal's cage at the zoo. A threadbare blanket was fixed over the window to block out the moonlight – a stray beam found its way through a rip in the cloth, but otherwise, the room was in darkness. A man was sitting cross-legged in the far corner of the room, with his head completely bowed down and his hands folded over his head and shoulders for protection. He was whimpering to himself.

For the moment, Nyquist left him as he was.

A photograph was pinned to the far wall, which the thin beam of light from the window seemed purposely to illuminate. The image showed a woman and a child, perhaps mother and son. The woman was Ava, the reader of *The Body Library* he had met in the penthouse suite, while the boy was the one who had run away from him on the stairs. Nyquist pulled the photograph from the wall and turned it over to read the inscription: *Ava and Calvin, happier times.*

"Don't touch that."

The cowering man had spoken.

"That doesn't belong to you."

Nyquist pinned the photograph back in place.

"Your wife and child, I take it?"

The man was breathing heavily, with some effort. Now he unfolded his arms and raised his head. His face was still hidden in the darkness.

"Stand up. Come on. Let me see you."

The man did as he was bid and raised himself to his feet. He glowered across the room. "You will be Mr Nyquist, no doubt. I was wondering when you'd find me."

"Is that so?"

"It is so. For I have seen it written." He spat out this last word as though it were poison in his mouth. "Written! Written in blood and ink, and piss and vomit and sweat and spit and every manner of bodily fluid. I have seen your story written, your journey, your coming here, your descent into the pool, your transformation, yes, all of it!" Now that he was roused, the man had the tone of an old-fashioned fire and brimstone preacher.

Nyquist waited, his body tensed and ready.

"You know my name. So what's yours?"

In response to this request, the other man's hand clutched at the blanket at the window and pulled it free. Moonlight streamed into the room. The figure cried out at his own action, a pitiful howl of despair and frustration. Nyquist saw the man's drawn expression, he saw the heavy eyes, the dirty teeth, the ink stains on his face and hands, and the tattered, unwashed clothing once so stylish, now a set of rags hanging off an emaciated body. He saw the wild uncut hair and the sniveling nose. The man laughed. There was no mirth in it, none at all.

He tried again. "Who are you? What's your name?"

A glob of jet black phlegm landed on the private eye's face.

"You little…"

The man laughed again, wildly now, madly. He wouldn't stop laughing. Nyquist took a step back. He wiped at his face with his jacket sleeve.

Revealed in the light, the room was as dirty and pitiful as the person who lived there: cheap unwashed bedding, a few plates and opened tins of food on the floor. Every surface was covered in dust. Nyquist's eyes returned to the occupant, who had by now fallen back into a state of helpless despair. He was a beetle-like specimen, tall and thin, his limbs sticking out at odd angles, his mouth surrounded by a black and grey goatee beard. His eyes were slightly too close together, the nose aquiline. He might have looked elegant, handsome even, in any other location: here, the sparseness and the filth of the room infected him. He looked more than halfway beaten, by himself, or the world, whichever got the blows in first. Obviously he hadn't eaten properly in a good while.

Nyquist said, "I'm not going to hurt you."

"Why not? What else can be done to me?"

"You live here?"

"Yes."

"How can we talk if I don't know your name?"

"Theodore."

"Go on."

"Theodore William Argyll Lewis. But I used to write under the pen name Louis Argyll. And then later on as Lewis Beaumont."

He looked proud now, as he listed his various names.

"You're an author?"

"I write books that few people read. Science fiction mainly, with a little fantasy on the side, to pay the bills."

Nyquist thought for a moment. "I was directed here, to this apartment. I'm looking for a woman called Zelda."

"Miss Courtland? Of course, yes, that all makes sense."

"You know where she is?"

Lewis hobbled up close. He studied Nyquist's face in great detail, taking in every line and crinkle, every pockmark. "What's wrong?" he asked. "Are you afraid? Or confused?"

Nyquist wouldn't let him have the satisfaction. "I'm looking for Zelda. I'm looking for answers. That's all."

"Oh, but I think you are afraid, John. I think you're wondering who you are, really. Isn't that true?"

Nyquist tried to shrug off the accusation. But Lewis wouldn't let it go. He said, "How's your backstory? Well, let's see. John Henry Nyquist. Late of Dayzone. Your mother dead at an early age, father missing, lost in the mists that plague that city. You were left to drag yourself up alone in a harsh, overbearing world. No wonder you find it so easy to get lost." He didn't give Nyquist any time to respond, adding, "But let me admit, I am at least partially to blame for your current circumstances."

"What did you do?"

"I wrote a book called *The Body Library*."

With this statement, Theodore Lewis seemed to lose even more of his strength. He fell back against the wall and leaned there, one hand pressed to his chest as he tried to control his breathing. With an effort he made his way over to the stool in the corner of the room where he sat down. Nyquist stood near the window and waited for Mr Lewis to speak. He knew it would happen, he knew the story would emerge. The author's lips moved and his tongue clicked at his teeth and he sighed. And then he spoke.

"So you've heard of *The Body Library*, yes? You know of it?"

"I've heard the title mentioned."

"But you're not a literary man, I take it?"

"Words escape me. They keep running away."

Lewis shrugged and settled back on his seat, his back against the wall. For the first time his face took on an air of calm. "That's fine. That's perfectly fine."

"Tell me about the book. Everything you know."

Theodore Lewis's voice took on the soft, awed tone of an arch fetishist describing an object of desire: "*The Body Library* exists as a typewritten manuscript of three hundred and fifty-seven pages, plus numerous offcuts and early drafts. Because of the unique nature of the book, there can only ever be one edition. There were no carbon copies made. Such a thing would be impossible. And this fact alone makes it very precious."

"And you did all this by yourself?"

"Myself and one other, a woman. Ava Beaumont." He paused momentarily at the name, and his voice, when he continued, was heavy with loss. "Ava and I were married. Actually, we still are, but our union is no more, not in any emotional or physical sense. For this reason, she has reverted to the name she was born with."

"How are the book and the tower related?"

"I don't know where to start."

"Try the beginning."

"Such thinking hardly applies to a book of this kind."

"Do what you can."

The writer nodded. He explained, "I was born to be a writer, telling stories from the earliest age possible. Because of this, most people naturally assume that I was born in Defoe."

"The exact center of Storyville?"

"Yes. It's thought that the very best writers come from that place. And that might well be true, but I fell into the world in a very different precinct: Graves. A sorry place, all told. A town where stories end, not begin. No writer would choose to be born there, yet such was my fate. I fell onto a grimy floor, with no known father and only a penniless drudge for a mother."

Nyquist noted how Lewis's style of speech had changed now that he was in storytelling mode. He spoke like an old-fashioned author might.

"From the dregs of existence I have crafted myself. So my stories were never concerned with the well-to-do, or the handsome or the joyful of heart; rather I wrote of and celebrated the destitute, the ugly, the downtrodden and the broken-hearted. These were my chosen subject matters. Now this approach afforded me some remuneration, but not much, for who would choose to read of such things? No, not many." He paused as he remembered a more painful time. "And my life would have continued on such a path were it not for my meeting with Ava Beaumont."

Nyquist waited for him to carry on. But the other man's gaze had drifted elsewhere, far away from this bare, dingy room in a dilapidated high-rise tower.

"I'm sorry," he said. "Sometimes it is painful to think of such matters."

"Was Ava Beaumont a writer as well, like yourself?"

"Not quite." He pursed his lips. "Perhaps you've heard of the Dadaists?"

"Weren't they a music hall act?"

Theodore Lewis smiled, the first such genuine expression he had shown. "No, no. The Dadaists were a group of artists prominent in the first decades of the century. They believed that art had become too academic, too bourgeois, and far too safe and comfortable. In opposition they worshipped chaos, and madness. For instance, they would cut up newspaper articles, photographs, romance novels and the like, and use the fragments to create a new painting or poem. They wanted to shock. They wanted to sever all links to the rational mind, to uncover the reality behind the mask, no matter how dark or hideous it might be."

Theodore Lewis's eyes were lit from within, glowing fiercely as he spoke.

"Ava Beaumont took great influence from them. And although the original Dadaists have long given up on their quest, Ava carried on through the years. Primarily, she's a visual artist, a true creator." His eyes blinked a few times. "She taught me one very important lesson. The truth of a story can only be revealed through violence, by cutting into the text, by wounding or even killing the narrative itself." He smiled again. "Of course, with such words being spoken, how could I not fall in love with her?"

"You said you were married?"

"We were, and we lived in a shared heaven for a time. She already had a child, a young boy, Calvin. I treated him as my own son, I really did. Strange and awkward though he was."

"So you and Ava worked on *The Body Library* together?"

"Yes. My career was going nowhere, my novels failing to sell. Subsequently, I was getting fewer and fewer readers. I was poor and desperate and open to any suggestions, any possibility. And Ava helped me, she taught me the way of the blade. Here. Let me show you."

He stood up and walked the short distance to his bed. He reached under a grubby pillow and pulled out a pair of scissors. He held these out in front of him, the blades reversed, pointing at his own stomach. "These are the scissors she used, her favored instrument. We had a pair each, matching pairs. We started our experiment using my own novels as the raw material, the seventeen books that I've published over the years. We cut into them. We attacked them, we sliced them open!" Lewis's face expressed the violence at work in the act. "We operated on them like highly skilled doctors, or like crazed murderers at their play." His whole body was taken over by a passionate fever. "Soon we'd exhausted the possibility of my books, so we started on other texts, on many others, stealing from here and there, building *The Body Library* word by word, phrase by phrase, page by page. We gouged at the books and slit them open and let the entrails spill out. Ava would do most of the cutting and slicing, while I worked on the fragments, teasing a kind of surreal narrative out of chaos. We made a fine team. Oh, it was exhilarating! It really was, after all the years of following the rules of literature, of being bound and gagged by grammar and syntax."

Nyquist was confused. "What did you hope to accomplish by this?"

"Why, to reinvent the novel, of course." It was a simple statement of fact. "To create a new type of novel more in keeping with the manic, disordered times in which we live."

"I can't imagine anyone reading such a thing."

Lewis explained in a firm voice, "Ava had a saying: *a novel is a labyrinth; a labyrinth is a novel.* That's a truth well hidden behind conventional narrative. But a certain kind of reader, we believed, would relish the challenge of this new book."

Nyquist leaned back against the wall. Theodore Lewis's growing intensity worried him; there was a kind of madness to it.

"So you finished the book. What then?"

"My wife left me, taking Calvin with her."

"And why are you here, in Melville?"

"I have no choice, I'm afraid. I am drawn here. But God knows, her child Calvin avoids me. He lives like a wild animal, darting from one apartment to another. And Ava..."

"What of her?"

"She has been banned from ever stepping foot in this place, until the ritual is complete, and the words are brought fully to life."

"I don't know what you mean by *ritual*."

Lewis didn't provide an explanation. Instead he said, "Ava sits alone in her little room far across the city, and do you know what she does, night after night?"

Nyquist already knew the answer: "She reads from the book."

"That's right. She reads *The Body Library* over and over, keeping the spell alive." He frowned. "You see, we all have our tasks, as given to us by Oberon."

"You make it sound like a grand plan."

"It's a spell. And believe me, Ava will do anything to make that spell complete. Legal or otherwise."

Nyquist lit a cigarette. He watched as Lewis brought his memories to the surface, an action both painful and joyous.

"Ah, that woman. She has such power. She sits like a spider at the center of her web, knowing every strand, every weave, every weft. And with a single twitch she brings one story into contact with another, or else she snips a thread here and there, making stories disappear entirely."

Nyquist pulled the piece of manuscript paper from his pocket. "Your wife gave this to me. It led me to this apartment."

Lewis stared at the page as though it might be a living treasure, a creature of beauty. "Let me see that." He took it from Nyquist's hands. "Ah yes, page nine. Oh, I love this page! It's one of my favorites." The brightened mood soon left him, and his face took on a bitter expression. "*The Body Library* was my life's work. Now it controls me. And it punishes me. And the cruelest of all punishments is that I'm still *real*, still of the world of everyday things. The book hasn't taken me, it hasn't made me one of its own, despite all the work I put in, and the sacrifices I have made in order for it to live and breathe, and for its pages to flutter gently as they prepare for flight. I am bereft!"

He was holding the page in one hand, and the pair of scissors in the other.

Nyquist asked, "Is that blood on the blades?"

"It is."

"Yours?"

"No."

"Ava's?"

"No. You really wouldn't understand, even if I told you."

"Try me."

"Ava has powers beyond any example of normal art. She's either a witch, or a great visionary. I truly believe she added some kind of magical effect to the manuscript, even as I struggled to write the words down."

"What do you mean by magical?"

In response the author opened the twin blades of the scissors and slid page number nine into the angle they made. The blades moved together, slicing cleanly through the sheet of paper.

Blood flowed from both edges of the cut.

As Lewis did this, Nyquist felt a searing pain in his hand. He looked at his palm and saw a straight cut from the base of the thumb to the edge of the third finger. He looked at the diagonal line in shock for one second until the blood came. He looked up at Lewis, seeking explanation, seeing only a cruel delight in the author's eyes.

"I will not write another word," he cried. "Not one!"

Nyquist stepped forward just as the scissors once more flashed and cut at the paper. This time he felt the pain in his midriff and he saw his shirt blossoming stark red on white, and he stopped where he was, in shock.

The scissors were poised along another diagonal.

Nyquist called out: "Wait!"

The blades met a third time. It took Nyquist a moment to find the pain on his body and he brought a hand up to the side of his neck and held it against the cut, hoping to stem the flow. He fell to his knees. The three wounds marked him, the three pains held him like a triangle of points on a graph of skin.

Theodore Lewis came close, brandishing scissors and paper as a threat, a weapon.

"I think one more cut will do it, what do you think? Perhaps the eye? Or the heart?"

Nyquist could hardly speak.

Lewis watched him, his face entirely without passion now. "I really am sorry to do this to you, but you have to understand... I will not write another word for that man, that creature! Do you hear me?"

"I don't..." Nyquist forced the words out. "I don't know what you mean!"

"I will not go back there, into that room. I will not write another word! I have done enough. Tell Mr Oberon that. Tell him!"

"I don't know Oberon. I've never met him. I'm working alone."

"I don't believe you."

Nyquist screamed at him. "I'm looking for Zelda. That's all."

Lewis's face was inches from Nyquist's. "Zelda is elsewhere employed and mustn't be disturbed. No, no at all."

"Where is she?"

"She has taken my job. For this I am grateful." Now

the madness truly took him over. The author danced a few steps back and forth and then around in a circle. "I shall never return to such folly. No, never." And he danced some more, singing gleefully to himself the whole time, the scissors raised in one hand, the paper in the other. "Never, never, never!"

Nyquist took his hand off his neck. He tried to get to his feet, but Lewis hovered near. The scissors gleamed in the moonlight – the blood was fresh on them, the blood of the story itself. He stopped his whirling and he faced Nyquist and he licked his lips and said, "One more cut, one more cut." He was mocking his victim, dancing near and then away, near and away. On the next close swipe, Nyquist reached out suddenly and grabbed the hand that held the cutting instrument.

The two men struggled. They fought over the scissors.

Nyquist should've won this fight easily, but the cuts and the blood loss slowed him down. And Theodore William Argyll Lewis fought like a tiger for his treasured possession. He yapped at Nyquist. He snarled and snapped and the twin blades opened and closed, cutting at air, at clothing, at flesh. In wild defense, Nyquist dragged the other man down to the floor and held on. The author was by now speaking nonstop, spewing forth words and grunts, splutters of spit and broken phrases, whistles and clicks of his tongue, words, words, words tumbling from his red maw of a mouth. Nyquist was fighting with a holy man, a speaker of snake tongues, of ancient languages, a wild witch doctor chanting rhymes and hexes. And word by word the spell had its effect; Nyquist was weakening further, the blood quickening at his trinity of wounds. His grip weakened on the other man.

Lewis took his opportunity. He slipped away, breathing heavily, resting on his hands and knees like a beast of the field, his lips still delivering the Babel of sounds. Drool splattered on the floor beneath him. His neck suddenly stretched tight and his head arched backwards as he sent a whole stream of invectives towards the ceiling. Then his head lowered once more, the horrible voice stilled at last, and his eyes drilled forward at Nyquist. Pure hatred rested within them, and fear, and desperation and insanity, the feelings merging and mingling like the book of death and life along whose course these two men now battled.

They faced each other, both on their hands and knees.

Between them lay the scissors, perfectly aligned with the floorboards, within the pool of light from the window. The gleaming blades were spattered with fresh blood: Nyquist's blood and the blood of words, mingling on the steel. One man moved towards the makeshift weapon, the other also, both at speed. Their hands knocked together, and the scissors spun away a few inches across the floor. But Lewis's hand darted out again and grabbed the scissors and brought them up, not towards Nyquist but to his own flesh, and he jabbed them inwards, the twin blades drawing blood from a wound in his neck, and he drove the scissors on again and again until the central vein was severed, and he drove the blades on further, as far as the handles would allow.

Lewis's strength faltered, his breath also, and the light dimmed in his eyes. The last of the words escaped his mouth as he both cursed and praised Ava and the child and the book and the tower and the person who lay behind it all, the one who controlled and took life as he pleased for his plaything. He cursed and praised Oberon, the king of spells.

Nyquist watched from a few feet away, as Theodore Lewis kept the scissors pressed deep in his own flesh and he waited, waited until the final pump of his heart had drained the life force clean away. At the end a kind of peace came over the man's face. He had freed himself at last from whatever curse had been placed upon him. And then his eyes blackened completely as though filled with ink. His body collapsed and he lay motionless on the floor.

The author was dead.

KEEP WRITING

Nyquist was lying on the floor, exhausted, freezing cold, his hands pressing down firmly on the floor as though by that means he might keep from sliding away. For a moment he had passed out. Now his eyes immediately fixed on one spot – the thick stain of blood on Theodore Lewis's neck, life's brief aftermath. He shifted his attention, following the blood trail from the neck to the floorboards, to join with the pool that had already formed there. The blood had flowed in a straight line out from the pool, and then turned a perfect ninety-degree angle. He couldn't understand how a liquid could do such a thing. He sat up and moved a little closer.

The blood had flowed into one corner of a pattern of recessed grooves cut in the wood, four grooves altogether, marking out the edges of a square shape set in the boards.

It was a trapdoor. A small recessed handle gave access. Nyquist got to his knees and pulled at the handle and the door opened and swung back onto the floor with a bang. He was now looking down into a shaft. There was no light, but he could see the top tier of a set of iron steps. He stood up, breathed easily, and took stock. The blood was drying on his left hand, his midriff and the side of his neck. The wounds were not too deep, and the pain was distant enough for him to ignore it.

"Are we going down there?"

It was Dreylock. He was standing in the doorway of the room, his eyes moving from Lewis's body to the hole in the floor.

"You're liable to get hurt," Nyquist answered.

Dreylock laughed out loud at this. "Any more than I am?"

Nyquist climbed down the steps, reaching a corridor that stretched away into darkness. He groped along it using his hands, one on each wall to guide his way. Turning one corner and then another he soon lost all sense of direction. He was somewhere on the ground floor of the building, that's all he could know. He still felt many miles away from the outside world, and escape, if such a thing was ever possible. He moved on, further down the corridor. A set of stone steps took him down to a lower level. He was now in the basement of the building. He could hear footfalls behind him, the dragging gait of Dreylock.

The walls were closer together and the ceiling lower, and water dripped from cracks in the concrete and brickwork; or perhaps not water, but some darker substance. It might well be ink. Not a trace of light to be seen, yet Nyquist's eyes were slowly adjusting and ahead he could see an open doorway. A heavier blackness lay within it, a blackness that seemed to be breathing, and Nyquist stopped where he was and reached out a hand in trepidation, expecting to feel the warm skin of a beast sitting in the dark. But there was nothing; only space, empty black space. He was about to step through when he heard again the sound of footsteps at his back. He waited for Dreylock to catch up. Somewhere along the way he had lost his walking stick and was now moving forward by will power alone, or just sheer madness. In fact, he looked stronger than ever, empowered by some final hope. The two men looked at each other in the tunnel. Dreylock's face was a mess: the stitches on his face had snapped and his wounds had opened. The blood travelled down the channels of his scars, dripping onto his neck and clothes. Yet his eyes glinted with life.

"Let me go first," he said. "That's all I ask."

"Very well. But be careful."

Thomas Dreylock nodded his thanks and then walked ahead along the darkness of the passage. Nyquist waited a few moments and then he too set off, entering the next room. He was now standing at the edge of a large chamber, roughly circular, lit from above with a soft light. It must've been some kind of storage room at one point, or a wine cellar. There was no sign of Dreylock, but there were three other doorways set in the walls at regular intervals, so he assumed the other man had already moved ahead through one of those. But Nyquist had reached his destination, he saw that straight away. A continuous scraping could be heard. *Scratch, scratch, scratch.* He stepped forward cautiously and spoke in a hushed tone:

"Zelda? Is that you?"

The woman sitting at a small desk at the room's center didn't respond in any way. She carried on with her writing, putting marks on paper. That ancient ritual.

"Zelda? Can you hear me?"

The pen scratched away. Her head was bent down, her hair falling forward to hide the face. The lace blouse she was dressed in, once white, was spotted all over with black marks. Nyquist called to her again and this time she reacted, making a slight movement of her head, setting the long strands of blonde hair swinging. He saw that this too was stained black in many places. It was ink, he saw that now. Zelda bent down and filled her pen from a kind of church font at her side; it was filled to the brim with midnight's ink. He saw that the font was fed by a series of pipes that ran across the floor, each flowing with the same black substance, an endless supply. And she needed such quantity, she really did, for the entire floor at her feet was filled with discarded sheets of paper, hundreds of them, or thousands – Nyquist could not possibly estimate how many – and every single one of them filled to the margins with tiny scrawled handwriting, the lines of script so close together that hardly any white surface could be seen.

Zelda finished the page she was working on and let it slide to the floor. The papers whispered against each other as this new arrival settled into place. Many of them had fallen into the channels and were soaking up the ink, becoming eclipsed. It mattered little, the words were being written one by one and what happened to the pages after they were filled up was of little or no importance.

Zelda lived only for that point where the pen's metal nib bit into the paper.

Scratch, scratch, scratch.

Nyquist walked over to the desk, where he read the lines of text that were currently being written:

He looks at the words that Zelda is writing and he touches her on the shoulder and she stops her work and turns and look at him...

Nyquist did exactly that; he had no choice. He touched Zelda Courtland on the shoulder and she stopped her action and looked up at him. They were, the both of them, described and rendered and brought to life by the words as written, each the subject and each the object of the same sentence.

Black ink dripped from the end of the nib, forming a small pool on the paper.

Not a sound was heard in the chamber.

Zelda's hands were raw from the act of writing, and her lips were parched, her skin pallid, her demeanor weak and her breathing shallow and drawn. Every visible part of her body and clothes was speckled with the ink. Nyquist's heart almost broke from the pain of seeing her like this. Yet her eyes were still lively, still bright. And she spoke to him in a quiet voice: "On the edge of town where the stories flow away, they stand alone..." At first he didn't understand what she was saying, and then entirely unbidden he started to join in, speaking the verse with her although he had neither heard it nor read it before this night, he was sure of that. They spoke as one.

They stand alone,
a man and a woman
covered in silence.

They spoke with one voice, and each word triggered a memory.

They walk alone
with only one word
left unspoken between them
one word unwritten.

In his mind a story was forming: another life, another world.

Until, on the border
where one breath meets another
a story begins in a kiss –
here, on the edge of town
where the words flow away.

And by the time the last line of the poem had faded, Nyquist knew the truth. He knew that his other self was lying in a bed, desperately ill, perhaps dying, damaged from a fall, infected by a virus of words, his mind and body taken over by the novel known as *The Body Library*. He knew also that Bella Monroe was sitting at his bedside, his narrative officer, talking to him, nursing him.

"I sent you a message," Zelda asked. "But I wasn't sure if it got through."

"Yes. I saw it on my typewriter."

"I wanted to put an X in the end, but I couldn't manage it."

"I know. That letter's broken."

Yes, down to the last detail he saw the truth as it was written, as it was lived.

Zelda's eyes closed and opened again and she looked at him and a smile came to her, and she said, "Johnny", and his heart leapt. She stood up from her seat and he took her in his arms, and for a moment they held each other's gaze. And in that moment Nyquist received another truth, a truth from the other side: this woman was dead. He had seen Zelda Courtland's body lying on a slab in the morgue. He had identified her for the police, and yet here she was, or a semblance of her. Alive. Yes, alive. Not fully, but as much as he was. Two equals. He struggled to speak, to express his feelings for her. But Zelda's attention was already drifting away, back to the task she'd been set: the pen, the paper, and the endless stream of words.

He held onto her. "Zelda, come away with me."

"I can't leave this room, I can't. He would kill me."

"Who would? Tell me."

"Oberon."

It seemed as though she might carry on from there and explain the spell she was under, but her writing hand started to twitch. She sat down and applied pen to paper.

"Zelda?"

She paid him no mind, but carried on with her work, the ink splashing on the paper as the lines of text appeared. Nyquist tried to get her to stop, but every action only caused the pen to dig deeper into the page, until the words almost broke the surface. He dared to look at the page, expecting to see Zelda locked in a description of the meeting that had just taken place between them, but she had already moved on, recording every single thing that was happening in the building.

And again Sebastian Vaughn walks out into the corridor to feed his cat, every night the same, the same cat every night, several times, or a different cat of identical stripe and coloring, it's impossible to tell. One cat many times, feeding. Or many cats each fed once only, an infinitude of cats, who can tell? But Sebastian loves this animal. The cat is his only friend. Sebastian lives alone in apartment 44. Sebastian lives alone except for the cat, Mr Peterson Smythe the Third, who lives in the corridor. This is the cat's name, Peterson Smythe the...

This is the job that Theodore Lewis used to do; now Zelda had taken over.

It was too painful to witness.

"Zelda! Stop!"

He reached for her but she shrugged him off and pushed his hand away violently. Her head was bowed down, her eyes fixed on the moving nib, her fingers flexed tight around the barrel of the pen. *Scratch, scratch, scratch, scratch.* Nyquist could do very little, without inflicting damage on her. The nib ran dry once again. Zelda dipped the barrel of the pen into the font to refill it. Nyquist used this small respite to make one last try; he whispered to her, cajoling her to come away with him. Zelda ignored him. The pen was now refilled and she started to write once more, the words flowing out endlessly across the page. In this way life in the tower block was recorded, each moment as it passed, each thought, each feeling, each and every action and reaction, the various characters moving here and there. The cat was fed and Mr Vaughn went back into his apartment, and so it went on, and Nyquist stood there, helpless, helpless.

A shadow moved in the chamber.

It was the boy, Calvin. He stepped forward. "Zelda won't leave here," he said. "How can she? Like yourself and all others brought here, she is under orders. There is no escaping it, I'm afraid."

"Why is she doing this?" Nyquist asked.

"All things must be chronicled. All the changes to the different stories, as they happen. Or else they vanish forever."

"But there's no meaning to it."

"None that you might understand." The boy smiled and tilted his head slightly. "But my grandfather has his needs. He desires people, characters, his *players* as he calls them, to move around, to keep him occupied in his long sleep." Calvin pointed towards Zelda. "The game is played, each with their parts."

"For what purpose?"

"Why, for the greatest purpose. Life, itself."

Nyquist thought about what this might mean. "Your grandfather is dying?"

"Oh, long dead, I'm afraid. Long, long dead." The boy's smile turned to a frown. "I call him grandfather only as a courtesy. His real lineage would bore you. You see, in reality he's my great great, great, great..."

"Save your words for later, kid, you might need them."

Calvin paused in mid-sentence.

Zelda wrote on and on. Ink dripped from the pen.

Scratch, scratch...

The boy's lips came together in a sullen pout. "There's no need to be so..."

"So what?"

"There's no need to tell me off." And suddenly the boy looked like a child, nothing more, all of his precociousness gone. He was small and alone and more than a little afraid.

"I need to see your grandfather."

"That can happen," Calvin replied. "Yes, why not." And here the smile returned in glee at such prospects. "After all, that's why you're here."

He guided the way to one of the doorways. A short passage led to the main part of the apartment block's basement, a much larger chamber. It only took one step into the lighted space for Nyquist to know immediately: he had been here before. The memories returned with a shock of anguish. In this room he had first fallen into the book's embrace.

Most of all he remembered the large, circular pool of ink that lay at the room's center. He remembered the shine of its surface, its texture and its pull on his eyes. He remembered the stones that lined it, set in the packed earth of the basement floor. Even now he felt drawn to the edge, and felt an intense desire to submerge himself within its black, unseeable depths. It drew him forth. It was a mirror in which he saw himself truly, both as he was a week or so ago – a man lost in a city that he could barely understand, chasing stories that never included him – and as he was now, changed utterly, a man not of the world, but of a book, a man of papery skin, of words in the blood, a man of fiction.

He remembered most of all the moment of change.

ONCE UPON A TIME

Nyquist lay in his bed, perfectly still, incapable of a single movement, both asleep and not asleep. He saw almost everything that took place in the Melville Tower; he heard most of what was being said by his fictional self and the various people he met on his way. He saw that Zelda was alive, and he longed to reach out for her, he longed for her to become real once more. He longed to be joined to her story once more, and for that story to carry on.

Once upon a time...

Now he remembered. He saw clearly the story of the last week, all the events that had brought him to this point. He saw clearly his first visit to Melville Five. He saw himself standing at the edge of the pool of ink, led there by the boy, Calvin. Zelda stood nearby, likewise hypnotized, bound by the spell. Nyquist looked around, taking in each detail: the rough stone walls, the patches of damp, the water dripping down from the ceiling pipes, the terrible smell of decay, of rotten flesh, of mildew, the alphabugs buzzing around their clay and twig nest in the lower trunk of the tree.

The tree. The one tree, the world tree. The word tree.

Once upon a time a man called Nyquist was led into an underground chamber. Here he saw the great tree of words, and the old king who ruled this realm.

Here the vast tangled roots of the building's tree grew up from the earth floor. Nyquist felt he was looking into the heart of the world itself: the fungal growths, the peeling bark, the wood rotting away, the roots, knotted together like some magical diagram, a mathematical equation of such complexity it was impossible to unravel, each tendril dark and clotted with further darkness in between, the absolute absence of light, yet filled with innumerable insects sparkling as they slithered: worms, bugs, flies, caterpillars, moths, all moving constantly like the thoughts in a brain. So that was it, the tree was the living brain of the tower, the root of all stories. Nyquist felt his own mind was entangled with the tree's nature: like Odin witnessing the letters of the runic alphabet in the roots of Yggdrasil, he too saw language at work, being formed and unformed amid the triple states of plant, insect and human.

A man was hanging from the tree.

His feet were held in leather straps nailed to the trunk high up near the cellar's ceiling, and his body was suspended upside down so that his head lay a few feet above the pool of ink. His arms hung down further, actually entering the pool, with both hands dipping into the ink completely, up to the forearms. The man's hair was yards long: Nyquist imagined it had been left to grow untamed for many years or decades or centuries, it was impossible to tell. Yet the thick insect-riddled strands of hair were black, jet black, the same color as the ink into which they sank at their lowest reach.

Once upon a time a man called Nyquist looked into a pool of ink, and fell into it, drawn by forces he could barely understand.

Nyquist moved a little closer, skimming the curved

edge of the pool. Some of the tree roots, like the man's arms and his hair, also dipped into the liquid. Everything in this place was feeding or being fed by the ink. Yet the upside-down man himself was rotten to the core: his skin shriveled and grey and his face and upper chest lined with folds of desiccated flesh. The clothes he wore were as old as he was and seemed to have fused with his skin; skin and cloth were made of the same leathery material. Where tree, flesh, clothes began and ended was impossible to discern. In fact, Oberon looked to be long dead. Yet his eyes were open and young and vibrant in their aspect, and they looked at Nyquist from the depths of the old man's ancient face, and they sparkled with life's central pulse. And from those eyes Nyquist received a message, not of words, but of impulse, the urge to obey, to follow the single pathway chosen for him. He did so, by turning back to the edge of the pool. Without a single thought he walked down a series of stone steps, into the ink, until his body was covered up to the neck. Zelda joined him, compelled by the same magic. There was a gentle pulling motion from below, from the liquid itself, and now his head sank beneath the surface. He was floating quite peacefully, suspended, still conscious, still breathing easily. He wasn't drowning. No, in fact the opposite: the ink was in some way giving him life, adding something to him, even as it took away an equal amount. Here was the story in its perfect moment; the long, tangled plot of his life up to then was held in the balance. Everything slowed. Everything was silence. He was aware of Zelda's body floating alongside his own, some few feet away. She too was at peace. He was aware of long strands of human hair waving slowly like fronds in the ink not too far away. He saw the old man's two hands submerged up to the wrists, glowing a spectral white, and he saw the deep cuts on each wrist. He saw the blood flowing continuously from the wound in the right hand, into the pool; and in exchange the ink entering the old man's body at the left-hand wound. Nyquist was aware, intensely, of the beauty of this system, how the story gave blood to life, and how life gave ink to story, and so it was and so it would ever be. At which point the book took hold of him. He was now inside the Library of Bodies. He was being read, and written upon, simultaneously. Words were given to him, words taken away. His own story taken, the ink's story given to him, infecting him.

Two beginnings, two endings.

Once upon a time a man stepped into a pool of black ink and his body was written and written again, over and over, until he became little more than the words that told his story.

And he rose up from the pool, suddenly gasping for air, for a good clean breath, knowing that he'd nearly drowned, nearly died. Zelda was there as well, as distressed as he was. The two of them floundered in the liquid, seeking a foothold on the steps. They climbed out, both shivering, holding each other for comfort. The man in the tree watched them through his unblinking eyes. Nyquist felt dizzy. The world belonged not to himself, but to the spirit of the building. The ink flowed off his body and clothes as mercury might off a looking glass, until he was perfectly dry. He separated from Zelda a little and turned back to gaze at the pool's surface. It lay perfectly still, poised, shining black, as flat and seemingly as solid as a slab of basalt. He couldn't believe that he'd been submerged there. He stared at the ink, and the ink spoke in silence to him. The liquid moved slightly. The smallest possible tide affected it, the moon's power almost lost down here in the basement of this strange tower. The ink shimmered. It glowed. Nyquist's eyes were drawn to it, held by it. The ink stared back at him and within its black depths he saw a figure and then one more, two bodies floating just beneath the surface, as he and Zelda had been, just a minute or so before. The two figures took on form and shape and features, even as he watched, even as Zelda came to stand at his side, to watch with him, as the two figures rose and broke through the ink's surface and floated there suspended: two bodies, male and female perfectly formed. In mirror-fashion he watched his own face take shape on this other body, as Zelda's features took over the female counterpart.

Fiction, Non-Fiction. He now occupied both states, simultaneously.

Nyquist felt himself weakened as he watched his reflection take on solid flesh and rise from the ink. He backed away from his living image in terror.

The boy Calvin approached. "It's time to go. The city awaits you."

Nyquist and Zelda had no option but to follow him, caught as they were in his charms. The last of the binding spell took them back up the stairs to the ground floor and from there to the tower's entranceway, and the very last traces of the spell got them as far as the limit of the tower's light, where Nyquist came to his senses and he fell and kept on falling and landed easily on a patch of dried glass and rolled over to break his fall. Confused, he struggled to his feet, only just keeping his balance, and wondering how on earth he had gotten here. His mind was a blank. He looked across the circle of towers and saw a woman walking away, her back to him. She was the only other person in sight. A single word entered his mind; the woman's name: *Zelda*. She glanced back and made a gesture, a signal of some kind, a wave. And then she turned and moved further on, into the shadows.

He was alone. It was like this sometimes, he thought: two people have walked the same story path for a short while, and then parted. *That should be enough. Surely, that was enough. Let it be enough...*

Nyquist lay in the darkness of his coma and thought of these events, these feelings, at last with full knowledge of what had taken place in the tower at Melville, and his lips parted slightly. A single word escaped the silence.

Once...

The rest of his body was still paralyzed; only his lips were moving. But for the first time in all that long night he had spoken, a gasp more than a word, a primitive utterance wrenched from deep within, from that veiled, sultry part of the mind where words are born. He tried it again, a little louder this time, even though it pained him.

Once upon...

He took in the world he could see, the tiny portion of the ward, the ceiling above, the lights blinking on the monitors. He was lying in a bed in a room in Kafka Court with Bella Monroe at his side. And he saw Monroe move towards him, towards his face. He saw her startled eyes, the movement of her lips: she was speaking to him.

"Nyquist! What is it? What did you say?"

Once upon a time...

Four words. It was all he could manage. A beginning.

He saw Monroe's hand moving on his face. Her touch. For the barest moment he could feel her touch on his skin, and then it drifted away once more. He tried to move his own hand in response, a single finger. It was no good. He tried to blink. He couldn't do it. Not yet. But he had to keep trying.

"John, I'm here. I'm listening."

He heard Bella Monroe calling to him, this simple admittance. A promise. *I'm listening.* It gave him hope. Here in the dark, in the stillness, someone is listening. It gave him hope and strength and he sank back into his mind and saw the world once more through his other self's eyes. He saw the basement of Melville Five. He gazed once more into midnight's ink.

WORDS UNWRITTEN

Nyquist drew his sight away from the ink. Within these depths he had split apart from his purely physical self and become a separate entity, a fictional form given body and blood and heat and life and soul by the power of the book. Everything he thought of as life had started here, just a few days ago.

Once upon a time: this was his place of birth.

Thomas Dreylock was kneeling on the ground on the other side of the pool, with his head lowered and his hands raised to cup his face. It was a pitiful gesture; all the anger had left him, leaving only this need, this wordless prayer. It did little good. The blood from his face dribbled through his fingers, quickly soaking into the earth floor.

Nyquist walked over to the giant tangled roots of the word tree and to the man who hung upside down within them, the dead man. It was their second meeting. Yet the sight still shocked him: the dried-up flesh, the exposed bones, the tattered and mummified clothing. By far the eyes were the worst, the only living thing in the entire body.

The insects made a constant buzzing and chittering sound as they slithered and crawled over the bark of the tree and the skin of Oberon.

Nyquist spoke aloud his first thought: "Will you let Zelda go?"

There was no visible reaction, not even a flicker of the eyelids, and his tongue lay dead in the silence of his closed mouth.

Nyquist turned to the boy. "What does he want? Tell me what he wants."

Calvin answered simply: "My grandfather needs your story."

"I've given it to him, already. He's stolen it."

"No. Not quite."

"He's taken everything!"

"One tiny thing remains."

"One thing?"

"You kept it hidden away."

"There's nothing else. I promise you."

"One thing. One tiny thing only."

Nyquist looked at Calvin. He looked at the man in the tree, at the pool of ink, at poor Dreylock. The whole chamber – with its stench of damp and rot, its haze of dust, the swarms of insects, and the constant rustling papery noise of the building, even the reader's faraway voice bringing it all to life, even the haze and hum of his own head – all conspired against him. He cried out, "There is nothing!"

Calvin looked at him with kindness. "You left something behind in the shadows. One part of your story. Oberon can sense it, hidden away. Something your father said to you."

"My father?" The word surprised Nyquist. "I can't remember." He was desperate now. He turned to the man in the tree and cried out, "There's nothing. Nothing at all."

But Calvin persisted. "One thing."

"No."

"Hidden away."

"Stop it! Be quiet."

But Calvin would not be silenced. He sulked and whimpered, "I only want to please Oberon, can't you see that?" His eyes sparkled with need. "I want him to look kindly on me, and to treat me as his favorite."

Nyquist saw the truth of this, but didn't know how to respond. He could only say again, so quiet as to not be heard:

There is nothing.

Calvin's expression darkened and his voice took on its older aspect. "Speak only of the missing story, and whatever you want is yours."

Nyquist stepped away from the tree, the pool, the boy. He saw the entranceway that led to the smaller chamber: he pictured Zelda at her neverending task, still caught in the spell that forced her to write down and record all of the tower's happenings, including this one, his struggle to find that part of himself that was hidden, hidden, hidden away – and in the space of a single thought he was back there again, a child of eight years, back in his home after his father had walked away into the mist, lost forever...

Nyquist hesitated. The pool of darkness glimmered at his feet.

"What is it?" Calvin asked. "Can you remember something?"

"Yes."

"Really?"

"Yes, it's clear now."

"Are you sure? Look closer. What do you see?"

Nyquist dismissed the boy with a wave, but the thought remained, sharp, in focus. He knew what was needed. He saw it plainly.

Calvin clung to the hope. "Speak. Speak again," he pleaded. "Speak on. More, more of the story, all of it. Speak!"

Nyquist could hear the rustling of the leaves from the whole of the tree as it reached up through the seventeen storeys of the building, up to the penthouse, the roof, where it blossomed into the night sky.

"I don't know how to say it."

"Not in words. Speak direct!"

The dead man in the tree stared at Nyquist with his dead eyes, the pool glistened, and Dreylock moaned from where he knelt on the packed earth, his ravaged face reflected in the pitch-black ink. Seeing these things as though for the first time, a change came over Nyquist, a calmness. He knew now what he had to do. And it wasn't about escaping, not at all.

He said at last, "In exchange then, but not for Zelda."

Calvin swayed back and forth. "No? What then, what do you want? Say it."

Nyquist skirted the pool's edge until he reached Dreylock and he held out his arms, taking the other man's hands in his, raising him to his feet. He didn't need to speak, not now. Everyone there knew what he wanted. He led Dreylock into the pool and allowed the ink to take the other man's body into its hold: Dreylock was floating easily, as Nyquist stood upright with his feet planted firmly on the bottom of the pool. And then he ducked down, taking Dreylock with him. The ink covered his clothes, his body, his face. Once more, for the second time in his life, Nyquist was submerged in this liquid, but this time he was fully aware of where he was and what he was doing, or at least trying to do. Dreylock struggled in his arms, but Nyquist calmed him and the ink washed over them both equally as they moved into a deeper part of the pool, and now Nyquist was floating too, alongside the other man.

All was darkness, all silence. All stillness.

Dreylock's body glowed with a soft, silvery blue light within the blackness.

Nyquist could hardly feel himself breathing. Not a thing in the world existed but for the two of them, in this place and this time. No more stories, no tales to tell, no consequences of action on plot or character. Only the ink itself, midnight's blood, as it made its circular route from the sliced wrists of the old man in his tree, down into the pool and around, through Dreylock's body, across his damaged face and flesh. And suddenly Dreylock tensed, and then relaxed, and Nyquist saw the ink at work, he saw the curing of the wounds, the skin patching itself together. Slowly, slowly, the scars merging into new flesh, the face reforming. Here and only here, on this one particular page of *The Body Library,* was the story remade, the pieces bound back together. With a shock, Dreylock lurched upwards, breaking the surface of the ink pool, reaching for breath and life with every fiber of his being.

But Nyquist waited. He waited until the pool had settled again and the surface reformed into its perfect mirror, upwards and below. His eyes closed, and he lay perfectly still, at rest, suspended within the blackness. He had no way of knowing which direction he was facing; all that mattered was the act of being, of being written, and of being read, one word feeding another. His whole life story was happening, happening again in the present, and there he was suddenly, back again, eight years and ten months old, coming home to the cold and empty house after his father had walked away, leaving young Nyquist entirely alone in life.

He saw the letter on the mantelpiece, the words inscribed on the envelope.

For my son.

He reached out and opened the envelope and read again for the second time in his life those first lines, written by his father all those many years ago.

Dear child, I don't expect you to understand this.

And this time he carried on.

In the endless night of stories, in the tower of stories, in the basement where stories are made and unmade, in the pool of ink from which all the stories flower, within the blood of Oberon himself, where stories flow back and forth from the heart, John Henry Nyquist carried on reading. He moved on from those first lines and the entire letter was seen by him, read by him, those words he had never dared to read, a father's final message to his son, the words he had torn into pieces and eaten and swallowed – he saw them clearly, these hidden lines that lay inside his body, never lost, never faded, not quite. The words that had always rested inside him in wait perhaps for this very moment.

He breathed in.

He breathed out.

The ink entered his mouth and coated his tongue.

He breathed in and he breathed out and those faraway words were conjured from his body and spoken aloud.

Ever since your mother died I have lived in such pain that I can hardly move without thinking of her. I no longer have any true understanding of life. Everything is darkened by her loss. My son, I know you won't understand this, not yet, not in your tender years, but I fear for my life. I fear that I may do something terrible, taking a step I can never come back from. I cannot say the words, they would hurt you so. All I can do is search for your mother's ghost. Nothing else will comfort me.

Please, John, please forgive me.

I will come back for you one day, and we shall all be as one again, a family.

I promise.

Your loving father, George.

Now the words left Nyquist's body and he watched with fascination as they issued from his parted lips, each separate word like a creature in the black ink, each letter illuminated in yellow or electric blue. They swam around his body and then formed into a pattern, and moved off together seeking out the open wounds in the white hands that held themselves in the pool a few feet away, the old man's hands. Nyquist saw his father's words entering at both wounds. It was that simple: the words were being read by Oberon's body.

And suddenly Nyquist was drowning, he couldn't breathe, the ink was in his mouth, his throat, his lungs, and his hands splashed and reached out desperately for purchase, for a ridge or a ledge to cling to. In the end it was a tree root that saved him, and he clambered up hand over hand until the clean black surface of the pool parted all around him, and he dragged in air, biting cold clean air, glad to his soul for the life it held.

He collapsed onto the packed earth beside the pool and lay there, breathing heavily. He could see the ceiling of the chamber, the patches of moss and mold on the stonework, the swarms of bugs that flew around. His heart raced and lights pulsed in his eyes.

After a moment he sat up and saw that Dreylock was leaning against the wall, at peace now, his hands touching at the scars that were still bonding and healing on his face. His eyes took in Nyquist and his expression hardly changed, but Nyquist could sense things beyond words, about all they had been through together: Dreylock was grateful. And Nyquist shared the feeling, because of the things he had learned about himself this night. He felt lighter on his feet as he stood up. Calvin was standing near the tree, looking up at his great ancestor, the man who stirred now in the roots and branches. The insects were making merry, the leaves rustled and murmured and the bark cracked and crackled and shuddered with new growth, with tiny stems of green wood. Already a red flower was seen amid the rot. And the old man stirred as well, his eyes brimming with tears and his hands and legs twitching, as the roots split open to let him free.

Nyquist had no desire to see the outcome of this process. He made his way back down the corridor to find Zelda. But the smaller chamber was empty, the desk and chair vacant. Sheets of paper were strewn all around. The ink overflowed the font and ran freely across the stone floor, seeking new words to write – but there were none. Zelda had vanished.

Nyquist made his way back through the underground tunnels, following the traces of ink on the walls. He pictured Zelda's hands leaving these marks as she steadied herself, seeking direction in the gloom. Ahead, a grey light shone. He walked towards it and came to the metal steps that led upwards into Theodore Lewis's apartment. The author's body still lay on the floor, another victim of this tower and its endless stories. The sliced and scattered pieces of page number nine were useless now.

Nyquist called out Zelda's name, but there was no answer.

He walked out into the first floor corridor. This too was empty. But as he made his way towards the elevator he could hear whispers from behind every door. These sounds grew louder as he walked along, until a tumult of voices reached him. He realized that the voices were not only coming from behind these doors, but from every apartment in the building, top to bottom, and from the air itself, from all around him. The building was speaking aloud. The voices followed him into the elevator car. It was quite easy now, easy to reach the ground floor. The spell was weakening. He walked out through the front entranceway.

At last he was free of the Melville Tower.

And he wasn't the only one: a good number of the other residents were crowded on the concrete forecourt, talking to each other or standing in silence. Nyquist recognized a number of faces among them, people he had met on his travels through the corridors and apartments. He saw the children from apartment 37, the ones who had sung and prayed around the word tree. He saw Alice from apartment 14, her face still haunted by the voices she was hearing in her head. He saw Sam Bradshaw from apartment 21, the cartographer of the building. Others were there as well, strangers to him, yet he felt he knew them all. Amber, Vito, Lionel, Vaughn. Some were scared, some worried, some exultant. Yet none of them dared to move any further. Instead they stared out into the night, into the darkness that lay beyond the glow of the forecourt's lamp. This was their limit, the borderline of their world. One of them, a teenage boy, was testing his courage, daring himself to take a step outside of the lamp's circle of light. But he never quite made it; every time he retreated back inside the safety zone. Nyquist recognized the boy: it was Benedict, the eldest of the worshippers. Nyquist nudged through the crowd and spoke to the teenager.

"What's happening? Why is everyone here?"

"There's a story going round," he said, "that we can leave now. Haven't you heard?"

"No."

"They say the old king has awoken. Our job here is done. He won't need us anymore."

Nyquist looked out to the circle of dimly lit space in the center of the ring of high-rises. All the windows in the other blocks were dark.

"Why don't you leave, then?" he asked.

"We're all scared. Maybe we'll die, once we leave the confines." The fear was real, written on the kid's face like a horror story. "And anyway," he continued, "we're waiting to see what happens."

"How do you mean?"

"To see what happens to the woman. If she'll live or not."

Nyquist had a bad feeling as he followed Benedict's gesture: a lone figure was walking slowly away from the tower. And he knew in the darkness of his heart that it was Zelda, that she was making her escape. He also knew that she was in danger, that her life was entirely held together by the building and its powers. Without the reader, without the author, without Oberon and Calvin and all the other spirits of the tower, what would become of her? And the fact that her true physical self was dead also added to his worry.

"Zelda! Zelda!" Nyquist's voice was lost in the night, carried away by the wind. Yet he kept on: "Zelda! Come back. Turn back! Zelda!"

Now the other people gathered around him joined in with their own calls.

"Zelda. Come back! Zelda, come back to us."

It was no use: the figure was already merging into the shadows. Nyquist had no choice. He stepped out of the light, into the grey expanse. He felt his shoes on the gravel path beyond the concrete of the forecourt. He felt grass and earth beneath his feet as he left the pathway, taking the shortest route across the central area. The other high-rises rose up on all sides like evil giants from one of the fairy stories his mother had read to him. He called again, hearing in response only the echoes of Zelda's name caught between the tower blocks.

The further away from the tower he walked, the more the details of his other life came to him, until it was all there in his mind: the case that had led him to the tower in the first place, all the different people he had met on the way – landlords, council workers, prostitutes, police officers. He felt again the sickening fear of his plunge from the rooftop, he remembered the swarm of words attacking him in the old, abandoned library; he saw it all. And he drew courage from this knowledge. He moved on until he saw her again, a figure in the shadows.

"Zelda! Zelda, wait for me!"

She was leaving the circular area, heading for Calvino Road. Once she crossed that limit, the city would engulf her in its twisted, darkened streets and she'd be lost to him, lost forever. Nyquist started to run. His heart was pounding now, and he felt the sweat break out on his brow, and his back, inside his shirt. Everything he knew, everything he had learned in the last few days, in the two bodies he currently occupied, fictional and otherwise, everything told him that he had to stop her. No, not that: he had to reach her. That was it! He had to do as she did, he had to be where she was. This was his story: whatever her fate was, his would be as well. And so he ran faster than ever. He tripped and nearly fell over a loose paving slab, but righted himself and hurried on, reaching the main road. Here he came to rest, for Zelda had stopped also. She was standing alone, but some distance away, across a patch of land where a number of buildings had been demolished, another woman was seen. Nyquist recognized her. Her name was Gabrielle, one of the prostitutes he had spoken to while seeking Zelda's killer. She was the one who claimed to have precognition of events that happened on the next page of life. Had this knowledge drawn her here, to help Zelda escape the tower?

There was a car parked nearby with its headlights on, turning the area into a theatre set. Another woman was sitting in the driver's seat.

Now Gabrielle waved to Zelda, calling her name loudly.

Nyquist called to her as well, and for an absurd moment he felt he was in conflict with this other woman, each seeking possession.

Zelda, Zelda, Zelda, Zelda…

The two worlds cried out to her: one real, the other a story.

One of them appealed more than another. Nyquist couldn't believe it; she was moving towards him. Zelda was walking back across Calvino Road. She was more character than flesh, and the character desired life. And he and she – two characters together – would live on together, they would make that happen.

Bathed in the glow of the headlamps, Zelda looked almost spectral, illuminated from within. She ignored the cries of Gabrielle; instead she came to Nyquist and embraced him. "Quickly," he said. "We have to get back." They set off, moving at a pace towards the Melville high-rises, towards tower five. A swarm of alphabugs flew ahead of them, lighting the way. Nyquist could see the group of residents on the forecourt: one of them made a gesture, a wave.

They were halfway across the central area when he felt Zelda slowing at his side.

"Come on, keep going! We're nearly there."

"I can't," she answered. "Something's wrong."

"What is it?"

But this time she didn't answer. She'd stopped completely. Nyquist did the same, he had no choice. "Zelda..." His voice trailed off as he saw what was happening to her.

It started on her face, in her hair, her clothes, her fingertips. They were breaking apart, crumbling away. In tiny pieces at first, then larger ones. And he saw that inside her body, in the fissures that were now appearing in her skin, the same process was at work. He saw the letters, the words, the phrases taken from the book, the sentences from *The Body Library*; this was her true nature, and without the tower's spell Zelda was nothing more than a series of words arranged in a certain manner. Nothing more.

One last time he tried to drag her along.

She couldn't move. There was no strength left in her.

So Nyquist stood there with her, and he held her tightly. He put his arms around her and tried to hold her body together, to keep the words from cracking apart, the sentences from breaking in two. It was no good. Her body fragmented. There was no pain, no expression on her face other than a sense of loss, and then even more than that: acceptance.

Now she was only words and letters in the air, caught for a few moments in the shape of a woman, a clouded shape that the alphabugs fluttered around and through, their darts of light like the final sparks of her soul.

And then the wind took her away from his arms.

Nyquist was alone.

Alone.

Alone in the story.

He took a few steps back towards Melville Five, towards the lighted forecourt and the people who stood there, watching him, waving to him, urging him to return.

The tower was his proper place, and these were his true brothers and sisters, fictionals, born of the word.

But then he stopped and he knelt to the ground, his hands covering his face. He felt like crying out, howling, but no sound would come: his mouth was empty.

Nothing more could be said.

And he waited. He waited until the process started in his own body. Here, at the center of the five towers, on this lonely, darkened, weed-strewn patch of ground in Storyville, he waited as his own body was taken back, into the book, into the library, into words alone. And then he could speak, he could speak to the air, to the city, to the life he had lost and the life he had gained or nearly so, and the love he'd held in his arms for so short a time, and he spoke aloud for the night to hear, and for anyone who might care to read these scattered words at some future date, yes, he told the story of his body as it broke apart, word by word, letter by letter, speck by speck, dust to dust.

PART FIVE
451 BRADBURY AVENUE

OUT OF SLEEP

He moved through one story after another, some from his life, some from lives he might yet live, or from lives he might already be living and not know about. Through the words of the sky he fell, through the pages, the tumbling, rustling pages; through a cloud of words he fell, through the rain that looked like ink spilling down on blue-grey paper. For the second time that day he fell and kept on falling until at last he landed in the book of his own flesh and lay there, scarcely breathing, looking out through his eyes as if he were hiding inside himself. He could see Bella Monroe leaning over him, he could hear the medical equipment bleeping and pinging, he could feel the tubes that entered his arms, feeding him, and taking from him all he didn't need. And most of all he could feel the letters moving in his body, the blood-red language of his flesh, the story of his body being written and rewritten, moment to moment to moment, and he clawed his way up through the layers of sleep and dream until his voice spilled over from his lips.

Bella...

"Yes, it's me," Monroe said. "Can you hear me? John? Did you speak?"

He tried to sit up in the bed but the various sheets, tubes

and wires held him back.

"Stay there, don't try to move." Monroe pushed him down gently. "I'll get the doctor."

"No, no, there's nothing wrong with me. I need to..."

But he couldn't for the life of him remember what it was he needed to do. On the edge of waking it had all seemed so clear, but now it drifted away, dreamlike.

"Bella, yes, fetch the doctor. Go on."

She nodded at him and smiled. "It's good to have you back."

The moment she'd left the room he ripped out the tubes from his arms and stomach and slipped away from the bed sheets. At first he could hardly walk, he had to cling to the bed for support. From there he stumbled over to a wall cupboard, where he found his clothes. He took off the hospital gown and started to get dressed. Blood was flowing from the openings where the tubes had entered, but he ignored this for now. It seemed to matter little, that he was losing vital fluid, when the words covered his body. They would keep him alive, at least for the time being. Every portion of him was covered, ever shifting, ever moving. What the hell was being spelled out? A narrative of some kind, but he had no clue as to its meaning, or what it might yet hold. But he knew one thing for certain: he was nearing the end of it. And then Zelda's face came to him: those final moments when her body had flowed away into words, pure language, lost, lost forever.

He was almost dressed by the time Monroe returned, with the council's chief medical officer in tow, alongside Overseer K. Nyquist pushed past them all without saying a word, and he took to the corridor, a long white pristine environment somewhere below the Grand Hall in Kafka Court.

Monroe shouted his name and came running after him.

"They don't want you to go, John."

"To hell with them!"

"It's not safe."

"It's not safe anywhere, that's a fact."

He turned to walk on but then stopped. He was suddenly tired, racked to his core by the long immobile hours in bed, and the events that had taken place in his mind during that sleep, the story of the night in the high-rise and all it contained.

"Bella, I need you to drive me. Will you do that?"

"Of course. Where to?"

He thought for a moment and then answered: "Where it all started."

"Melville Towers?"

"No, not there. The real beginning."

"Where? Where are we going?"

But Nyquist was already walking away.

A BOOK OF SPELLS

It was half past three in the morning. The streets were silent, deserted except for those few nocturnal creatures who preferred the night's tales. Monroe drove her car at speed, following Nyquist's instructions. He was sitting in the passenger seat, holding his arm where the blood had already congealed, where the words had already done their job and sealed his wounds with their letters. His mind was clear, the clearest it had been for many a week: the vanishing point lay ahead and he was heading straight for it.

"Will you please tell me what's happening," Monroe said.

"I'm still not sure."

"Is that true? You're not holding back from me?"

"It's the truth, Bella. I'm putting it together. But something is taking place tonight, in the city."

She pulled up at the stop light of a traffic sign. "I feared as much."

"Bella, you spoke of people coming together with one purpose, the chosen ones. The messengers, you called them. You told me about the story coming alive..."

He stopped speaking.

"John, are you all right? You don't look too good."

"I'm fine. Just keep driving. No, wait. Stop here."

She did so and Nyquist climbed out of the car. He walked across the street and entered a telephone box. Monroe waited for him, keeping her eyes on him the whole time in case he tried to slip away. But he finished the call after a few minutes and came back to the car and they set off once more.

"We're nearly there," he said. "The next right."

"Who did you call?"

"The police."

He would say no more. She tried to engage him in conversation, to no avail. He was either weakening, or finding some hidden strength; she couldn't decide which. But a change was definitely taking place.

"Turn here," he said. "Drive down the street a few yards, and then stop."

The car moved slowly. "Here?"

"This will do it."

Monroe turned off the engine and the quiet crept in around the vehicle. They were the only living souls awake on the street; all the lights were off in the buildings on both sides.

"What now?"

His answer surprised her: "Turn away, Bella. Don't look at my face. Please."

"Nyquist, you think…"

"Don't look at me!"

She wouldn't do as he asked, so he did so himself, turning away from her in the seat. But her hand sought out his features. Her hand moved over his face, tracing the shapes of the letters that moved on his skin.

"I've been watching you all night."

"I know, I know that. I heard you. The words…"

"Well then?"

"I'm grateful to you."

"But now?"

It took a while for him to answer. "I'm ashamed," he said. "I don't know what you've been reading."

"Your face, your story. All that I could manage."

"I heard you. Speaking to me, telling me things. You were a lifeline."

"Well," she said. "It works both ways."

He turned to her directly and held her gaze, and she did the same, eye to eye. Nothing was said for a moment, not in words. And then:

"There were two women. Both called Zelda."

"You were close to them both?"

He nodded. "Yes. One was like me, suffering in the same way." He indicated the words that moved on his raised hand. "And she was murdered. It was staged to look like a suicide."

"And the other woman?"

"The other? The other Zelda died a short while ago, in my arms."

He said it in an almost matter-of-fact way, but Monroe could sense the deep emotion hidden behind the words. She let the moment go by and then asked: "Is that why we're here?"

"I need to find out why this happened." He pointed over to a building across the narrow street. "And the answer, I believe, is waiting for us in that office."

Monroe followed his direction. The place was dark. But then she noticed a tiny flicker of light at one of the windows on the upper floor.

"Shall I come with you? Only..."

"What?"

"I'm not very good at staying put."

He smiled at this, but then his expression changed;

the words grew more agitated on his face, and his eyes screwed shut.

"What is it? Are you all right?" Monroe reached out to him. "Does it hurt?"

"I think... I think..."

"Yes? John, speak to me, please. Speak to me!"

"I think they're killing me."

"They? You mean the... you mean...?"

"The words." His eyes opened wide. "The words are killing me."

"No, no that doesn't make sense. When you were under, in the coma... they kept you alive."

"Then I don't know. But it's not a good feeling."

And with that, he got out of the car. Monroe followed suit, joining him as he walked across the road.

"What is this place?" she asked. "A. P. Linden Associates?"

"Antonia Linden employed me, right at the very beginning of this case."

He pressed on the door buzzer and waited. The last time he'd been here, he'd broken in like a burglar. Now he suspected that Linden was in residence, and he also suspected that she would have to welcome him: there was no other choice. He pushed on the door and it opened easily under his touch.

"Not very secure," Monroe whispered.

"She wants us to visit."

They entered the small reception area and walked past the desk, looking into the main office. It was empty. They carried on down the corridor, towards the kitchen. Antonia Linden was sitting at the kitchen table in the near dark, smoking a cigarette and taking sips from a glass of red wine.

"How nice to meet you again," she said, her words ever so slightly drawled.

Nyquist didn't have any time for niceties. "Where is it?" There was an edge in his voice. "Upstairs?"

She didn't even bother to nod.

Halfway up the stairs his pace slowed, he couldn't help himself. The whispering could already be heard. As they reached the landing he saw a flickering light coming through the open doorway of the smaller of the two upstairs rooms. Monroe started to speak, but he shook his head. There wasn't a single question he could possibly answer. They entered the room together. Nyquist remembered his first visit here: the same blue and yellow flowery wallpaper, the same desk, the chair, the art deco lamp which was currently switched off. Despite the lack of artificial light, a soft glow permeated the room, emitted from the object that lay on the table in plain view.

The Body Library.

He had heard so much about it, seen so many pages torn from it, or offshoots of it, and he'd witnessed and been deeply affected by its magic: now the real thing was in his sight.

Monroe made a wordless sound.

The manuscript was opened out flat at a middle spread. The pages were either single ply, or made of two or three layers where different parts of other books and magazines had been glued down, or stitched or stapled into place. The whispering was heard again, as a page of the book turned of its own accord, blown by a ghost's breath.

Nyquist and Monroe could only look on in wonder.

They saw stories, images, fragments of poems, attached objects, trinkets, feathers, bits of cloth, empty cocoons, pressed flowers, leaves, the iridescent wing cases of beetles. The sentences tumbled over the pages in a wild fashion, the cuts between phrases as jagged and as primitive as the ones that had occupied Thomas Dreylock's face. Nyquist felt within his own body the book's profound magic, and the words in his flesh responded to it, like to like, species to species. He felt himself becoming lightheaded, that old spell taking him over, but far more powerful than the words he had chanted at the secret meeting of the believers, and more powerful even than the word tree and its natural energies. Here was the source itself, the wellspring from which a rebel language rose up, seeping through his skin, through the bloodstream, up the nerves of the spine, into the brain, there to explode into one story after another, moving continuously into new variations.

Monroe gasped. "It's alive," she said. "The book's alive."

Indeed it was. They could hear it breathing, they could see the pulse of the pages, the heartbeat. Nyquist could feel the heat generated by narrative itself as it wove through the paper. Yet when he reached out to touch the open page his fingers tingled cold from the contact, as though from a jellyfish's skin, or a spider's web in a darkened cellar. Most of the stolen sections were typeset, but at least a portion of each page was handwritten. The words trembled slightly under his gaze. A fine array of veins was visible in the parchment, both red and blue, ready to flow as blood should a pair of scissors come near. Nyquist caught the scent of fog and dust and flowers and animal fur and a slight tinge of decaying flesh, and whenever another page turned he might hear the human whisper or a crackle of autumn leaves or the sound of wings softly beating in preparation for flight.

A single touch had stained the tips of his fingers black with ink. It made him think of the pool beneath the Melville Tower and its mysterious substance, the blood of Oberon. The very same blood was used to write *The Body Library*. And midnight's ink never quite dried on the paper, the story was never complete, there was always another word to write, another incident, another character to add.

Nyquist stepped back from the desk as Antonia Linden joined them in the room. She stood just inside the doorway.

"I don't know what to call you anymore," Nyquist said. "Linden, or Beaumont?"

"I was born Ava Beaumont, if that's of any use to you."

"So right from the start, you were using me?"

"You were a character, one of many. And yet a willing one, as I recall."

"I didn't know the real motive for your employing me."

"There were pressing matters at hand."

"You had it all planned out."

"Not all. No, that's not possible. There's nothing certain about this endeavor of ours, even with Oberon's exquisite eye for all the city's stories. Chance will always be a factor. But by careful consideration, a nudge here and there, a word in someone's ear, one person forced to meet another without either person knowing why... in this way the tale unfolds."

Nyquist looked back at the book on the table. Its spectral glow reminded him of the penthouse suite of Melville Five.

"I saw you earlier tonight. In the tower."

She smiled at this.

"I saw through my other self's eyes, Ava. You were reading from the book."

"Such is my task. I do it every couple of nights, if I can manage it, for a few hours or more. It's very tiring. I sit here at the desk and the book transports me to the tower. And I feel that I'm there, I really do. And I read, one page after another. It makes everything more..." She chose her words carefully: "More *real*."

"You pointed the way forward, told me how to find Zelda. Even then, you were urging me on."

"I had to get you down there, in the basement."

Nyquist shook his head in disbelief.

Ava shrugged. "I felt for you, John, I really did. I tried my very best to help you, to keep you alive. We needed that final element, the words you swallowed, a father's message that lived on inside your body. That vital, dark energy that you carried within. John, you do know now; it's why the book picked you out."

Nyquist felt cold, his feelings pushed aside.

Ava continued: "There were many others chosen. Some proved themselves worthy, others failed."

Monroe had been quiet up to now, listening to the conversation. But hearing this last statement she stepped forward and asked, "Is she referring to Patrick?"

"She is. Among others."

Anger crossed over Monroe's face.

But Ava stood her ground. "There's very little either of you can do now." Her voice had taken on a lilting quality. "Only the final chapter remains to be told. And then, at last, we shall all be free. I only wish that my little Calvin could be in my arms once more. I would like to sing to him one last time. Alas, it will never be. His grandfather needs him more than I do."

Her eyes closed as she performed the first verse of the "Crooked Man" song, the most perfect and tender-hearted version Nyquist had yet heard. Even the words on his skin were calmed a little by the song. And he knew that Ava Beaumont was herself a victim: her son had been given up to the book, his absence a necessary sacrifice, and all at Oberon's bidding, no doubt.

Nyquist spoke urgently: "Ava, you needed me to go back to Melville, in spirit at least, to guide my other self through the corridors and rooms of the tower. Is that right?"

"One of you wasn't enough. No, we needed both of you, working together, both sides of the page, fiction and non-fiction." Ava smiled at her own success. "It all worked out remarkably well, considering the chances I took. And then you kindly visited a library, and it was all very easy from then on."

He stared at her. "And for all this to happen, you needed to set me on a task."

"By that point I knew how to provoke you, how to make you commit." A half-drunken smile settled on her lips. "You never could resist the search for truth, Nyquist, especially when it concerns the death of love."

His final suspicion was confirmed.

"I talked to your husband, Ava."

"How thrilling for you."

"He told me about your personality, your passion, that you would do anything at all to bring the spell to its rightful conclusion."

"It's true."

"So you murdered Zelda Courtland. It was you. Maybe you had a little help from your assistant, for the nastier aspects."

Ava Beaumont gazed at the book on the table. "It was all for the one purpose," she said. "A purpose beyond any of your petty comforts."

"You should know," Nyquist replied, "that I've already called the police."

"It matters little. My work is almost done."

There was a weight to her words, a darkness.

Nyquist put his hand on the open page of *The Body Library*. He held the paper between forefinger and thumb.

Beaumont drew her strength towards her and said in a stately voice, "Our family has always ruled over the story of this city, back to when Storyville was little more than a few huts beside the river, and the story first flickered into life. Long ago, the seeds of the word tree were planted.

Each of us contains the spirit of that same story, the grand story. We are moved by its magical properties, and each tells it in his or her way, passing on the words down the generations." Her voice rose up, filled with pride. "We shall yet prevail."

Nyquist tore at the page, feeling the tear inside his own flesh as the words reacted.

Beaumont laughed out loud, her own body reveling in the pain.

Monroe said. "You've done your job, John, as Overseer K asked. You've found the book."

"Not quite. She wants me to destroy it."

He tore out another page. He wanted to tear out page after page until the whole book was nothing but shreds of paper on the floor, but something stopped him. The room seemed smaller suddenly, and he felt suffocated. The words were burrowing madly under his skin, worse than ever. Panicking, he tried to reach the door, only to be blocked by Monroe. She was speaking to him, asking him if everything was all right, but he couldn't hear her properly. His own writing was too loud, far too loud, the phrases and sentences were crying out in pain from his skin and that was all he could feel, all he could understand, nothing else, his body was a book of skin, bone, muscle and blood. The glow of light around the manuscript was brighter now, pulsating, and his own blood pulsed to the same rhythm. Words were rising from the pages of the book, the same ones taken from his body earlier, they were rising up in a cloud, filling the room. His father's message. Nyquist stared ahead and he saw within the cloud a place, a field, an overflow pipe, a tree.

A body swinging from a branch.

The words spoke to him.

ONE MORNING IN STORYVILLE

They left Ava Beaumont to her drink and her cigarettes, her precious book of cut-up magic and her empty, lonely rooms, and whatever ending her story might reach. Bella Monroe drove out towards the east of the city. Nyquist was drowsy, his head filled with visions, his eyes opening on other worlds beyond the road ahead. And all the time he was mumbling and giving out directions, following the words' instruction.

It was almost dawn by the time they turned down Plath Lane. Monroe parked the car by the farm gate and they both got out. She looked around.

"What is this place? Why are we here?"

"Marlowe's Field," he answered. "This is where Zelda Courtland was murdered."

They walked across the open land, feeling the sodden, marshy ground underfoot. Not a soul was in sight apart from the two of them. Birds sang verse and chorus from trees and bushes as the sun rose over the edge of the world.

"Nyquist, you're not going to do anything silly, are you?"

"I don't know why I'm here."

"You don't?"

He stopped walking. "Every single ounce of my being is

telling me to be here, now, at this time. There's no hope of resistance."

She waited for more information, but her friend was quiet. He held up a hand as though testing the day's warmth. Then he shielded his eyes with the same hand and said, "There, do you see, Bella? We're not alone."

Yes, she saw them now: dark figures moving in the early morning mist, other people coming from different directions across the fields, by different roads, in different vehicles from different lives and situations, but all with the same purpose. Nyquist moved on, urging Monroe to keep up. He walked with determination, his body controlled from within by the script that wrote out each moment for him, line by line. The many words glowed on his skin and for the first time he welcomed their presence.

The others were drawing near, a hundred or more of them, men, women and even a number of children, all heading for the same location: the tree by the wastepipe, the hanging tree. He remembered what the two young kids had told him: Marlowe's Field was the site of a gallows pole, three or more centuries before. He imagined a hamlet in this field: dirt roads, villagers, the crowded square, the hangman going about his business, the final words of the condemned man.

Alphabugs fluttered in, hovering above the heads of the gathering. Monroe by instinct stood back. She was not part of this. Nyquist looked at her, and she waved him on. He could see the others clearly now; all were marked on the faces and hands, and no doubt over their entire bodies, with the new lexicon, the words and letters of the spell. He recognized some of the faces from his time in the Melville Tower; but these were not the residents, these people were real, born of flesh and blood only. Gathered in the field were the poor men and women who had been taken over by the virus. Even Thomas Dreylock was there. All were now drawn forward.

And then he heard Monroe shout out. He turned, to see her approaching one of the men.

It was Patrick Wellborn, his face covered in lettering, but recognizable.

Monroe stopped a few feet from him. Nyquist could see the look of shock on her face. The man she had once loved, that she feared was dead, was now standing in front of her. For a moment she looked as though she might strike him, or shout abuse at him, or at least argue with him. But the anger left her face as quickly as it had appeared, and now she simply stood there, staring at him. The mists of dawn wreathed about them both.

She turned away and came towards Nyquist and then stopped a little way off. She was waiting, as they all were.

For Nyquist's part, although Patrick Wellborn had pushed him off the rooftop in Lower Shakespeare, he felt little animosity toward him. Some other impulse had taken over them all, and for the moment they were joined in one action, one purpose. Of the infected, only Zelda Courtland was missing.

Nyquist moved closer to the old tree. The others did the same, forming a circle around the bent and twisted trunk. A breeze rustled the leaves. Here two stories joined together perfectly: two trees, two bodies. One female, one male. One upright, hung from the neck, the other upside down, suspended from the feet. One young and one very, very old.

Nyquist looked over to the wastepipe with its swarm of alphabugs: the night's broken tales ended up here, amid the mist, the dew on the grass, the sparkle of birdsong. It made him think of everything he had lost, both recently, and in the distant past.

On the edge of town where the stories flow away.

A man and a woman are covered in silence. They walk alone, with only one word left unspoken between them, just one word unwritten.

He had never said the word to her, to Zelda, the one word that mattered.

His thoughts were interrupted.

The words stirred within his body.

The spell was beginning.

Nyquist wasn't the first to feel it. Across the way a young woman suddenly screamed. She bent over double and clutched her belly with her hands. Then she screamed again and lurched upright, her backbone arched over at a dreadful angle. Another, an older man, copied her movements. He howled in pain as his body went into seizure. Nyquist felt himself taken over by the same actions. It began as a sharp pain in his stomach and then grew outwards from there, quickly reaching the outer layer of flesh. His skin burned as the words writhed madly about, slithering over each other in their desire to escape his body. If he screamed or made any noise at all, he wasn't aware of it: his body had been taken over completely. He, like all the others present, was at the mercy of the sickness. The entire circle was suffering in the same way.

Monroe stepped back, her nerves on edge from what she was seeing and hearing. It was a terrible sight to behold, so many people, each one in the throes of a possession. That was the only way she could think of it: a demon had taken refuge in their bodies and was now eating or bursting his way out, through the flesh. Poor Nyquist: he had dropped to his knees in the dew-wet grass and was pressing the sides of his head with his hands, the better to keep whatever it was inside from breaking free. Monroe moved a little way towards him and then stopped, for what could she do, truly? She was human to her bones, unaffected, without any true knowledge of what was taking place here. All she could do was witness the events and pray to the gods of the city that some good came from this, that the story ended well, not in despair, or loneliness, or injury or death. A glimmer of hope in the last few sentences, this was all she wished for.

Nyquist sank further down, into the grass. He felt his hands clutching at the earth, the damp soil, the insects within the soil; he felt the water below oozing though the ground, he felt the roots of the tree reaching out in a network of growth, seeking food, nutrients, energy; he felt himself as part of the roots, the system, the tree, the earth, the air, the field, the words that flowed from each to each, and the pain, the pain that coursed through him, making his nerves sing, sing aloud with the long epic ballad of the world. And then the pain was gone. It happened like that, in an instant, and he stood up slowly, testing his limbs, his muscles. Everything was fine, in fact his skin tingled with delight. He breathed easily, and his mind was free of thought, cleansed. He stood up tall and proud and strong and saw that the others had done the same, and that their expressions were purged of all cares. And he saw also that their faces and hands were now clean, free of the words that had plagued them over the past days or weeks. He looked at his hands to make sure; yes, the palms and backs were empty, the skin returned to its natural hue. Yet he could still feel the letters inside him, in his head, in his skull, gathering there.

A hush fell over the field. Not a sound was heard.

The hanging tree was lit at its topmost branches by the rising sun.

Not a leaf or branch rustled, not a stalk of grass stirred. Not a bird sang.

The bugs hovered motionless in the air.

The mist haunted the fields.

The whole land around was holding its breath, waiting.

Bella Monroe felt it herself from where she was standing, off to the side. Everything she could see in all directions across the wide flat expanse, from the tree to the hedgerows and back, lay quiet and still. Even her own breath, her pulse.

She was the witness.

A few seconds passed and then a single flicker of light was seen, as an alphabug clicked into flight. The wind and the leaves and the grasses and the birds were brought back to life. Nyquist saw it all at that point, the knowledge sound and pure in his mind: the people gathered here were the hosts, the transport system, that's all, nothing more. They had been given the words in the pool of ink with the sole job of carrying them into the city. The words had grown within their bodies, where they reached maturity, and had now been carried to this place at this time, in this moment. And one by one he felt the letters leaving his body, via the top of his skull, the fontanelle momentarily unsealed. He saw the black letters in the air, dancing around him, whirling, floating. He saw the same effect on all the other people, their heads and bodies already clouded with words: hundreds, thousands of them taking to the air, many thousands. It was a book not yet written, a story in waiting. A living story.

Monroe saw it too. She watched in awe as the words joined together in many different formations, seeking new phrases, sentences, breaking apart, starting again, erasing, writing, editing, the very air their paper. And then, on the patch of ground next to the tree, they started to work as one, building out of themselves a shape, a form, a figure, a man of sorts – more a ghost to begin with, until the words gave him texture and color and flesh, the mass splitting into the four limbs, forming the torso, the head, the long strands of hair. From first letter to last, the words wrote him into being. His edges were fuzzy, jagged, and then smooth as the letters buzzed around, putting the finishing touches to his body, the details, the dashes, commas, speech marks and full stops. And last of all, made from the word *air*, the breath that brought him to life.

The spell was over. Nyquist was returned to his normal self. He saw the world through his own eyes, and acted as his own person. He gazed in wonder at the figure beside the tree, wondering just what it was they had created. He took a few steps forward until he was standing only a few feet away from the written man. And as the newcomer's face took on its final features, Nyquist recognized him. It was Oberon. He was alive once more, given flesh, a flesh of words. The man blinked his eyes a couple of times, testing them out. He raised a slow hand and examined it, and then shook it. A few letters fluttered off, and then reattached themselves to the whole.

Nyquist heard sounds from all around the circle, cries of surprise, or shock. The people were coming out of their trances, one by one. All eyes were now fixed on the apparition who stood before them. How could this be? Working together, they had created this person.

But Oberon was there only for a moment.

Even as Nyquist looked on, the figure started to disperse, his gathered body taking off in flight as the words carried him back towards the city in the dawn light.

There were other stories waiting to be told.

BEGINNING

The people came from all directions, from all parts of the city and beyond, to witness this new phenomenon. They gathered in the streets, at the speaking posts, in the bookshops, the libraries and in private houses and clubs, all to listen and to read, and to feel the power of language flooding their veins. Yes, it was a drug; and they could not give up on it, not until they were overwhelmed. Then they would fall down as though drunk and wake up hours later lying in an alley or on a park bench, and yawn and groan, as they tried to clear their heads of last night's words. Some would leave Storyville before their visit was officially over, seeking easier tales with easier endings. But many stayed on.

Nyquist kept away from such pleasures, if such they were. His business had picked up since his involvement in the Melville Affair, as the newspapers and radio stations called it, and despite his refusal to be interviewed or photographed, his name was known: he was a discoverer, a direct line to the Muse in the Sky, or whatever they deemed it this week. More than once he had passed a raconteur in the street only to hear his own name mentioned, and his own story described: *One night in the late summer of 1959 a young courting couple were seeking a place of calm and secrecy.* It made him laugh: the name Oberon had been taken up, the spell maker, but really the man in the tree was still an unknown character. But he was happy to take the new cases on, and to be paid for it. The city was his home. He'd even gone back to the high-rise tower a couple of weeks ago, but the place was abandoned, the corridors and rooms uninhabited. The magic had drifted away. Bella came with him and together they made their way to apartment 67. Monroe joked that he was one of the few people to have actually killed a fictional character in real life. He let it pass. The bedroom was empty, the patch of blood and hair real enough, but fading now. Nyquist realized that he missed the residents, and he hoped that somehow or other they lived on, perhaps in another book by a different writer. They went down to the basement. They saw the roots of a dead tree, and a drained pool littered with bits of paper, sodden leaves and animal droppings. In a year or two all this would be just another story told at school, something to excite the pupils, or to scare them. Of course, the evidence remained in full view, whenever a novel or a short story collection was opened, and the words shifted around on the pages. Probably the kids would grow up accepting that as the normal way for a story to be presented.

Let it be.

Ava Beaumont was found lying on the floor of the storage room in Chaucer Town, her face contorted into a fierce delight. Her last act had been to set fire to the manuscript of *The Body Library*. By the time the police got there, the entire upper floor was filled with smoke. Beaumont had destroyed her greatest creation and breathed in its essence; she has yet to awaken from her coma. The spirits of the book have taken possession of her.

Let it be. Keep on. Keep writing.

Nyquist met with Bella once a week or so. They chatted, went out for dinner, drank a little. Once or twice something had almost happened between them. Perhaps it would, one day. There was time. Zelda, of course, was never mentioned. In truth, he tried not to think about her too much. Tried, sometimes failed. But like the poet had once said: *Another day, another story*. With the help of such platitudes he got by. Mostly he lived for the early hours of the morning, when the casework was done and the city taken over by silence. He would sit in his office apartment at 451 Bradbury Avenue and start typing. Even the letter X had been fixed on the machine, not that he used it much. He'd abandoned his first attempt at a novel and was now working on another story entirely. Sometimes he would struggle with the plotting, and then at others times the words would flow easily, and several pages would be written without him realizing it. He would look up at the sheet of paper and see the lines and lines of black text and wonder where they had come from. Still, he was grateful.

Sometimes the words would change shape, or shift their position on the page, even as he watched, and he knew that some other force had taken charge. Oberon was at work, the editor, the muse, the author of all we hold dear: take your pick. Nyquist welcomed the effect, for invariably the story came out better in the new rearrangement. There was no such thing as a fixed story anymore, not in this city: non-fiction books and papers were unaffected, but every novel and short story floated freely in a kind of liquid haze, and every time a book was opened, the events and characters changed a little: narrative was in flux. And that was good. Oberon lived on in the city's texts. For now, at least. Some people even claimed to have seen him at large, a body of dark shimmering words in the neon haze at midnight. Always in these sightings he was accompanied by a child, a young boy, who held his grandfather's hand almost as if to stop Oberon from drifting away.

Let it be. Keep writing.

After a time, Nyquist realized that his new novel was really an attempt to give Zelda Courtland another chance at life. Nothing magical, or supernatural, just words on paper: events, characters, dialogue, memories, emotions. She was his focus, this woman who arrived on page thirty-nine of his manuscript, entirely unannounced, unbidden, taking on more of her qualities and quirks as the days passed, both in the real world, and in the fictional world he was creating. In this novel, Zelda would not be murdered, she would not attempt to leave the tower. And even if both of these things did in fact take place, despite his best efforts – for the words would always transform themselves on the page – then at least he knew that somewhere deep in the story, deep down, a chance had been taken, a word of love spoken in the night.

ACKNOWLEDGMENTS

Thanks beyond measure to Marc, Penny, Phil and Paul, and all the amazing team at Angry Robot for steering this novel from its first inkling all the way to the final full stop.

And thanks to Edwin, Graham, Hayley, Kevin, Steve, Sarah, Lane, Rikki and William for support and advice and most of all friendship, both now and over the years.

PREVIOUSLY...

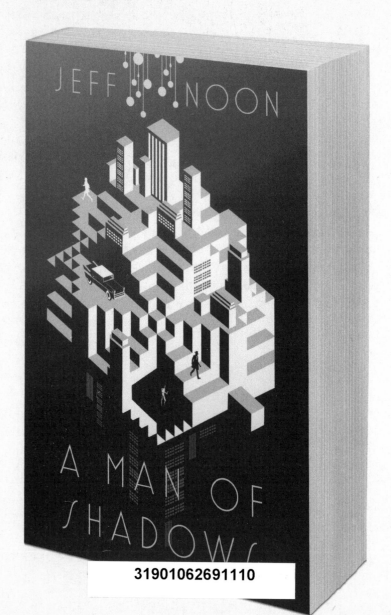

31901062691110